# TWIN FLAME JOURNEY
# FROM A MAN'S PERSPECTIVE
## GUIDING THE COLLECTIVE INWARD

Terrence Johnson
Johnson Craftworks LLC
2023 © All Rights Reserved

# TWIN FLAME JOURNEY FROM A MAN'S PERSPECTIVE
## GUIDING THE COLLECTIVE INWARD

Terrence Johnson
Copyright © 2023
United States of America

Cover art, book design, and interior art by Terrence Johnson.

**ISBNs**
eBook: 979-8-9877194-2-8
Paperback: 979-8-9877194-3-5

Published by:
Johnson Craftworks LLC

# HIGHLY SENSITIVE
# CONTENT WARNING

This guidebook contain highly sensitive, non-pornographic contents. The contents within this guidebook are not age appropriate for those under 18 years. It contain sexually explicit, non-pornographic contents. This guidebook is not sold by the author or Johnson Craftworks LLC to those under the age of 18 years. **DO NOT share or expose the contents within this guidebook to those under the age of 18 years.**

The contents within this guidebook may contain topics, phrases, concepts, terms, facts, statistical data, acknowledgement of historical events, and acknowledgement of certain social movements which may trigger the reader emotionally. **READ AT YOUR OWN RISK.** This guidebook does not contain slander or defamation of any kind. This guidebook does not contain any information with regard to the LGBTQ community, as the author is a traditional heterosexual male, and is not affiliated with the community in any way.

This guidebook WILL trigger you, especially if you are a woman. Due to the women in Twin Soul collective having a significant presence on the internet, this guidebook is naturally geared more toward the women of the Twin Soul collective. This guidebook is only for the strong at heart, and the mind that is willing to ingest painful truths that are easy to ignore or pretend do not exist.

This guidebook is only for those who are willing to self-reflect, rationalize, and make changes to their way of thinking, behavior, and lifestyle with regard to their Twin Sou journey. This guidebook is not written to destroy the value, integrity, social status, life, or emotional well-being of any persons.

**If you are unwilling to be triggered emotionally, please return this book.** If you wish to proceed, read when you are in a good mood, and take breaks if and when you get triggered.

# OFFICIAL LEGAL DISCLAIMER

All information, knowledge, recommendations, and procedures in this guidebook are not designed to replace your following of doctor, lawyer, spouse, soul guide, coach, and soul guide directions. They are not designed to replace the law. They are not designed to replace or substitute the training, information, and instruction given by any doctor, lawyer, spouse, soul guide, coach, or soul guide. They are not designed to change any laws, regulations, or school training. Always follow the laws and regulations as designed by the international, federal, state, city, county, and local governments.

Johnson Craftworks LLC is owned by Terrence Johnson. Johnson Craftworks LLC, and its owner are not liable for any person or entity who misuse the information, knowledge, recommendations, and procedures within this guidebook.

Johnson Craftworks LLC and its owner are not liable for any person or entity who use the information, knowledge, recommendations, and procedures in this guidebook to break any law, or cause any kind of harm (physically, emotionally, verbally, ext.) to any person, animal, or entity, including themselves.

The legal names of particular persons will not be revealed in this guidebook. They have a right to privacy of their identity. All persons and examples are only used as examples, and not provided to degrade or pedestal any person's reputation, business, health, status, or life.

The information, knowledge, recommendations, and procedures in this guidebook are not designed to degrade or pedestal the reputation, legality, debt, or profit of any business, contract, law, regulation, agreement, exchange, person, entity, or organization. Johnson Craftworks LLC and its owner are not liable for the degradation or pedestaling of any business, contract, law, regulation, agreement, exchange, person, entity, or organization due to the contents of this guidebook.

# ABOUT AUTHOR
## INITIATED

It happened when I was just three years of age. I woke from an intense and vivid dream. I was drenched in sweat. My body was so hot, I felt like I was on fire. I pulled my clothes off quick and ran to the bathroom. I turned on the shower head with cold water to cool down.

It was the first of a series of very intense and vivid dreams I had at the age of three years. In this dream, I was in a car with my mother and the car moved through a lake of fire. The location was actually a real life apartment complex my mother used to live. In the dream, skeletons came for the car and raked the windows and paint with their fleshless hands. Eventually I found myself standing outside of the fire looking down a road. Unfortunately, my mother didn't make it out alive. Little did I know, I had been initiated on a soul journey.

In another dream, I found myself on an island. There were 3 others with me. In the middle of the island was a large tree. The tree was surrounded by a huge body of water in the shape of a circle. Two bridges allowed crossing over to the tree from one end to the other. The water looked murky.

We walked over the bridge and to the tree. I noticed one of the people was a red-haired woman. The second was a man just a little taller than the woman, and also had short black hair. The third of them was a short woman with long black hair. I didn't see their faces, but I certainly felt familiar of them.

At the body of water, I remember wanting to see my reflection. I got close to the water. I saw my reflection for a second before the water turned clear and I saw a horrifying scene. Under the water were dragons which were sleeping. I was not aware that the lake was deep enough to hide them under the surface, as the water looked very dirty. I was so frighten, I fell into the water. I woke just as I was going in, and again, was drenched in sweat. This time my body was very cold, and I needed a HOT shower.

## THE DOUBLE LIFE

Over the years following the series of dreams, I experienced even more otherworldly things. I figured it all by high school, that I was very different than most around me. I had also developed the gift of foresight. I also had the ability to sit in a quiet, dark room with my eyes closed and see people and things in real time, and even non-physical entities. This came from years of sitting by myself after school and at night due to high stress levels from life and family issues. It was just a coping mechanism, but I didn't know I was actually engaging in a practice called meditation.

I had a realization early on that I was born in a not so friendly environment, and that the world around me was not as it seemed on the outside. I experienced the best of the metaphysical world while in meditation, but saw the worst of the human world. I found myself living a double life, each life of a different experience. The human world, as I saw underneath, was very backwards in a lot of ways, but the non-physical world was somehow connected with the human world in a mysterious and profound way. This non-physical world became a place of escape for me.

# A FRESH START
# LED BY THE MOST HIGH

When I turned 18 years of age, I was forced out of my mother's house and began my adult life with nothing but two pairs of shoes, a week worth of clothes and my art book. From there on, I had to navigate a social-economic environment which looked advanced and well-organized on the outside, but I found that it was actually very toxic underneath.

I didn't have but $40 in my pocket (not a lot to live off at the time) and the job which I worked refused to move me to full-time hours. But they were comfortable with working me one day a week. I didn't have anywhere to place my belongings, except temporarily at someone's house I just met that same day. I saw a hotel while riding the bus to work one day that was only $40 a night; cheap, but still too expensive to live long term. I figured I would just get a room for one night just to have a place to sleep and to clear my head. In the room, I remember feeling stressed about the whole situation. So, I sat in the bed, as I have always done to escape, but this time was different. "Most High Lord, if you exist, do something with my life. I have nothing. My Father is dead, and my mother removed me from her life. If my life has any value, take me and do something good with it."

The next morning I received a phone call from the job I worked that an employee had been fired and if I wanted to take their place. I stated that I need more hours, and they uttered "You are full-time now, you have all the hours you can get." So I stayed in the hotel until I worked and saved to get an actual apartment.

While learning to navigate the toxic and unfriendly world, I came to realize another thing. I also had the gift of influence and leadership. It seemed that people LOVED me, at least once they got to know me. People from all walks of life. *"It's because you don't judge people and you are so easy to talk to, Terrence."* one woman said.

This is when I began feeling an intense inner well of energy to be of positive influence to the people around me. I made a commitment to myself and The Most High Lord Ahmen that I would do what I could to make this world a better place, even if it's just one person. I found myself writing short stories, drawing pictures, and writing Bible-based content on the internet. I quickly drew an audience and realized that I needed to mix my creative abilities with technology to make that positive impact. So, over the years, I taught myself how to write and use technology, and I did what I could to keep myself healthy and out of trouble.

**GUEST** – *"Wow! That's all so wonderful!"*
**GUEST (2)** – *"Mr. J, I'm not a Twin Flame or Soul Twin. Would this guidebook still be good for me to read?"*
**MR. J** – "This guidebook is for everyone. It's a soul guidebook, a book about soul ascension, and not just a Twin Flame book. As you will find out, everyone has a Soul Twin. It is just that people go looking for 'the one', or for a specific physical person. But the reality is that not everyone experience their Soul Twin as a specific physical person. Most people are younger souls. Their Soul Twin manifest only in energetic form. That means that they will have many relationships and marriages throughout many lifetimes. Whatever energetic frequency they live in, a person will come which reflects that frequency. As they learn and ascend, people will come and go which match their current energy."

It is the more mature souls which have to undergo what is called a soul split, or soul spread. This soul split or spread give the soul the ability to incarnate in two bodies. Once a soul reach a certain frequency of vibration, it cannot incarnate in only one body. The body will not be able to handle the energy. So, the soul splits, or spreads. Once split or spread, it can incarnate into two bodies. So, you now have One Soul in two physical bodies. These are called Soul Twins. Twin Flames have a different meaning and purpose which you will learn later in this guidebook."

**GUEST** – *"I didn't know everyone has a Twin Flame, I mean Soul Twin!"*
**GUEST (2)** – *"But not everyone meets their Twin as a specific person? Some people meet their Twin as an energy, depending on how their energy is at the time?"*
**MR.J** – "Yes, that's correct! I can tell you all will learn quick. Let me share more about myself and life before we get started. It is important to know your leader or guide. We are still human in a certain way too. We just have come to a place where we want to help others along their life and soul journey."

## THE SOUL JOURNEY ~ NOT WHAT IT SEEMS

In my younger years, I went to church with family, and a few times by myself. I read the Bible. I also met people of other religions and spiritual beliefs over the course of my life. I had my own mystical and mysterious experiences that caused me to be unable to deny that life isn't just physical and material.

Eventually I found myself using the internet to look up various information on all things spiritual, metaphysical, and etheric. But life got in the way, as most have experienced, and I found myself struggling financially, keep a place to live, and bills paid. But I wasn't going to give up, because I knew that if The Most High Ahmen was real and took me up to make something of my life, I needed to be serious about this.

So, I began reading books and watching videos online about money and business. I also had the privilege with certain jobs I worked and a business I owned to meet and engage with wealthy people. That is when I learned that working a job is not the way to riches, or a stable financial life. One thing in particular I always wanted to learn was investing in passive-income-producing assets and speculative investments. I wanted to learn myself, and also stay up-to-date with the markets as I learned...

...which eventually lead up to meeting a particular woman on a certain social media platform...

# INTRODUCTION

**GUEST (3)** – *"From a man's perspective? Is this guy sexist or something?"*
**MR. J** – "Absolutely not! I actually got the name from a few female Twin Flames on an online writing forum I write on. I kept hearing the same thing:"

*"It's so good hearing this journey from a man's perspective!" "Oh, a DM is on here sharing his perspective! We could use the experiences and perspectives from more male Twin Flames." "Thank you for your perspective on this crazy journey, especially because you are a man. Most of our Twin Flames are not on here and don't open up about what they are experiencing."*

So, I created my own space on the forum and named it 'Twin Flame Journey From A Man's Perspective' and actually gained a loyal following. This is also where the title of this book came from, just to keep things consistent and transparent. It works!

## WHAT TO EXPECT

This is a guidebook. It hold valuable information, knowledge, recommendations, and procedures that will aid in your Twin Soul journey.

If you are reading this guidebook, you may or may not have a physical (incarnated) Soul Twin, but your Twin may be in purely energetic form. But this guidebook is written in a format which works for everyone, whether their Soul Twin be incarnated in another physical body, or is purely in energetic form.

It is of utmost importance that you always engage with your Soul Twin and those of the Twin Soul community in a respectful and courteous manner. At no place, time, or circumstance should you engage in any behavior that is illegal, unsafe, or cause of conflict to others or yourself.

This guidebook is filled with many useful stories, examples, illustrations, and wisdom (personally from me) which will be the meat, veggies, and potatoes. It will be a full, heavy, and hard to digest meal, but it will nourish you for decades and even lifetimes. We will begin with my personal Soul Twin experience and some appetizers before the full meal is served.

Call-to-actions are important. Emotions come and go. Talking is easy. Anyone can say they want to or can do something. But to actually do it, and do it in a way which bring profound and lasting results...not everyone can DO that. Usually, a person's ability to act and make positive changes reflect in their personal well-being, state of mind, and their ability to engage others in a healthy way. This guidebook is filled with call-to-actions which will help guide you in your soul journey and ascension.

Also, to be upfront and forward, I have labeled the woman I met in 2020 the 'supposed Twin' because I came to realize she is actually a past life connection, not someone to be with in this life.

**LEGAL DISCLAIMER:** "The recommendations and procedures given in this guidebook should ONLY be performed with permission from your doctor, lawyer, soul guide, or soul guide, and only in a way that is safe, do not break any laws, and do not cause any kind of harm or conflict with any person (including yourself). The author and Johnson Craftworks LLC relinquish liability."

This is Twin Flame Journey From A Man's Perspective! So, let's get to those appetizers, and remember, "It's Union Season™!"

# LIST OF CONTENTS

# MY SUPPOSED 'TWIN' EXPERIENCE

Here, I will share my personal Soul Twin experience. It has been both a simple, but also very complex journey. Certain information will be restricted from this guidebook, to protect *her* privacy. All written within this section and guidebook about *her*, I, and our journey are not for the purpose of degrading or pedestaling any person's name, reputation, status, well-being, or identity. All written within this section is only for the sharing of limited information on our personal journey for enterjoyment and educational purposes only. I don't want to make my Supposed 'Twin' (or any woman) out to be a horrible or undesirable woman. But I do want to write this to allow the Twin Soul Community a reconsideration on the running/chasing issues, or what we have been told is running/chasing, and the causes of such.

## IN THE BEGINNING
## TIME: MARCH 2018 - AUGUST 2020

In 2020 I was living at a particular family member's house, a place I did not want to be. I was around people I did not want to be around. I was stuck in a difficult situation in 2018 and had to choose between being homeless for the second time in my life. Or I could at least have a bed to lay in and roof over my head, but in a place I did not want to be, and people I did not want to be around.

From early-mid 2018 to May 2021 I lived in that house. I planned on getting out of there as soon as possible. But that would prove to not be the case. I started to suffer from serious health problems, mostly heart related. This led to me being unable to maintain a job (it was already difficult for me to get one). That led to financial issues. Then I felt truly stuck. It wasn't enough to just exercise or change my eating habits. I knew there was something going on beyond my control.

My mother passed away in August 2019, due to heart issues. That was the last straw for me. I was so sick, broke, in debt, everything going missing, breaking down, or not working. I wanted to give up. I didn't know what to do. The only thing that kept me going was a large amount of money that I was able to get from her passing.

Since I wasn't able to work, I started self-educating on cryptocurrencies and investing in the stock market in late 2018. I started with small amounts of money and learned within a few months to multiply that money with an 80 to 90 percent rate guarantee. With the money I got from my mother passing, I was able to take care of the things that cost money, such as paying off consumer debt, putting the car in the shop, catching up on bills, ext. I also began weightlifting, long walks at the park, and was able to afford healthier ways of eating.

This eased my health problems enough I was able to work full-time if I chose. I invested most of the money that was left over and was able to profit enough money every week that I could keep up with bills and still have money left over. This gave me enough drive and optimism to keep me moving, although I was still stuck in that house in a way.

# THE MEETING
## TIME: AUGUST 2020 TO SEPTEMBER 2020

In 2020 I created a Twitter social media account to stay up to date on events and advances in the stock market and cryptocurrency technology. At least two or three times a day, I logged into that account. Now anyone who has used Twitter know it can be annoying to use if not set up correctly. You'll find you keep getting notifications and feeds which you are not interested in, are filled with click-bait, scams, and people posting ridiculous comments. That was before Twitter had some improvements.

I specifically set up my account so that I could avoid the annoyance. I streamlined it perfectly. Or so I thought...

One day, I just happened to come across a comment that had nothing to do with money, investing, or cryptocurrency. It was from a particular woman, and the comment read *"God is a woman"*. Normally, such things wouldn't bother me. But this one random comment seemed to turn my surroundings into a black vortex, and everything disappeared. For a moment, nothing existed except me and this woman, and this one comment which would be our first interaction.

I was a bit put off by it, because for one, I didn't want to see something like that when everything on my Twitter was set up only for things related to money, stocks, and cryptocurrencies. Additionally, it was during a time when *"God is a woman"* was something which was mentioned by some celebrities, advertisements, models, and even the woman at the grocery store. It was a statement that I saw as lacking rational and soul awareness.

I remember telling *her* (not in the nicest way to be honest), that if God is a woman, I won't be worshipping her because I had observed women very carefully all my life, studied, and researched their nature and came to the truth that women are inherently unable to handle their own emotions, are deceptive, and far worse than men as far as manipulation and using other people for their own gain at the expense of others. A mouthful, I know. And you know what? *She* actually AGREED!

*She* replied - *"Yes you are right, God in all her perfect ways"*. At that point I knew it was time for me to get off the phone, but I was drawn to look at her profile picture and that's when I was hit with a heavy dosage of what most in the Twin Soul community call 'soul recognition' and 'soul familiarity'. On a deeper level, *the woman* looked like a female version of myself (no, *she* doesn't look like a man, but is actually very feminine and gorgeous looking). I was lost for words and didn't know what to say.

When I looked at *her* eyes, I fell into the picture and then found myself in outer space (I closed my eyes at this point, because well, it is just a picture and thought I was seeing things). When I came back to myself, five minutes had passed. What felt like two seconds, was actually five minutes. Looking at her eyes, even though a picture, was an intensity that is hard to describe, and can only be felt. This was the first 'sensation' I felt from this *mysterious woman.*

Then I looked through *her* page and read *her* tweets and was astounded by *her* level of wisdom and perception. It reminded me of myself. Then I came across two videos of *her* talking, one *she* was reading a book. My jaw dropped when I heard her talking, *she* spoke in a moderate passed, well-spoken manner, just like I do.

*She* had a unique voice I never heard before, soft and gentle, yet direct and bold. *She* had the same body type that I do as well, the ectomorph. I noticed in one of *her* pictures that *she* was kneeling in a way exactly the way I have kneeled all my life, and still do today. I thought maybe I had went crazy for a moment. I followed *her* page, because *she* was deep into politics and government stuff that I knew anything about.

## DRAWING CLOSER

As the days passed, I'd comment on tweets *she* posted and eventually we drew closer together, talking more about ourselves and lives. I did notice *she* eventually started tweeting about *her* personal life, and this is when I realized that this *woman* wasn't very fond of men. It was apparent *she* felt like men were the source of all the problems in our society, aggressive like wild animals, and that only women and children are innocent by nature.

Again, flawed, because all men were once children at some point in their lives. If boys are innocent, at what age, and under what circumstances, or parenting do they become toxic, abusive, and sex-crazed? If girls are innocent, at what age, and under what circumstances, or parenting do they fail to retain their innocence in a gynocentric society which REWARDS women for shaming and destroying the lives of men?

Now, at this time in my life, I had already known and met many women who are like this. So, I wasn't surprised or put off. I didn't want to share personal stuff to the public. So, I decided to send *her* a DM, a picture of myself and short description of who I am. *She* said that I was handsome and then I didn't hear from *her* for a while. I messaged *her* to see what *she* was up to, and *she* said *"sorry I didn't respond. I have a lot of feelings to process."*

I thought "Well dam, was it not a good idea to send a picture of me? At least it's not a dick pic!" Ha! After that we talked literally every day through the message system on Twitter. *She* lived in a certain state I always wanted to visit, which I thought was interesting because I always wanted to go there as a vacation point of interest. We also played the same video games and *she* had invited me to go to that particular state to meet *her*. Now, I did have the money, I could have caught a flight and stay there a few weeks. But for me, I have to get to know someone before I make moves that bold. This would later on turn out to be a wise choice...

## SOUL TWIN TELEPATHY

Now, I did not create that Twitter account to look for women to be with. I could have just downloaded a dating app if I wanted, or even better go to a local bar or club. And no, the Twitter account I currently have now is not the same one we met on.

Well one day I was sitting in bed and the strangest thing happened. I was looking at my phone, and the sensation of someone being behind me looking over my shoulder was very strong. Looking into the screen of my phone I sensed that *she* was looking back at me, but through my phone. I had not even gone into Twitter. When I did though, *she* had tweeted that *she* owned Twitter. I thought that was funny.

But with what I had learned about this *woman* so far, I knew *she* was the kind to watch out for. *She* also tweeted something about how *she* doesn't like men giving other women attention, and that the man *she* loves needs to protect *her* heart. It was said in a way as if *she* had a boyfriend that was flirting with a woman at the cash register or somewhere, and *she* was very upset.

I didn't know (until later) that *she* hacked into my twitter account. *She* was able to see all of my DMs. Most of them were just cryptocurrency scams that I didn't reply to. Ha! But there was one person on there I made friends with before meeting *her*. She happened to be a DJ and a model from the UK. She also was into politics and government stuff, which I knew nothing about, so she was educating me on it. This was before the Trump and Biden presidential election, and she was trying to persuade me to vote. Being illiterate in politics, and feeling antsy about both parties, I wanted to vote for neither to be honest! I met this friend because she was also into Bitcoin and crypto, and we crossed paths on a certain Tweet about cryptocurrency.

I do think that me talking to this woman made *her* jealous and triggered. At this point I already knew *she* liked me. *She* also had a massive need for attention (mentioned directly from *her*). The thing is, I was trying to figure out whether or not *she* was still married or not. A woman and even a man, can and will tell you all sorts of things to avoid saying the truth. I didn't want to be with another man's woman. Plus, I still had not met *her* in person.

So, I wasn't making any advances due to not being sure what *her* relationship/marital status was and not knowing *her* well enough. But business wise, *she* being in certain professional fields, I wanted to meet her. We both had big plans in life but had financial issues, so working in tandem would have been an interest for me.

## BAIT AND HOOK
## TIME: SEPTEMBER 2020

After *she* hacked into my Twitter account, *she* wasn't the same after that. Most of *her* tweets turned into man-hating tweets, and 'women are better' tweets. Then *she* wanted to leave twitter permanently, as *she* sent me a DM about someone who was causing her too many problems.

I was confused as to who. I did ask and try to clarify who, what, when, where, and why, but *she* either avoided the questions or didn't give me direct answers. I sent *her* my phone number and told *her* to contact me since *she* was deleting her Twitter. I figured, because reading through the comments of *her* tweets, it appeared as if *she* was in conflict with others on twitter, men of course.

I didn't realize until it was too late that *she* was talking about me the whole time and *her* inability to handle me talking to another woman as a friend. Now before *she* 'deleted' *her* Twitter *she* mentioned that *she* didn't want to even talk to me. So, I logged off my own Twitter account for a few days because I was annoyed by the whole experience.

When I later logged back on, *she* had been tweeting on and on about some disturbing stuff (most not about me or related to me). *She* never called or texted me, so I took that as *her* not wanting to talk. One day, another weird thing happened. Whenever I picked up my phone, I had that same intense sensation as before as if *she* was looking back at me through the phone. I heard *her* voice as well, but it had a reverb sound to it.

I hadn't been on Twitter. But this time it felt like *she* was reading my text messages in my cell phone. I didn't want to ask *her* directly if *she* hacked my phone because communication between us turned into a crazy game of indirect communication because *she* was afraid to share *her* feelings and be upfront about anything. Not something I'm interested in doing. But I wrote a bait message in a way that only *she* would understand and know that if *she* seen it, it confirmed that *she* had hacked my twitter account and my phone. I even included her favorite emojis (call me, and unicorn emojis).

The same day, and not long after sending the message to one of my mother's friends on my phone, and again to the woman I was talking to about the Biden-Trump election, *she* posted a tweet that *she* was *"found out"*. I thought it was funny. *She* even posted a picture of a surveillance camera, which I found even funnier. *She's* got a dry sense of humor, just like me! Although I wasn't laughing. I was both angry and disturbed that *she* hacked into my phone. According to *her* profession, *she* should know that it is illegal to invade people's privacy without a warrant or permission.

I baited and hooked *her*, and *she* didn't even know. Game over. At this point, I no longer want to be around the person or even talk to them. It becomes endless gameplay, and not *her* and I's favorite RPG – Elder Scrolls: Skyrim. So, I stayed off Twitter. Until one day a terrible thing happened. And I knew it was from *her*. This time *she* baited and hooked me, and it nearly killed me.

## PROTECT MY HEART
## TIME: SEPTEMBER 2020

My father died in 2009 due to heart issues. My mother died in 2019 in August (yes, exactly 12 months before meeting my Supposed 'Twin') due to heart disease. I suffered from undiagnosed (doctors always said I was healthy) heart issues all my life as well, which was the worst from 2018 to early 2020. By summer of 2020, I had gotten my health to where I could at least work part-time. I still had unusually low energy, trouble getting out of bed in the morning, and pain in the heart and chest.

One night in September 2020, I ended my day like I did all the previous days. I was exhausted and hoping that my life would improve. I was depressed, like I did everything I could to live at least a half decent life, but I was just dealt a bad starting hand and luck wasn't on my side. That night I didn't know I'd be in for the ride of my life, literally.

Being in a car or truck, and especially driving always made me happy and feel like I'm home. Not this ride. This was the ride that would nearly kill me. Nighttime is not normal for me as it is for other people. I don't just dream, I detach from my body and experience a world that most would see as beyond belief. It was heartbreaking experiencing the passing of both my parents.

I laid in bed, at a certain family member's house alone. It was very quiet. I smiled, thinking I was going to finally get at least one good night's rest. I fell asleep. **THEN IT STARTED.** I was in the back seat of a car on the passenger side. This was interesting because I did drive for a rideshare company on and off part-time, which *she* would have known if *she* hacked my phone, and also knew my GPS location. Although as a rideshare driver, I would be in the driver seat and not the passenger. In the back seat of this car, I sat. It was nighttime and the road was not busy with traffic.

Strangely, I noticed the car was swerving and driving about in an uncontrolled way. When I looked over to the driver's seat to see who was driving, it was my mother! The thing is, my mother was dead in real life. In this dream, my mother's hands looked like they were tied to the steering wheel and her body and head flopped around in the seat as the car tumbled and jerked sit-to-side down the road. I was terrified, not because the car was out of control, but because my dead mother was about to kill me as well, or what it looked like...

The car swerved recklessly down the road, even driving into the opposite lane of traffic, twice almost front-ending an oncoming vehicle. Then the car drove to the left side of the road, in the opposite lane. There was a very deep cliff, about 25 feet off the road. The car swerved back and forth a few times as if it was intentionally wanting to drive off the road and down into the ditch. The third time, the car turn hard left and drove off the road, all four wheels free, and headed down into the dark unknown.

Right before hitting the bottom, everything disappeared, and I saw *her* face looking at me angrily for a split second. After, an image of a heart with blood squirting out of it appeared, then I woke up.

*Someone had just performed witchcraft on me, cunning and secret attack...*

I was drenched in sweat, it was still nighttime. My chest felt very tight, and my heart was so much in pain, I screamed. I could barely breath and fell off the bed. A bottle of water I sat hours before on the end table fell off. I grabbed it and drank the whole bottle and tried breathing deep breaths. I went in the kitchen to get some food then laid in bed, being exhausted, and having no energy. I was trying to grasp what just took place. I knew I had just been attacked and there was only one person who came to mind, *her*.

I went onto Twitter and noticed *she* had posted up pictures of *herself* playing with weapons, sharp objects, and even a doll, yes ones typically used in voodoo. I assume *she* mistook when I told *her* one of my ex-lovers had a .45 ACP handgun and other weapons, but she never used them to threaten me. But no, *she* wasn't mistaken. I did go to the doctor, and as always, *"You are healthy, we can't find anything wrong with you."*

**GUEST** – *"Wow, what a story! Why are you always drenched in sweat when these happen to you?"*
**MR. J** – "Well, the metaphysical realm and dreamscape is purely energy. When these things happen, there is too much energy involved for the body to handle. So, the body heats up, and sweats to try and keep cool."
**GUEST** – *"I get that. Are you mad that she did witchcraft on you? Thankfully you are still alive!"*
**MR.J** – "Keep reading, you'll find out."

## THE DAY I 'RAN' - FED UP

I wrote a goodbye message to everyone on my Twitter page, that I wouldn't be on there any longer. She Tweeted a picture of herself saying goodbye back. It was obvious she was very heartbroken and sad, trying to hold back her tears. After that day, I could feel a heavy sense of anger, sadness, and grief that I shouldn't have been feeling. Where was it all coming from? I'm not an emotional person.

I wasn't able to actually delete the page, so I was left to deactivate it. This is when the obsessive thoughts most in the Twin Soul community mention, began. I couldn't get *her* off my mind. Every so often I'd reactivate my account to see what *she* was posting, and of course, it was *her* being very aggressive and defensive. Eventually I left Twitter for good and never looked back.

## "WHAT THE HECK IS THIS???"

Various strange events (seeing repeat numbers, seeing people who look like *her*, hearing *her* voice in my head, smelling the food *she* ate, feeling *her* emotions, ext.) and other things took place over the course of 10 months after leaving *her*. It also included very intense dreams of *her*, weird body pains, sounds of air flow and popping sounds coming from my midsection, a high/drunken feeling while walking, and constant malfunctions with any electronic device I came near, including my own cell phone and cash registers at various stores.

I went online to find out what it was I was experiencing with this *woman*. I remembered a few years before, I ran into a picture online that said "Twin Flames" at the top and below a description. I was reading various stuff like kundalini awakening and how the early 21st century way of living disconnects us from God and how nature reconnects us to God.

I thought nothing of the Twin Flame picture I saw, it wasn't me or something I knew of. But in late August I did search 'Twin Flames'. The more I read the more it lined up with what I was experiencing from my short but intense and deadly encounter with *her*. Even after leaving *her*, I still researched Twin Flames, looking for answers. Eventually I found myself on a writing forum called Quora.com, and since then became a writer on the subject and experience of Twin Souls.

## BEGINNING OF OUR 'SEPARATION'

It became an every night occurrence. I would go to bed and have intense dreams of *her* and I. Usually, they were friendly interactions, sometimes we played in the grass and trees as kids, others, *her* and I seemed to avoid each other. Over the summer of 2021, I met a fellow Soul Twin in person from the online Twin Flame community on Quora.com. We became friends. Months later, she somehow found *her* phone number.

At this point, I wasn't interested in contacting or seeing *her*. *She* deleted *her* Twitter, and I wasn't able to reach *her* by phone. I attempted to do that months prior. But this person from the online community insisted that I at least try. Of course, upon reaching out to *her*, no response. I wasn't surprised. I did more than enough research by this time to become aware of a widespread issue amongst other Soul Twins, where they had trouble getting ahold of their Twin once they separated.

In the summer of 2021, I worked a full-time job and had a business which I started. I was still investing in the stock market and cryptocurrency. I wasn't thinking about *her* much, until this person from the online Twin Soul community persuaded me to at least try to get in contact with *her* and 'send her love'.

At the time, I gained a loyal following on Quora.com. I was also very much into helping other Soul Twins by this point. I realize I managed to pull my energy from *her* and focus on my life, something many of the female Soul Twins struggled to do.

It happened again in 2020. I met another person from the online community who somehow found *her* phone number, this time a different one. I wondered, though, why should I have to be the one calling *her*? It became obvious *she* was not fond of men, there was some miscommunication (and lack of) between us, and then the whole witchcraft thing at the end which made me not want to talk to *her*. If anything, I saw it as *she* needed to contact me to apologize.

Then I moved out of my hometown with the help of one of the Soul Twins from the community on Quora.com. I began a new job, and my life took a different direction. I started writing books while working a full-time job, this guidebook being one of them. Over the course of being engaged with the online Twin Soul community, I got to hear lots of interesting stories from other Soul Twins. I even met a few in person, which further made me realize that I encountered something which was not normal, and certainly does not happen to everyone.

## MORE TO COME...

I have nothing against *her*. I don't regret leaving. But what an intense experience! Although, other things would happen over the course of the next three years. One thing though...I do hope *she* forgives herself and finds peace in *her* life. I don't enjoy seeing other people stress, struggle, and self-destruct. If I found a better way for myself, I know *she* can too. I will add other parts of my experience with *her* in the other sections of this guidebook.

## MY SOUL TWIN MIRRORING

Upon coming across the comment on Twitter which *she* posted, the 'mirroring' between us became obvious. It was the first time I ever looked in the mirror and was 'triggered'. Due to not knowing what I was about to get into (Soul Twin mirroring of behavior), I lashed out at *her*, not knowing who *she* was or why *she* posted what *she* posted, something I normally don't do. I did not know at the time that we were mirroring each other's behavior.

I noticed *her* picture and was drawn to it. When I clicked on *her* profile to get a clearer look at the picture, I was shocked. The woman was GORGEOUS. But what started pulling me in was looking into *her* eyes. Eyes are my favorite part of a woman's body. I know what I need to know by looking in them. *Her* eyes were eyes that I only seen on one woman before. They were glossy, deep, mysterious, and definitely eyes that see EVERYTHING.

I noticed right away looking at *her* other pictures that *she* had every single physical attribute I have always found attractive in a woman, down to the freckles on *her* face. From *her* long black hair, *her* eyes, pretty face, light-mid tone skin, to *her* slim but still curvy body, the way *she* dressed and even sat crisscrossed. We had the same smile and direct eye contact. We even had similar facial features. I read some of *her* other postings and was in awe at how perceptive, wise, and soulful she was. It reminded me of myself. The more I looked through *her* page the more everything I saw and read reminded me of myself. A few of *her* pictures gave me extreme DeJa'Vu.

What took me home was when I watched a video of *her* talking. I clicked on the video not being prepared for what I was about to hear. *She* had the most unique voice I ever heard from a woman, so soft and gentle but still womanly and strong. Even the way *she* spoke had me tearing up and feeling a little struck. *Her* voice sounded familiar and echoed inside me. I had to get off *her* profile because looking at it was too intense for me and started to confuse me. In a way, it was like this *woman* had been with me all my life, carefully observing my behavior, likes, dislikes, what stirs me, what calms me, what turns me on, what makes me happy, sad, angry, ext. It's like *she* lived with me all my life and copied me in every way.

I had to get off Twitter. I told myself I must be imagining things. Or *she* must have been secretly spying on me for years and knew everything about me, and was copy-catting me. No way, it couldn't be that of course! Grrrr, get off Twitter already!

"Who the heck is this? Am I going crazy?" I thought to myself. I tried not to think too much of it. I followed *her* anyways because I thought we would be able to relate on a lot of things. I wasn't expecting to make any friends on Twitter and definitely not begin what I would soon after learn was my Soul Twin journey. It started simple and small, just a few comments here and there I made on some of *her* posts. I didn't know why, but all of a sudden, since the day I first engaged with *her* on there, I had not been able to free her from my mind.

I ALWAYS thought about *her*. It was strange. Her name and face stayed in my head. This never happened to me with any woman I had ever met in my life. I don't get attached. But with *her*, it was less than a day. This was the beginning of me learning and experiencing what attachments are.

Those few comments on *her* posts turned into lots of comments and deeper conversations. It got more strange, and my curiosity was through the roof. The more we talked and learned about each other, the more I felt like this *woman* was someone who had learned everything about me, even my secrets and learned to mimic me. It was strange, but somehow so addictive and pleasant experiencing this *woman*, even thousands of miles away from each other.

I wrote a list of all the things *she* and I had similar and I eventually stopped because I just kept finding things and the page was already full. I wanted to know more about this *woman*, on a deeper and more personal level. I told *her* I was going to DM and did just that. Things got really intense. So intense that the triggering increased, and I could not remain engaged with *her* without the pain and intensity becoming unbearable. I could tell the same was happening to *her*.

This was around the same time I had the second dream of *her* that I still remember today vividly. In the dream, *she* was standing on a sidewalk, in front of a building. *She* wore what looked like a graduation gown. *She* had long, black, silky hair, a very pretty face, and had the same smile that I did. Looking into *her* glossy, deep eyes, I saw all my own thoughts, feelings, desires, fears, trauma, beliefs, and energy. I was looking at the *female* version of myself. Myself in a *woman's* body. Neither of us exchanged words in the dream, but the energy alone and eye contact was highly intense.

Whoever *she* was, *she* knew everything about me. There was nothing I could hide from *her*. The idea of a secret no longer existing or being something that could exist. I was embarrassed, guilty, and ashamed of myself, and so was *she*.

I had more intense and mysterious dreams of this *woman*. So much so that I continued to try and figure out what I was experiencing. I had done a lot of reading on Quora.com on Twin Flames (Quora comes up a lot on Google "Twin Flame" searches) and decided to create an account and have feeds go to my notifications.

The more I learned, I eventually came to a place of accepting this *woman* and the intense energy that I couldn't run from. Since then, I have learned so much about myself, healed, and changed my life in a way I wasn't able to do before meeting her. I'm no longer confused about *her* or what all this is. I know exactly who *she* is, and what all this is about. *She's* me. And this is about experiencing the Oneness that is everything and everyone. This is a soul journey to ascension back to Union, or as I call Oneness Consciousness™.

## MY SOUL TWIN DREAMS

About those series of intense and vivid dreams I had when I was 3 years old...In the one which I was on the island and saw the dragons under the water, those other three people...one of them actually was *her*. The energy and presence of the long black-haired *woman* was the same. The other two, I met one of them as well, actually in person. The same hair, hair color, height, small body frame, ext. Did I not mention before I have the gift of foresight? This gift causes me (yes it still happens!) to see people in dreams before I meet them in real life.

It all connects. My whole life experience, the dreams, the soul journey, the Soul Twin meeting, ext. It all connects. I see the big picture. The journey to Union, Oneness Consciousness™, or a conscious state of awareness that everyone and everything is One Energy.

In another dream, I met *her* at an airport. I get lost in places like airports, and I figured *she* would have a better time finding me. I stood in a spot looking for *her* and felt a tap on my back. I turned around and there *she* was, smiling back at me.

In another dream, *she* texted me that *she* missed me, never forgot about me and was so sorry for ignoring me for so long and *she* wanted to know if I could forgive her, and if I did, *she* wanted to see me in person.

A few days after I had a different dream, I was standing near what looked like a barn or a shed, and when I turned and looked over, *she* was running towards me and jumped on me to hug me.

## MY SOUL TWIN ~ LEARNING TO LOVE

I was tired from running errands and helping my first client in my business. I took a shower and went to bed. I fell asleep.

In the dream I sat down in the yoga standard pose with my eyes closed. When I opened my eyes, I noticed I was sitting in a large grass field where the grass was cut really low but it was still full and fluffy. I noticed a little *girl* sitting directly in front of me. *She* had black hair and wore a dress. In the dream I knew who the *girl* was. But *she* was behaving in a way that had me concerned. *She* was playing with a doll which every time *she* stabbed it or said something mean to it, *she* felt a big pain in her heart.

I asked *her* "why are you hurting yourself?" *She* replied *"I hate you. You hurt me. I need to kill you!"* *She* attacked the doll more. *She* cried tears of pain, because every time *she* attacked the doll, *she* felt the pain in *her* own heart, in *her* soul. I asked the *girl* "There is no way I could have hurt you. I've been sitting here in a deep sleep for a few thousand years, and you are obviously a younger soul than I am. Can you please stop hurting yourself?" *She* replied, *"Leave me alone!"* *She* then attacked the doll even more, still crying from the pain *she* felt. I told the *girl* "The pain you are feeling in your heart and soul, you are causing by trying to harm me. I'm sorry to say but you are hurting your Self. The one you are attacking when you try to hurt me is your Self."

The *girl* got angry and threw the doll away from *her*, and the items *she* used to attack the doll. *She* turned *her* face away from me, with *her* arms folded, with *her* eyes closed and head up, still angry and dropping tears from *her* eyes. I knew the *girl* would be okay. So, I closed my eyes. I don't remember how long my eyes were closed, but when I opened them, the *girl* was sitting in front on me looking at me smiling! *She* had a different dress on, one that caught my attention, it was very pretty and elegant. They went along perfectly with *her* braided pigtails. I noticed some flowers (roses and lavender) planted in front of me.

I asked the *girl* "You are happy this time. You learned how to love yourself. You learned every time you sought to hurt someone else, you caused your Self the pain. I am proud of you." The *girl* said *"I'm sorry I tried to hurt you. Oh, I mean, I was trying to hurt myself. But I am sorry anyways."* I said "Lesson learned. But why did you plant these flowers in front of me?"

She replied *"Because roses always make me happy. I wished the man who truly loves me would give me roses, so I know it's him. I planted the roses as a gift for you because when I was hurting myself, you were the only man who was concerned about me. You loved me when no one else did. You even saved my life, I was about to kill myself and didn't even know it. Thank you for saving me and truly loving me. These roses and lavender are for you!"*

"You are right. Another lesson learned! Good student! But how did you know I like lavender?" I asked. *She* replied, *"I know who you are!"* I asked, "And who is that?" I asked. The *girl* got a sad faced and looked down. "You don't have to tell me, it's okay." I said. *She* replied *"I didn't know before, but you are him! You are me. I finally found you! I'm sorry I tried to hurt you."* My eyes closed shut again. When my eyes opened, the *girl* was gone. I looked to the left, *she* wasn't there, I looked to the right, *she* wasn't there either. I looked ahead and only the roses and lavender where there. A light breeze passed through, and I heard the voice of a *woman*.

Then a *woman* walked in front of me from behind me. *She* sat down in front of me, smiling. I noticed, the *woman* looked like the little *girl*. *"I love you."* She spoke. I replied, *"You mean you love yourself? But thank you for loving me, I honor that."* She replied *"Oh yes, you taught me how to love my Self. But I wanted to love you in return, because you taught me how to love my Self, and I want to share this love with you."* I replied "Well it's only us here, we can. Yes."

The *woman* leaped forward at me and gave me a hug. We both started to rise upward above the ground, still hugging.

## REBIRTH (TRANSCENDENCE) DREAM

I was in a house full of people. Some I know, some I don't. I wondered why there were so many people in the house. I held a baby (baby symbolic for birth or something new). The baby was happy and giggly. Then I happened to be in a room. *She* walked up to me like *she* was going to hug me. *She* was very happy and excited. The energy from *her* was intense! I woke up right before *she* touched me because that happens whenever I see *her* in a dream and the energy gets too high.

I woke up and heard the masterpiece of a song - Bob Marley's song "Could you be loved" as if it was playing from a speaker in the room.

Unhook.

# SECTION TWO
## A PARTICULAR WRITING FORUM

While trying to figure out what I was experiencing with *her,* I consistently found myself on the writing forum, Quora.com.

This writing forum would serve as the place I learned a lot about Soul Twins. It also has been the place I have engaged with other Soul Twins, met a few in person, and eventually created my own space. I experienced the worst, the best, and all in between. But it also showed me a lot of things which most people performing internet searches about Twin Flames and Twin Souls might not be aware of...some things that can be jaw dropping, undeniable, and triggering.

I realized the reality of Soul Twins is not the roses and sunshine many pictures, videos, and writings paint them to be. But then again, you easily come across content on the internet from female Twin Flames, tarot card readers, energy channelers, psychics, and even undercover witches about how toxic and unavailable the male Twin Flames are. But it's much deeper than that...

## NOT SO WELCOMED to WELCOME

Although I first joined Quora.com wondering why I was experiencing all the wild and intense things from my encounter with her, I found myself helping other Twins with their journey. They were mostly female Twins, more than 97%.

The Twin Soul community online, and especially on Quora.com was heavily dominated with female Soul Twins. It felt like I was the only male Twin in the room filled with nothing but women. I did seek to find some male Twins on there, but they were either unreachable, or rarely online.

This is when I realized a heavy majority of the female Twins were struggling with the Journey. *"He won't even reply to any of my text messages." "Why is my Supposed 'Twin' Flame running from me? I tried telling him how much I loved him, but he blocked me." "The night I went over to my DM's house, we talked for hours, and it felt really good, we had sex, and after that I never heard from him again. It's been weeks but I can't get him off my mind. Why am I going through this?" "He did it again. Every time me and my Supposed 'Twin' Flame get close, he runs off and gets into a relationship with another woman. Why is this happening to me?" "What can I do to get my DM to share his feelings? I know he loves me but every time we start talking deeper, he pulls away."*

It was so common to see these types of answer requests and comments on other writer's posts. Then it hit me. Something was very different here. I wasn't the one running or avoiding the connection. It was her. I was the one online, seeking answers, engaging others, and wanting to know what was going on and why I experienced what I did with her.

This is when I began sharing my experiences, dreams, and the intense energy I felt from her. The female Twins caught on, and I found myself surrounded by female Twins, all asking questions and for me to share more. But it wasn't all pleasant. There were also female Twins who I saw as being very masculine, rude, and defensive, simply for me being a male Soul Twin. They told me that I was toxic, stupid, and in my 'ego'. I ignored it for the most part, and sometimes finding myself having to put my foot down.

## HELPING & BEING HELPED BY MY OWN KIND

Sometimes it got so bad that I was told I was just in my feelings and that my journey didn't mean anything or hold any weight. The same I desired to be helped by and help, pushed me off the forum. I know I needed to take a break. But then I decided that I should throw it all in the trash, that I was wasting time. Maybe they were right. I just needed to clear my head. Plus, I never met the *woman* in person any way. Was I stuck in a coma dreaming all of this or something? I needed to wake up.

But one night I had a dream, yes, another one...The Most High's favorite way of communicating with me. In the dream, I saw Earth from a distance, in space. *she* and I appeared from a sea of dim lights. As we ascended up into the sky and into space, I noticed the dim lights grew brighter. A small group of the lights followed under us, forming what looked like an umbrella which covered the Earth. As *her* and I ascended, all of the lights across Earth grew brighter, and eventually the light was so bright they all merged into one big light, then I woke from the dream. I asked aloud, "What was that?"

I immediately felt a strong urge to get back on Quora.com. I surely didn't want to, but I know what that dream meant. I was led to be on there for a very important purpose. Upon getting back onto Quora.com, I was repulsed by the same things which initially made me leave there. That's when I remembered something. The female Twins who did enjoy what I shared, mentioned a common thing, an appreciation for my perspective as a male Soul Twin. It stuck to me – Twin Flame Journey From A Man's Perspective.

Then I realized I could have my own section within the writing forum, called a space. This meant that I would not have to write or comment on other's content. Guess what I named the space? Of course – Twin Flame Journey From A Man's Perspective!

I uploaded a picture of watercolor art I made, a photograph of a creek I took In West Virginia, and began writing posts. But I did manage to find a few of other's spaces which enjoyed my writings, so I made sure to comment on their content. My space grew a small but loyal following. A few times, due to the same reasons as mentioned before, I attempted to leave. But I kept being pulled back to write on Quora. So, I stayed permanently.

In 2023, I felt pushed to write a book to help Soul Twins. With all that I experienced with *her*, engaging the Twin Soul community online, meeting a few Twins in person, and a handful of dreams I had, I knew I needed to not only share my experience, but reveal some truths to the world. Soul Twin – a connection most desire but few understand in its entirety.

## DIVINE MASCULINE OR DIVINE FEMININE?

Another thing which stood out to me was the usage of the terms Divine Masculine, Divine Feminine, DM, and DF. DM is short for Divine Masculine. DF is short for Divine Feminine. Of course, men are the masculine (they should be in theory), and the women the feminine (should be in theory). But DIVINE masculine and DIVINE feminine? What does that mean? I don't think anyone should call themselves Divine unless they actually know what it mean, and they are willing to bear the responsibility. I'll explain more in the next two sections of this guidebook 'What Are Twin Flames' and 'Seeking: The Beginning Of The Stages.'

## END OF JEALOUSY AGAINST SOUL TWINS

Believe it or not, I was subjected to jealousy coming from other Twins on Quora.com. Now, I know this journey isn't easy, and the love and pull toward our Twin can be intense. But eventually we all come to the point where we realize that we aren't in 'separation' from our Twin, we just got a glimpse at ourselves in the Divine Mirror. Another side of this, we also get to see our love and attachment to behaviors, lifestyles, and beliefs which are deemed 'toxic', unpleasant, and unhealthy. We then have an important choice to make.

We have to either set boundaries against such things, or we have to throw them away. This is not just a Soul Twin thing, but it is with everyone we encounter. Many of us did not fully know ourselves inside and out...good, bad, and fugly, until after we met our Twin.

It is a journey for all of us to increase our awareness to see that, and find the strength to change. This change could mean different eating habits, choosing friends that keep us out of trouble rather than those who get us into trouble, leaving abusive family members, letting go of addictions that are not healthy for us, and picking healthier romantic partners to share our life and energy with. We have to make a choice to move on from or set boundaries with our Twin, if they are toxic, unresponsive, abusive, and/or emotionally unavailable.

But me personally, the Soul Twin journey had not been easy for a different reason. I assumed that other Twins would understand and be a support. But even in the Soul Twin community, there exist jealousy.

See, moving on from a Twin (or anyone) is not running from them, although running from them isn't moving on from them either. Moving on does not mean jumping into another relationship or trying to ignore or push away the person.

Moving on simply is a conscious choice to no longer accept toxicity, emotional unavailability, abuse, and non-existent communication.

It is a decision that is not made out of anger, frustration, or hate toward your Twin. It is a choice made when you realize that you cannot change your Twin's behavior or lifestyle. You can't force them to accept the connection or to be with you. You understand that if they want to remain where and how they are, but you do not, it is YOUR choice to move on.

Moving on is not about finding a different person to be with or to have sex with. It is not done to make the Runner Twin jealous, to seek revenge, or to make them see you happy with someone else so that they chase after you. Moving on is a choice. It is not accepting less than a good life. It is also not chasing after and accepting those things that don't make you whole, at peace, and abundant.

I had conflict with certain female Twins from the online community because as their words, *"Why are you waiting for your Twin to come back? You need to stop chasing her and waiting for her and find someone who accepts you for who you are." "Someone is out there waiting for you while you are waiting for your Twin to come back." "She is running from you because you are still chasing her. You need to stop chasing her and find someone else to be with."*

Now, when I heard these things, I wanted to laugh. Because first, I know I am very well at explaining things. And I for sure do not have any reason to chase after anyone, or run from anyone, including *her*. I let go of it all seven months after meeting her. I realized that this *woman* was not going to miraculously stop running. No amount of love, communication, sending letters, gifts, prayer, or anything was going to set me free from the attachment to the very things I do not like. The problem here was an attachment to a *woman* I never met and who obviously did not care about me. This attachment to *her* needed to somehow be broken and I didn't see anyone talking about how to do so. I'm not talking about the infamous cord cutting rituals either.

Allowing yourself to chase after and be attached to people and things that are unhealthy and destructive is a reflection of your own unhealthy and destructive behavior, beliefs, and lifestyle. I wasn't going to do that. I know better than that. I struggled for seven months with this attachment. Until one day I broke free..

I was not going to hope for her return. I decided to move toward a healthier me, a healthier life, and healthier choices. I was only going to use *her* as a mirror to show me what all about myself was toxic, out of balance, or unhealthy; that 'I' was going to proactively make changes in those areas. And as for *her*, I wished no harm on *her*, and only for the Most High to keep *her* safe and keep working to bring her out of the self-imprisonment *she* put herself into. Life was still working on her.

Since then, my life and much about me completely changed for the better. But the difference is that it is not just a verbal "I have healed". I have real and tangible proof that I had not been chasing or waiting for some *woman* to come towards me, on top of me being "healed".

Over the years following leaving my Supposed 'Twin', I lost weight, eliminated ALL of the health problems, made significant changes to my eating habits, went from living in someone else's house to owning my own home, I went from jobless to starting a profession in truck driving, and turned my financial well-being for the better.

I also opened my second LLC, started my 'mission' (EXCELLENCE on Fire!) as far as leading others into a healthier life and healing of their minds, hearts, and souls, and began making preparations so I can start a family. I certainly was not sitting around waiting for a *woman* to come back to me. I worked 100 plus hours a week and spend a lot of time around other people and literally had no time, energy, or thought to chase a woman who was MIA (missing in action).

But yet, there are those who were seemingly trying to tell me that I need to stop sitting around waiting for her and needed to move on. Yea, I 'moved on' long ago, and I have actual things to show for it. But I realize that some in the Soul Twin community still struggle to accept the fact that they can love someone so much and that same person not love them back or want to be with them. They hate the fact that they have tried everything to either move on or get their Twin back. Nothing worked.

They still fight and wrestle with the emotions and the connection they feel, continuing the running and chasing from their end. They still think they need to make their Twin come back or they just need to wait. Or that they need to be in denial and run into someone else's arms after they realize their Twin does not love them and is not coming back to prove that they have moved on.

See, being a young man (I was 29 years old at the time) and having only been on the journey for 2 years, it was assumed by some that I didn't know what I was doing. It was assumed that she was running because I was chasing still. Many others have been on the Journey for 10, 15, and even 30 plus years! But see, I am aware that age and time alone does not determine maturity, progress, or the number of lessons learned.

Sadly, I had been subjected to jealousy from other Twins because I wasn't stressed out why this and why that. I simply didn't care anymore. I moved on, bettered myself, bettered my life, and they were jealous of that. They could have done the same, but why didn't they?

## TAKE TWO ~ A DIFFERENT PERSPECTIVE

I learned very quickly and early that your Soul Twin is not someone to chase after or run from. They are simply a mirror of your Self. If they do return, it is just another opportunity to look in the mirror, not necessarily for a relationship, marriage, or anything of those matters. I liken it to going in the bathroom to clean your skin and do your hair. You look in the mirror and decide what you want to do. Then you take some supplies and run it through your hair. You might take a comb or brush to straighten your hair. You might apply oil to damaged ends, or even curl your hair so that it is wavy. Or you might decide to put it into a hair style. You apply a scrub pad and cleansers to your skin to remove dead skin. Then you apply creams to your skin so that it looks healthy. You might arch your eye brows, tweeze hairs, or apply make-up. The end result is a healthy and pretty you in the mirror.

Your Soul Twin is a mirror for your Soul, mind, emotions, life, and energy. If you don't like what you see, you have to make the necessary changes, and for many, that is very difficult for various reasons.

A couple months after meeting my Supposed 'Twin', I bought a $1 journal from a local store, so I could write down everything she mirrored back to me. This was so that *I* could make the changes I needed to make for my own good, and not for her to come back to me.

There is no need to be jealous of another Twin's progress or judge their lack of progress. We are all where we need to be to learn what is beneficial for us. I know Twins who are in communication with theirs, who are married to theirs, and those who get to make love to theirs, and yet I had nothing! I learned the lesson, she served her purpose, and my life completely reflects it.

## CAN WOMEN BE TOXIC?

I saw how obvious it was. The male Twins had nowhere near the same presence online or on Quora.com. The place was full of female Twins wondering why their Twin ran from them, or why their Twin won't reach out to them, or why they were on bad behavior. I made it part of my day-to-day routine to seek answers and to talk with other Twins about what they experienced. I figured I could help the women since that's all I had to work with.

The only way through as far as I could see, was that no matter what they believed about their Twin, their Twin was simply mirroring their own soul back to them. I was met with a lot of resistance by most, and a sense of relief by others for suggesting a different perspective on looking at their situation. But that resistance, what was it?

I noticed over time, that many of the female Twins were unable to see and admit that they ALSO were guilty. It wasn't only their DM that was on bad behavior. I felt their energy, their fear, anxiety, insecurities, need for attention, lies, entitlement, need for control, lack of introspection, impulsive reactions, low self-esteem, lack of self-worth, ext.

**GUEST** – *"Come on Terrence! Women are innocent creatures! Where do you get all that from? You sound crazy and like a woman hater!"*

Oh, I have heard it all! The truth doesn't hurt, it's resistance to accepting the truth that hurts. Mr. J – "It's the rock in our shoe that gives us a foot cramp, that won't rid the foot cramp until the rock is removed and the foot massaged™". But what about the reality that women, even in the Soul Twin community, are not all innocent and free from doing as much harm as their DMs?

Men don't run from women. It's not natural and we all know that. Nothing makes a man get on his knees other than his desire for a woman. Even God is jealous that a man kneels his body, heart, and soul in desire to a woman. Male animals don't run from the female. Why are the men turning their backs and leaving the women? Something has been going on and it is not what we think it is.

If Soul Twin love is so pure, profound, and life-changing, why don't the male/Runner Twins want it?

I have long believed that relationships and connections are a two-way street. And two-way streets are built for traffic to flow in both directions. In the same way, energy flow in both directions in any connection between two people. A cycle is created. I remember having this conversation with my Supposed 'Twin'. She believed firmly that only men are abusive and destructive. I argued against that. What comes first, the chicken or the egg? If chicken but no egg, once the chicken dies there are no offspring to grow into another chicken to lay more eggs. If egg and no chicken, well that's obvious.

You can't have the egg without the chicken. The chicken and the egg BOTH come together and at the same time. It is called the cycle of life. Everything is a cycle and in cycles. If the woman be the chicken, and the man the egg, they both come together. Life is experienced by both, and passed along by both. And in the same way, abuse in relationships is experienced by both, and passed on to the next by both. Although here, we are asking why predominately the male Twins are avoiding their female Twins.

You have heard it so many times. *"He is afraid of love, that's why he is running." "He just wants to sleep around with other women and not me, why doesn't he love me?" "He won't talk to me, this is the third time he has ghosted me." "He won't leave his karmic for me."* It is always seen as if the male Twins have walked away because they have a problem.

But here, I am suggesting that if your Twin doesn't want to be with you, around you, or even communicate with you, it might be time to look at yourself in the mirror. The most difficult thing for a human to do is admit their own wrong doing and harmful behavior. And I think women, even Soul Twin women struggle with that worse than anything in their life.

I know that many women may have a deep need for attention, control, and an easy life (less burden emotionally speaking). Sometimes, maybe more than they realize. These needs go so far out of hand, one will even destroy or get stuck to people and relationships which are toxic and unproductive. The need can linger and never go away, even when attention, complete control and the feeling of being loved is present.

The men aren't the only ones who have been on bad behavior, some of the women are also guilty, in their own ways. But if someone is truly toxic and narcissistic, you have to ask yourself how can you be so deeply in love with such an individual? That would say a lot about you. If someone doesn't want to be with you and blocks or restricts communication, why don't you get the message that they simply aren't interested? If they have trauma and need healing, then let them do that and let them be. If they are married, have kids, or are already with someone else and they prefer to remain with them, then that is their choice, not yours.

We all took the same test and so few saw it for what it was. I know what it was for me. I needed to let go of fears, heal my traumas that kept my masculine energy down. I needed to see somethings that exist in all women that most don't talk about or know about and usually the only ones who do are women themselves. How could I ever be a happy man, especially with a woman, not knowing the nature of half the human population? I think for women, learning to not need attention, relinquishing control, and realizing healthy connections with sane and present people is the way to happiness. If only it was that simple...

No one wants to be forced into your life, or forced to love you, or pay you attention. I think for men, prioritizing their own physical health and financial growth is most important alongside having a strong backbone. I think it is wise the DMs walked away. Men are supposed to stand up for themselves, even if that means walking away from someone they love. I have met a few DFs in person, and I know it is possible for Soul Twin women to be toxic, just like the men they initially raved on about, and loved so deeply.

The men outside the Soul Twin community also turn away from women when the women are on bad behavior. I'm not surprised if Soul Twin men do the same. Learn the lesson! Hear the wake-up call and take action! If you want to be the woman that your Twin will want to kneel to (you know what I mean by that) you have to become that woman. But do it for you.

That's all this journey is. A mirror to look back at ourselves. You do it to put make-up on and to do your hair, why not for you soul? The Soul Twin is nothing more than a living mirror image of ourselves. When you look at them what do you see? That is all you!

One thing that I initially found astounding in the Soul Twin Community was the endless complaining from DFs about being emotionally weighed down by their DMs not showing love back or no communication. For one thing, we all have a right to remain silent, second, no one is obligated to love you except yourself, your parents (birth right), and your married spouse (vowed).

A lot of DFs have reached out to me for help, and I have helped as many as I could. I have seen dozens of DFs do a 180 and turn their lives around by simply looking at the situation for what it is and not shaming or demonizing the DMs because they aren't getting what they want out of the connection. I have seen a few who have truly brought themselves out of despair and shifted their focus on looking at themselves, and what they can do about making their own lives better.

No one can tell me that it is only the DMs that are the cause of why the Soul Twin community was in so much confusion, separation and conflict. "It takes two to tango" still ring true, even for Soul Twins.

I have said for a long time, your Twin isn't someone you NEED to be in a relationship with. They are simply a reflection of yourself, good, bad, and fugly. We always put the good of ourselves in the spotlight while sweeping the bad and fugly under the rug. But our Twins pull that rug to expose the bad and fugly things we hide, and then they run like hell with that rug never giving it back for you to cover up what you attempt to keep in the shadows.

The Soul Twin community initially didn't see Soul Twins coming together physically across the board, because unfortunately most in the community were still stuck in the same unhealthy cycles. And it's no one's fault except their own. And it isn't only the DMs side, it's on the DF's side as well. Those who realized that and made a change for themselves, they know what came afterwards. We are responsible for our own lives, and the lives we create. Nothing really change or improve in one's life until they take that finger pointer and point it at themselves rather than at other people.

I think the Soul Twin community initially had it all wrong. The community screwed up by creating so much content on the internet about the DMs being toxic and narcissistic. How welcoming is that? If you had some serious life traumas and walked away from an amazing person you met to avoid hurting them, would you want to walk into a room full of people who want you to love them and give them attention, but yet they have so many bad things to say about you?

I think we forgot that the DMs needed healing for their soul, and not be in a relationship they weren't ready for. Have DFs created a welcoming space for them? A lot of DFs won't admit it, but they are part of the cause of why their DM ran and hasn't returned. Where are the DMs going to go? The world hated and mistreated them already, and in the spiritual community they had more added to their shoulders.

You can change that. Be mindful what you share about DMs on the internet, and in the community. Don't support DM-bashing. Create a fresh and welcoming environment for the DMs to come to!

# SECTION THREE
## WHAT IS A TWIN SOUL?

Highly controversial in the Soul Twin community are the questions *"What are Twin Flames?"* and *"What is a Twin Soul?"* You will hear a variety of responses. This make it confusing for people to determine if they have a Soul Twin. Some deny its existence and say that it is just New Age nonsense. I thought that myself at one point...until I was shown otherwise.

**NOTE:** While studying this guidebook, keep in mind about the Self. The Self can express itself in two different ways: the Higher Self, and the Shadow Self. They are also known as the Higher Self, and the Lower Self. We all have a Higher Self and Shadow Self. As you study this guidebook, you will come to learn that Soul Twins are a manifestation of the Higher Self and the Shadow Self. One Twin will embody the Higher Self, while the other will embody the Shadow Self. It is important to understand that we all have both aspects. Therefore, we cannot judge our Soul Twin as 'evil' or 'toxic', because they are our Self in another body. They are YOU. If you feel that your Twin is toxic or a narcissist, you are simply looking at your Shadow Self. They are a reflection of the Shadow Self within you.

The same is true for the Higher Self. One Twin will embody the Higher Self. No, it does not mean they are arrogant or pretend to be above other people. Remember, they are YOU in another body. But you may feel like your Twin is an angel, as if they are too good to be true. This may trigger you and make you feel unworthy of them, or like you don't deserve them. Understand that when you look at your Twin (if they are embodying the Higher Self), you are looking at the Higher Self which is within you. There is no need to feel unworthy or not deserving. You ARE worthy?

So, a Twin Soul incarnate as Twins, one embodying the Higher Self, and the other the Shadow Self. But essentially, the two are actually One entity.

**NOTE:** While studying this guidebook, keep in mind of what I call the Mirrored Self. The Mirrored Self is just that. The Self looks at itself in the Divine Mirror. This is where we get the perception of polarity and Masculine/Feminine energies. Really, the Self is being revealed as having two major components of itself, or two expressions. The Self can manifest in a masculine expression and in a feminine expression. This means that the Self is the Oneness of Masculine and Feminine energies. It is the Oneness of the Higher Self and Shadow Self. This explains why we see men and women. This explains why men are masculine in their natural state, and why women are feminine in their natural state. For the Self to incarnate in this Universe and Earth plane, it must do so as the Mirrored Self. One body takes on the masculine/male expression, and the other body takes on the feminine/female expression. This is also why birth rates are generally 50% male, 50% female. Really, the man and the woman are the physical representatives of each component/expression of the Self.

The masculine/male represent the Higher Self (Sun, light), and the feminine/female represent the Shadow Self (Moon, dark). The Higher Self seeds the Shadow Self. The Shadow Self receives the seed and the Self is rebirthed as offspring. The Light shine in the Dark. The offspring continue the Mirrored Self, Higher/Shadow Self, Masculine/Feminine, and Male/Female expressions.

## THE TRUTH FROM A REAL SOUL TWIN

To understand what a Twin Flame or Twin Soul is, we will need to take a look at some foundational realities with regard to creation, life, soul, and soul behaviors. It's important to know that a Twin Flame or Soul Twin is not New Age, or something that has recently come about. The reality of Twin Flames and Twin Souls are ancient, they stretch much farther back, and much deeper than any rabbit hole.

A Twin Flame is a multiplying pair-bodied soul. This mean that the soul has the ability to incarnate within multiple, paired physical bodies. This is different than regular souls which can only incarnate in a single physical body at a time. In this section, you will learn how the Twin Flame soul is different than single souls. Twin Flames, as flames suggest, can multiply. A soul can actually incarnate as a large group of people. The energy and complexity of a soul can get so high, that it must incarnate in a group of physical bodies, and not only one or two. There can be multiple pairs of a Twin Flame.

What you see online, are people actually talking about 'Soul Twins', which are different than Twin Flames. There can be multiple pairs of Twin Flames, yet there is only one Soul Twin. I don't use the term 'soulmate', because souls don't have a need to mate (have sex). Souls can polarize, but they don't have sex organs. There can be physical mating with sexual creatures, but soul-mating doesn't exist, as there is only One Soul. What we are actually talking about is a Soul which can polarize into masculine and feminine and incarnate in two physical bodies. The Soul is still One entity. There is never a separation or division. There can't be sex because the Soul is always One entity already. Soulmate describes something different which you will learn shortly.

## THE ORIGIN OF LIFE

Let's take a look at the origin of Soul. Since Soul Twins are a soul, it is necessary to understand the origins of Soul.

Whether you believe in God, Source, The Lord, (or whatever term you use), it is necessary that an original, living, and eternally sovereign entity exist. This is because what we call life, the Universe, and souls must all originate from somewhere (or something). I will use the terms 'Source' to describe this original, eternally sovereign entity. Even though most are familiar with the term 'God', the term 'God' has a different meaning and origin.

How did souls come about? Everything that is created comes from the Source. The Source is Oneness. It is pure consciousness, intelligence, and void. It is mental energy and the material which mirrors the mental energy. The Source is One, yet has two distinct characteristics, which is commonly called Masculine and Feminine. I will say that Masculine and Feminine certainly are One energy, and not two. I have always seen that Masculine and Feminine is actually One energy, it's just that It is expressing Itself in two different ways.

But for the sake of helping you to gain understanding, I will put an 's' at the end of 'soul' for now, and we will work the 's' out, so that you can come to understand the Oneness of all. This is because there are not multiple souls, or multiple lives, but simply one Soul.

## MASCULINE AND FEMININE COMPREHENSION

There is commonly confusion with regard to understanding what is meant by 'masculine' and 'feminine'. Most people assign 'masculine' and 'feminine' to the sex organ of people, and that is incorrect. Remember, masculine and feminine are an expression of a single energy. So, it doesn't matter if someone is a man or a woman, they each will have both masculine and feminine energy. It is also true that a man can behave 'feminine' and a woman can behave 'masculine'.

But we THINK that one belong to a man, and the other to a woman, because of what we see, and how our brains process this reality. When most people look at a man and a woman, their brain process the information captured by their senses, and render the man and woman as two separate entities, one which LOOKS masculine, and the other feminine. This is called duality consciousness, also known as separation consciousness. But how can you be conscious of separation if everything is One? So, I use the term 'Separation Illusion™'. When someone sees a man and a woman as two separate entities, this mean that they are not conscious that a man and a woman are the same entity. They are not conscious that masculine and feminine are the same energy, just that it is behaving in two different ways.

So really, we should say that the man symbolize the masculine expression, and women symbolize the feminine expression. At least in theory that is how it should be. Of course, in the real world, we all have masculine and feminine behavioral characteristics. This can be natural, due to upbringing, culture, religious teaching, entertainment, and societal conditioning.

The only difference between feminine and masculine energies, is that they are the same energy but expressed in two different ways. I define masculine energy as 'action' or 'movement' and feminine energy as 'substance' or 'tangibility'. The substance part is not necessarily physical. They exist and function together. They are inseparable because they are one energy. This bring us to Source creating the Universe. Uni = one, and verse = expression. Put the two together and you get Uni-verse, or one expression. Although it is called 'universe', because of the human mind perceiving duality, the person must awaken to the truth of the universe, that everything and everyone is One entity.

## UNI-VERSE (ONE EXPRESSION)

This Universe we live in was created by Source. Because of this, Source's own characteristics are part of the Universe. The Universe function under 'Oneness', and not duality as commonly taught by many gurus and spiritual coaches. It is said that this Universe is one of duality, but that is incorrect. It is only because the common man and woman are not in Oneness Consciousness™, that they see the Universe as dual. It is not the Dual-verse, or Di-verse, but the Universe! I don't use the term 'Unity Consciousness' because you cannot unite what is already one. So, I use Oneness Consciousness™ instead.

One must take the spiritual journey toward Oneness Consciousness™ so that they become aware that everything and everyone is all One. Everything is One. We are all One. Because Source's own characteristics are part of the Universe, the Universe is also made of, and function with masculine and feminine energy. **Substance + action = energy (or substance) in motion.** This is why the Universe expand and contract, why stars explode, and why the Universe is full of life and things moving and transforming. The universe is a living entity.

All humans, animals, insects, and other lifeforms which take on a physical body, take up physical substance from the Universe. Because Source, and the Universe have both masculine and feminine expressions, so do the physical bodies any souls. But what are souls, how are they created, and what are their purpose?

## ORIGIN OF SOULS

Where do souls come from? It would not be far from truth or reality that Source is the original, eternal Soul. Souls can be created individually, and each soul can be given the ability to incarnate in a physical body. So, if Source is the original Soul, souls would then come directly from Source. I find this to be true based on what I have seen during meditation, and from directly asking The Most High. We really are the children of the Most High, or souls of the Soul.

Souls are pure energy. They are not material, but are immaterial and incorporeal. Souls are purely consciousness, intelligence, and mental. Souls also have both masculine and feminine expressions. This allow them to move, and also have tangible characteristics.

## SOUL POLARITY

I see that this is also a difficult topic for those to understand. It can also be difficult to explain. Let's look at polarity first. I know it is easy to think that polarity means 'two'. But remember, everything in life and the Universe is One.

**GUEST** – *"If everything is One, how is it possible to have polarity?"*
See, that is where the masculine energy (aka movement) come into play. You likely already know that everything moves and vibrates. This vibration happen in patterns. These vibrational patterns create what look like two separate things which are opposite. The vibrational patterns usually take a circular or oval shape.

Suppose you have a man and a woman to stand 10 feet from each other, facing opposite directions. You then instruct them to walk in a circle, having them to walk the same radius. It will look like they are walking in opposite directions. But they are actually both walking the same path and in the same direction. This is what we call and perceive as polarity. So, then polarity is not 'two' separate things, but actually one, with movement in the form of vibrational patterns. Really, polarity is about the vibrational PATTERN, and not about two of anything.

You can say that masculine and feminine are the same energy, under a vibrational pattern. This is where you get soul polarity from. The soul has both masculine and feminine characteristics. They look polarized because the energy has a vibrational pattern. All souls have a vibrational blueprint and pattern, just as Source does, the Universe, and everything else. Source contains all vibrational patterns, in all frequency possibilities.

# SOUL TYPES

**SINGULAR SOULS** – The most common soul type, usually Earthling and young souls. A soul that is young simply is a soul which is created at a lower vibration. The soul's journey is to increase its frequency through life experiences, schooling, and learning lessons. As the soul ascend in frequency, it becomes closer to Source frequency.

**MONAD SOULS** – Monadic Souls are commonly what people call 'soulmates'. A monad is a singular energy which come from Source. Souls can be birthed from the monad. There can be many monads, and they can take on various frequencies and characteristics. Souls from the same monad are known as 'soulmates'. Soulmates are commonly Twin Flames, as monadic souls can multiply, since that is the primary characteristic of a monad – being able to create multiple offspring souls of itself. Monadic souls can be Earthling souls and also StarSeed or cosmic souls.

**STARSEED SOULS** – These are powerful souls which most call 'angels'. They are Soular Souls, which is why they are called StarSeeds. They are very close to Source frequency by default. Since they begin their lives with so much power, in order to incarnate on the physical 3rd Dimension, they would either have to split or spread and incarnate into two bodies. They can also be Twin Flames, as flames suggest fire, which stars and suns create plenty of. Twin Flame StarSeeds are very common on Earth since our home star is a Soul Star. Many StarSeeds are also Melanated people, because of their connection with the

Stars and Soular energies. Melanin gives them the ability to absorb and expel Soular and solar energy without being destroyed by the intensity of energy.

**COSMIC (ET) SOULS** – Another type of angelic soul, cosmic souls are also very powerful. They take on many different forms, frequencies, and characteristics. The universe is full of entities which only few on Earth know of. We call them cosmic souls because they come from far out in the universe. Cosmic souls can be either singular, or usually monadic, or StarSeed souls.

Most souls on Earth are single souls. They are usually in the third dimension or Earth plane. As of the beginning of the Age Of Aquarius, newer single souls are upgraded to at least fourth dimension. But there are souls which come from an 'over soul' or a monad. The monad soul is a soul, but of higher vibrational energy and 'size'. Source can create different over souls with various energetic DNA and blueprints. Souls can then be 'birthed' from the monad. These type of souls are called soulmates. For more information on soulmates, visit the section in this guidebook named 'Soulmates & Karmic Warfare.'

The mating of soulmates is simply the mutual resonance of the same frequency. This means that it is pleasing (emotionally, mentally, and energetically) to be with a soulmate or Twin Flame. Since the energies are the same, there is an energetic resonance that amplifies the energy they both feel between each other. They both 'resonate' and resonate *with* each other.

You only have ONE Soul Twin, but can have many soulmates. Please do not leave someone claiming they are a 'false Twin Flame' and then go looking for your 'real Twin Flame'. You only have one Soul Twin. Everyone has a Soul Twin, but can have many soulmates or Twin Flames if they were born from a monad or are a StarSeed. Many get confused when they meet a soulmate and confuse them for their Soul Twin. They might abandon their Soul Twin to be with a soulmate only for the relationship to not work, yet still love and want to be with their Soul Twin. Others might leave their Soul Twin (they were behaving bad or unavailable) to be with a soulmate and the relationship worked out fine. Please, do not go seeking to be with someone just because they are a soulmate or Twin Flame. Do not chase after people. You will know in your soul who is reasonable, healthy, and productive to be with, and it won't necessarily be a Twin Flame, karmic, Soul Twin, or soulmate.

Monadic souls can birth what are called Monadic Soul Twins. There are also Earthling (Earth-bound) Soul Twins, StarSeed Soul Twins, and Extraterrestrial (ET) Soul Twins. Earthling Soul Twins are created on the 3D physical plane of existence, or in the Earth. StarSeed and ET Soul Twins are not Earthlings. StarSeed and ET Soul Twins are foreigners to Earth and the third dimension. They tend to come from higher dimensions, commonly from 4D up to 12D. StarSeed Soul Twins are home to the stars and Soular energies. Cosmic and ET Soul Twins are home to the cosmos of this Universe, or other Universes. There are also Multiverses, but they will not be discussed in this guidebook.

Due to the higher energetic DNA and blueprint of StarSeed and cosmic (ET) Soul Twins, they are not created in the third dimension or on the Earth plane. They are created in higher dimensions.

# SOUL SUBTYPES

**SOUL TWINS**
**TWIN FLAMES**
**KARMICS**

You will learn more learn more about these three soul subtypes in the section of this guidebook named: Soulmates & Karmic Warfare.

# SOUL CONTRACTS

All souls are living, vibrating entities. They all have a sense of consciousness, intelligence, and mentality. Imagine soul contracts like contracts and agreements we sign throughout our lives. There are business contracts, agreements for job duties in exchange for compensation, the marriage contract, agreements made by roommates to share house chores, and various other contracts and agreements.

In the non-physical realm, there are also contracts and agreements between souls and Source, and between souls themselves. Usually, contracts made between souls and Source will have to do with what you may have heard as soul ascension. All souls want to ascend. I liken this to the desire to earn more money each at year at the same job, or to have healthier and more fulfilling relationships as we move through our years. This can also be like the desire to improve a skill or ability.

The Source-to-soul contract or agreement will allow the soul to go to certain dimensions, worlds, and planes of existence, each with their own challenges and rewards. Souls ascend by 'experiencing life' in different dimensions and worlds. They will have challenges to overcome. They are usually are placed in environments and situations which will require them to 'become aware', use their sense of intelligence (as a non-physical tool), and their mentality to make choices which produce a favorable outcome.

Soul-to-soul contracts and agreements are when two or more souls agree to help each other for the challenges. There are also souls who may agree or make a contract to actually increase the complexity of the challenge, or through additional problems. This forces the soul into a 'greater risk, greater reward' situation where the soul can ascend at exponential rates.

# THE 'EGO'

Now, I have heard the term 'ego' from so many people, and with so many different meanings, that I don't even know what it is. I personally don't know what ego is. I have tried to grasp the meaning, and even asked the Most High what is ego, but I still find myself looking at a blank sheet of paper.

But one thing for sure, ego, at least in its original design, has a sure meaning. I have come to learn that ego is something that Source has placed with each soul as part of their ascension. The ego is an internal challenge which the soul must overcome, so that it can ascend. So, there are 'external', and internal challenges each soul can utilize for its ascension.

**GUEST** – *"Why do souls want to ascend?"*
**MR. J** – "Well, we have to go back to the original, eternal Soul to answer that question. See, Source isn't stagnant or complacent. Source is self-sustaining, self-sufficient, and omnipotent, omnipresent, and doesn't require outside validation. Source is Home. All souls want to make their way back home, to pure consciousness, intelligence, and mentality. The soul's greatest challenge is to transition from unconscious to conscious, from animalistic ways to intelligence, and from impulsive-choice to logical choice. Source also ascend. Because Source also ascend, this phenomenon trickles down to all souls, in different ways."

Some use the term 'ego' to describe what is called arrogance, which is not the same thing. Ego is meant to be something that a person need to not be influenced by. Or, you can look at it as ego is meant to be balanced. Extremes can be problematic. Someone with a balanced ego, as an example, will be able to accomplish great things while remaining humble and honest. There is no sense of needing validation from someone else. There is no need to look at others as below himself or herself just because they have accomplished more, or something that others have not.

The ego is simply an internal challenge, and internal obstacle which one must overcome. You must learn to not be led by the ego, but by the Higher Self, and by the Ahmen Most High.

## SOURCE INCARNATED

Since souls come from Source, and our physical bodies are made up of substance, which was also created by Source, it's not wrong to say that we are Source incarnated here on Earth. Or at least, we are created to behave and live like Source. In a way, we are Source experiencing Itself, in the form of souls in physical bodies. This would also create the challenge for souls to transition from Separation Illusion™ to Oneness Consciousness™.

## SOUL TWINS ~ SPLIT AND SPREAD SOULS

A Soul Twin is a soul which has 'split' or 'spread'. The soul split or spread, allow the soul to function as if it is two separate souls. This give the split-soul, or spread-soul the ability to incarnate in two separate physical bodies simultaneously. The Soul Twin is singular, but can exist in two physical bodies, which is why it is called a Soul 'Twin'. ONE soul, but in two bodies. Because of this, the soul experiences itself in the Divine Mirror. The Divine Mirror is simply the splitting or spreading of a soul. The soul is able to experience itself in what looks like another entity.

'Relationship' as most people in the world use it, mean *two* people together. The dictionary meaning suggest the 'connecting', 'attaching', or the affairs between *two or more* individuals. But a Soul Twin cannot be brought together, or have a relationship because it is already one being, just in two bodies. When we see the two bodies together, it looks like it is two people in a relationship, but really it is the Twin Soul experiencing itself in the Divine Mirror.

There is no need for a relationship if the soul is one. We call this Union, the soul (masculine and feminine) is One.

Soul Twins are soul counterparts. They can be a split-soul, or spread-soul. Of course, we can see one as the Masculine polarity and the other as the Feminine polarity of the soul. I don't use the term 'other half' because Soul Twins are not half of a soul, but a whole soul functioning as the Masculine and the Feminine. Your Soul Twin is NOT your other half, unless you only have one arm, leg, one eye, half emotional, half logical, ext. Your Soul Twin is your WHOLE Self. They are a living, breathing mirror of your entire being. Also, Soul Twins will have greater emotional and mental depth, and their body/DNA will be a little different. This is necessary in order to handle the intense energies of the ascended soul.

# THE 'DIVINE' IN
# MASCULINE AND FEMININE

If you go on the internet or meet a Soul Twin, you will commonly hear them reference themselves and other Twins as Divine Masculine and Divine Feminine. You have gained a better understanding of what Masculine and Feminine are, and where they come from. But what is the 'Divine' part?

Although many Twin Flames, Soul Twins and others in the spiritual community call themselves 'Divine Masculine' or 'Divine Feminine', they cannot be used freely. Not just anyone can call themselves a DM or DF. Divine Masculine and Divine Feminine are in reference to men and women who consciously choose to live in their Divine state (conscious, intelligent, and of a healthy mind) over their animalistic impulses and worldly following. This mean they no longer are influenced by worldly view s and beliefs. They don't live their lives according to what is popular, or what they are told. They don't live by impulses, or whatever they feel in the moment. They don't follow the crowd and do what everyone else does just because everyone else is doing it.

They live purely by Divine will. All men are born representing the masculine energy, and women representing the feminine energy. Through life experience, an initiated spiritual journey, and spiritual practice, they can move into the Divine Masculine and Divine Feminine state of being. It does not come just because someone likes the name, because it is popular, or because they 'feel' Divine. It does require work, experience, and maturity.

# THE RACO™ SYSTEM COMPREHENSION

In this guidebook I will be using the term RACO™ in place of the term 'RACO™'. This is because the term 'RACO™' sounds like 'chock' and 'ra' which means to stop energy from spinning or rotating. When I used to drive big rigs, we were usually told to 'chock' the trailer wheels while the trailer is getting loaded or unloaded. Chocking the wheels prevents a driver from pulling the trailer from the dock door while being loaded/unloaded, which could result in damaged merchandise or injury to the forklift operator. This made me think why people referred to our energy wheels as 'RACOs™'. I thought that was backwards, so decided to call the energy wheels RACOs. I am also releasing this disclaimer that I am not using the term RACO with any relation or affiliation to any company or business.

Remember Source is pure energy. Pure consciousness, intelligence, mentality, and imagination. Due to these things, energy doesn't necessarily behave erratically without purpose or a sense of intelligence. Energy is within purposeful control and move about in a way which allow life to have an intelligent, conscious sense of behavior.

The RACO™ structure and system are organized in the form of energetic passages and meridians (aka junctions). Meridians are like large meeting centers for many passages. The RACO™ system is depicted using flowers to represent the main meridian areas. All souls and entities have a RACO™ system. When a soul or entity incarnate into a physical body, the RACO™ system will become more complex and intricate. When a soul or entity is not inside a physical body, the RACO™ system will be more simple and less intricate.

Throughout this guidebook, the RACO™ system will be mentioned with regard to certain aspects of the Soul Twin dynamic and journey.

## INTRODUCING THE 9-RACO™ TRIPLEX™

When it come to RACOs™, the most popular recognition has been the 7-RACO™ system. It consist of the root, sacral, solar plexus, heart (center as we call it), throat (voice as we call it), third eye (hidden eye as we call it), and crown RACOs™. This 7-RACO™ system has been used for a long time and has benefited many generations of people. But I have uncovered something deeper, more profound, and more useful than the 7-RACO™ system. That is the 9-RACO™ Triplex™. Now, I am not doing this to undermine the 7-RACO™ system or place the 9-RACO™ Triplex™ as better than its 7-RACO™ sibling. But let's take a look so that you can innerstand why it is more useful than its sibling.

Also, recognize that there are DOZENS of RACOs™ within the body and outside the body, although most of them are smaller. The 7-RACO™ system notes 7 of the major RACOs™, and the 9-RACO™ Triplex™ notes 9 major RACOs™.

So, there were some issues with the 7-RACO™ system I noticed while studying the metaphysical benefits of gemstones. It started with a conflicting area with black, brown, and red colored gemstones being labeled as 'root' RACO™ gemstones. Anyone who has studied light, color, and how different frequencies appear as different colors know that the color black and red are two completely different frequencies, and they affect the body and mind even more differently. The color black is associated with grounding, protection, and transvibing negative energy into positive. The color red is associated with love, blood purity, passion, protection, Earthly resources, and feeling 'rooted'. But the question I asked myself was "What does the root RACO™ root the body into?"

I thought of how plants, flowers, and trees are all rooted in one way, and blossom in another way. They have lower roots that dig into the Earth to pull water and minerals out of the soil. They also have upper roots known as blossoms (leaves, flowers, buds, and fruits) that open up into the 'heavens' (the sky) to receive sunlight, fresh air, release negative ions into the surrounding air, and to cool the surface of the Earth. The cumulation of leaves, buds, branches, flowers, and fruits can shade parts of the Earth, and trees bunched up together help regulate the surface temperature of Earth.

That is when I realized that the root RACO™ IS associated with the color red, but NOT with the color black. I did some research and came across some forums that spoke of the 'Earth Star' RACO™. I thought, "Why is this not commonly mentioned?!" It made sense. Roots go into the Earth. The roots of flowers, plants, and trees have to go into something, and that is the Earth. You can't have roots just hanging in the air! Now if the human body has a root RACO™, there must be an Earth RACO™ that the roots can go into. The Earth RACO™ is just below the feet. This is the RACO™ that grounds the body to the Earth grid and removes static and negative energies from the body. Now you know why you feel so much lighter emotionally, mentally, and physically after walking barefoot on the beach or in some soil!

This made me think of something else. I very much enjoy working with clear quartz. It is my favorite gemstone. The more you read about clear quartz, the more you realize why it is called the master gemstone. It has SO many benefits, and other interexciting things such as the ability to be programmed with our intention simply by speaking some words and thinking some thoughts while looking at it and holding it in the right hand. I always looked at clear gemstones (such as clear quartz) to be true energy amplifiers. It is as if they 'turn on' the energy. They clear out the smog and clutter from our body, aura, mind, and emotion so that the energy can flow freely and smoothly.

The crown RACO™ has to open UP into something to be able to receive, and that is the Soul-Star RACO™. This RACO™ represent the receiving of sun and soular energies. Like an electric circuit, black represent ground, red (or clear in the case of the Soul-Star RACO™) represent the power. The other RACOs™ and colors are like different kinds of resistors, capacitors, switches, fuses, ext., and your body is like the device. The gemstones fine tune the frequencies and energies of your body, soul, and mind.

This made me see a different and bigger picture of the RACO™ system: a metaphysical electric circuit! If you look at it as a 7-RACO™ system, sure you have clear gemstones as the power source, but then it is usually labeled under the crown RACO™ with white and silver-colored gemstones and minerals. And sure, you have the black gemstone, but it is usually labeled under the root RACO™. Sometimes I wonder if those certain people who have ruled the world didn't want people to know the true RACO™ system layout, because it would cause people to be too energetically free and powerful. People who are free and powerful are very difficult if not impossible to control. Think about it!

But looking at it from a 9-RACO™ perspective with the clear as the Soul-Star RACO™, and the black as the Earth (aka ground) RACO™, we see some very different and profound things! It looks JUST like an electric circuit! Now before I give you more of the juicy stuff, let's look at some common gemstones and match their colors to the 9-RACO™ Triplex™:

Soul-Star – clear quartz
Crown – white jade
Hidden Eye (aka third eye) – chevron amethyst
Voice (aka throat) – angelite
Center (aka heart) – malachite
Solar plexus – citrine (not heat treated)
Sacral – carnelian
Root – fire quartz
Earth-Star (aka ground) – shungite

**GUEST** – "Wait, where do brown color gemstones fit, such as smokey quartz, brown tiger's eye, and brown petrified wood?"
**MR. J** – "They fit in between the Earth RACO™ and root RACO™, although they can somewhat take the place of the Earth RACO™. There are also the minerals silver. They are related to the RACOs™ above the Soul-star RACO™, although silver is also related to the crown RACO™."

Now, with these 9 RACOs™, let's put together some gemstone combinations and see what they would do. Let's take black tourmaline, clear quartz, and green aventurine. Black tourmaline is grounding. When put with clear quartz, this form an electric circuit with your body being the device. But we know that electric circuits at least require a resistor to function properly. So, when you include the green aventurine, it behave as a resistor or capacitor in the center RACO™ area. Let's say you struggle with emotional outbursts. The green aventurine alone will help to balance your emotions. BUT where does all that pent up, negative energy go?

This is where the black tourmaline come in. It grounds that energy and either sends it away from the body into the Earth, or it transvibe it to a positive energy. Without the black tourmaline, you may only temporarily feel better emotionally while working with green aventurine. Or the energy from green aventurine might feel aggressive, like your emotions are difficult to handle. This is because the green aventurine is bringing those emotions to the surface. The black tourmaline rounds this off and rather than feeling like you are being tackled by a football player (emotionally speaking), it feels more like someone is simply pushing you. This would make it easier to process those emotions so you find the underlying cause and triggers so that they don't return to you later. This is why I also enjoy working with black colored gemstones.

Now, with the clear quartz, it is more than just amplifying the energy of other gemstones. Remember clear gemstones are clear, they represent the removal of energetic, mental, and emotional clutter and fog. So, with black tourmaline and green aventurine, the clear quartz clears out the emotional clutter from the center RACO™ and the black tourmaline helps to direct that energy out of the body. The clear quartz also represent an energy source. So, it can behave as if it is pushing foggy, cluttered energy out, and pulling fresh, clear, and high vibrational energy in. Clear quartz is also programmable.

Let's say a recent breakup with your ex has left you angry and emotionally uneasy. You could grab a black gemstone so there is something to absorb and either send away or transvibe that energy. With the green aventurine, it opens and rebalances the center RACO™. With the clear quartz, you repeat the words: "Peaceful. Happy. Joyful." 8 times and then say "programmed" while looking at the clear quartz and holding it in your right hand. Now you have programmed the clear quartz, and since "peace, happiness, and joyful" are related to emotions and to the center RACO™, the now programmed clear quartz can push out those angry emotions and replace them with peace, joy, and happiness!

So, if you have a black gemstone, a clear one, and any of the major 7 bodily RACO™ colors, you now have a triune of gemstones working together. This is very powerful, yet gentle in another way! The three gemstones all work together, each bringing different abilities and properties to the table.

So, the root RACO™ and crown RACO™ are the bottom and top openings of our energetic and auric bodies. So, these major 7 RACOs™ are the bodily RACOs™. The Earth-star RACO™ and Soul-star RACOs™ are outside the body, yet again, roots need something to be rooted in, and a crown needs something to blossom up into to receive. So black gemstones and clear ones are also directly part of the 7 bodily RACOs™ even though they are outside the body! Now, using the 9-RACO™ Triplex™, I'm going to show you another thing I have discovered. Look at this!

**The 3 RACO™ Triplexes (body, soul, mind)**
Mind Triplex (identity) = third eye, crown, and soul-star
Soul Triplex (action) = solar plexus, center, and throat
Body Triplex (possession) = ground, root, and sacral

Do some research on the number 9. 9 is a very powerful and foundational number. Those who have studied numerology or the Hebrew language know exactly what I am saying. Just like with clear quartz, the more you learn about it, the more you will see just how important and powerful it is. 3 is a major component of 9, so it is also interexciting how the 9-RACO™ Triplex™ can be divided into 3 triplexes, each triplex having 3 RACOs™. Each triplex relate to the 3 specific parts of our being: body, mind, and soul.

Notice how the Earth (aka ground) RACO™ is part of the body complex. Also, the root and sacral. The human body in itself is nothing more than an accumulation of Earth in very specific minerals and substances in certain proportions, structures, and rations. And just like with plants, the roots have to go into the Earth. The sacral and the solar plexus are directly tied to each other. The sacral is the lower half of the solar plexus. The sacral RACO™ is like the open door for a soul to incarnate into a physical body. It is the upper RACO™ of the body complex. Note also they are warmer colors (like cooled down fire embers: red, black, and orange.

The soul complex is our soul, which take residence in your physical body. The soul allow conscious thought to be transvibed into electrical pulses the body can receive so that movement of the limbs can happen. A body without a soul is an empty-minded and unconscious vessel moving about. Kinda scary huh?! Maybe that's why some people behave so crazy and have no sense of embarrassment, guilt, or remorse!

The soular plexus represent the light energy from the sun, the energy that make things vibrate and move. It is also the same energy we feel through our heart RACO™ as emotions, and our voice RACO™ (aka throat) as talking, singing, and other forums of manipulating air using our lungs, throat, mouth, and vocal cords. This is why people who sing very well are considered to be 'soulful', people who love strongly felt to be soulful, and people who have a lot of energy to be soulful. There is something invisible, yet powerful, and obvious than just a body walking about!

The mind or mental RACO™ complex has to do with the mind. The mind is really what controls the body. We move, behave, and talk based on our mentality, thoughts, and mental programming (or lack of programming!). Notice how the hidden eye (aka third eye) is part of the mind RACO™ complex. This is because focus and sight (aka consciousness) create imaginations in the mind. As our physical eyes take in code (unprocessed light) from the matrix and send it to the brain for processing, so does the hidden eye. But the hidden eye takes in more subtle light which people call invisible or unseeable. This hidden eye sends that light to the mind, where the mind receives the light as impressions, just like how a camera record and store light in the form of pixelated impressions on a film, which form a picture which can be seen.

The crown represent the portal which the hidden eye is able to receive the more subtle, invisible light. The crown is also the upper opening (*openings* for women as they have a split crown RACO™ with two smaller openings) of the body. No, you won't see a hole in the top of your head! But you might notice your hair spirals outward from a particular spot on the top, somewhat rear of your head. The crown RACO™ allows the body and energetic system to receive higher forms of energy and intelligence.

This is where we get to the Soul-Star RACO™, the highest part of the mind. It is the part of the mind where The Most High is able to be communed with. It is the RACO™ where we 'receive downloads'. It comes in through the Soul-Star RACO™ first as undefiled energy and intelligence. Then the crown RACO™ cools this energy so it can be received into the mind and hidden eye RACO™. This is why crown RACO™ openings are commonly felt with cooling or warming sensations, depending on the frequency of the incoming energy.

There are warnings on the internet about not mixing certain gemstones together because their metaphysical properties can interfere with each other and cause some not so good things. But with the 3 RACO™ complexes, gemstones of the same complex can be mixed together. There are some gems, such as my second favorite: chevron amethyst, which contain 3 and somethings even four 'crystals' in one. Chevron amethyst contain amethyst, white quartz, and clear quartz all in one! Sometimes it will also contain a 4th called smokey quartz, which is brownish in color. That is all three of the mind RACO™ complex colors together: purple, white, and clear.

Black, red, and orange, also go together, not just visually appealing, but also energetically, as they are all the lower bodily RACOs™ and warm in color. Now you may be thinking the soul RACO™ complex would be an energetic mess with all those different colors! But in reality, yellow, green, and blue can and do mix together well. There is a reason why indigenous Americans were once called the colored AND soul people, and literally dressed in colorful, vibrant clothing. The soul is very much tied to the energy the sun project, and its happy, uplifting, vibrant, and youthful energy. It represent the colorful and vibrant part of ourselves: yellow solar plexus is our inner youthful energy, green heart RACO™ is our deep passion and empathy for each other, and the blue throat is our voice being used to communicate with each other and sing soulful music with our bodily musical instrument = our voice.

**GUESTS**: "That's all easy to understand! WOW! But do gemstones REALLY Have metaphysical or health benefits?"
**MR. J** – "Most people don't believe they do, and of course scientists, health 'professionals', and the US government will deny they do. But why is clear quartz a requirement in many computers and electronics? Think cell phones, clocks, music players, microchips, and microphones. Why do people who take silver particalized drinks remain free from colds, the flu, and other sicknesses? Why do the wealthy invest in silver if they are nothing more than shiny rocks and for 'wealth preservation'? We are talking about MILLIONS of ounces of silver! Why were the pharaohs of Egypt and priests of ancient civilizations adorned with gold and gemstones? Why does our body REQUIRE dozens of minerals including gold, platinum, copper, iron, and silver to properly function?

Look at how much silicon, carbon, calcium, phosphorus, and water is needed to create the human body. Why are we so attracted to gemstones to begin with when there are rocks in our backyard, we don't even give a first look to? There is more going on than what we are being told, as with most things in life. As I always say, do your own research. The deeper you dig, the more you will find. The dots will always connect!"

**GUESTS** - "What are the most powerful gemstones?"
**MR. J** – "The most powerful gemstones to any person will depend on various factors. But green gemstones have a different kind of 'hit' to them. There is a reason why Superman was made to be weak to Kryptonite. Like with so many things, the people who have ruled the world DO NOT want the average man and woman to have access to the things which would make them free and powerful. Why would a movie and comic series be made about a superhero whose weakness is various varieties of green gemstones? That was always very odd and different about the superman movies."

Black gemstones may represent ground, and clear ones the power of an electric circuit. But I call the heart RACO™ the center RACO™ for a reason. Because it is the middle RACO™ of our body and RACO™ system. It is like the middle point of a balancing beam. Because it is in the middle, the energy and flow of green gemstones can afford to be much higher than of others without unbalancing the person who is handling or wearing a green gemstone. Imagine a 5-pound weight on the end of a barbell and nothing on the other side. That is a small imbalance. But if there is a 50-pound weight on one end of the barbell, and a 5-pound weight on the other end, the disproportion of weight will cause you to tip to the side of the 50-pound weight and possibly injure yourself or damage your spin!

This is what it would feel like with a gemstone of the RACOs™ other than the center RACO™. Some people feel like carnelian make them anxious, or amethyst makes them calm, it is only that the energies are polarized above and below the center RACO™. The lower RACOs™ other than black and brown gemstones feel energizing, while the upper RACOs™ feel calming. You are experiencing the effect of different frequencies as they relate to the different dimensions we experience. Because we live in the physical 3rd dimension, red and orange gemstones feel energizing. But the 'calming' gemstones are also energizing, just with higher dimensions. Amethyst is calming to the body, but energizing to the mind, which is why it makes you feel like you want to meditate or sit and think.

Since green gemstones resonate with the heart (aka center) RACO™, they can afford to have a higher flow and weight of energy. This is like lifting a barbell with 50 lbs of weight on each end. The weight is perfectly balanced in the middle, so you can lift the weight without being pulled to one side of the other.

Some powerful green gemstones are: serpentine, moldavite, and malachite. Moldavite is renowned for its high energy considering it is actually a tektite. Serpentine relate to our kundalini energy, and it makes sense for it to be a powerful gemstone since it is green and not red or orange. The green color allow it to push the kundalini to a high resonance without feeling like you are being tackled by a 300 lb football player. Malachite has lots of copper, and we know that copper is a high conductor of electricity! Since it is green, that energy can be strong while you remain balanced.

## THE DIVINE RACOS™ ~ PURE CONSCIOUSNESS

There are 3 more major RACOs™. They relate to the other 3 RACOs™ outside of the body. They are the Void RACO™, the Union RACO™, and the Imagination RACO™. Here is how they look with the 9-RACO™ Triplex™:

**The Complete 4 RACO™ Triplexes (body, soul, mind, consciousness)**
Consciousness (the imagination) = imagination, union, and void
Mind Triplex (identity) = third eye, crown, and soul-star
Soul Triplex (action) = solar plexus, center, and throat
Body Triplex (possession) = ground, root, and sacral

The middle or core of the Consciousness triplex is the Union RACO™. This is the RACO™ that is associated with the common statement "All is One and One is all." This RACO™ is the very center, birthplace, and eternal continuity of life. All things and all beings spring out of this eternal continuity. It is the highest vibration and frequency a being can experience and realize.

The 'two' parts of the consciousness triplex are the Void and Imagination. The Void is the Divine Feminine in Her highest frequency, the Divine womb, and the energetic empty place which Imagination can exist. Imagination is the Divine Masculine in His highest frequency, the Divine movement and expression of energy. The Lord Ahmen (aka Source Frequency, The Divine, The Most High ext.) communicate to us through the imagination RACO™. The imagination RACO™ is linked to the Soul-Star and crown RACOs™. This is why when a person experiences a crown RACO™ opening, they will either feel cooling, heating, pressure, or tingling sensations on the top of their head.

These sensations are The Divine seeding the person's mind with divine intelligence and high frequency energy from the imagination RACO™. The Divine Feminine Void and the Divine Masculine Imagination are in Union, and always One. They work and function as one. As you raise your frequency and awareness, you will one day clearly see that there is no separation between man and woman, no separation between above and below, no separation between within and outside, and no separation between the Divine Masculine energy and the Divine Feminine energy. We don't have direct access to this 4th RACO™ triplex, only we have to work with the lower 9 RACOs™ so that we can open our being to receive the energy and divine intelligence of The Divine through our crown and Soul-Star RACOs™.

# ENERGETIC CORDS & MIRRORED ENERGY

Once souls incarnate inside a physical body, the body and lower dimension act as a veil, which create a sense of 'separation'. The physical body's brain and its senses also aid in creating a sense of separation. This create the challenge for the soul to transition from Separation Illusion™ to Oneness Consciousness™.

This is also how energetic 'cords' are created. Really, the cords are actually the Oneness in all. The cords prove that all life is One. All souls are actually One Soul, and not separate individual souls. Whether someone is your Twin Flame, karmic, Soul Twins, or soulmate doesn't matter, you have a cord to everyone. It is just that, because of the veil and body's brain, we perceive that there is no connection between ourselves and others around us. That is until there is a sexual, social, or sensorial exchange. At that moment, we FEEL connected to someone. But this is only rooted in the body's hormones and senses.

What happens is that, we think when we FEEL a connection to someone else, it is because somehow we gained an attachment or connection with them. In reality, you have only become aware of the Oneness you are with that person. There is never a gain or loss of connection or Oneness. There is also awareness and sensing of the energy flow between you and another person. The soul journey and practices are so that a person can realize they are conscious, so that they SEE, KNOW, and EXPERIENCE that they are One with every person. Everyone is capable of this.

Soul Twins prove this. Usually, before Soul Twins meet in the 3rd dimension, Earth plane, their awareness and sensing of their Soul Twin is blocked by the veil and their body's brain/mind. Once they meet in the 3rd dimension in any given life time, they are 'awakened' to the eternal Oneness with their Soul Twin. This begins the Automated Default™ soul journey. The Soul Twins will find themselves overwhelmed with the connection and energy the feel with their Twin.

Usually, one of the Twins will attempt to run from the connection and energy, while the other Twin will chase after the running Twin. This behavior is the Soul operating in unconscious choice and Separation Illusion™. The Soul must transcend Separation Illusion and transition into Oneness Consciousness™. Once the Soul realize it is attempting to separate from itself, chase after itself (like a dog chasing its tail), and break or force the connection, then the Soul has graduated.

Automated Default™ mean that someone is automatically placed on a one-way pathway of ascension back to Oneness Consciousness™ and Source frequency. All Soul Twins are on an Automated Default™ soul journey. When the soul decided to split or spread, it was due to a contract or agreement the soul made to take the most difficult of soul journeys and at an accelerated rate. These split and spread Soul Twins would be the college graduates. They would have already completed elementary, middle, and high school, and passed through the beginning of college.

Because Soul Twins originate from the same soul, energy, feelings, sensations, and even life experiences are reflected on each side. This will happen even though the soul has incarnated in two different physical bodies. Even if the physical bodies are on opposite sides of the Earth, even if they grew up in different cultures, or religions, they would find that their life events and experiences have been mirrored. For more on mirroring, visit the section in this guidebook named "Twin Soul Mirroring, The Living Mirror."

## THE REAL SOUL TWIN

**GUEST** – *"Terrence, a Twin Flame coach told me that everyone has a Twin Flame."*

Not everyone has a twin flame. They would have to be born from a monad or be a StarSeed. I think what they mean is that everyone has a SOUL TWIN. But your soul will need to split or spread to become a Soul Twin. If the soul has not split or spread, what it would experience is meeting different people throughout their lives which reflect their current frequency. This is why humans are polygamous and not monogamous. As people ascend, the person they are with will have to be changed out to match their new frequency. This is why relationships and marriages end up stale and boring because one or both people have ascended beyond the frequency of their first meeting.

Remember, we live in the Universe. The Universe is not dual, divided, separated, or split in two. The 3rd Dimension Earth plane and physical body's brain/mind, create a veil. The veil is what we see when we look and think that everything is dual, separate, or divided. The veil is not real. It is an illusion.

What Twin Flame coaches should say, is that all souls have both masculine and feminine polarity as a SINGLE unit. The soul has not split or spread. Because it has not split or spread, the soul cannot incarnate in two physical bodies, or incarnate partially (one polarity is in a body while the other is not).

Soul Twins are different because the soul has split or spread. This means that most people on Earth (who are singular souls) have both their soul polarities in one body. But the Twin Flame can have one polarity on one body, and the other in a different body. This is what defines a Twin Flame, and differentiate them from other souls.

Every soul can split or spread if it chooses to do so. Unfortunately, most souls do not or are not able to do that so early or fast. There are various reasons why. Most souls find it difficult to ascend, or they get caught up in the veil and Earth School. It is very challenging to take the soul journey all the way back to Oneness Consciousness™ and Source. But the souls which decide to split or spread take the challenge head on, and that is actually a very small percentage of people.

**GUEST (2)** – *"But Terrence, a different Twin Flame coach told me that everyone is my Supposed 'Twin' Flame. I'm confused now!"*

**MR. J** – "That's a good sales and marketing strategy! But it has left so many in confusion. The confusion arise because too many Twin Flame coaches, online writers, and Vloggers will tell you completely different things. You'll find yourself stuck with *two* or *three* different people trying to figure out which one is your Twin. One person could look gorgeous with money, but you might not feel anything, another could be unattractive to you, but bring endless orgasms in the bedroom and you feel emotional intensity with them."

It is nothing but sales and marketing to sell more books or courses. If everyone is your Soul Twin, then why would you need to buy a book or course to try and find out who your Twin is or how to get them to stop running?

You will also learn from this guidebook that the Soul Twin connection and journey is not about romance, wet-panties sex, or a free ticket to an easy life. In fact, it can actually the opposite. You will learn why many Twins are not married or together. You will learn why many of them are in some degree of conflict with each other, and find the connection overwhelming and burdensome. It is also common for one or both Twins to actually not want the connection, and go to great lengths to sever or run from the connection, and their Soul Twin.

## HOW TO KNOW YOU ARE A TWIN SOUL

You will hear various things like: *"You will meet someone, and they will fall deep in love with you." "You will share a powerful connection with someone." "They will be 8-foot tall." "You will see them in your dreams, or you will see a lot of repeat numbers after meeting them." "They will drive a blue car." "They will have a lot of money, or you will find them physically good looking." "The sex will be amazing!"*

The main issue with all of these kind of responses is that you can experience them with ANYONE. There has to be (and are) specific things which will reveal to you whether or not you have met your Soul Twin. Since everyone has a Soul Twin, that means that you are a Twin Soul. If I were to tell you "You will be on a spiritual journey" or "You will be the outcast of society" or "You will have weird dreams" I would be lying to you. Anyone can experience those things. There are Twin Flame writers, 'coaches', Vloggers, and others who purposefully lie so that they can gain more followers, sell more healing services, or sell their course to more people. I'm going to be the rock-in-the-shoe and speak some hard to accept truths and provide some information which will be of truth and for your benefit.

## HOW TO KNOW THEY ARE YOUR SOUL TWIN

As far as my personal experience meeting my Supposed 'Twin' and being involved in the Twin Soul community, I have come to learn three distinct characteristics which reveal the real Twin:

- No matter how many minutes, decades, or lifetimes pass, you still feel their energy, run into them unexpectedly, and crave their presence and touch. The connection never goes away and at times can get very intense and annoying. You will still and always feel their emotions, hear their thoughts, and feel their energy.

- A deep and inescapable knowing that you and this person will never be able to separate from each other and will be together.

- The mirroring of your own soul and being, not to be confused with love-bombing, copy-cats, or 'have a lot in common'. This person will seem to be a living, breathing mirror image of your soul and being. There will be an endless number of similarities and opposites. The opposites come from *inverted* mirroring. The similarities come from non-inverted mirroring. Even life experiences, mannerisms, eating habits, and various other things will be mirrored.

**NOTE:** Your Soul Twin will not necessarily be the kind of person, you think or feel they should be. It is possible (and I have observed this with some in the Twin Soul community), that your Twin might not have all the physical, social, financial, or sexual attributes you look for in a sexual or romantic partner. Not one is perfect, and that hold true even for Soul Twins. Just because a particular person has everything you want doesn't make them your Soul Twin, and likewise, just because someone isn't your 'type' doesn't mean that they are not your Soul Twin. Please review the three specifics above again.

## HOW IT'S LIKE BEING A TWIN SOUL

Mostly, we are just like everyone else. We eat, sleep, bathe, work, and seek a better life just like other people. We experience our own life difficulties, trauma, ups & downs, and challenges. But we also experience a lot of good things. Some of us have perfect health, psychic abilities, easier time making friends, and for some of us climbing the social-economic ladder is easier, and various other things.

But we are also different than everyone else, and it is obvious to us. Some people notice that, and others are oblivious to it. But it is common for us to either be outcasts, or we actually don't enjoy the craziness and chaos of human society. But we do the best we can to have a good life. Our Twins can make all of this more or less of a problem.

## TWIN SOUL LOVE & ONENESS

Soul Twins always love each other, despite what may be seen on the outside. Although there are two bodies, they will both experience a constant and sure love for each other. Non-Twin Souls don't experience a constant, sure love for someone else due to the constantly changing nature of hormones. Instead, they will experience a changing love for other people throughout their lives, the years, and even within the same day. This is because hormones change depending on various factors such as eating habits, age, stress-level, sex, medication, and other factors. Non-Soul Twins can 'fall in love', but they can also fall out of love with others. Soul Twins always feel love for each other.

There is a such thing as someone loving (emotionally speaking) another person so much, it actually cause them to run, or pull away. This is because they might not feel good enough for such love, they are overwhelmed by the love, or having to manage a connection with that level of depth is too much work they are willing to take on.

The 'Runner' Twin has been notorious for experiencing love for their Chaser Twin that cause them to feel insecure, not good enough for such love, or they are overwhelmed by it. The love that Soul Twins feel for each other will always be more intense than with normal people. This is because the Twin Soul is incarnated in two bodies. That is double the hormones! Normal people only experience hormones from one body.

Unlike normal people, Soul Twins always experience Oneness Consciousness™ with each other, especially after they meet in the 3rd Dimensional Earth plane. This Oneness Consciousness™ will continue to expand until it is at Source Frequency, encompassing everyone and everything. Normal people will have to engage in practices or be initiated onto a soul ascension path to transition into Oneness Consciousness™. But Soul Twins are on an Automated Default™ soul ascension path.

**GUEST** – *"But how do I know if they are my real Twin?"*
**MR. J** – "You'll hear various answers like: "You will love them a lot," "They will be 8 foot tall." "They will wear shoes made out of pure gold." "You will have the same hair color." "You will both be left-handed." "You'll both have a lot in common."

The issue with these things, is that non-Soul Twins can also be tall, or left-handed, or have the same hair color as you. They can also make you feel happy and have a lot in common."

## TWIN SOUL AND THE CONCEPT OF MARRIAGE

Marriage in the modern day world is man-made. It has become based on signing a contract that gives the man-made government, court system, and law authority over the husband and wife of the marriage. Rather than the Ahmen The Most High having that authority, it is given to another man, and man-made governments and systems.

In its original form, the idea of marriage was created due to Separation Illusion™ and ego being influential as souls incarnated in the 3rd Dimensional Earth plane. The Separation Illusion™ and ego creates a veil of illusion. This veil of illusion cause men and women to look at each other as separate entities, and not as One.

So, the institution of marriage was created as a ceremony and ritual to keep the men and women together in peace, harmony, and humility. But without The Most High heading the man and woman, man-made marriage fails and pulls men, women, and children away from Source, from The Most High.

But with Soul Twins, we see Union in its original format. Since Source is the Oneness of the Masculine and Feminine, there cannot be a marriage. Marriage is about bringing *two* together, to make them one. Since Soul Twins are one soul, they are already One. They cannot be married, because they are already One, and that which is already one, cannot be married. Marriage is for younger, lesser souls who need marriage to keep them on the path of ascension. Man-made marriage is not necessarily a bad thing if used in a certain way. But for more mature souls, marriage loses its use. The mature soul realizes it is already One with everything and everyone.

Once a soul decide to take the soul journey all the way and split or spread, the soul no longer needs marriage. The soul automatically comes back under the Oneness of The Most High, and Source Frequency. Now if one or both Twins decide to marry someone, or each other under then that is not an issue. Even mature people and ascended souls still go through the marriage ceremony.

But in our modern world do you see and hear how many marry and then divorce? See how much conflict is in our society between the men and the women? The marriage doesn't look so healthy, does it? If two people are One, they are always One, there is nothing or anyone that can separate them. What happens when people marry, then divorce and break up the family? Trauma, fragmentation, and baggage is produced. That is the consequence for attempting to separate those who have been brought together. Modern day view of marriage is warped and unnatural. There need to be a change. Marriage, although man-made, can still be a useful tool if used a certain way, and people are educated on how to maintain it.

**GUEST** – *"Does a Twin Soul make a better lover?"*
**MR. J** – "Twins CAN make a better lover, but that will depend on their level of maturity and how much trauma and fragmentation they have. It is important to realize that someone's love for you isn't necessarily dependent on what type of soul they are. Even younger souls can have a lot of love that is more innocent and child-like, free of expectations and demands. But Soul Twins are always going to be of higher intensity due to the soul having split or spread, and due to having double the hormones with the soul being incarnated in two physical bodies. Higher intensity of energy can mean more pleasure, sensation, and a stronger bond, but doesn't always mean more or better love."

## FALSE TWIN FLAME SYNDROME

*"Terrence, I think I have left a False Twin Flame. When will I meet my real Twin Flame?" "I am dating two guys, but I'm confused which one is the False Twin and which one is the real Twin." "I had sex with my False Twin Flame and it was amazing, but my real Twin Flame, he runs after we have sex. How can I get him*

*to stop ghosting after sex?" "My ex abused and assaulted me, does that mean he was a False Twin Flame?" "How do I know when I meet someone if they are a False Twin Flame or my real Twin Flame?" "I got into an argument with my False Twin Flame and he blocked my, but my real Twin Flame is dating other women and doesn't talk to me, what should I do?"*

Over the years of being involved in the Twin Soul community, these types of questions were so common, it made my head spin. But I wasn't surprised. In the beginning of my journey, when I met my Supposed 'Twin', I thought at one point too, that there is a false twin which precedes the real one. Until I learned otherwise...

It is one thing to meet people we connect or feel something with. It's another thing to attach labels to someone and then change that label when it is felt like they don't measure up to it and then attach that same label to someone else. It's already overwhelming and a huge chore having a Soul Twin. Having more than one Soul Twin, or different types of Soul Twins would be over kill, and actually defeat the purpose of the journey. The Twin Soul journey is a unique one, and one which is not experienced with everyone.

I wondered why anyone would want or need a false twin. They don't exist. It's not wise or right to go around calling people 'false' just because the relationship with them did not last or they were on bad behavior. I personally would never call someone false. Every person you meet is a real and alive being. They may not behave the way you want, but why does that make them false? Then calling them a false twin after meeting someone else that is easier to get along with? Can we look at this a little deeper?

For a long time, I have said that the Soul Twin primarily has nothing to do with love and romance. But they have everything to do with reflecting your whole being back to you, inside and out. It is truly a soul journey. That doesn't require two, three, four, or a dozen twins to achieve that. You only have one Soul Twin. Having a false twin would mean you could have multiple Twin Souls, and then if you could have multiple Twin Souls, this would take away from the whole purpose of what the Soul Twin is for.

I have seen many who go from one person to the next, calling each of them their Twin Soul, initially. But when problems arise they do not want to deal with, or the person does not want to be with them, or the person does not love them the way they want, then they want to leave and go to the next person. Or they meet someone they have a better connection with and call the previous person a 'false twin' and look at the new person as their real Twin, until the same happen as with the previous person(s).

Something I found interesting are the people (not surprisingly mostly men) who wrote online complaining about meeting women who called them their Twin Flame and proceed to force love or a relationship out of them. Those people (not surprisingly mostly men) are walking, living proof of what I call 'False Twin Flame Syndrome™'.

False Twin Flame Syndrome™ is when and individual believe they have a Soul Twin, and seek to find the person, along the way calling those who they didn't get along with or were abandoned by, their false twin. They continue the search to find 'the one' only to never find them, but to have a trail of failed relationships.

There is no 'the one'. The only thing there is, is your Self. The Soul Twin is nothing more than a mirror to reflect your Self back to you, not for a relationship. Why would someone chase after their Self? Why would they chase after a mirror image of their Self? They might not innerstand the journey or the nature of non-physical things.

If you didn't get along with someone, you simply didn't get along with them, no labels needed. If someone was abusive, they simply were abusive, no labels needed. Some feel the Soul Twin cannot be abusive, have addictions, or engage in toxic behavior, and that is far from the truth. We all had some level of trauma, abuse, or abandonment in our lives that caused us to handle relationships in a way that wasn't healthy. We needed those things revealed to us so we could make some adjustments.

The Twin Soul journey is a privilege, and a huge blessing to those who realize and understand its purpose. There are some who are in a relationship with their Soul Twin, and they are in harmony with each other, and that is also a huge blessing. There are others who are not in a relationship with, or married to their Soul Twin, and that is also a blessing in its own way.

I don't approve of calling anyone false. Some want to find their Soul Twin, but they have trouble making normal relationships work. It is important they ask themselves why they want to find their Twin when they could destroy that relationship like they have the others. An unchanged person will do the same things, and if they hadn't worked before with others, why would things be different with their Twin?

There is no such thing as a false twin. You can only have one Soul Twin. Those other people were just relationships that didn't work. Or you could look at it from a different perspective and say they were there for lesson learning, which everyone experiences. It has no relation to Soul Twins. We need to stop taking normal everyday events and relationships and try to sculpt them into a Twin Soul connection. You will absolutely know that it is real and who they are.

## FALSE TWIN FLAME SYNDROME AND SOCIAL DRAMA

Some people use the Twin Soul phenomena as a reason or excuse to be obsessed with or control people. When they say Soul Twins are rare, that is true. I am talking about the split-souls and spread-souls that are incarnated into physical bodies, not the energetic form of Soul Twin.

I have observed that this is especially a problem for women, as they have a drive for love, romance, and intimacy, and will take on things that relate to them. Some people and social circles thrive off drama, stringing people along, jealousy, resource extraction, and sexual escapades. Injecting *"They are my Supposed 'Twin' Flame"* into the mix give even more social drama and leverage over people. It's unwise behavior, and makes the real Twin Souls look bad.

Most people do not have an incarnated Soul Twin. They only attract people based on their current emotional, physical, energetic frequency, and mental maturity. Their upbringing, environment, social circle, and entertainment intake also influence this. Real Twins also have this, but after Soul Twins meet each other, the attraction is reversed. This mean that they lose attraction and attachment for people who are not their Soul Twin, but will be intensely drawn toward their Soul Twin. If they attract someone other than their Twin, it won't 'feel' the same, and it certainly won't be the same. Many Twins can relate to this.

People believe in Twin Souls because they want to experience intense and pleasuring relationships with others. These are natural desires, but they believe that if they can tell themselves they have a Twin, they will meet the person and have that intense connection. All that happen is they obsess over toxic and abusive people. They might try to force people to be with them who usually want little to nothing to do with them.

**GUEST** – *"Do people meet a false twin or catalyst twin first before meeting the real Twin?"*
**MR. J** – "There is no false twin or catalyst twin. There is only one Soul Twin. All the others were simply other people who are not your Soul Twin. The others are either a karmic or soulmate."

## IF SOMEONE LIED ABOUT BEING YOUR SOUL TWIN

Has someone lied to you about being your Twin? Has someone impregnated you after convincing you that they are your Twin Flame and you are supposed to be together? Were you manipulated you into a relationship by a man or woman who kept sending you memes, quotes, and Twin Flame website links after telling you that you are their Twin?

You may have met someone who is obsessed with the IDEA of being with a Twin Flame. This person may actually be a Twin Flame, but you are not their Soul Twin. They may be running from their Twin. They might be trying to get into a relationship or sexual activity to seek vindication over their Twin. They might try and 'get over' their Soul Twin by getting with you. What a spilled bowl of cereal! This is a mess!

I think this would be an issue with the courts and lawyers, maybe even a joke to them. But unless the person has committed a crime listed under the law, it might be difficult to win that lawsuit. The court system does not care if someone is your Twin Flame or Soul Twin. The phenomena is either unknown by the court system, or they see 'twin flame' or 'Soul Twin' as terms which hold no value or importance. They will certainly want to make some money off you though. Those legal fees pay their bills, finance their new car, and fund their family vacations.

If you are pregnant, or they are pregnant, or you two have birthed a child, you may find yourself in family courts getting DNA tests and fighting for child custody. Just know that if and when you mention anything to do with twin flames or Soul Twins, you may not be taken seriously.

If a crime has been committed or you have been abused/assaulted by them, contact the local authorities.

Personally, it has happened to me two times, a woman was claiming me to be her Twin Flame. But I already know who my Supposed 'Twin' is. I found it to be both troubling and funny. I don't think it is wise for anyone to pretend to be someone's Twin. Don't walk down that road.

## THE DIVE INTO HIGHLY SENSITIVE TOPICS

Throughout the rest of this guidebook, there are subsections which will deal with certain aspects of the Twin Soul journey which may be unique in comparison to other Twins. Examples of these unique aspects include: being married to someone other than the Twin, Soul Twins with a wide age gap, Twins who are dealing with a Twin who display narcissistic behaviors, and various others. Here is a list and description of each subsection topic:

## FOR MARRIED TWINS

I remember how common it was in the Twin Soul community. One or both Twins will meet each other when they are married to other people. This can create a variety of problems, such as affairs, lying, jealousy, and even domestic violence or murder. But usually, the marriages end in divorce, and fewer remain married to those who are not their Twin.

I know it may be difficult to believe, but cheating and affairs happen even amongst Soul Twins. Usually one, or both Twins refuse to leave their marriage. But they will still get involved with their Soul Twin emotionally, sexually, or a relationship outside of the marriage. Being married to someone, and then meeting your Twin can wreck you marriage, and your life.

I have commonly heard from married Twins (or previously married Twins) that after meeting their Soul Twin, they lost attraction and feelings for their wife/husband. The Twin Soul connection will always override all other connections. It won't matter if you marry someone else, have sex with someone else, if they have more money, or look better (to you), the Twin Flame connection will still override them all.

Some cultures and religions prohibit divorce, and some criminalize, or even severely punish (such as killing), cheating and affairs. This can wedge a fork, and cause more confusion and stress between Twins who feel the everlasting connection and intense energy they share with their Twin.

## FOR TWINS WITH CHILDREN

Just like with marriage, some Twins meet their Soul Twin when they, or their Twin has children with someone else. This add a layer of complexity. Usually, if they are still married to, or in a relationship with the father/mother, they might want to stay. This is, until they meet their Twin, and the overriding of the Twin Soul connection changes everything.

When there are children involved, this can be seen as a form of baggage. Children are not free, they cost. They are a liability. They cost money, time, energy, and planning. Having a child, or children can also cause issues between Twins. One Twin may not want to be with someone who already has children. Or one Twin may not want someone else fathering/mothering their children.

Another issue is that the child's mother/father may not want someone else fathering/mothering the child they have had with your Twin. If you try to bring the children around your Twin, the father/mother might get jealousy or create drama.

But it is more likely your Twin will welcome the children, and accept them as their own. I have also heard of situations where the child actually attempts to bring and keep the Soul Twins together. In other situations, you may feel like your Twin will make a better step-parent than your child's father/mother. In another kind of situation, you might feel a need to keep your children from your Twin, if your Twin engage in addictions, crimes, are toxic behavior.

Depending on the energetic vibrance of the family members, you or your Twin may feel like the children are your own, and their own. This is because your Twin's soul blueprint is in them, and Twins share the same soul blueprint.

## FOR TWINS WHO ARE FAMILY MEMBERS

**GUEST** – *"Can Soul Twins be family members?"*
**MR. J** – *"There are Soul Twins who are family members. And no, this does not mean that they are sexual or romantic with each other. Remember, the Twin Soul journey is not about romance or getting married to someone, but is about the soul choosing to take the journey of soul ascension all the way. The soul is choosing to finish school and all of its lessons so that it can graduate."*

# FOR TWINS WITH A LARGE AGE GAP

Twins can meet each other at any point in their lives. They can also be of varying ages. They might have a large or small age gap. One or both Twins could be under age. In most societies, people desire and get with someone who is close in age as themselves. I know there is a thing amongst women where they might prefer the man to be older than them. But it is rarely 20, 30, or 50 years older. Due to age laws, there is also a legal age limit with regard to sexual conduct and certain romantic behavior between people. If you or your Twin are under the legal age, this can be a major problem.

In some cultures, religions, and countries, it is prohibited to have large age gaps, or underage people to be together at all.

ALWAYS follow the law with regard to legal sexual conduct age, and age restrictions. Never engage in sexual behavior with someone who is underage, regardless how you feel about them. Even if you think they are your Twin, if they are underage, do not engage in any sexual behavior with them.

If you and your Twin have a large age gap, you don't have to remain quiet about that. Mention that to your Twin. It may or may not be a problem with them, depending on their culture and religion. Despite the large age gap, Twins will STILL feel the intense connection, strong sexual energy, and magnetic pull toward their Soul Twin. This may or may not be a problem. But regardless of age, the Twin Soul connection will override all other connections. It won't matter if your Twin is older and married with children. It won't matter if your Twin is younger and you are triggered and feel insecure (because you don't feel good enough for someone younger with less experience and baggage). It won't matter if you are retired, and your Twin is busy with college and a part-time job. The Twin Flame connection will always override other connections.

# FOR TWINS WHO ARE A CELEBRITY OR PUBLIC FIGURE

This one is something I never thought of until I met a few Twins online (and one in person) who either was a celebrity/public figure, or their Twin was.

Normal people already craze over celebrities and aspire to be like their favorite public figure. But throw a monkey wrench in the Twin Soul journey and add another layer of complexity by making one or both of them a public figure or celebrity.

If your Twin is a celebrity or public figure, you probably found them to be completely unreachable. They likely were already married, or dating someone. This can cause extreme insecurity. You might like the fact that your Twin is a celebrity or public figure.

But what happens when you feel an unbreakable connection, intense energy, and chaotic feelings for them, yet they are completely unreachable and unavailable? This can be very stressful. You may be in a situation where you may actually be able to reach your Twin, yet they are emotionally, sexually, or romantically unavailable to you. You may also find that you have full access to your celebrity (or public figure) Twin Flame, and this could pose other issues and benefits.

Either way, most people (literally) can only dream and fantasize about being affiliated or involved with a celebrity or public figure. You are dealing with this on a completely different level if your Twin IS a celebrity/public figure. If you are able to be in contact with them, and be romantically, or sexually involved with them, it is a dream come true, whereas for others, it can ever only be a dream.

Yet, just because your Twin is a celebrity or public figure, it won't mean that a relationship with them will be easy. It doesn't matter how famous, rich, or well-known someone is, no one is perfect. We are all still human (in a certain way) at the end of the day. It's important to approach your Twin with humility, respect, and patience, as you should anyone else.

If you are a Soul Twin, and have met your Twin who is not a celebrity, you may find some enjoyable or not so enjoyable things about them. Your Twin may not be able to handle the fact that you are a celebrity AND their Soul Twin. They may likely be severely insecure, doubtful, or overwhelmed. It is not because you have done something bad to them. Most people cannot handle themselves with or around a celebrity or public figure, and you already know that. But your Twin might not have an issue with it. Some people, more or less, are not overwhelmed or overjoyed by a celebrity or public figure.

You may find that, out of all of your fans, haters, and supporters, it is that one person (your Twin) who always capture your attention. Unlike with others, you actually feel a connection, and huge attraction toward them. You dream about them, see their name EVERYWHERE, and can't stop thinking about them. Don't worry, all of those are completely normal, and experienced by all Soul Twins.

If you and your Twin are both celebrities and/or public figures, the journey will be different for the both of you for different reasons. Unlike those who are not public figures or celebrities, all eyes (and cameras) are on you. You and your Twin both know that you simply cannot just behave and do things anyway you want. Your career, business, and status are all, and always on the line.

You and your Twin may find it difficult to come together smoothly mainly due to being in the spotlight. You both may also work in entirely different industries or work in industries with opposite or conflicting natures. How can you two come together smoothly without all the paparazzi coming after you or ending up on someone's hitlist? Keep studying this guidebook, and the pathway will be laid out smooth and clear for you, just like the red carpet under you shoes (heels for the ladies! Ha!).

# THE 'NARCISSIST'

Narcissism is widely misunderstood. Take Soul Twins, another widely misunderstood phenomena, and try mixing the two together. You might as well go on a journey looking for a unicorn! Narcissism is a hot topic. Many people use and throw around the term freely, not knowing what it is, and where it come from. Unfortunately, those who are not mature or on a soul path, also attach narcissism to Soul Twins, not realizing that the two cannot mix. I commonly see people using narcissism to verbally attack other people.

Narcissism is clinically described as a PERSONALITY disorder. Personality is commonly also misunderstood, without a firm meaning. So, I will translate 'personality' with 'actions' and 'behavior'. So then narcissism is a person with a behavioral disorder. This mean that their actions, way of living, how they treat others, and their behavior is OUT OF ORDER. Or as I say, is BACKWARDS. This mean that narcissists behave in a way which is out of order with life, with nature, and with the Most High's Divine order.

The worst case scenario, your Twin might have one or two narcissistic ATTRIBUTES (which are not permanent and can be changed), but they can't actually be a narcissist. Once a Soul decides to split or spread to take the soul ascension all the way, any narcissistic behavior or attributes must fall away.

Narcissism has become a topic of huge confusion and misuse. It is so common to hear *"Yea, my ex was a narcissist."* *"He is so toxic and narcissistic!"* *"I just ended my 10-year marriage with a narcissist."* *"All men are narcissists by definition."* *"Yea man, that woman was so crazy, she must have been narcissist."* *"He asked you out? Be careful, he might be a narcissist."*

I cringe when I hear people use the term. I have come to realize that many people actually don't even understand what narcissism is. They just use it to attack people, and bring people's name down, usually those they did not have a good relationship with or get along with. Here, I don't lie or care about what the social norm is. I will give you the truth and nothing less than that. Too many people lie to support their hidden agendas, to 'fit in' with others, or because they only follow social norms without regard to what is actually true and genuine.

In this guidebook, I will use the abbreviations 'NARC' and 'NARCs' in place of 'narcissist' and 'narcissists' respectively.

NARCs are rare, and unfortunately the term is being thrown around too loosely and freely. It is important not to confuse a Soul Twin who has trauma, baggage, and fragmentation with a narcissist. Soul Twins cannot be NARCs. At the most, they might have one or two attributes of a NARC, but that does not make them one. NARCS cannot and do not change from their ways due to something they have no control over. Only if the origin of the NARC behaviors is changed, can a NARC change. It is possible for a NARC to change, but the underlying issue must change. That is more of a medical and psychological issue of the brain I will not get into in this guidebook.

Having insecurities alone is not enough for one to qualify as a NARC, because we all have insecurities, to some degree. Being emotionally immature alone isn't enough for someone to qualify as a NARC, because we all start off with some degree of emotional immaturity (especially as children). We all must mature into emotional stability and health. Lacking logic/reasoning alone isn't enough for someone to qualify as a NARC, because someone can lack logic/reasoning, yet not be insecure and actually care about other people.

It is also important to not confuse narcissism and codependency with attachment. Attachment is commonly deemed narcissism, codependency, or a NARC-empath dynamic. Attachments will be discussed in the section of this guidebook: Seeking ~ The Beginning of Stages. Attachment is normal and can be healthy in certain situations.

In this guidebook, the subsections which mention narcissism, will only be used to describe a Soul Twin who has one or two BEHAVIORS similar to that of a NARC. They will not be used in a manner which suggest that they are a NARC. But by the time you are finished studying this guidebook, you will have a firm and sure understanding of the Soul Twin connection.

And remember, it's Union Season™!

# SECTION FOUR
## TWIN SOUL MIRRORING
## THE LIVING MIRROR

Many Twins don't overstand or have never heard of mirroring. Experiencing the mirror myself from my Supposed 'Twin', it is too intense and too obvious to miss it. The mirroring is my favorite thing about this connection, and it is what I have used to my advantage to heal and better myself. Mirroring is a definite way to identify your Soul Twin. But be careful! Energy vampires, NARCs, soulmates, and even karmics can partially mimic (or copycat) you. I didn't say mirror, because only your Soul Twin can mirror you.

INTRODUCING:
**TWIN SOUL PAIR EXAMPLING WHAT NOT TO DO**
*B-male* and *Y-female*

**TWIN SOUL PAIR EXAMPLING THE CORRECT WAY**
*A-male* and *Z-female*

I will use the above pairs to create examples of what not to do, and recommended call-to-actions. These will be for the purpose of helping you to better understand Soul Twin mirroring.

## TWIN SOUL MIRRORING COMPREHENSION

We all know what a mirror is, and have used one at least a few times in our lives. Such a simple object has a profound meaning when tied to that of Twin Flames. Mirrors have the ability to reflect ourselves back to us at a 1:1 ratio, with certain acceptable effects and alterations. These effects and alterations include inversion, concave, convex, and warpage.

Inversion is when an object or thing is in the opposite position as it appear it should be in real life. Convex is when objects appear larger than normal as they become closer to the mirror. Concave is when objects appear to be upside down, and of a different size.

A Twin Soul is a split or spread soul in two bodies. Because there is One soul, when the soul incarnates in two physical bodies, there is directly a mirroring effect. When you look at your Twin, you are only looking at your Self as a complete, living, breathing mirror image of your own being.

Mirroring between Soul Twins can be very interesting and even make one or both Twins feel crazy. It might make you feel crazy because you cannot stop thinking about this person, they behave just like you, they may look like you, and you both will notice similarities in life experiences. At times the mirroring can be pleasant, as you find things that both you and your Twin share. But at other times the mirroring can be annoying, especially the inverted mirroring. This is because you may find that certain things you do, your Twin does the opposite.

**NON-INVERTED MIRRORING EXAMPLE**
*Z-female* has struggled to find a man who is as sexually expressive as she is. She has also struggled to find a man who can stimulate her mentally. That is...until she met *A-male*. The very moment she met him, she felt tingles in her body, purely off his energy and handsomeness. But it was during their first conversation when she knew that *A-male* could possibly 'wow' her sexually, simply off the captivating conversation with him. A few weeks later, *Z-female* found herself OBSESSED with *A-male*. Not only was he highly sexually expressive as she, but he constantly stimulated her mentally. It overwhelmed her to the point she eventually needed to keep *A-male* at arm's length. She felt like she lost herself in the conversations and sex, like nothing else was important. This is non-inverted mirroring.

**INVERTED MIRRORING EXAMPLE**
*B-male* and *Y-female* have been arguing. *Y-female* feels like *B-male* never share his feelings, as if he has something to hide from her. *Y-female* is very emotional, and expressive. She is not used to men being emotionally unavailable, although she lose attraction easy to men who are emotionally available. She has assumed that if she share her feelings with *B-male*, he will with her. But, *B-male* constantly avoid sharing any feelings. *Y-female* still loves him and is attracted to him, but she is annoyed that he is emotionally closed off. This is inverted mirroring.

## DYNAMIC, REAL-TIME MIRRORING

Twin Soul Mirroring is not the same as a copy-cat, someone mimicking your behaviors, or having a lot of similarities. Go into your bathroom, or stand in front of the mirror. Move around and make faces. No one is copy-catting you, no one is mimicking you, and no other person is there who has the same similarities. You are simply observing a mirror reflection of yourself. This is who your Soul Twin is. Although, they certainly have a physical body you can touch! And the mirror is not on the wall, but they are the mirror!

Mirroring by itself is NOT an indication of meeting your Twin. Twin Fame souls experience some mirroring between each other, especially if they are monadic Twin Flames. But with your Soul Twin, you will notice the mirroring is dynamic. Dynamic means that it is subject to change. That change can happen at any time. Twin Soul mirroring is live, in real time.

For example, *B-male* and *Y-female* both argued a lot when they first met. Now, neither of them argue at all, but now find themselves always laughing and enjoying each other's company. *A-male* was unemployed when he first *met Z-female*, while she was an assistant manager at a retail store. A few weeks after they met, *Z-female* was unemployed, and *A-male* got a full-time job as a manager at a construction company.

# NON-INVERTED VS INVERTED MIRRORING

Mirrors have inversion and non-inversion characteristics. The word *invert* mean to reverse in position or attribute. If you invert the screen on your cell phone, everything will flip the opposite color. The location of your right hand in the mirror is inverted. The color of your shirt in the mirror is non-inverted; meaning, if your shirt is pink, it appear pink in the mirror.

So, what things are mirrored between Soul Twins? Emotions, energy, thoughts, behavior, physical looks, personality, food choice, childhood experiences, and various other things are mirrored between you and your Twin. If you only smoke a particular brand of cigarettes, your Twin will also smoke the same brand of cigarettes. Or, they may not smoke cigarettes at all, but work at the company which make the brand of cigarettes you smoke! I know it sound crazy, but this is why many Twins, at least after first meeting their Twin, feel crazy about the Twin Soul connection.

It is common for Twin Flames to share similar traumas and life challenges. Both Twins may have grown up without their father, or both were sexually abused, or both may have had 3 failed marriages. Both Twins may have been homeless at the same time, or they may have the same life-threatening cancer or disease. The opposite is true as well. There are some things which one Twin may experience, while the other has no experience with it at all.

For example, one Twin may have had a lot of previous relationships, and been married twice before. But their Twin may have never been in a relationship or marriage. One Twin may have been bullied in freshman and junior high school, while their Twin bullied many of their peers while in high school.

**GUEST** – *"How can my Supposed 'Twin' Flame be mirroring me if he is so toxic and I'm not?"*
**MR. J** – "This is going to hurt either way. To put it clearly, your Twin is either mirroring your own toxicity, or they really are toxic (while you are not), and this is still unfortunate. Remember non-inverted and inverted mirroring. Remember that souls who choose to split or spread, do so because they want to take the soul journey all the way back to Source, to Oneness Consciousness™. Split and spread souls will have to relinquish their identification with EGO, pay off their karmic debt and will have to transition back to Oneness Consciousness™."

What is 'toxic'? I am sure you hear that word being used and thrown around all the time. This is especially true if someone is talking about their ex, or someone they did not, or do not get along with. Everyone may tell you something different. The dictionary defines the word *toxic*. But here, I want to define the word *toxic* with relation to people, to their behavior, and how they handle social situations.

Toxic as I will define and use here, is the selfish, destructive, and unwise actions (or words) of a person with regard to themselves, others, and social interactions.

If your Twin mirror you own toxicity, this is non-inverted mirroring. Your soul journey will take a certain path. If your Twin is toxic, while you truly are not, this is inverted mirroring. Your soul journey will take a different path. Understand also that most people will always deem themselves as not toxic, and as 'good'. But they will certainly and easily point their finger at someone else and say that person is toxic, or not good.

It is easy to FEEL or think that someone else is toxic, and that you are not. But the Twin Soul connection has proved otherwise from my own personal experience, and observation of other Twins in the Twin Soul community. Most people will simply not want to admit that they have engaged in toxicity, or they will make an excuse to justify their actions. I am all about being honest and realistic.

If your Twin is toxic, and you truly are not, this is an unfortunate situation. You may have to live your life without your Twin, as their toxicity will make it impossible to have a healthy relationship with them. That is, unless they choose to take the soul path. This will be the same for you also. It is part of your ascension. Will you take and accept a toxic and unhealthy reflection of yourself? (Shadow Self) Or will you say, "I am better than this, I am worth more" and see that your Soul Twin's toxic behavior is something that you must choose to walk away from? (Higher Self). It won't matter how much you love them, how amazing the sex is, or how they make you feel. You need to walk away from people who are toxic and abusive, Soul Twin or not.

## TRIGGERING COMPREHENSION

What is triggering? I am sure you have crossed this term on the internet or while conversing with someone. Triggering is an intense emotional and impulsive response to certain stimuli. Usually, this stimuli is the perception of someone cheating us, being attacked, or a fear of loss. Anyone can be triggered, and what trigger them can be a variety of different things. Triggering is intense. It can cause verbal and emotional outbursts. It can cause one to behave erratically, completely without reason, restraint, and acknowledgement of other's boundaries.

Triggering between Soul Twins is a reality. Don't let anyone tell you that Soul Twins cannot be toxic, or engage in destructive or abusive behavior. Triggering between Soul Twins can be MORE intense than with normal people. This certainly can and does cause wild arguments, abuse of various kinds, and domestic violence. Mirroring can make the triggering worse. The good news is that most Twins are able to manage the triggering, for the most part. Some

Twins will still end up abusing each other or experiencing domestic violence. Murder would be very rare.

*"That isn't true, Twins won't want to harm each other!"* *"Your Twin Flame will only love you and could never do anything to hurt you."* Oh how much I would want to believe that! But fortunately, I live in reality. It is certainly possible for one or both Twins to harm the other.

The majority of Twins never go that low, fortunately. Usually, Twins separate from each other for extended periods of time, and this prevent Twins from doing serious harm to each other. Because Twin Soul love is so intense, usually Twins love each other too much to do such damage.

Twins especially trigger each other in the beginning of their journey. The triggering is intense enough to cause separations. The Twins will separate from each other. The triggering subsides as the years and decades go by, depending on how soon one or both Twins decide to take the soul path. The soul path is relinquishing identification with EGO, paying off karmic debt, and transitioning back to Oneness Consciousness™. That transitioning is also known as transcendence.

## THE RACO™ SYSTEM
## SHARED WITH YOUR TWIN

All Soul Twins share a RACO™ system. Remember, the RACO™ system is energetic, and not physical. You may find on the internet, or in other Twin Soul books that Soul Twins experience a 'RACO™ merge'. Since Twins are one soul and one energy, they can only have one RACO™ system. What happens is that the Twins are not in Oneness Consciousness™ to be aware that they share the same energy. As they go up the soul path and ascend, they experience strange and intense energetic upheavals and restructuring. This is 'merging', not to be confused with bringing two things together to make them one. But this is a soul 'merge'. It is experiential.

The energy you feel with your Twin, is that of your own energy. The energy you feel from your Twin is influenced by your own energetic state of being, mentality, awareness (or lack thereof), and any impurities in your energetic field. Notice I didn't mention anything about emotions, because emotions are more so tied to hormones and controlled by mental processing power. Change how you think, and your emotions will follow. But you may FEEL energy from your Twin in the form of emotions.

The connection you feel is of your own energy coming back to you. You are feeling your own energy and intensity from your Twin, who is a living, breathing mirror of your entire being. The energy is direct and shared by both Twins. Resisting the connection, trying to push them away or chase after them is a resistance within yourself. You would simply be attempting to run away from or chase after yourself.

# DON'T HATE THE MIRROR

Your Twin's behavior can be hurtful, confusing, and annoying. But you don't have to walk around an emotional wreck. It is what it is. You can't change the fact that you have a Soul Twin. You can't change their behavior...at least not by going to them and telling them, or manipulating them. You can only bring change to your own Self, and life. You are only looking back at yourself. Don't hate the mirror. You use the mirror in your bathroom to clean and your skin and apply makeup. You use the mirror in your room to see how your butt look in that skirt. Why not take this mirror and use it to see how you are emotionally, mentally, and especially energetically? But again, if the person you are feeling something with is toxic or abusive, you don't have to stay or put up with that. It doesn't matter who or what they are. Don't accept abuse and bad behavior in your life.

## MIRRORING BETWEEN MY SUPPOSED 'TWIN' AND I

- she's short, I'm TALL (inverted)
- similar facial structure (non-inverted)
- same eyes, lips, forehead, and smile (non-inverted)
- both slim body type, aka ectomorph (non-inverted)
- I wear dark colors, she wear bright colors (inverted)
- both like to dress up (non-inverted)
- both omnivores (non-inverted)
- both love horses (non-inverted)
- she eat pork, I cannot eat pork (inverted)
- same text messaging style, very expressive (non-inverted)
- I'm an introverted, she's an extravert (inverted)
- she's emotional, I'm logical (inverted)
- both like to read (non-inverted)
- both want to save the world, SUPER HEROS! (non-inverted)
- both LOVE the Medieval times theme (non-inverted)
- she's the matrix Twin, I'm the soul Twin (inverted)
- she is child-like, I am adult-like (inverted)
- both sit crisscrossed (non-inverted)
- both had very traumatic childhoods (non-inverted)
- both dry sense of humor (non-inverted)
- she's older in age but younger in soul, I'm younger than her but older in soul (inverted)
- both love nature and the natural way of living (non-inverted)
- both are not fond of small talk (non-inverted)
- both play the same video games (non-inverted)
- both watch anime (non-inverted)
- both are fond of the idea of aliens and make alien jokes (non-inverted)
- she know how to instill fear in others, I know how to instill confidence in others (inverted)
- both like roses (non-inverted)
- she communicate indirectly, I communicate directly (inverted)

- both hate online advertisements, Grrr! (non-inverted)
- I have neat handwriting, she has scratchy handwriting (inverted)
- both need alone time (non-inverted)
- both have penetrating eyes (non-inverted)
- she can stir up the energy in a room, I can calm it down (inverted)
- she's turned on by a man's words, I'm turned on by a woman's actions (inverted)
- she has to process emotionally, I have to process mentally (inverted)
- we are both physically good looking (non-inverted)
- we both squat with one knee low and the other knee higher (non-inverted)

WOW! That's a lot! I had to take a deep breath after finishing this list, ha! And this isn't everything! I can't give away too much.

Now, there are a lot of things which my Supposed 'Twin' mirrored back to me which were not so pleasant. I knew what I had to do. On that particular writing forum, and with Twins I met in person, I saw how much they struggled to connect their Twin's behavior with themselves. They were so sure that only their Twin was toxic, abusive, had personal issues, bad behavior, or insecure, and not themselves. I did not want to live every day of the rest of my life like that, so I did something which changed my life. I bought a $1 journal from a nearby dollar store. In the journal I wrote down all the things I saw in *her*. I then took them all as my own, and relinquished them from my own being a life.

Then I needed to work on my financial life and physical health. I was in a much better state of being, a firm frame of thought, and of better behavior. So, I made changes in every area of my life. I became so consumed with making changes, that I found myself living a new life. Everything was different, in a good way. I lost some friends and family along the way, but also gained some new ones. I went through a huge career change, and my social life also improved. I understood early in my journey that *she* is ME. *She* is not someone I was supposed to chase after or confess love to. *She* was not someone sent to destroy my life. I knew *she* was actually the playbook to a better life, a healthier me. I took that journal and used it to iron out all of my own personal problems. It worked!

## FOR MARRIED/DIVORCED TWINS

**GUEST (2)** – *"My Supposed 'Twin' is also married to someone else, how am I supposed to be with them if we are both married to other people?"*

It is not unusual if you have met your Twin, while you both are married to other people. The inverse can be true, and you may find that whenever you are married, your Twin is single, but whenever you are single, your Twin is married. How frustrating right? You may also find that as soon as you divorce or exit a marriage or relationship, your Twin jumps into a relationship or gets married to someone else. As soon as you get into a relationship, or get married, all of a sudden your Twin wants to talk to you and express feelings. How frustrating!

Moving in and out of relationships and marriage has become normal. But when that means your Twin is always in a relationship or married when you are single, this can be a problem. Not everyone is polygamous. Many people want monogamy, or they want the person they are attracted to, to be free of a relationship and marriage. But the constant switching back and forth, availability and then unavailability can be very annoying.

In this situation, it is important to be honest with yourself about your feelings and what you want. It is not wise to cheat or have an affair, but it is recommended that you communicate to your Twin (if possible) about how you feel without crossing boundaries. If your Twin, or their partner does not want you and your Twin to be involved with each other, then you may have to leave the situation alone. For some of us, our journey is to not *chase* and to not *need* our Twin. If we find ourselves chasing a relationship or validation, or needing them, this will cause cycles of running and chasing.

It won't be the same forever, fortunately. Remember, Twin Flame mirroring is dynamic. We all would love to be with our Twin and have them all to ourselves. But the nature of life and reality does not always permit what we want, and how we want it. But at times, we may find great opportunities right in front of us, all for our taking. You may find one day, all of a sudden, both you and your Twin are single, and not in a relationship. You may find yourself on a date with them, kissing and rubbing all over each other. Weeks later, you are together!

Never stress about not being able to be with your Twin, for whatever reason that may be. All of us, at some point during our journey, will have to experience 'separation' from our Twin. At some point though, we also will get to be with them.

## FOR TWINS WITH CHILDREN

Some Twins will not have any children when they meet. Others though, may find that their Twin has exactly the same number of children as they do. Or if their Twin has all boys, they may have all girls. The Twin Soul mirror is a mysterious thing!

**GUEST** – *"Are the children Soul Twins have with each other special?"*

I would say that all children are special. All children are born undefiled and without trauma and baggage from life and relationships. Children are special to the man and woman who birthed them. But Twins who have children with each other will certainly know they have to put in time, energy, money, and love to raise healthy, secure, and productive children, just like everyone else. They will of course feel a special bond with their children.

Twins who have children with each other will certainly know their children are different than others, on a certain level. That is on a DNA level. Because Soul Twins have a different (not necessarily better) DNA than other people, the children they birth will also be a little different.

## FOR TWINS WHO ARE FAMILY MEMBERS

I know it sound funny. If Twins are born of the same mother and father, wouldn't they already be 'twins'? Well not all children born of the same mother and father are twins. But Soul Twins who are born of the same mother and father certainly will have a different experience than if they were not Soul Twins. Even though many children of the same parents have lots of similarities and opposing differences, this will be even more true of Soul Twins.

If you and your Twin are family members, you will still experience all of the typical mirroring that other, non-family membered Twins experience. This can be interesting, or very chaotic, as some family members already may fight and argue a lot, or get into trouble. If your Twin is one of your children or parents it won't be as bad as siblings.

## FOR TWINS WITH A LARGE AGE GAP

Most people assume that if someone is older, they are more wise and mature. Most people assume that if someone is younger, they will be more naïve and immature. This may be true in some instances, and to some degree, depending on the person. The Twin Soul journey may proves otherwise. It is not unusual to meet Twins where the younger Twin is just as wise and mature as the older Twin. It is common for Twins of a large age gap to have more issue with the large age gap itself, and not really with who is more or less mature.

Soul Twins of a large age gap will still mirror each other. Both Twins could be extraverted, or both introverted. Both Twins may work in the same professional industry, in the same corporate position. They could have the same personalities and even both be well spoken. The inverse is true as well. One Twin might speak very loudly, while the other speaks with a low voice. One Twin may live with only fun in mind, while the other Twin is highly self-accountable and serious about everything.

The large age gap may also create awkward situations. The younger Twin may think their Twin looks like an older version of themselves, and the older Twin may see their Twin as themselves, decades younger.

## FOR TWINS WHO ARE A CELEBRITY
## OR PUBLIC FIGURE

Many celebrity fans and supporters can only wish to even meet their idol. But imagine a fan and their celebrity actually being Soul Twins. Usually, celebrity and non-celebrity lives do not mix well. If your Twin is a celebrity, you may find it strange that this somehow is different for you. You and your Twin wears the same brand of designer clothes. You both have personal trainers, coaches, and financial assistants. You both have the same type of business. You both have A LOT of people who treat you like gods. Yet you may still find them unreachable, unavailable to you, and difficult to meet. I recommend you not stress about it. Understand that no matter if you are a celebrity or not, you must live your everyday life in an honest and productive manner. Things also do change, and one day you may get a chance to meet them.

The journey for you here is to not allow insecurity, anxiety, anger, and any other emotions to overtake you. Don't look at your celebrity Twin as above you, or out of reach. Your journey here will be to understand that your Twin shows you the luxurious and wonderful life you potentially can live. But it won't come from chasing after them, not feeling good enough for them, or beating yourself down because they are unreachable or unavailable.

In another situation, you may have meet them and get to see them regularly. Their celebrity status and the spotlight may overwhelm you. You may find that you are constantly learning new things about yourself, people, and the world that you have never been taught or considered. This is a good thing. You have experienced one side of life here on Earth, and now you are experiencing another side of life. You may also come to learn and see some things about yourself, people, and life which may seem unfair, dark, and just *different*.

In this situation, I recommend that you allow the journey and process to take you to these new places, experiences, and knowledge. This will be important for your soul ascension, as well as your Divine Mission here on Earth. If you find yourself being overwhelmed or triggered by your Twin, and/or their celebrity status, it is important to take baby steps. There is nothing wrong with taking time alone or away from places, people, and things to process and rebalance. Your celebrity Twin likely understands, as celebrities know people may get overwhelmed, too excited, or even triggered in their presence.

If you and your Twin are both celebrities and/or public figures, I guess you can call yourself Celebrity Twins! Your journey may seem more like you both are having to always work as a team to accomplish things. It is also likely that if one of you experience a career advancement, a new gig, or some controversy, the other experiences the same. You both may also work in opposite industries. Those industries may conflict with each other. If they do, this may make it difficult to see each other, be together, or work together. You both may work in opposite industries which fit like puzzle pieces and work well together. This may cause you two to always be around each other, whether that is a good thing or not.

I recommend that, in either situations, you both communicate what is going on. A lack, or inefficient communication is a great conflict creator, and destroyer of relationships. It is okay to be honest. It is not good to be quiet about problems, and drag them on. This is a stressful way to live. It is also important to communicate to them in a way which will not create undesirable controversy or drama. The spot light has no mercy.

## WHAT IS NARC BEHAVIOR?

B-male is angry and annoyed by Y-female. She has called him narcissistic because she feels like he is self-centered, only caring about himself. This cause B-male to keep Y-female at arm's length, further making her feel unloved and abandoned. B-male isn't a NARC, but he does enjoy being alone sometimes, and isolate himself from others he think disrupt his peace. He thinks Y-female is a NARC because she is emotionally immature and impulsive. They both see each other as NARCs.

But neither of them are NARCs. They actually have a simple misunderstanding. B-male doesn't understand that women are emotional creatures by nature, they can't help it. Y-female doesn't understand that men don't have a NEED for emotional intimacy, as they are more logical and physical about things. This simple misunderstanding cause them to fight and argue a lot. Even though the make-up sex is beyond amazing, they constantly get back together and break up.

A-male is stressed because he thinks Z-female used him, and strung him along. He missed the amazing sex and conversations he had with Z-female. He thinks that Z-female is a NARC because she love bombed him for a few weeks, then all of a sudden began to ghost him, and not communicate nearly as much. Z-female feels like A-male is a NARC. She had been sexually and emotionally abused by a previous romantic partner. Her female friends told her that men who are sexually and emotionally abusive are NARCs. She also read a book, and watched two movies where she saw women being emotionally and sexually manipulated.

Z-female felt like the sex and conversations with A-male were TOO good to be true. It triggered her heavily. It brought back feelings of shame, regret, and disgust she experienced with her previous romantic partner. She felt like A-male was emotionally and sexually manipulating her. Although she loved him and enjoyed his presence and words greatly, she found herself pushing him away. She needed to keep him away from her...she feared of getting used and abused again. A-male and Z-female both see each other as NARCs.

What A-male doesn't understand is that women who have trauma and fragmentation actually run away from love. These women find it difficult to trust men. It doesn't matter if he doesn't physically hit her, call her derogatory names, or gaslight her. Women who have trauma and fragmentation might find good men to be too good to be true. Z-female doesn't understand that men are primarily made by nature to be physical and logical. She is also not used to a man who says all the right words, and man who has a strong voice about his standards, respect, and what he believes. Z-female doesn't understand that men also are sexual beings, just like women are. She doesn't understand that men voice their beliefs and concerns, just like women do, just not in the same ways.

Here, simple misunderstandings cause people to believe the other person is a NARC. These simple misunderstandings and issues are further amplified by the two looking at each other as NARCs. *B-male*, *Y-female*, *A-male*, and *Z-female* all have experienced their own fears, assumptions, and trauma mirrored back to themselves.

It is important to understand that you and your Soul Twin are not NARCs. You must separate anything to do with narcissism and their behavior. Your Twin is mirroring your own internal issues, whether that be fear, trauma, or false beliefs. On the flipside, your Twin truly may have a lot of personal issues that you don't. In this situation, pay close attention to how you RESPOND, and are AFFECTED by their behavior. If you find yourself responding out of anger, hurt, and frustration, this is non-inverted mirroring.

You must not respond out of hurt, anger, and frustration. This will only cause your Twin to continue to behave the way they do toward you. If you find that you are negatively affected by your Twin's behavior, this may be due to you taking their actions too personally, as if it is an attack on you sexually, emotionally, or verbally. It is likely that you have inner fears, trauma, and insecurities which cause you to be affected by your Twin's behavior so much, it negatively impact your health and life.

In a situation like this, disassociate their behavior with anything to do with you. You must not accept their behavior as bad treatment toward you. You must see their behavior as not belonging to you, and not because of you. It is important to release those fears, insecurities, or traumas out of your being, so that they do not cause you to respond to people and their behavior out of anger, hurt, and frustration.

# SECTION FIVE
## SEEKING THE BEGINNING OF THE STAGES

**Introducing:** *PhatPhat* and *Ms. Wonka*! No, *PhatPhat* is not a fat woman, and no, *Ms. Wonka* has nothing to do with chocolate! *PhatPhat* and *Ms. Wonka* are two defining relationships I had in my early-20s and mid-20s which completely changed what I thought I knew about women, and how I perceive them. I am introducing them as my own personal examples. These examples will be for the purpose of teaching the difference between karmics, soulmates, Twin Flames, and Soul Twins.

*PhatPhat* is and *Ms. Wonka* are their nicknames, not their real names. Neither of them wanted their real names identified in my books, obviously. *PhatPhat* was a woman I met while moving furniture. She is exactly the same age as I am, and her nickname was given to her by others in her neighborhood because she had a big butt. But don't be confused, she was not 'ratchet' or ghetto at all, but very classy. She walked like she owned the Earth and had long black hair, which I have always found attractive on a woman. She also had a slim, but model worthy body and smooth skin.

*Ms. Wonka* on the other hand, was a country woman who was crazy about me. I still don't know why until this day, but again, she was one of the women who changed everything I thought I knew about woman. She was slim, and had long, coiled hair. She was always smiling and happy. Her nickname was given by me, because she used the word 'wonky' a lot. She used the word to describe things she felt weren't up to her standards. Whether it was a wonky chair about to fall apart, or a wonky phone application that had too many bugs.

*PhatPhat* was a karmic (single soul), *Ms. Wonka* a soulmate (monadic StarSeed soul), and my supposed 'Twin Flame' was a past life connection. I am sure the one I am to be with in this life is my actual Soul Twin (aka Twin Flame).

Before we dive into the Twin Soul stages, we first need to gain a basic understanding of the design and nature of humans. The way humans are designed, and their nature, is also part of being a Twin Soul.

## ORGIN OF HUMAN NATURE

There is a part of all of us which come from our physical parents. But then there is another part of us which come from a different Entity. There is a difference. We all have two distinct *natures* within us. Nature, as used here is not talking about the Earth, but about human behavioral tendencies influenced by hormones. The physical aspect of us come from various animals. There is a different kind of nature to this as well, just like two sides of the same coin. The other side to this, is Divine Nature. This Divine Nature does not come from hormones, but directly from Source, from Ahmen The Most High. Whether you call it the Holy Spirit, the Kundalini, Divine Nature, or whatever else, it is essentially Source frequency. In this guidebook, this will be called Divine Nature.

## AS ABOVE, SO BELOW

Really, we are soulful beings. We are Soul beings, and some of us are Soular beings. The soul is an invaluable possession. Our physical 3$^{rd}$ Dimension body is simply a projection of our own mind. The physical body is simply energy that is very dense and held closer together. Since we are Consciousness, we are aware of that projection. Because humans have a Divine Nature, and an animal nature, humans are hybrid entities. Humans are a hybrid entity which is half animal but wholly Divine. The animal part is = mammalian predator (sexual) with a serpent brain. The predator part is not related to eating meat, but to being social predators. This mean that humans are always looking for ways to gain social position and influence, in some way, and to some degree. The Divine Nature is = consciousness, intelligence, mentality. These two natures have similarities and differences. Our Divine Nature is the ABOVE, and our animalistic nature (flesh, mortality) is our lower, or *below* nature.

**As above, so below. I'll add an extra part = "As within, so without."**

The two natures are similar because they both cause humans to have behavioral 'tendencies'. Both tendencies come from somewhere, the animalistic one from bodily hormones, and the Divine one from Source. The animalistic nature push us to eat, sleep, desire sex, resource extraction, and survival (protecting the physical body). The Divine Nature in us push for a sense of sovereignty, power, discipline, and influence. All of that sound cool right?

**GUEST** – *"Humans are badass!"*
**MR.J** – "I'll take that as a yes. But there is an important twist…"

See, these two natures are at odds with each other. Humans were created to have internal challenges to overcome. One of those challenges is two different natures which are in conflict with each other. The two natures are placed at odds with each other. One nature is concerned about animalistic endeavors, while the other is concerned with the things of The Most High. Mixed together, with a lack of Oneness Consciousness™ and a sense of ego, and now you have a human who is born into conflict with themselves. Before the human even engage with another person, get into a relationship, get a job, have sex, or compete with others, they already have internal conflicts within themselves.

This is part of each individual person's soul ascension, and life lessons. We all have challenges to overcome. We all have things to experience and learn in life. We are not here just to be here. The two natures exist on good purpose. And if we learn more about those natures, we can gain awareness to align those natures so that we can have a more favorable and productive experience of life, and so that we can see just how powerful we are. We must realize the power of CONSCIOUS choice over ourselves, and over our lives. We stop pointing our finger pointer at other people, and we take accountability for our own behavior, outcomes, and life.

The ABOVE, or Divine Nature part, is the soul journey to bring us out of being controlled by our animal nature, and be led by our Divine Nature. It is not that our animal nature is bad or evil, it is just that the Divine Nature of The Most High is above animal nature. Divine Nature and Source is truly where we find protection, love, peace, joy, and fulfillment. We conquer our animal nature by becoming more conscious, intelligent, and mentally healthy. When we step out of our animal nature, and become more conscious, we recognize both natures. At this point one can CONSCIOUSLY choose to live in Divine Nature, and not by the hormonal animalistic nature. Now eating, sleeping, having sex, and the like are still necessary in a way, but they do not rule over you or primarily influence your choices.

The seeking stage is when someone attempt to marry the animal nature and the Divine Nature with external vices. It's when they are at the beginning of 'waking up', not necessarily looking for love. But because the two natures are different, and opposite, they cannot be mixed without conflict. So one must choose to prioritize animal nature or Divine Nature. Choosing Divine Nature does not mean starving yourself to death, forbidding sex, or not protect yourself physically. But it mean that you do not allow those things to control you and your life. You become sovereign. You become led by The Most High and Source, and not by hormones and physical cravings.

# MATESHIP

You may have heard the term 'the game' before from a dating coach, or from someone mentoring you about human sexuality and mate selection. What is The Game? It wasn't in your middle school or high school curriculum. Your mother likely didn't tell you, and your father may not know at all, or wasn't around to tell you. The Game is not to be confused with dating, courting, or looking for a marriage partner. The Game is when sexual entities engage in the process of looking for, finding, and mating with another of its kind for the purpose of continuing its species, while passing on the good things from its generation. I call this Species Continuation. Since humans are sexual creatures, The Game is part of and necessary for their continuation.

It is not dating, courting, or looking for marriage. Those three things are man-made procedures. The Game comes from Nature, and is for sexual animals and for humans. It is different for humans, because we have an animal nature AND Divine Nature. This Divine Nature adds a twist to The Game. But, The Game is a way in which the males and females do what they can to get what they want or need from the other. This isn't always as simple as agreeing to exchange one thing for another thing. The Game is complex, and unfortunately, most people actually go without getting their core physical and non-physical needs/wants met in the way they truly desire. Sometimes people do, sometimes they don't, and other times they find themselves desiring MORE.

## HYPERGAMY

This MORE is called hypergamy. Hypergamy is part of the Species Continuation programming. Because of the drive for Species Continuation, there is a continuous need to do better, be better, have better, and get better. Hypergamy is part of our animal nature and Divine Nature. It cause us to always want and look for better. This could be higher quality of food, better shelter, a larger social circle, more resources, better quality of sex, a healthier/stronger body, more social approval, and various other things.

Hypergamy is not bad or evil. It is part of The Game, and part of our core programming. It is actually beneficial to all animals, at least to those who engage in hypergamy consciously and with discipline. Hypergamy can also cause stress and conflict in any species. This is because those who are not hypergamous, do not ascend. They are too easily comfortable, too easily content, and don't strive to do better and be better. When others are hypergamous, the same individuals will find themselves at the bottom to the selection pool. This can cause stress and conflict between others, even of the same species and kind.

You may think that The Game is about finding love or getting married, but that is not the case. Those things are taught by social engineering, entertainment (movies, TV shows, ext.) and society. The Game is centered around Species Continuation. It is programmed into all of us. Species Continuation is the process of looking for, finding, and mating with another for the purpose of continuing its species, while passing on the good things from its generation. The mating births offspring, passes on of the good, and continue the survival skills and technologies which benefit the species. All humans are pre-programmed with hypergamy. This cause humans to desire to look for and mate with someone. These desires are mostly animalistic. Humans must have sex and produce healthy, strong, intelligent, and CONSCIOUS offspring so that the human race can continue and pass on the best of the best.

Before meeting *Y-female*, *B-male* had issues keeping a girlfriend. It made him frustrated. *B-male* was never taught hypergamy or The Game. He figured that as long as he treated women well, they would love him and want to be with him. This is until he met *Y-female*.

*B-male* realized that his previous girlfriends left him because he didn't strive to be much in life. He settled for less and did not care about anything but basic day to day things like eating, sleeping, and going to fun events. This initially drew *Y-female* to him, because she had a stressful life, and going out to have fun and restaurants took her mind off life stress. But after a few weeks, it hit *Y-female* hard that *B-male* had no drive or ambition. When she felt this, she immediately called one of her guy friends for a fling. She needed to get over her feelings for B-male, and look for a man who was more ambitious.

This triggered B-male and caused him to become severely confused, frustrated, and angry. Y-female and her male friend ended up in a relationship, a man who she felt could take better care of her. Her male friend (now boyfriend) worked a job, had a business on the side, and lived in a large house. At the same time, B-male had a realization. His father was never present in his life because his mother pushed his father out the house. His mother resented his father because he spent a lot of time working to pay the bills. He wasn't home much and didn't go out to eat or fun events because he'd be too tired from working. B-male grew up around his mother, who was all about having fun and not caring about any of the important things in life.

B-male bought some books to read and enrolled in school so that he could learn to be more ambitious, and establish something for himself. Meanwhile, Y-female and her new man began having issues. Y-female found him to be very responsible and mature, but he was not fun. Again, Y-female found herself stressed and bored. She missed B-male at this point and began wondering how he was doing. She found B-Male online in the Metaverse and social media. She saw that B-male got a bachelor's degree, opened a business, and had a job as a manager. She was shocked. She contacted B-male, but did not hear back from him. B-male had gotten married to one of his colleagues and didn't respond to Y-female.

Y-female engaged in hypergamy by leaving B-male for a different man she felt could make her life better. B-male also engaged in hypergamy by becoming more ambitious and striving for more in life. They both engaged in hypergamy, for different reasons, and achieved different results.

## THE DIVINE NATURE TWIST

But humans are different than animals. Humans are indwelled with Divine Nature. This Divine Nature put a twist to The Game. It becomes more than just eating, sleeping, and having sex. Humans, through Divine Nature, can develop emotional attachments. Animals mostly do not get attached, unless they are specifically breed and taught to do so. Emotional attachments are more than just hormones making you want to have sex. They are not what cause a female animal to feel bonded and protective of her offspring. That is Species Continuation in animals. But in humans, emotional attachments come from Divine Nature. The Divine Nature in us prolongs hormonal and emotional phenomena.

Through attachments (prolonged hormonal and emotional phenomena), a man and a woman has the POTENTIAL to mate and live together until they die. These attachments allow a man and woman to live together without the primary reason being to have sex for the purpose to mating, but simply for companionship and presence. This is the only way humans could be monogamous. Humans are polygamous by default. This is unlike many animals who come together only to mate, or stay together temporarily. Animals who stay together long-term due so because the wild is full of danger, and staying together is safer. It has to do with safety and survival, which are essentials. In humans, it is a luxury and a convenience. It is also because humans are social creatures.

Because of hormones, and humans being sexual creatures, they have a tendency to look for a suitable mate. But as with all things, there are groups of people where this is deferred. There are those who only want to mate, those who want companionship, and those who want a combination of the two. Everyone is different, and no way is wrong, just different. Most people also change from wanting to mate, to companionship, and back to mating throughout their lives.

Everyone seeks mating, companionship, or physical pleasure to some degree. At times, we seek a combination of the three. Everyone is also looking for a sense of sovereignty, power, discipline, and influence. This is our 'above' or Divine nature. Soul Twins still experience all of these things: animal nature, Divine Nature, The Game, Species Continuation, attachments, and hypergamy. All of these things, in some way, and to some degree, are still part of Soul Twin's lives, and part of their soul ascension.

*Z-female* is attached to *A-male*. She has become obsessed with him. She has intense feelings for him. She adore the fact that *A-male* is so driven and has the desire to better himself and the world around him. *A-male* is also attached, but not to *Z-female*. *A-male* is attached to a purpose in his life, and attached to The Most High, Source frequency. *A-male* wakes up every day with new ideas, things he wants to achieve, and refreshed confidence that he will make the world a better place. It is on his mind all the time. *A-male* is always in *Z-female's* emotions. *Z-female* and *A-male* have a healthy attachments.

## ALPHA MEN VS BETA MALES VS STAGNANTS

You have likely heard the terms 'Alpha male' and 'beta male' before, either in a book, online somewhere, or from a dating coach. They hold important meanings. Here, I will describe them in a basic sense without the modern day clutter.

Alpha men basically are the males which consciously choose to be hypergamous, and choose to become attached to the Most High, and Source frequency, and not to the females. Alpha men are self-sufficient. They are hypergamous, and so they choose to separate themselves from the herd and look for higher quality food, better shelter, cleaner water, a stronger body, and improve their survival skills. They do not settle for mediocre. They are aggressive, in a good way. Alpha men are mature. They also seek to improve the environment and living quality of everyone else. They are generous and empathetic.

beta males either do not choose to be hypergamous, or they choose to chase after the females. They become attached to looking for the females and 'fit in' with the herd. They rely on others in the herd, including females, to protect them, and provide their needs. They are not hypergamous, and so they don't seek adventure and risk, in order to find and obtain higher quality food, better shelter, cleaner water, a stronger body, and improved survival skills. They play it safe or they have too much fear to take risks and seek new terrain. They are immature. They usually don't seek to improve the environment and lives of others.

I want to add a new term, and this is the *stagnant*. Stagnants are just that, stagnant. This is either due to pure laziness, a lack of drive, a sever disability, or simply carelessness. Stagnants only care about eating, sleeping, and excrement. They are pure animal nature and do not utilize the Species Continuation program or hypergamy. They lack drive, desire, or ability to have sex and procreate.

Most men are born beta males. They can ascend, and become Alpha men, but they have to break their desire to chase women, and become attached to the Most High, and Source frequency. They have to gain the drive for a better quality of life outside of chasing a woman. Only some men are born Alpha men. They already start off aggressive, not wanting to chase after females, and not wanting to fit in with the herd. They want to take risks, seek new ground, and become physically and mentally strong.

beta males are not necessarily bad or unimportant. They actually benefit women because it is easy for the a beta male to work for resources and give women those resources, which women do want and need. The women will gladly take those resources. Women do need resources for their offspring. So, beta males serve a purpose. As I say, "No shame in the game!™"

## PURE-HEARTS™ VS *OTHER WOMEN* VS STAGNANTS

Remember the Divine Mirror? The man is a mirror reflection of the woman, and the woman a mirror reflection of the man. Men in their Divine Nature are gods. They are caretakers and protectors of life. That is why I use a sword to represent the Masculine. Women in their Divine Nature are Pure-hearts™. When a god looks at His Feminine, He sees His own Heart, His own Soul. That is what She represents. So, She is His Heart. When She sees Him, She sees her Masculine. She sees Her Protector and Caretaker. Women in their Divine Nature represent life-giving and the Earth. Life comes through and from the woman, and men are the protectors and caretakers of life and the woman and their offspring.

Pure-hearts™ are women who consciously choose the Divine Nature within themselves over the animal nature. Rather than living to eat, sleep, extract resources, and engage in social conflict, they seek Alpha men to procreate with and engage in Species Continuation. Because Alpha men have an attachment to the Most High and a higher quality of life, Pure-hearts™ find themselves attracted to Alpha men. They are also attracted to Alpha men's desire to improve the living environment and quality of everyone else. Pure-hearts™ use hypergamy to its fullest to become attached to and support the healthiest, strongest, and most intelligent male they can – the Alpha man.

'other women' are females who seek Alpha men as well. But there is one issue. other women avoid the Divine Nature within themselves, and operate under the animal nature. They only care about eating, sleeping, extracting resources from other males (usually beta males), and engaging in social conflict. Since Alpha men consciously engage in hypergamy, they usually don't mate with just any kind of female. They have options, but they are selective. They desire their Pure-heart™ a woman who also consciously choose Divine Nature over animal nature. Just because an Alpha man will have sex with other women does not mean he wants to have offspring with them.

This leaves the other women who don't qualify for the Alpha men (for whatever reason) to engage in various trickery. This trickery, at its foundation, is to try and get their needs met from multiple males, rather than an Alpha man. The trickery might also involve attempting to get the Alpha man to get her pregnant, or get his resources, either without him knowing, through manipulation, or trying to trick him.

Since Alpha men are few, and beta males are many, other women find themselves doing what they can to get what they need, since the Alpha men don't want to commit to them. But other women don't want beta males. No female WANTS a beta male. Females want a COMPLETE men, a man who has it all, is capable of all, and who is attached to the Most High, and Source frequency. They want the man who has the drive for a higher quality of life. This is because all females are created to birth and be the primary caretakers of the offspring. Females NEED provision, protection, and some guidance from an Alpha man. Alpha men can take care of all of those things for a woman.

other women, just like beta males, find themselves in a difficult place. other women want Alpha men, but Alpha men don't want them. beta males want Pure-hearts™ and other women, but they don't always want them. beta males chase after women, but women usually don't want beta males because beta males are too concerned about women and fitting in with the herd. This is all very conflicting and stressful for those who are not Alpha men and those who are not Pure-hearts™.

What ends up happening, is beta males and the other women stay in a toxic cycle of chasing, deception, resource extraction, and social conflict. The women don't want beta males, but they will use beta males for whatever resources, food, shelter, and attention the beta males have been able to obtain. It is not uncommon for the other women to exchange sex for resources and social approval with beta males, which is why they are called other women. Pure-hearts™ don't do this with Alpha males, because Pure-hearts™ WANT to be with Alpha men, and Pure-hearts™ qualify for Alpha men's standards. The beta males can become stressed that the *other women* and Pure-hearts™ don't want them, and so they chase women for sex and social approval (validation).

This is all part of Species Continuation, hypergamy, and The Game. Keep this all in mind while studying this guidebook, as it is important to understand, even for Soul Twins. All Soul Twins grow up in this environment. This can cause various issues for Twins during their lives, before and after they meet their Twin. Karmics and soulmates are not necessarily beta males or *other women*, and soulmates are not necessarily Alpha men or Pure-hearts™.

# SOUL MATURITY

Just as there is Species Continuation, there is also soul ascension. Although Species Continuation deal with sex and procreation, soul ascension deal with the maturity of a soul. Soul maturity is the transitioning out of being unconscious and into consciousness. It is transcendence. It is also transitioning to conscious choice. Souls do not mature by time or age, but by transitioning into conscious choice through experiencing life and learning lessons. Through life experience and learning lessons, souls mature...at least in theory. Many souls resist maturing, or they get so caught up in life drama, that they sidetrack their soul ascension. Here are the grades of soul ascension from a baby soul, to an ascended master:

**ASCENDED MASTERS (SOUL ASCENSION MASTERS)**
**OLD SOULS**
**MATURED SOULS**
**young souls**
**baby souls**

Most people on Earth have baby and young souls, with a smaller percentage being matured souls, and even smaller percentage old souls. It is not possible to skip grades. Souls have to ascend through each grade. Soul Twins are old souls which decided to 'graduate' and take their soul ascension all the way, which is known as 'Going Home' or reaching Union. Union is Oneness Consciousness™.

# TWIN SOUL JOURNEY & STAGES

If you do an internet search, you will find various 'Twin Flame Stages' photos and blog. They each will list different (and some similar) things within the list. This can make it confusing to know where you are in your own journey. If the stages do not connect, and flow from one to the next smoothly, it can also make it difficult to know what is needed to transition to the next stage. From my personal experience with my Supposed 'Twin' and from being involved in the Twin Soul community, I have carefully formulated a unique list. This list only has the most important stages. They all flow easily from one to next, and it is easier to identify where you are on your journey, and what's needed to transition to the next stage. This unique list is below:

**TWIN SOUL STAGES:**
1.  SOUL SPLIT/SPREAD
2.  DUAL INCARNATION
3.  YEARNING/SEEKING
4.  THE MEETING/RECOGNITION
5.  REALIZATION (Awakening)
6.  SURRENDER (Losing identity with ego, and with the body)
7.  ASCENSION (Turning Inward)
8.  UNION (ONENESS CONSCIOUSNESS™)
9.  DIVINE MISSION

I say that seeking is the first stage, because this is the first stage we consciously are aware of first. To us, we start off *seeking* 'the one'. But there are very important stages which come before. Below is a breakdown and explanation of each stage, as defined by me personally, through my experience and observation:

1.  **SOUL SPLIT/SPREAD:** This is the moment when a soul decides to split or spread. This must happen for a soul to be recognized and classified as a Twin Soul.

2.  **DUAL INCARNATION:** Incarnation is when a soul takes up consciousness in the 3$^{rd}$ dimension using a physical body. It must fall and descend to a frequency which it can engage which physical reality. This happen inside the womb of a woman, sometime after conception. Once a Twin Soul incarnate in two physical bodies, then it is recognized as Soul Twins, because it looks like two people which share the same soul. They are Twins, Soul Twins. Remember, a Twin Soul has the ability to incarnate in two different physical bodies. This allow a Twin Soul to ensoul the fetus two different mothers. Once incarnated in two physical bodies, a Twin Soul is now classified as Soul Twins.

3.  **YEARNING/SEEKING:** All humans experience yearning and seeking. This yearning and seeking, is due to the Species Continuation programming, and The Game (the mating game). This happens through bodily hormones and brain impulses. The yearning is the hormonal desire and impulse to have to procreate. The seeking is the desire to find the most suitable mate to procreate with. With Soul Twins, this is taken a step further, and this is the soul itself yearning for and seeking Union (aka Oneness Consciousness™).

4.  **THE MEETING/RECOGNITION:** When Soul Twins first meet each other, they experience recognition. This recognition is the soul 'waking up' or seeing itself for the first time. This is not to be confused with meeting another person. No, the soul has met its Self in another physical body. The meeting is essential for complete soul ascension. The dreamscape is where all humans other animals dream. It is not

enough to simply dream, or become conscious of other dimensions and planes of reality. There has to be a 'place' for this to happen. The dreamscape is like a wall-less room we enter, where we are able to become less conscious of this physical reality, and become aware of other dimensions and planes of reality. This wall-less room allows that to happen. The dreamscape is also where people see other people, and where Soul Twins can see their Soul Twin.

5. **REALIZATION:** When the soul becomes aware it is attempting to separate itself, run from itself, or chase after itself, it will enter the Realization Stage. In this stage, the soul has transitioned enough into consciousness, and conscious choice that it 'realizes' it is one. The Soul Twins here will take a different path. One or both Twins will all of a sudden experience extreme changes in their lives, and within themselves. Their entire life will begin to change. On the surface, these changes may not look the same. It may seem that one Twin's life change for the better, while the other Twin's life change for the worst. But all of the changes are a path redirection. All of the changes are for the long term good, and the bringing back together of the Twins. But when they come back together, it will be while they are both in Oneness Consciousness™ and not in Separation Illusion™.

6. **SURRENDER:** This is the middle point between the Realization stage, and Union (aka Oneness Consciousness™). All stages before the ascension stage are the *transitioning* out of Separation Illusion™, and into Oneness Consciousness™, and conscious choice. Surrender is when Twins no longer run and chase after each other, and they no longer try to separate from each other. They are free to live their lives without any Separation Illusion™, and without trauma, baggage, or fragmentation.

7. **ASCENSION:** (Turning Inward). Ascension is not really a stage, but the conscious choice to raise your frequency. It is about being better, living better, speaking better, thinking better, and behaving better. It is not a stage between Surrender and Union. All souls are ascending, and under some degree of soul ascension. But Soul Twins are on an accelerated ascension path. They are graduating.

8. **UNION (ONENESS CONSCIOUSNESS™):** This is pure consciousness, intelligence, and mentality. The soul is no longer fighting and wrestling with life or with its Self. It is no longer 'blind' to the things, places, and entities which are in place to give it the challenges in order to help it learn and ascend. The soul is completely aware, and instead use the challenges to ascend. In Oneness Consciousness™ a soul can be an ascended master. Here the soul gain the privilege to guide, challenge, and help other souls along their ascension path.

9. **DIVINE MISSION:** Once one or both Twins are in Oneness Consciousness™, they are qualified to engage in the Divine Mission. What is the Divine Mission? On the surface, it will be different for everyone. But generally, the Divine Mission is rooted in living your life in a way that is rooted in pure conscious choice. This pure conscious choice will be of positive benefit to yourself and everyone around you. Your life will no longer only be about taking care of yourself or being your own priority. The Ahmen Most High will become your first priority. Being of benefit to others will become your first priority, because you are now aware that everyone is YOU. Everyone is a reflection of yourself. You will find yourself living your life to help others along their life and soul journey. This is different than a normal person, where doing things for others are commonly out of obligation, peer pressure, social adherence (herd mentality), incentive, or selfish endeavors. Your helping of other people will be of pure conscious choice, and for the benefit of everyone around you.

## HOW YEARNING/SEEKING AFFECT OUR RACO™ SYSTEM

While we go through life, our energy system is affected in many ways. This will happen due to eating habits changes, the social environment, ecological environment, level of stress, exercise (or a lack), relationships, sexual activity, and body health. It is also due to cosmic changes and changes in our Soular System. While yearning and seeking, our energy will experience many fluctuations, blockages, and energetic impurities. At times we may think or feel that nothing we do improve our physical health, our emotions, or life experience. Many do not take into consideration their energy body, because energetic health is not taught in schools or by most parents.

We go through life thinking it is food, money, or a better romantic partner which will better our health and life experience. Although that may be true on some level, to some degree, and in certain circumstances, it is our own energy which influence our life experience. What we think is a stressful life or a life of lack, is actually a life in which we are creating through our own energetic health. Our energetic health influence our entire lives, in every way. Our RACO™ system will generally not be of optimal health and cleanliness while we are yearning and seeking (to go Home, Oneness Consciousness™. But as we take the ascension path, we come to see the places, people, things, and activities which keep our energy at a low vibration.

## QUICK QUESTIONS

*"Can a Soul Twin marry someone else if they have a Soul Twin?"*
Twin CAN be married to people other than their Twin. Nothing really stops them from going to the courthouse or a church and marrying someone. Will they be fulfilled, have their needs met, and be productive (in a positive way) in that marriage? That is something to consider!

### *"How do I find my Supposed 'Twin' Soul?"*

You cannot 'find' your Soul Twin. Your Twin is YOU in another body. Unless you are talking about finding your other body! But no, you can't and won't 'find' your Twin. You only become aware and conscious of your own soul when you meet them. You don't and won't meet them until the appointed time as you both agreed before incarnation. Usually, Twins don't know they are and have a Soul Twin until AFTER they meet their Soul Twin. Usually, we don't know until after we meet them in the physical 3$^{rd}$ dimension, in the dreamscape, or energetic channeling by a medium. I suggest living your life and not worry about how to find your Twin Flame. Twin Flames are rare and an extremely small percentage of the population.

### *"How do I attract my Supposed 'Twin'?"*

You can't attract your Self. You already are your Self! It's just a matter of becoming aware that you are what you have been looking for. YOU are your Twin, and your Twin is YOU. Trying to attract your Twin will actually do the opposite because you are operating under Separation Illusion™. If you try to attract your Soul Twin, you will prolong Running, Chasing, and Separation Illusion™. Don't try to attract your Twin. This is a lesson of itself. Instead I recommend that you study the rest of this guidebook for alternative solutions to trying to chase after or attract your Twin.

## FOR MARRIED/DIVORCED TWINS

Probably the worst feeling is to be married and still feel a yearning to be with or find someone. Most people think or feel they have married 'the one' and that getting married will take away the yearning. But what do you do when you are married and feel like something is missing, or that you have married someone who has not taken away the yearning. For Soul Twins, the yearning has nothing to do with getting married, finding 'the one', or satisfying the yearning. The yearning and seeking is a soul one, different than that of humans. Humans have to ascend, and go through life lessons to progress through the soul maturity grades. Their yearning and seeking is rooted in hormones, for the purpose of coming together to produce offspring. As they ascend though, eventually they will find themselves on the soul journey.

Twin Soul seeking is due to the soul desiring Union. Twins take it a step further from Species Continuation. If you are married to someone other than your Twin, they may satisfy Species Continuation programming in you. But they won't satisfy your soul craving for Union. You might think that your Twin is 'the one' and you need to divorce your wife or husband. Stop right there! Remember, your Soul Twin is YOU in another body. Getting divorced and going after your Twin wont satisfy your soul craving for Union. You might actually push your Twin away! They may actually run from you!

This is because you can't and won't experience Union chasing after or pedestaling a person, even if they are your Twin. Union is Oneness Consciousness™, NOT a relationship with another person, and definitely not with your Self. You can't even have a relationship with your Self, because you are already One, and you are already your Self. It is important that you are not hasty to divorce, get married, or jump into a relationship upon meeting or after meeting your Soul Twin. It is important to CONSIOUSLLY choose to be with someone, and not out of hast, command, or hormones.

## FOR TWINS WITH CHILDREN

Having children is a dream and goal for many. For some, having children was not planned, and they actually may dislike the fact that they have children. But by having children, you or your Soul Twin, won't cancel the yearning and seeking. Both you and your Twin could have multiple children from each other and other people, but STILL experience yearning and seeking. Having children is not Union. Having children will not get you to Union.

But having children could make the journey to Union prolonged, and even stressful. Children are a liability. Children cost money, time, energy, patience, and attention. Children can only become an asset after years and at least a few decades of rearing, teaching, and guidance. If they survive and do well, then children can do things which benefit you, and this is only when children are an asset. Children can be an asset if you have a legacy to pass on to them. They can also be an asset if the human population were to become minimized. Children are our future. They increase and extend the populations and generations. That is what can make them an asset.

If you are a Soul Twin, the yearning and seeking you experience doesn't happen because you want to be with your Twin. But it is because your soul wants to realize Union. You and your Twin are already One and you must realize that. Your Twin is YOU.

## FOR TWINS WHOSE TWIN IS DECEASED

**GUEST** – *"If my Supposed 'Twin' died, how come I still yearn for them?"*
**MR. J** – "The yearning you feel is likely hormonal and emotional in this situation. All of us experience sadness, grief, heartbreak, and sometimes anger at the passing of a loved one, or someone we cared about. But even if your Twin died, it does not automatically lead to Union. You still must progress through the stages. But if your Twin died, your journey to Union may be expedited, as your Twin is not in a physical body, and they are no longer subjected to gaining trauma, baggage, and fragmentation from the chaotic life on Earth."

## FOR TWINS WHO ARE FAMILY MEMBERS

Family is a blessing to have. They are the first ones who teach us some things about life. They are our first experience of society. They are the first people we love, and are loved by. But even having family won't rid that yearning you feel. It won't matter how big, loving, rich, or present your family is. You can and will experience a longing. This longing is for Union, Oneness Consciousness™.

## FOR TWINS WITH A LARGE AGE GAP

Most people do not yearn to be sexual or romantic with someone much older or younger than them. But is your Twin might be much older or younger than you? You are not yearning and seeking to be with your Soul Twin, but for Union. You might be triggered by your Twin if they are underage, much older, or much younger than you. But it is not because you are desiring sex or a relationship with them, but because you are desiring Union. As stated before, DO NOT engage in sexual activities with a minor.

## FOR TWINS WHO ARE A CELEBRITY OR PUBLIC FIGURE

I know what you are thinking – Who doesn't yearn for or seek a celebrity? Well, Twin Soul yearning and seeking is not about celebrity status, being famous, or great wealth.

If your Twin is a celebrity or public figure, you may have a yearning for them due to their celebrity status. They may be your idol, or you may be a fan of theirs. But on another level, they cause a different kind of yearning in you, and that yearning can't be fulfilled by their new hit song, their reality TV show, YouTube channel, or by meeting them in person. This kind of yearning can only be fulfilled by realizing Union.

In another situation, if your Twin is a celebrity or public figure, you may not even care that they are. But you feel this intense desire and yearning for them. This is your desire for Union, which is Oneness Consciousness™.

If you are a celebrity or public figure and you Twin is not, you may find it strange that this person has sparked such desire and yearning in you. You may think that something is wrong, or that 'it can't be right'. But surely, even you, as a celebrity or public figure, can be on the Twin Soul journey, a type of soul journey. But that desire you feel, is to reach Oneness Consciousness™ and not to drop a new music album , star in a new movie, or make a new episode on your YouTube or in the metaverse.

If you and your Twin are both celebrities and/or public figures the connection you have with them can be intense. It could make it difficult to go about your business without the paparazzi noticing something is different between you and them. You know that what you feel for them isn't because they also are a celebrity or public figure, because you have met many others who are. But it is because you have a yearning in you for Union.

## NARCISSISM AND LOVE

Narcissism and love are two different things. But depending on a person's level of trauma, baggage, fragmentation, and even their upbringing or social programming, they may find themselves attracted to those who have NARC behaviors. It is important to not confuse the two. Love is an emotion. But narcissism is not an emotion.

No one goes out and seek to be with a NARC. But some people find themselves with someone who they assume or claim to be a NARC. If you have called your Twin a NARC, STOP doing so. It is not healthy or a mark of maturity to call someone a NARC who you have feelings for, or experience a connection with. It is important to understand that calling your Twin a NARC does not make them a NARC just because you want them to.

Calling them a NARC would be calling yourself one, and why would you do that if you are not willing to call yourself one? Calling them one just adds more confusion, stress, conflict, Running, Chasing, and Separation. Why would you want to live like that? I recommend you stop calling them a NARC if you have. If you continue to, then that is actually you calling yourself a NARC. Remember, you Twin is YOU in another body, not some guy, or some woman.

# SECTION SIX
## THE MEETING ~ CHANGED FOREVER

It is one thing for two souls in separate bodies to meet, but imagine a single soul, split or spread into two separate bodies. In the physical dimension, the soul meeting itself through two different bodies is a mysterious, confusing, and addictive experience.

*Strange* things began happening upon meeting my Supposed 'Twin', even while not in person. The first thing was how she looked, like the female version of myself. I found myself saying "If I were a woman, I'd look like her!" The first picture I looked at, at her eyes, I *fell into* her eyes, and ended up out in the Universe. I was no longer surrounded by 4 walls, a ceiling and roof. It all disappeared. Then, the obsessive thinking started a few days in. Every single day, she was the only thing on my mind. This was strange, because I never had a problem with remaining detached from women. Even *PhatPhat* and *Ms. Wonka* couldn't get me attached even though they were very feminine, treated me well, and the sex was amazing. How the heck could my Supposed 'Twin' consume my mind and I hadn't met her in person yet or talked more than a few days? Something wasn't right here...

Then, after I 'ran', I had a very vivid dream of her. She stood across the street from me, wearing a graduation gown. She looked directly at me, with her characteristic mischievous smile. I walked across the street in the dream and stood right in front of her. Her hair looked as if she just left the hair salon, long, straight, and with a luster. But looking in her eyes, I didn't see eyes, I saw the cosmos. After that there were many vivid and intense dreams of her. I figured it would go away after a few days. But months and YEARS after leaving, I still saw her in the dreamscape.

## MEETING YOUR OWN *SOUL*

There is no such thing as 'meeting' your Soul Twin in the sense you might assume. You are not meeting a separate entity, but your own soul in a different physical body. You simply saw your own soul. All you did was look back at YOU. Or you could look at it as, it was the first time you 'opened your eyes' (energetically speaking), and when the eyes open, behold! You saw your own soul in another body.

Only you will know if you are a Twin Soul and have a Soul Twin. The 'knowing' is beyond the mind and emotions. There is an intense connection with them that does not go away no matter what you or they do, or who else you or they are with. Only you will know. There isn't a checklist of things to look for to tell when you meet them. It is a profound and undeniable inner knowing. You won't know by their hair color, personality type, dress style, age, popularity, skin color, accent, or shoe size. When you meet your Soul Twin, you will be thrown into a soul journey. Your life will change and you as a person will change, fortunately for the better.

Meeting your Soul Twin is your soul awakening. You are forever changed. The meeting is usually intense, life changing, and for a short time. Some Soul Twins first meet in the dreamscape before meeting in person. Twins don't always meet under the most ideal situations. Many Twins are already married to someone else, live thousands of miles away, have familial or financial obstacles, or may be in a place in life which make physical meeting temporary or non-existent.

## SOUL RECOGNITION

Soul recognition is not meeting someone who looks like you, or someone you find attractive. It has nothing to do with physical looks. Soul recognition is what it sound like. It is when you recognize your own soul in your Twin. You have one soul, and that soul has also taken residence in another physical body. The body may be different, but the soul is the same.

When Twins meet for the first time, the soul recognition can be very intense. You don't know WHY you feel drawn to them. They seem so familiar, like you have known them all your life. But you have just met them. This can be confusing, cause anxiety, or create excitement and impulsive action. At this point you may already have begun chasing or running from your Twin and not even realize it.

Soul recognition happens the moment you meet them, especially when you first look IN their eyes. The energy Soul Twins feel amplify when looking in each other's eyes. I have heard plenty of cases where some Twins cannot look into each other's eyes for a prolonged time, or at all, because they energy gets too intense. Meeting your Twin can spark confusion or anxiety, especially if your Twin does not have the physical attributes you are normally attracted to. All of a sudden, you find yourself feeling so familiar with them, and drawn to them. You may also get so excited by the recognition, that you already begin chasing after them. The inverse is true, as excitement itself can cause fear or trigger a Twin into running. This is because you simply are caught off by them, and they intensity you feel so soon.

## CAUGHT OFF GUARD

Your Soul Twin will be your idealistic mate, or the opposite of your ideal mate. They may have ALL the attributes you find attractive in a mate. This can actually throw you off, as such a person is commonly glorified. But most people do not know what to do or how to respond upon meeting such a person. This is because emotionally it is easier to become attached, triggered, and insecure. If this is the case for you, it is important to work out your insecurities and attain the ability to be emotionally open without being triggered. There is no need to feel insecure or be triggered, your Twin is YOU, your own soul.

They may also have the opposite qualities of your ideal mate. You feel an attraction toward them, yet they don't have the qualities you are normally attracted to. You may find yourself not wanting to be with them, and not want to share a connection with them. This could cause you to run, jump into relationships with others, or treat your Twin poorly. Here it is important to understand that just because we don't like someone, or they are not our ideal mate, doesn't give us the right to treat them poorly or look at them as less than.

My Supposed 'Twin' has all the qualities I look for in an ideal mate. She had the other non-physical things, but because of her baggage, trauma, and insecurities, we were unable to get along with each other. I took part in it as well by adding fuel to the fire, enabling her in certain ways. Luckily I put an end to that, as I realized I was making things worse for the both of us. I knew I needed to change my own behavior.

Soul Twins do not always meet under ideal conditions. Most people imagine meeting 'the one' under ideal conditions. This could be while at a social gathering, while dressed nicely, while being happy, having all the material things they want, making a lot of money, or while single. It is common for Twins to first meet each other under conditions which are not considered ideal. Some Twins do meet each other under ideal conditions. These could be at a classy lounge, a music rehearsal, museum, vacation spot, on a cruise, at a bar, or club. It is important to not have an assumption in your head that you can only meet a good person (even your Twin) in certain locations, and under certain conditions. We can meet someone anywhere, under any circumstance.

When you first met your Twin, were you caught off guard? Did you meet them in a location, and under conditions which you deemed to be *ideal*?

## SOUL TWIN ATTRACTION & ATTACHMENT

What is attraction? It is not lusting after someone's looks. Attraction is something, or someone you moderately can't escape. Entrapment is something you can't escape, unless the device or condition which has someone trapped change. Attraction is someone or something you find difficult to escape. You feel a pull to them, whether it be hormonal or purely energetic. You may find it difficult to keep your Self away from your Twin. You want to talk to them, hear them speak, be touched by them, engage in sexual behavior with them, and even be with them romantically.

Attraction is not the same as attachment. Attachment is rooted in emotions for someone where you are already *caught* by them. Attraction is the difficulty of escaping a PULL toward someone. Attraction happens first, then attachment afterwards. Someone can be attracted to you, but not attached to you. Attraction can happen physically, meaning you find them good to look at. Attraction and attachment can be sexually, meaning you experience high sexual chemistry and functionality with them. It can be emotionally, meaning they stir emotions within you that you find pleasing. It can be mentally, meaning there is mutual psychological comprehension. It can be energetically, meaning there is non-physical resonance and harmony.

Soul Twins feel both attraction and attachment. This is even if your Twin does not have the qualities and attributes you are normally attracted to. There will always be an attachment between you and your Twin, because you both are the same soul. Even if you or they don't feel attached, the connection is still there and active. A lack of FEELING attached to your Twin begins in the Realization stage, continue through the Surrender stage, and is permanent in Union. There connection is still there, but it is free from inner conflict and resistance.

Twin Soul attraction is very intense, and can cause triggering, running, chasing, and insecurities to arise. If you have experienced these, it is part of your soul ascension. After some time and work, the intense attraction and attachment will seem to disappear. They have not gone anywhere, you are simply harmonized within. The attraction you feel toward your Twin will be different than with other people. The attraction will be near instantly upon meeting them. It will be intense, or grow more intense as the days pass. You will find yourself attracted to them, sometimes without words to explain.

## HEART PALPITATIONS

When I was little, I began having heart issues. I knew exactly where they came from: high stress from family and life, poor eating habits, and overeating. This unbalanced my hormones, caused me to gain weight, and gave me heart issues. The heart issues ranged from painful tings, to a complete drain of energy. I did my best to take better care of my health, and I eventually lost weight and had better health. But then my father passed away in 2009 when I was in high school due to heart failure. Then, ten years later, my mother passed away in 2019 due to heart disease.

I was devastated. Worse, during the time, the heart issue returned. I was worried I was next in line to be laid into a coffin. Again, I did what I could to better my health, especially my heart health. Then in August of 2020, *it* happened. It was the day I met my Supposed 'Twin' online. The very day, I began experiencing a different kind of heart problem, or what I thought was an issue. In the Twin Soul community, they are called *heart palpitations*. I remember the feeling, and still until this day, experience them. I could describe it as my heart doing a kind of flutter. It is not painful at all, but does cause laughter when they are strong.

Since that day meeting *her* on a certain social media platform, these heart palpitations signify the connection we share. I thought it was just me, until I read constantly on Quora.com and YouTube, that other Twins experienced heart palpations. The more I read on Twin Soul heart palpitations, and the more Twins who I asked about it, the more I was convinced *she* wasn't just a random woman I met a certain social media platform.

Heart palpations come from the shared soul and RACO™ system. All Soul Twins are one soul, and have one RACO™ system. Since the physical heart has its own energetic field, it is affected by Twins' RACO™ system. The heart palpitations can be experienced with both Soul Twins. This can happen when one or both Twins 'look' for each other, emotional upset, and when Twins are close distance from each other. Looking in the eyes, becoming sexually aroused by the other Twin, and physical touching can amplify the heart palpitations. Heart palpitations can be experienced with your Twin, even if they are thousands of miles away.

If you experience heart palpitations, don't make any assumptions. I recommend you go to the doctor or a clinic and get checked out. Never assume that just because you have met your Twin, or you feel their energy that you don't have heart issues, or other health complications. You will not experience heart palpitations with karmics or soulmates. But you may experience trauma or stress-induced heart pain, skipping beats, or irregular rhythm. It is important to not confuse any energy you feel in your heart or chest with meeting your Soul Twin. Everyone has the possibility of having heart problems.

## TWIN SOUL ATTACHMENT

Your Soul Twin is someone you cannot stop thinking about. You keep feeling their energy, hearing their thoughts, and have a magnetic draw toward them. You can't break the attachment or connection you have with them. Twin Soul attachment cannot be broken, unlike with karmics and soulmates. Twin Soul attachment is Divine, and beyond hormones. Because Soul Twins are one soul, but in two bodies, the attachment cannot be broken. Their being one soul creates the permanent, Divine attachment.

Fortunately, Twin Soul attachment can be redirected, but not broken. No matter what you do, you won't be able to severe or destroy the connection you feel with them. Attempting to do so will cause yourself, them, and others unnecessary harm. There is another way. That is, to redirect the attachment. We all have attachment to things and people, in some way, and to some degree. It is possible to redirect attachments, even the one you have with your Twin. This is very important, especially if your Twin is toxic, up to no good, or they are unavailable (physically, emotionally, ext.)

Due to the Divine Hierarchy, it is good for women to have an attachment to a man. But the man must be healthy, strong, and doing good things for himself and others. It is not good for a woman to have an attachment to a man who is toxic, physically abusive, engage in addictions/crime, and does harmful things to himself and others. It is good for men to have an attachment to The Most High, to Source frequency. It is also good for men to have an attachment to things which are good for himself and others. It is not good for men to have an attachment to women for various reasons which will not be included in this guidebook.

If you are a female Soul Twin and are attached to your Twin who is on bad behavior or unavailable, it is good to redirect this energy toward something else. This could be a hobby, positive social activity, or a career which is fulfilling. If you are a male Soul Twin and are attached to your Twin, it is good to redirect this energy toward Source frequency, The Most High, a hobby, business, or career. This will be regardless if your Soul Twin is toxic, ext. or not. It is beneficial for males to not be attached to women.

The process for redirecting attachment is complex and will be different for each person. But on a basic level, it is about redirecting your time, attention, and energy toward something or someone else. Redirecting attachment away from your Twin will not break the connection, cords, or energy you feel from them. Simply, you no longer are overwhelmed or influenced by them. An attachment you have with anything and anyone must be one that is healthy and beneficial for you. It must be one which does not cause you to engage in harmful or illegal behavior. I recommend you sit and think about where (and who) you have your energy directed. If it is with someone or something which is not healthy, beneficial, or of harmful/illegal nature, redirect the attachment.

## CHANGED RACOS™

When you meet your Soul Twin, you will experience a number of energetic, physical, and emotional changes. You RACO™ system will go through a variety of purging, clearing, grounding, and realignment. This can be intense, painful, or overwhelming at times. This is not a bad thing at all, but part of the soul journey and ascension. It is necessary. We are all (including Soul Twins) energy. We all have an energetic system. This energetic system can be subjected to impurities, blockages, and misalignment as you progress through life, and through lifetimes. It is important for these impurities to be dissolved, blockages opened, and misalignments realigned.

Remember, Union is Oneness Consciousness™. Oneness Consciousness™ is a state of consciousness. It is a harmonic, blissful, and abundant state of being. It is important to have a clear and aligned RACO™ system free of blockages to realize Union. As you live through life, experiences with the environment, social programming, other people, life events, trauma, abuse, and other things can influence and alter your RACO™ system. It may not always be influenced or altered in a beneficial way.

Grounding, clearing, and realigning your RACO™ system is possible. It can come through a variety of ways. Meditation, eating habits change, being around different people, living in a different geographical location, exercise, removing or changing social media intake, bare feet in soil or sand, daily showers, clean clothes, and healthy music all clear and align the RACO™ system.

The impurities usually come from being emotionally, energetically, and sexually involved with other people who have 'clutter'. It is important to take energetic showers to keep this clutter from building up in your RACO™ system.

Blockages can come from trauma, abuse, and physical or emotional ailments. Blockages can be open by healing trauma, removing yourself from those who abused you, and improving your physical and emotional health.

Misalignments usually come from social programming, certain social media/entertainment influences, your childhood upbringing by those who looked over you, adherence to social norms (aka herd mentality), poor eating habits, and emotional attachments to people or things which are harmful for you. Misalignments can be realigned by removing yourself from the above said people, things, and social influences. Regular time alone (to meditate) is beneficial here.

## TRIGGERING

**GUEST** – *"How were you triggered by your Twin and the connection?"*
**MR. J** – *"She triggered me in a few ways. For example, one day she stated "You will get EVICTED" on a random post I uploaded, in the middle of a conversation. It had nothing to do with housing, living arrangements, or a residential lease. I was confused by it, but remembered a time when I was in high school and feared my mother kicking me out homeless, which actually did happen. After the years though, I got rid of that fear, or at least I thought..."*

It was like she knew all of my fears and insecurities.

In another way, *she* clearly (and personally stated) her deep issues with the opposite sex. It caused her to get into unnecessary arguments and conflict with others. I knew that eventually, this would be directed toward me, since I am a man. It was just a matter of time, she was a loose cannon at that time. Then, one day it happened... the black magic attack which I wrote about earlier.

**GUEST** – *"I been researching black magic and witchcraft since you told us about your Twin using witchcraft on you. I am surprised that it is a real thing and people actually practice it. Even more, people post all of their business online! I would think if someone is doing black magic or witchcraft it is something to keep secret!"*
**MR. J** – *"That is great you all are researching things outside of this book. Remember, your learning and ascension do not stop here. This is just a stop along the way. I am giving you some meat, veggies, and potatoes! But the rabbit hole is even deeper than all I share with you."*

I was also triggered by the attachment that developed toward her, a woman I didn't know and hadn't met in person yet. This was before any dates, sex, or relationship. That is impossible, or so I thought... No other woman in my life, no woman I ever dated or had sex with, not even *Ms. Wonka* or *PhatPhat*, were able to create an attachment on me. Fortunately, I was able to redirect the attachment away from my Supposed 'Twin'.

**GUEST** – *"How was your Twin triggered by you and the connection?"*
- She didn't feel good enough for me (a shocker for me!)

- She was surprised by how I am always happy and peaceful despite having a bad start in life with abuse, trauma, and loss
- I triggered her trust issues, me being younger than her, and by having female friends
- Due to her opposition of the opposite gender, she didn't like that I am testosterone filled with a high sex drive
- She felt like I am 'ahead' of her as far as emotional and soul maturity
- I was too aware of certain things which most men don't know about, such as how women can be manipulative. This meant that she would not be able to manipulate or get over on me in any way.
- The day I left, it hurt her deeply. She thought I wouldn't turn my back on her, but I had to. It's not healthy for a man to be attached to a woman, especially not one who had an opposition against men
- Her perception was that only women are innocent, and men are guilty of all, yet I don't possess the attributes she thought men have by nature (violent, crime-driven, liars, misogynistic, emotionally aggressive toward women, physically abusive, drug addictions, ext.)
- She experienced an attachment to me, someone who doesn't LOOK like her ideal mate on the outside, yet is one underneath. Looks can be deceiving, sometimes in a good way
- I was kind to her, when others were not

## MEETING IN THE 3D PHYSCIAL

**FRIENDS** – After meeting your Soul Twin, you likely became close friends. Not all Soul Twins become romantic or sexual, and some are even family members. Because Soul Twins are the same soul in two bodies, they make easy friends. You find that you and your Twin understand each other better than anyone else, even parents or siblings.

Twins can experience issues with each other, even if they are only friends. It is important to BE a friend to your Twin and not just want them to be your friend. You must still treat them with respect, honesty, and understanding.

**BUSINESS PARTNERS** – Twins who don't live off-grid or have enough passive income to not work, likely work jobs or own a business. Soul Twins also have bills and expenses like everyone else. Being a Soul Twin does not prevent bill collectors from wanting their money. Soul Twins who are entrepreneurs or business owners may end up working alongside each other. Many Twins met each other at a job they both worked at.

Twins are still able to use someone or each other for money or undermine the other's business. Although not common in the Twin Soul collective, it is still possible. It is important to know that however you treat your Soul Twin, whatever you say about them, will be reflected back to you. Never take advantage of, use, or undermine your Twin and their success. Keep business professional, legal, and mutually agreed.

**DATED** – Soul Twins also desire to feel love, companionship, or the pleasure of romance. Twins who meet in person and are not family, may find themselves dating or courting. The high attraction, the magnetic pull, and the feeling of being Home, can cause Twins to seek more than friendship and business with each other. Dating your Soul Twin will be a unique experience unlike any other. You will already feel an attraction toward them, have a deep sense of familiarity with them, and easily become emotionally and sexually aroused when around them.

Dating your Twin might still bring problems commonly experienced by normal people. There can be miscommunication, manipulative games, usury, pulling back, unavailability, or a lack of progressing things forward. Ensure that you communicate your needs with your Twin and understand that this connection also requires work, just like with normal people.

**HAD SEX** – Soul Twin sex is also unique, and not like that with karmics or soulmates. Soul Twin sex is also part of the merging process mentioned earlier. And no, there is no incest here. There is one soul, but TWO different bodies, and most of the time those two bodies are born from different parents.

Soul Twin sex is of the highest intensity, above karmics and soulmates. It can actually be addictive, unlike with karmics and sometimes soulmates. The sex also never gets old, boring, or stale. More than a few times I have heard of older Soul Twins who are together, who STILL have sex and enjoy it as if it's their first time! Soul Twin sex is the kind of sex we all dream of and imagine. No, it is not necessarily porno kind of sex. It is the kind of sex which involve the complex mix of intense energy, highly pleasuring physical sensations, being emotionally connected to the other person, speaking the right words (dirty talk), the right stroke, and actually being attracted to them. Soul Twin recognition and familiarity just adds more on top. This creates the kind of sex that leaves one still feeling the pleasure days and even weeks after.

But Soul Twin sex can cause issues. One common reason I have heard are the sex being so intense and pleasurable that it brings out insecurities, which can lead to running. Another is the sex triggering one or both Twins. They have never experienced sex on this level, especially not with someone they are actually attracted to so much, and feel so familiar with, even just after meeting each other. This can cause one of both Twins to feel like it is 'too good to be true' and develop trust issues. One or both Twins might make assumptions about a third party, cheating, lying, leading them on, or feeling like their Twin is love bombing them for a hidden agenda. The intensity and pleasure of the sex can compound, and become overwhelming for one or both Twins. It just feels so good and so right that it can become too much. This will stabilize once Twins Surrender and realize Union so that it does not cause triggering and overwhelm.

It is important to not make assumptions of your Twin cheating on you or having a hidden agenda. They are likely not love bombing you or trying to manipulate you using sex.

**IN A RELATIONSHIP** – Just like with normal people, Soul Twins usually seek some kind of commitment or relationship with each other. Some people call this 'Reunion'. But I don't like using the term ReUnion here because it suggests that Union is about Twins being together physically, which is not true. If the whole idea of Union was to bring and keep Twins together physically, it would defeat the purpose of the soul splitting/spreading and the soul journey.

There is no ReUnion. There is only Union, and everything before that is a journey toward realizing Union. It is not about a physical relationship with another person.

But it is a wonderful experience when Twin Flames are able to be together physically. Most Twins will require some time together physically in order to progress through the stages to realize Union. This is even more true the more lessons they have to learn, and the more trauma and baggage they have to release. They simply need to spend more time 'looking in the mirror' to work out all of those issues, and learn those lessons. Earthling Soul Twins will require time together physically, as they are Earth-bound souls. Earthling Soul Twins are home to the 3D physical Earth, even when they transcend the 4th dimension or higher. ET (cosmic) and StarSeed Twins do not necessarily need to be together in the 3D physical, and most only need a few days to catalyze the merging, triggering, and ascension process.

Soul Twin relationships can be intensely fulfilling. Because of this, Soul Twins who have been together in a relationship may find it impossible to have the same or better experience with a karmic or soulmate. But as with other things, Soul Twins may find themselves having relationship problems which are common with normal people. Just because you get into a relationship with your Twin does not mean the relationship will be perfect or last longer. It is important to not be careless with the relationship, thinking it will work out no matter what you do just because they are your Twin.

**MARRIED** – This is what most people think of when they read or hear about Twin Soul Union. They relate Union to marriage, even though the two are not related and actually contradictive. It is impossible for Union to mean getting married. Marriage is bringing two together to make them one. Union is Oneness Consciousness™. Union has nothing to do with bringing two people together and uniting them. Union is a state of consciousness. If there is already Oneness, there can't be a marriage.

But, going to the courthouse or a church and marrying your Twin can still be a good experience. Although most Twins will not get married, the ones who do, have their *dream come true* moment. It is important to not assume that being married to your Soul Twin is Union or the end of the soul journey. It is possible for Twins to be married, yet not in Union. Even if you and your Twin have been married for 10, 20, or more years, how long you have been married still does not determine whether you are in Union or not.

**HAS CHILDREN WITH THEIR SOUL TWIN** – Pregnancy happens, whether planned or not. It happens to normal people, and it can and does happen to Soul Twins who have unprotected sex. Meeting your Soul Twin and then having a baby with them can be a fulfilling or problematic experience, depending on the situation. Having children with your Twin can be another *dream come true* experience. It can also cause additional conflict between you and your Twin, especially if you or they are the Runner.

**DIVORCED** – Normal people can and do divorce, and so can Soul Twins. You might think that the end goal for Soul Twins is to meet each other, get married, and that marriage is Union. But it is common amongst Twins who have gotten married to end up divorced. It can be a stressful situation and painful for Twins who thought that getting married to their Twin was Union. But some find out the hard way that marriage itself is not Union, and is not related to Union. It can create grief, heartbreak, bitterness, and mistrust when a Twin has been divorced, or choose to divorce their Twin.

If you marry your Twin, it is still a dream come true experience. Ensure that you are grateful for it and make the best of it. Maintaining a marriage can still be hard work even for Soul Twins.

**GUEST** – *"How is it like meeting your Soul Twin in person?"*
**MR. J** – "There is a great sense of familiarity, calm, love, mutuality, sexual arousal, attraction, and of course mirroring. There is a knowing that you and they are going to be together. You get along so well with them and it feels like you and they have known each other for all your lives. Everyone disappears when you are around them, as if it is only you and they who exist."

## MEETING OTHER SOUL TWINS

A fellow Soul Twin is someone else's Soul Twin. They are not YOUR Twin, but they are someone else's. I call them fellow Twins. And no, it is not another type of Twin. You only have ONE Soul Twin. But fellow Twins are those in the Twin Soul community. You can find them online in certain places, and you might meet them in person. But since the Twin Soul collective is so small, you are more likely to meet other Twins online, in certain groups or social media platforms. Treat your fellow Twins with respect and never judge them. The Twin Soul journey is not easy or smooth for any of us.

Personally speaking, meeting fellow Twins in person and online can bring some confusion. If you have met more than one person who you think is your Twin, you likely have met a fellow Soul Twin. There is some mirroring, intensity, and recognition between fellow Twins. This is because we are ALL Soul Twins. We are all split souls, or spread souls. This cause fellow Twins to share certain characteristics between themselves, common in all Soul Twins. This also cause fellow Twins to *stand out* from normal people.

If you are confused about who your Soul Twin is amongst two or more people, it is likely you are actually a Twin Flame and have met those from your monad. A Twin Flame soul is of a different kind than a Twin Soul.

You might feel intense or very calming energy with fellow Soul Twins, and they will also seem 'familiar' in a way. There will be some degree of mirroring, because all Soul Twins are split or spread souls. You will find a lot of similarities and opposing differences between you and fellow Soul Twins. Because of all of these things, fellow Twins will behave or feel like soulmates to you. If you and a fellow Soul Twin were to get together romantically, sexually, or in a relationship, you both will feel like soulmates. They are not your Soul Twin, but would take the place of a soulmate.

It is possible and has happened where a Soul Twin has met someone else's Soul Twin but confused them with their own Twin. It is also possible and has happened where a Soul Twin has met a soulmate and confused them for their Soul Twin. Karmics can also be intense connections, but in different ways. Because karmics hold a lot of Earth energy, sexual and emotional intensity is common. I personally experienced this with *PhatPhat*, a karmic I met in my mid-20s. The sex was amazing, and she felt an emotional intensity, while I had a large increase in confidence and drive to succeed (the male equivalent of emotional intensity). Don't assume that karmics are dull, boring, and unfulfilling connections.

Because soulmates hold a fair amount of both Earth and Cosmic energy, they also can be intense, and exciting connections. With *Ms. Wonka*, there was never a dull moment. We both connected on all levels, and it was a life-changing experience. It is common for some Soul Twins to meet their Twin, but if they are dating or having sex with other people, become confused as to who their Soul Twin is. Unfortunately the internet is filled with confusion and lack of right knowledge with regard to the differences between karmics, soulmates, Twin Flames, and Soul Twins.

If you are dating or having sex with multiple people, this will only create confusion and stress. This is even more true if you are a woman, as being involved with multiple people cause you to become too *scattered* emotionally. This will make it difficult to recognize who your emotions are with. Remember, your Soul Twin may or may not be your ideal partner. Just because one of the people you are dating or having sex with has all the qualities you like in a mate, does not automatically make them your Soul Twin.

I recommend to keep your dating and sex life as clean and simple as possible to avoid becoming confused and scattered.

# THE 'CATALYST TWIN'

Just as there is no 'false twin', there is no catalyst twin. You can only have one Soul Twin. Your Soul Twin IS your catalyst. There is no need to have a second Soul Twin to function as a catalyst. The catalyzation happens upon soul split/spread, and upon meeting in the 3rd Dimension. There is also catalyzation which take place with Twins the first time they have sex, whether in the 3D physical or in the dreamscape.

All Soul Twins catalyze each other after meeting. It's part of their ascension process. Catalyzation is the purging, opening, clearing, and realignment of the RACO™ system. It is also, the soul transitioning into Oneness Consciousness™. It is when the soul triggers its own awakening.

Only you will know if you have an incarnated Soul Twin or not. No one can tell you who, where, how, or why except you. You have to be careful, as some tarot readers, energy channelers, witches, coaches, and others might give you misinformation. Most of these individuals perform their work honestly, but some do it with fault or ill intention. But one thing for sure, when you have the initial meeting with your Soul Twin, you will know without a doubt.

# SOUL TWIN MEETING

If you discovered Soul Twins online or heard it from someone, it could be you just happened to come across information about them. It would be useful to sit in a quiet place and ask The Most High why you discovered the phenomena; there is likely a purpose for you in it.

After the Soul Twin meeting, both will have their entire lives wrecked and rebuilt from the ground up. It is not going to pass you by and leave you guessing or just believing.

There is a connection with Soul Twins on all levels. The Twins are usually not aware of the connection until after they meet. They experienced life under the veil of illusion. They awaken after they meet. Then they experience life while in Oneness Consciousness™. Most of them will not feel the connection until after they meet, and they are then catalyzed into the ascension process. Whether or not they are aware of the connection, there is always a connection in the non-physical, and in the soul. You are just feeling it, and becoming activated, which mean the blocks are being removed, so that you FEEL and SENSE the connection as well as the energy you share with your Twin.

Have you ever heard women say *"I want a connection"* when asked what it is they want from a man?

That's not really what they want. What they MEAN to say, is they want to FEEL something with a man. They want to experience an exchange and flow of energy, power, and passion that they can FEEL. It's not enough to just have a connection. Imagine this actually happening. You just happen to meet someone, and from the very moment you laid eyes on them, you were engulfed and pressurized by an intense familiarity and energy that you can't describe in words. This is a connection mixed with the flow and stimulation of energy.

Twins even more so have an intense and deep energy exchange with each other. This is due to the *connection* (aka oneness) AND *energy* they share as one being. Upon meeting, their RACO™ system is activated, and this system activation ignites the love they feel for each other. Since Twins are connected at the energetic system (aka RACOs™), they are shared in the heart space, sacral, solar plexus, root, throat, and 3rd eye. This means that they share the same love, sexual essence, power, and consciousness at a foundational level.

Synchronicities are part of a soul awakening, and they can happen to anyone who is on the soul journey, but they do not have to have a Twin Flame. Do not think seeing synchronicities or having a soul awakening conclude that you have met your Soul Twin. They have nothing to do with what we are experiencing. What we experience is 100% because of our own soul awakening.

## QUICK QUESTIONS

*"Is it possible to fall in love with someone else after I have met my Supposed 'Twin'?"* You aren't supposed to fall in love with someone else, not after meeting your Twin. Upon meeting your Soul Twin, it is time to move on from being romantic/sexual with others. The Soul Twin journey and connection is purposeful, and not a random occurrence, or someone we need to run from to go be with someone else. That defeats the whole purpose of the journey. Twins ARE meant to be together. The unbreakable connection, the intense love and heart pull towards them, the sexual cravings for them, thinking about them day in and day out, being madly in love with them,.....none of those signify needing to abandon the connection to be with someone else. Those are all obvious signs of who we need to be with and why.

If one has spent YEARS and DECADES being in romantic and sexual connections with karmics and soulmates, WHY do they need to go back and be with more karmics and soulmates after meeting their Twin? That would be so unnecessary and backwards; in that situation, it would have been better for them to not have a Soul Twin, and never meet them so that they can remain with their karmics and soulmates.

After meeting your Soul Twin, it isn't possible to have the same depth and intensity of love and connection with someone else. It is an unbreakable connection after all... All Twins desire in some way to be with their Twin. It is perfectly normal.

*"Do Soul Twins have to meet in person to feel the connection?"*
Twins don't have to necessarily meet in person for them to feel the deep and powerful connection. It doesn't take much for the soul recognition and energy

system activation to take place. The connection is not limited by distance, time, or the lack of physically meeting.

### *"Why did I meet my Soul Twin?"*
You meet your Soul Twin for the purpose of initiating you on a complete soul journey to Union. It's time to graduate! It's Union Season™!

### *"How is it like meeting a karmic and a soulmate?"*
Karmics are abundant, soulmates not as much. But karmics are not bad people. You work with them, they are in your class, you drive next to them down the road, you go out on dates with them, they are your lovers, and friends. Soulmates, while a smaller percentage, are also 'normal people', with a Twist. Because soul mates are not souls created individually, but born from an energetic monad, they behave and feel different than karmics. This does not necessarily make them better than karmics, as you will learn in this guidebook.

I describe karmics as *easy* and *simple* connections. They are a good balance. They aren't always intense, but they aren't dull either. They won't push you to greatness and deeper soul discovery. But karmics are everywhere. Karmics make smoother relationships (in theory) because the energy is not as intense. They are also baby and younger souls, so karmics tend to favor social activity and having fun over purpose and responsibilities. Younger souls may take on more purpose and responsibilities naturally than baby souls. Meeting a karmic can be like meeting someone you know will be a lot of fun. It can also be like meeting someone you feel like you have to babysit or micromanage a lot, well...because they are younger souls and find themselves easily in trouble or needing guidance. Karmics really are a mixed bag, it depends on the person. Karmics give us most of our life lessons, which is why most of our friends, loves, and colleagues are karmics. They are necessary for our learning and ascension.

Soulmate connections are more intense. This intensity can come in different forms, sometimes alone, or in a few areas. Soulmate connections tend to have more sexual energy, soul depth, and psychological stimulation. Soulmates can be baby souls, young, old souls, ext. Soulmates usually mature fast, and find themselves in leadership, management, and community service, or they will be very connected to the Earth and natural life, and not so much follow the crowd. Meeting a soulmate is like meeting someone you instantly get along with and feel like you have known them forever. There is a high degree of chemistry, attachment, and emotional stimulation.

### *"Is it possible to connect with my Supposed 'Twin' without meeting them physically?"* Not all Twins meet in person, at least initially. Remember, Twins 'separate' to later meet, while normal people meet to later separate. So, if you have met your Twin through video chat, an online messaging system, a dating application, or any other non-contact means, don't feel like you can't be connected to them. Even talking on the phone with your Twin and sending

pictures of each other is enough to catalyze Twins on the soul journey. You will meet in person later when you least expect it.

### "Was meeting my Soul Twin an accident or destiny?"

You may feel like meeting your Twin was an accident if the relationship didn't quite turn out well. Remember, the Twin Soul journey is not about getting into a relationship or getting married. It is about a soul journey. If your Soul Twin was toxic, married, or didn't want anything to do with you, you might feel like it was all an accident. But honestly, it is part of your soul ascension. The soul journey is not always an easy one.

You may feel like meeting your Twin was destiny because it seemed like you were going to meet them either way. You probably felt like because you cannot severe the connection or stop thinking about them, you two were meant to meet. You are correct here. There is a grand purpose for Soul Twins splitting or spreading and then incarnating on Earth.

# FOR MARRIED TWINS

Did you meet your Twin, but the meeting happened when you (or they) were already married to someone else? This is an unfortunate situation. Most people will want to protect the integrity of their marriage and not divorce or cheat.

But the Twin Soul connection provide a different, and even more difficult issue. This is because the Twin Soul connection will never go away after the initial meeting. You will feel them, think of them, and crave to be with them. But then, you are married, and that is a contracted, life-long commitment. Now you find yourself in an impossible situation. You feel like you are being torn apart by two different people, and two different worlds. On top of that, your Twin might ghost you or not respond to you contacting them. But the connection is ever strong, the feelings won't subside, and you are still married. But then, the issue is that they are your Soul Twin, and now the question is: who do you belong to now? Husband or Soul Twin? Wife or Soul Twin? Again, an unfortunate situation.

In this situation, I recommend to not make any hasty or emotionally-driven decisions. You need time to process what has happened and what is going on. I'm not going to tell you to leave your married spouse to be with your Twin, or ignore the Twin to stay with your spouse...that is YOUR choice.

As I tell other Twins, the only reason you should divorce and leave a marriage is if the marriage is putting your life at risk, the children's life, or negatively impacting the other areas of your life through no fault of your own, but from your married partner. You should never leave a marriage just because you think you have met someone who you feel strong emotions for, Soul Twin or not.

Commonly though, I have heard from so many Twins who were married to someone other than their Twin, who ended up divorcing anyways. This was usually because the marriage already was not working out and having a lot of issues. In another way, it also has been common for the married partner to already be cheating, abusive, or no longer want the marriage. In another situation, I have commonly seen where the Twin is no longer able to be with their married spouse after meeting their Twin. All of a sudden, they no longer have any attraction, desire, or want to be with their married spouse, even after trying to make it work. But yet, they are intensely drawn to their Twin. All of these situations though, never involved the married Twin divorcing their spouse just so they can be with their Twin. Keep this in mind.

## FOR TWINS WITH CHILDREN

How could meeting your Soul Twin while they have children affect you? Not everyone wants to be involved with someone if they already have children. This is especially true if you or they are younger. Those who are older may not care, as they expect those in their age group to likely already have children. Some people don't mind. But having children before meeting your Twin can put a twist in your connection and journey. It is possible that your Twin may have left you or not want to be involved if you already have children. You may have not wanted to be involved with them if they already had children.

Having children from others can put a hold on you and your Twin coming together. This is especially true if the children's other parent does not want them to be around someone else. This can create problems. But most people, if they feel a deep enough attraction to someone, may waive the fact of them already having children. Most people prefer to have their own children with the one they love. Some are willing to take care of or look after someone else's children. It is important to not assume your Twin left you or does not want to be involved with you if you have children. Never tell yourself that you are 'damaged goods'. If you live every day while feeling like that, that can put a hold and create separations with the other person you have feelings for or an attraction to, including your Soul Twin. Communication is key. Never assume.

## NARC BEHAVIOR EXPOSED

Most if not all of us have some degree of desire to meet someone who we get along well with, feel an attraction to, and want to be with. We envision how they would look, dress, talk, and behave. But imagine meeting this very person. In the beginning, everything is just so perfect. They say the right words, they dress nice, and you feel safe and comfortable with them. But one day, sometimes too deep in, you come to a terrifying conclusion. You've known for some time that this person is your Soul Twin,. But you could not have imagined they'd have NARC behaviors.

You spent a lot of time, energy, love, sexual energy, and possibly money on them. You are completely in, both feet. Now you are stressed, angry, and grieving that your Twin has NARC behaviors. Their behavior make it difficult to have anything meaningful, productive, and fulfilling with them. You've tried and tried. They either gaslight you constantly, only care about themselves, are emotionally immature, or pedestal themselves while putting you down. What do you do? It's hard to walk away, you still love them. They are your Twin. How do you handle this?

Sometimes the hardest thing to do is walk away. We all have to have our own standards. When someone isn't treating us with respect, patience, love, and in a mature manner, how we handle the situation say a lot about ourselves. People with NARC behaviors are impossible to deal with, they make life stressful, and they seem to never change. Actually, they get worse whenever you try to make things better. If you have met your Soul Twin, and they display NARC behaviors, the first thing I recommend is to not attack them in any way. Those with NARC behaviors FEED off other people attacking them. This is why trying to seek vengeance or harm a NARC actually make their behavior worse, sometimes to the point the NARC may actually seek physical violence against the attacker. It is wise to walk away from anyone (including your Soul Twin) who display NARC behaviors.

Rather than attacking them or seeking vengeance, walk away from them. This is the only way to take the power back. Notice, I didn't say block them or jump into another relationship. This will only cause your Twin to increase their bad behavior. All you have to do is not communicate with them, increase physical distance from them, and ignore their bad behavior. This is a much more mature and effective way to handle your Twin if they are displaying NARC behaviors. Never seek vengeance or an attack against a NARC, they will make sure it come back to you one hundred fold.

# SECTION SEVEN

## INTENSE SEX SENSATIONS

Remember The Game mentioned earlier? All humans are sexual creatures, the males and the females. Sex is foundationally for the purpose of producing offspring. But there are deeper levels with humans which go beyond having sex for the purpose of procreation. Because all humans have Divine Nature within them, this allow the possibility for humans to engage in sexual behavior for purposes other than procreation, and engage in these behaviors out of conscious choice. A big part of this is having sex for the purpose of physical pleasure, but then there is a deeper part. This level of sex is with the purpose of aiding soul ascension. It involves merging and Kundalini awakening.

Because Soul Twins have physical bodies, they are subjected to hormones just like everyone else. This means that Twins also have sexual desires and cravings. But because Soul Twins are one soul in two bodies, their sexual activity between each other has other purposes and a higher intensity. It goes beyond having sex to make babies or for physical pleasure. Many Twins, especially Earthling Soul Twins, will need some degree of sexual activity to trigger each other and their ascension. Other Twins who are already soul aware may not need sexual activity with their Twin.

## TWIN SOUL SEX AND THE RACO™ SYSTEM

Because Soul Twins share the same RACO™ system, they also experience the same sexual energy and sensations. Because Soul Twins are one soul, the energy, emotions, and sensations one Twin experience will be felt by the other Twin, and vice versa. The energy, sensations, and emotions are shared and experienced by both Twins, in their own ways. This is also true sexually. If one Twin is having sex with someone other than their Twin, they will feel some degree of sensation in their genitals, and other areas of their body. When Twins have sex with each other, they will experience sex beyond words. The intensity will be the highest they've ever felt. This doesn't necessarily mean the sex is *good*, but it will surely be more intense than with karmics and soulmates.

## SEX: DEEPER KNOWLEDGE

Contrary to popular belief, no one makes you feel anything. What you feel is 100% your own energy, and 100% processed sensorial input through your brain and nervous system. What you feel is your own energy, not really someone else manipulating your energy. Sure, those who learn certain energetic practices CAN manipulate energy, but it is not their own energy they are injecting into someone else. It is not that they are forcing you to feel anything. The only thing that happen here is your nervous and energetic system receive input, and that input is then processed as an energetic rise or change.

During sex, the sensation you feel is the rise and excitement of your own energy. Imagine if someone took full accountability for the sexual stimulation and arousal they experience (or don't experience). They would not wait or expect for someone else to make them feel good. They would take better care of their body and will put their own energetic influence into the sexual experience with someone else. Now if you put two people together who are like this, they both will have intense and immersive sexual experiences. This will be because neither of them are expecting the other person to please them. But they both will surely add in their own influence to the sexual experience. Let's look at the sensations one feel during sexual activity. **SENSATIONS:**

**PHYSICALLY** – Even though the body itself isn't directly responsible for the energetic sensations felt, it is still an important part of the experience. Physically, the body is the vessel which hold energy. It is a thin barrier or transfer. It also change the structure and complexity of the RACO™ system, which allow energy to pool and flow more in certain areas of the body.

**VISUAL/AUDIBLE** – As we all have eyes, we take in visual stimuli (information). We also take in audible stimuli through our ears. This is lustful arousal. This is received by the brain and nervous system. Sound is energy. Energy is substance in motion.

**EMOTIONALLY** – If you find that you can only enjoy sex with someone through emotions, this is emotional arousal. Emotions are the result of certain hormonal activity in the body.

**THOUGHT** – This is mental, post processed sensorial input from energetic, visual, and audible arousal. It is a more refined version of the two. Our ability to think and hold in memory aid in the sexual sensations we have. Our reality and experiences are based on our thoughts, even our sexual experiences. A healthy mind is important for a stimulating sex life.

**ENERGETIC** – The energy in its raw form, what you actually feel. This energy is not limited to the 3D Physical. It is the energy itself changing on a vibrational level which we experience as sexual pleasure and stimulation. These vibrational changes can be intensity, changes in patterns, and 'weight'. The nervous system is an important aspect of feeling this energy. We all have a nervous system. Certain parts of the body act as passage ways for energy to flow and resonate through the nervous system. It is the information input into our senses and through our nervous system which give us the pleasurable sensations and feelings. Really, when people have sex, they are tuning in to each other's energetic frequency, and then stimulating that frequency. It is like tuning two instruments to the same tuning and so that when one instrument is played, the other instrument sounds through mutual energetic resonance. All of these combine to create the energetic sensations you feel while engaging in sexual activities.

# ASTRAL SEX

Astral sex is the energetic phenomena you experience in a way which take place outside of the body, yet is sexual. It is the experience of true Oneness, which is profound, blissful, ecstatic, and highly pleasurable. This is a place where non-physical, purely conscious and energetic experiences happen.

All Twins will experience astral sex, to some degree, and at some point in their journey. This has a Divine purpose, and aid in the Twin's soul ascension. This can take place while having actual sex with your Twin, or directly in the astral plane. Below is an example of a personal and simple astral sex experience I had in the astral plane with my Supposed 'Twin':

**PERSONAL ASTRAL SEX EXPERIENCE**
About a year after meeting my Supposed 'Twin', one night I climbed into bed after a long day of work. I went into a deep sleep. I 'left' my body, and looked back at myself sleeping in bed. After leaving my body, I immediately was out in the middle of the Universe, my Supposed 'Twin' right in front of me. We looked back at one another and spun around each other as we came closer. Then we had sex, and merged into one energy. Everything started to glow really bright before turning completely into pure light, everywhere. Then everything went dark, and I was back to where my body was, and entered back into my body. After waking up I was horny beyond imaginable!

# END OF FRAGMENTED SEXUAL ENERGY

We are all born mostly undefiled. I say mostly, because those who are aware, know that energy, influence, and memory can be carried over into someone's next life. But usually for most people, our memory and the influences from previous lives are blocked or wiped clean until a certain level of soul maturity is reached. We will just say that we are all born undefiled sexually. This mean that we are born with no sexual trauma or clutter. We are 'clean' and pure. We all start off life being sexually secure. This sexual security also tie heavily into emotional security, especially for women.

But oh, if life could be perfect enough to never allow sexual trauma to happen! The reality of life is that sexual and emotional trauma and social programming that is very harmful does happen. These things can cause one to engage in unhealthy sexual behavior. This will only compound the sexual and emotional trauma they have, rather than allow them to heal the trauma, and release the programming. But thankfully, as a Soul Twins, you have agreed to take the soul ascension all the way. This will allow you to heal your sexual and emotional trauma, and reprogram back to a secure, pure, and conscious sexual energy. This will attract completely different sexual and romantic partners to you. This is because you'll be operating in secure sexual energy, and you will consciously choose mates who are also sexually and emotionally secure. We only attract people based on our frequency and mentality.

Sexual and emotional trauma and unhealthy social programming can cause one to become sexually and emotionally fragmented. This fragmentation mean that a part of yourself (energetically and/or emotionally) has been stuck with a previous sexual or romantic partner. The inverse is true, and a mate who had sexual and emotional trauma could also have a part of their energy stuck and left in your body and energetic field.

Fragmentation can cause one to continue to engage in sexually and emotionally harmful behavior, creating a positive feedback cycle which is difficult to get out of. This cycle can go on for years, decades, and even lifetimes. At some point, you ask yourself why you keep getting in the same toxic relationships and the same toxic people over and over. Fragmentation is like leaving behind residue from yourself. It creates energetic cords and ties to people you have had sex with.

**DIFFERENCES BETWEEN SECURE AND FRAGMENTED SEXUAL ENERGY:**
**SECURE SEXUAL ENERGY:**
- Healthy
- Heals yourself and the person you engage in sexual behavior with
- Promote wellness on all levels
- Rooted in sexually sharing with your partner (not being a selfish lover)

**FRAGMENTED SEXUAL ENERGY:**
- Unhealthy
- Cause physical, emotional, mental, and energetic imbalances
- Usually rooted in using someone (for social, financial, or emotional gain at someone else's expense)
- Cause trauma, baggage, confusion, and scattered energy

I have found it common that Twins trigger each other sexually, in some way, and to some degree. This is for the purpose of healing sexual and emotional trauma. This triggering will allow regaining your fragments, while releasing other's fragments from your energy. This is a timely process and usually does not happen overnight. If you have had sex with your Soul Twin and it brought out insecurities, fear, or stress, this will be different than if it happened with a karmic or soulmate. This triggering will create positive change in the long run.

## CHEATING VS ACKNOWLEDGED OPTIONS™ (AKA OPEN RELATIONSHIP)

*"Your Twin will not cheat on you if they are your real Twin Soul!"* I have heard this so many times. Unfortunately, many Twins have had to learn the hard way. See, it is possible for your Twin to cheat on you, just like anyone else. They are still susceptible to human life and human ways. Cheating though, is different

than what I call Acknowledged Options™. Acknowledged Options™ is when the other person has stated that they WILL be engaged in sexual and/or romantic activities with other people, even if you and they get together.

Some people confuse this, as they assume that humans are monogamous entities, which is far from the true. How many people do you know who have only had sex and been in a relationship/marriage with one person all their lives? Monogamy is rooted in only having one mate all a person's life. Most people have multiple sexual and romantic partners throughout their lives, and some even withing the same year. Humans are mostly mammals, and the heavy majority of mammals are not monogamous.

Some people also assume that societal programming of monogamy and 'faithfullness' is a universal, mandatory social law. So, when they get into a relationship, marriage, or sexual connection with someone, they assume that the other person will not be with anyone else sexually or romantically. This can happen even if the person clearly stated that they will continue having sex and/or romantic activities with someone else. But in this situation, it is very immature to call the other person a cheater.

They are not a cheater, they have Acknowledged Options™. They choose to retain, and verbally (or written) state that they will keep their sexual and/or romantic options open. Cheating, on the other hand, is lying about (and not acknowledging) having other sexual and/or romantic partners. This IS not a mature way to engage someone else. It is important to let the other person know (beforehand) that you will keep your sexual and/or romantic options open.

Has your Twin cheated on you? Were they exercising Acknowledged Options™? Did you confuse them exercising Acknowledged Options™ with cheating? Both cheating and Acknowledged Options™ can and does happen between Twins. Cheating is not right, whether they are a Soul Twin or not. Cheating between Soul Twins create more unnecessary conflict, delays, and trauma against their ascension. But is exercising Acknowledged Options™ wrong? Again, if it is acknowledged, you knew before getting involved with them. If you wanted to be exclusive with your Twin, did you state that from the very beginning?

It is important to not be with someone if you want exclusivity, but they want to keep their options open. This can later cause undesired issues in the relationship.

If your Twin has cheated on you, it is important to let that go, and not hold on to it. You don't want to walk around feeling angry, used, and insecure. This is not a healthy way to live. I agree with you that cheating is wrong and never justified. But still, you have to let it go, and not hold onto what they did. This does not necessarily mean that get back together with them. But it does mean you choose to not allow it to affect you anymore.

If you have cheated on your Twin, for whatever reason, it is important to forgive yourself and change your ways. This is regardless if you felt it was justified or not. It is never mature, wise, or a good idea to cheat on someone. This is different with Acknowledged Options™, as you specifically state at the beginning, before taking things further with someone, that you will keep dating other people, even if you get together. With Acknowledged Options™, it is not wrong, because both people are aware, and agree that one, the other, or both will keep their options open to other people.

If you have cheated on your Twin, this can cause a variety of issues. This alone can be a reason for them running. It can also be the reason for them becoming attached to you, and not giving you any space. They may not leave you alone and always try to control the connection or dictate your life. Cheating between Twins is harmful, just as it is with normal people. It cause stress, confusion, insecurity, jealousy, anxiety, anger, and even vindicative behavior.

## BEGIN ON, HOT & OPEN INTIMACY

*"I need stability"* said *Y-female*. *"But B-male is so hot and cold, I don't know what to think of him."* Said *Y-female*.

Has your Twin been distant or bouncing between 'hot' and 'cold'? What is meant by these open/closed, hot/cold, on/off, and distant/close behavior from your Twin? These could be the result of a variety of things. It can range from your Twin being unsure of you as well, to them loving you but being busy with life, and all the way to behaving like this due to trauma/fear, and doing it intentionally to manipulate you.

These back and forth energy and behavioral shifts are usually normal. We all do these to some degree, and in some way. They add tension, excitement, and attachment to a connection or relationship between two people. But taken to the extreme, they can cause unnecessary conflict, confusion, and even the two people breaking up or separating. If they are happening out of trauma, fear, or manipulation, one or both of you may not want to take part in it, and leave.

It is a good feeling to be close to your Twin, to feel their warmth. It is great when they are open about their feelings. But let's be honest, any relationship and connection would get boring if that is all there was. There has to be a healthy usage of time apart from each other, time which feelings are not shared, and when things are more 'serious'. It is easy to notice when our Twin is distant, cold, and closed off. But rarely are we aware when we are closed off, distant, and cold. The reason why your Twin could behave this way may even be because you have so yourself. It is important to know that a healthy connection between you and your Twin require investment on both sides. If you are closed off, distant, and cold, how can you expect your Twin to be warm, open, and close? They might be initially, but eventually, they will remove their energy and presence.

I do not recommend trying to get your Twin to open up and share feelings and be closer. I also don't recommend trying to push your Twin away, or intentionally become closed off and cold. This never create a healthy connection between two people. It is important to understand that trying to force someone into doing something is not an appropriate way to get what you want. Your Twin has to choose themselves to open up to you, and be close.

If your Twin does not want to open up, or they are distant, don't wrestle them into opening up or being closer. This will just push them away more, and keep them closed off. Not all Twins are warm, open, and free flowing when meeting them. A good thing to do is to let them be. If they choose to be distant, closed off, or cold, let them be. If they choose to open up to you, be warm, and close, then enjoy that with them. Either way, it is important that you can reach a place of inner peace, self-secured, and inner joy. It is important to maintain this regardless if your Twin is all over you, or they are keeping you at arm's length.

## ENDING SEX WITH KARMICS, BEGIN SOULMATE SEX

No matter how you see it, no matter your beliefs, most Twins will not be virgins when they meet each other. It doesn't matter what your spiritual or Biblical beliefs are. It doesn't matter if you think or someone told you that Twins are not supposed to have sex with those other than their Soul Twin. Who people (including Twins) decide to have sex with is their own choice and consequence. But one thing for sure, the sexual experience between karmics, soulmates, and the Soul Twins are vastly different.

Due to karmics being younger souls, their energetic system is of a certain vibrance which do not permit high intensity sex. The Soul Twin is on the opposite end of the spectrum, as the energetic system is more complex and is of a vibrance that is high frequency. The Twins also being incarnated in two bodies also amplify the experienced sexual pleasure and intensity. Soulmates will be somewhere in the middle.

Now, this doesn't necessarily mean that YOU will enjoy sex more with your Twin, and less with a karmic. This does not necessarily mean that sex with a soulmate will be less pleasurable and intense to YOU. Sexual preferences, physical health, attraction, lust, attachment, seduction, investment, physical attributes, chemistry, experience, body odor, emotional intensity, dirty talk, eye contact, stamina, stimulating certain areas on (and in) the body, and being in the correct energy (masculine or feminine) all affect your sexual experience. Do you see how much is involved in sexual activity? And I am sure I didn't even name it all! I don't claim to be a sex expert, but I do have enough experience, knowledge, and overstanding to know that sex is very complex in a way.

I understand from my experiences dating a few karmics and soulmates that it can be hit and miss, regardless if they are a karmic or soulmate. I have had sex with some karmics who 'got me off' and left an impression, while one of the few soulmates I was with just couldn't keep me up. Your sexual experience will be the same with different people. Isn't that interesting? You can be the same person, and do the same things with each person, yet some people get you off so well, while others just can't. And then there are those in-between who are not good but not bad either. At the end of the day though, you will still to some degree enjoy sex more with your Twin than with karmics and soulmates. If you want a better sexual experience, you must look at your own energy, and investment in the sexual experience.

Some Twins may even find the sex with their Twin ADDICTIVE. This could result in stalking, chasing, and even running behavior. *"Who would run from sex that is SO good?"* Someone who has sexual trauma, fear, trust issues, and someone who is insecure. The feeling of 'not good enough' and being undeserving come to mind.

Soul Twin sex can cause Twins to not enjoy sex with others anymore after meeting. This is because the level of intensity and soul connection is too high with their Soul Twin. Twins who attempt to find a better sexual experience outside of their Twin may find themselves frustrated, confused, sad, and even angry. They want to have at least the same if not better sexual experience with someone else as they did with their Twin. This is especially true if their Twin was abusive, toxic, unavailable, deceased, or not their desired mate.

Having sex with someone other than your Twin to try and get your Twin to chase you, push them away, or be vindicative is also not healthy or mature. If you are having issues with your Twin, I recommend that you two sit with each other and discuss those issues and make some changes. If one or both of you are unwilling to do this, then how can you have a healthy connection with them?

In the other situation, if your Twin is engaging in these behaviors and refuse to change, you have to stand up for yourself and stop allowing your Twin to get over on you. You do this by not putting up with them cheating or using sex with others to hurt or control you. You might have to get out of the relationship with them and move on with your life. If they beg for you to come back, you have to not succumb to the immediate emotions to want to run back to them. They could be doing this temporarily to reel you back in for more abuse! If someone (including your Twin) want to change, they WILL change. It's not enough for someone to just apologize and beg you back. Their behavior need changing!

## SEX AND KUNDALINI AWAKENING

There is a relationship between sex and Kundalini energy. The sex organs alone are passive. The don't do anything by themselves. They need energy (and not just blood flow) to function. This energy is Kundalini energy. Not everyone's Kundalini energy will be the same. And just because someone has sex, does not mean they will have a Kundalini awakening.

I remember hearing it commonly when I was little. If it wasn't advertisements about a pill to help erectile disfunction in men, it was a TV show where someone mentioned men losing energy after sex. Losing energy after sex? How could men have such a strong drive to have sex, enjoy it much when they get it, only to lose energy, and even fall asleep afterwards?

Remember earlier when I mentioned I began unknowingly meditating when I was little? Well, meditation has a way of opening up closed doors and hidden knowledge about life, people, and even yourself. One of the things I experimented with was Self Hormonal Manipulation. This is being able to manipulate a certain aspect of your own hormones without the need of food, sleep, stress, or external excitement. It is done by changing the way you think and perceive something or someone. I realized that we really do create our own reality, even our inner reality by the contents of our mind. I was stressed because I was choosing to be stressed in my earlier life. Once I realized I had some control over certain aspects of my hormones, I knew I could keep myself peaceful, calm, and alert 97% of every day of my life, no matter what was going on. Even in very stressful situations, I was able to keep myself from becoming stressed uncontrollably.

Then I realized I could also do this sexually. My first sexual partners I experienced the 'tired after sex' and 'sleepy after sex' phenomena. But one day I wondered if I could flip this the other way, to be completely full of and even overflowing with energy after sex. I experimented with *Ms. Wonka* and it actually worked! Maybe too good. In fact, I ended up having trouble sleeping because I had too much energy. I would only get 2 hours of sleep every night. This could be from just having sex once a week. After sex, I couldn't go to sleep. I found myself up and cleaning the house, washing the car, running errands, and various other activities. *Ms. Wonka* sure liked the extra stamina and staying power! Those two things she could never describe as 'wonky'! Ha!

I did not realize I was opening the door for my Kundalini to excite and expand. I was already on the soul journey, on the ascension path. My Kundalini was active and strong. I had Kundalini awakenings just from having regular sex! It was beyond an intense orgasm. Since then, I can situate myself to have sex once every two weeks and just overflow with energy and drive. I can get so much stuff done. I can even go without sex entirely because the Kundalini is so active. It also makes astral sex very vivid and realistic. There is never an erectile issue.

Have you had issues with your Twin and erectile disfunction? Do you feel they are lazy, have no ambition, and go straight to sleep after sex? They might actually have low testosterone. They should go to a doctor for that. But if you and your Twin have not had sex and you decide to, it does not necessarily mean their Kundalini will become active and they will become superman or an Alpha man. But sex with your Twin should activate their Kundalini. Most people who are on the soul journey and ascension, even women, have more and more active Kundalini. It does make you more horny, but it also gives you more energy and drive to get up and get things done. Even women need some amount of testosterone and an active Kundalini to be healthy and vibrant.

## THE 4ᵗʰ DIMENSION

The 4th Dimension? What is that? That's what I was thinking! You'll read a lot about 5th Dimension and 3rd Dimension, but what about the one that brings the two together?

4D is the bridge that connects 5D and 3D. If you don't have 4D, you can't get any denser energies to stabilize. Even if you have met your Twin in 3D, 4D is still a big part of the connection and even the telepathy Twins share. The best way I can describe 4D is that 5D can resemble purple color, 3D green color, and 4D blue.

Also, you can't skip over dimensions. You can't go from 3D to 5D. THINK, use your brain. Even though the whole '3D vs 5D split' thing has become popular on social media and in various spiritual circles, you have to innerstand that it is necessary to go from one dimension to the next lower or higher one. Even advanced souls don't skip over dimensions, because each dimension is connected to the other, and there are important energies, experiences, and beings which they can engage as they travel interdimensionally.

4D is difficult to grasp because the human brain has not been made to see life as ONE. The brain process this reality as duality and like to divide things in a manner that is extreme on one end or another. Unless you have a certain level of awareness, 4D is not easy to innerstand.

4D is the most dense energy can get before it is 'physical', or what we perceive as physical. 4D and 5D are also commonly traveled by angelic and demonic entities. Angelic entities who wish to manipulate the physical world without incarnating can utilize 4D and 5D. Demonic entities can and do utilize 4D and 5D to influence people. Demonic entities want to hide their identity and not let their presence be known, so rather than incarnating in a physical body, they use mental and emotional manipulating to possess and control people. Scary, I know!

## TELEPATHY

To understand what telepathy is, we will break down the term. 'Tele' means communication. 'Path' is an open space where people or things can move through. The dictionary definition state that *telepathy* means 'communication through extrasensory means from one mind to another'. Extrasensory mean senses which are not physical (eyes, ears, smell, ext.). Extrasensory are non-physical senses. So, telepathy is a direct, mental means of communication with someone else or another entity. This communication is non-physical and does not require the use of cell phones, computers, or radios.

Anyone can ascend to become aware of their ability to telepathically communicate with someone else. But this does not mean the person you send the communications to will 'hear' them, or have the soul maturity to recognize them. Since a Twin Soul is a soul in two bodies, telepathy between them is active by default after the initial meeting. The Twins will hear their Twin's voice and mental chatter coming from their Twin. This chatter is your Twins thoughts. Their thoughts are also your own thoughts. Your thoughts are also their thoughts. Your Twin will hear your voice and mental chatter from you as well.

Overstand that telepathy alone does not determine whether someone is your Soul Twin or not. It is possible for you to experience telepathy with karmics, soulmates, and Twin Flames as well. But you will surely experience telepathy with your Soul Twin!

## REMOTE VIEW

This has happened to me so many times, and even today. I will be driving or doing chores around the house and for a quick second or two, I'll see through my Supposed 'Twin''s eyes. She'll be walking, sitting on her couch looking down at her phone, driving, or talking with someone. There have been times where I have read messages she was in the middle of typing to send to someone. This is called remote view. It is a psychic gift. I can utilize this during meditation, although I haven't found a purpose for using it intentionally. I don't have a need to spy on anyone.

Remote view by default, is a standard with Soul Twins. Because there is one soul in two bodies, even the physical senses can be experienced by Twins. The sense of sight, touch, hearing, and others all can be felt by the other Twin. It is not uncommon for Twins to feel their Twin is touching a certain part of their body, having sex, eating, walking, taking a shower, or scratching their skin. It is the second most thing I enjoy about the connection with my Supposed 'Twin'. I can feel when she is walking if my feet are not on the ground, or my feet are suspended, or not pressed against anything. I can feel when she showers, because all of a sudden my body temperature rise, and the sensation of water running down my body. I have also smelled the food she eats, and at the same time unintentionally remote viewed her eating the same food I smelled.

**GUEST** – *"Doesn't that drive you crazy?"*
**MR.J** – "It was annoying in the beginning. But as with all things involving this journey, it doesn't bother you anymore after some time. There isn't anything I can do, except live with it."

## THE CLAIRS

Welcome to the Clair Family! It is a family of non-physical senses. These are non-physical senses. Anyone on a soul journey or the ascension path will gain access to one or more of these non-physical senses.

**CLAIR-AUDIENCE** – *clear hearing*, hearing voices and sounds. You may hear people talking even if you are the only one in the room, your phone is off, and no one else is nearby. You may also hear music playing and other sounds which seem to not come from anywhere in your immediate or distant environment.

**CLAIR-SENTIENCE** – *recognizing emotions*. For those who are very emotional, women in particular, clair-sentience will cause you to feel other people's emotions. It is like telepathy, just with emotions rather than thoughts. You can also 'feel' things before they happen, or while they are happening.

**CLAIR-VOYANCE** – *seeing images and physical movements*. Similar to our ability to see this 'physical' reality, this one allow you to see things which could be thousands of miles away, events taking place in real time, and other images. You will be able to 'see' things with your eyes closed. And no, this will not be your imagination or thought.

**CLAIR-COGNIZANCE** – *clear knowing*. This is the ability to gain knowledge without having to read anything, watch a video, someone tell you directly, and any other common methods of gaining knowledge. It is possible for someone who is clair-cognizant to even gain knowledge seemingly out of thin air. They just KNOW things. They can also gain access to what is on a cell phone, written inside a book, or even what someone is doing behind closed doors, out of sight.

Personally, I am heavily clair-cognizant, with a fair mix of clair-voyance and clair-audience. If I sit and meditate, I can intentionally boost my clair-voyant and clair-audient capabilities. I have no clair-sentience ability at all, except with my Supposed 'Twin'. I am able to feel her emotions, whether she is happy, sad, angry, stressed, ext. and at times know why.

**NOTE:** In the beginning of my journey after first engaging the Twin Soul community, I ran into a problem. I noticed that most of the people who either channeled my energy or attempted to connect with my energy, actually saw my Supposed 'Twin' as me. This created a lot of confusion and conflict. It was normal for these people (as much as they were trying to help me) to tell me that *"You are in your ego", "The only thing that is stopping the two of you from coming together is your fears", "Your Twin is waiting for you and wants to work together", "You have 3rd party people who you need to get rid of, they are blocking and keeping the two of you separate", "You don't trust anyone due to fear and trauma, but you allowed that to separate yourself from this person who is very trustworthy", "Your life has fallen apart and won't get better until you reconcile with this person. You did something to them to cause them a lot of pain and distrust. You have to go back and fix things."*

This all confused me so much because all of these things were not me at all, and had nothing to do with me. At first I thought they were confusing me with someone else, and then I realized they were channeling my Supposed 'Twin'! Then it all made sense. But since then, I stopped letting others do channelings for me. A handful of them either blocked me, stopped talking to me, or lashed out at me because they felt threatened by me. They didn't realize they were channeling my Supposed 'Twin', and not me. This also creates another layer of complexity with the Twin Soul connection.

# QUICK QUESTIONS

*"If Twins are supposed to be together and are Divine partners, is it considered cheating if they have sex with or marry someone else?"* It is not considered cheating. Cheating is when it is agreed that one or both partners cannot be sexual and/or romantic with someone else, and these boundaries are crossed. It is also when it is not talked about or agreed upon, but assumed that two people are monogamous. So when one or both decide to be sexual or romantic with someone else, they feel slighted and cheated. This is what cheating is.

Sex, relationships, and marriage is a CHOICE. Even if Twins are 'supposed' to be together, they BOTH have to CHOOSE to be together. It is a mutual choice. But it is not cheating. Now, if Twins are together, and one Twin decides to have sex with someone else, or have a mate on the side, this IS cheating. That is, unless they mutually agreed to an open relationship, or that it is okay for one of them to have other mates.

*"My Supposed 'Twin' runs after we have sex. I won't hear from him for weeks. What should I do?"* This can be for a variety of reasons. You will have to ask your Twin, as they will know why. I know they might not tell you, but only they have the answer. In situations like these, it is common for the one running from sex to not feel good enough, to be insecure, have some sort of sexual or emotional trauma, manipulating the relationship, or they are feeling the connection too intensely after sex and pull away to not be so overwhelmed.

Don't feel bad when they run after sex. How you respond to this situation is very important. You can't change your Twin's behavior, but you can change how YOU respond to their behavior. Don't pressure them or try to get them to come back using sex. It doesn't matter if they are a man or a woman. You can't force things onto people. That is not mature or wise. But if they have sex and then leave for long periods of time, how is that going to become a healthy connection? Is that the kind of relationship you want to be in the rest of your life?

*"I feel like my Supposed 'Twin' only wants me for sex. I want to just be friends for now, but he pushes for sex and runs when I say no. how can I keep both of us together without it only being about sex?"* If your Twin is a man, then you wanting to be friends is the cause of all of this conflict. Men ARE NOT women. We are not emotional. When we are dealing with a woman we like or feel a connection with, the energy does not go to our heart first. It goes to our sacral, THEN back up to the heart. With women, the energy is the other way around. It goes to heart, THEN down to the sacral. Since women are the

ones who control sex in relationships, and sex is the deepest form of intimacy, a woman who restricts sex from her partner is a woman who is closing the door to the emotional intimacy she desires. Neither partner will get their needs met.

The man can give the emotional intimacy, but needs the physical intimacy first. The woman can give the physical intimacy, but needs the emotional intimacy first. Do you see how nature has the sexes at odds? This is part of The Game and hypergamy. Not everyone realizes they have to actually put in the work and invest into the relationship. What makes this worse is when women restrict sex from their partner. This shuts down the entire circuit. I am not talking about a woman restricting sex from a stranger or a man she doesn't know or just met. For Lord's sake, don't sleep with a stranger or someone you just met! It's good to have standards, and you should have standards!

There has to be sex, just as there has to be some kind of emotional intimacy or stimulation. Men don't want to be friends with the woman they like and feel and connection with. We want the deeper connection, which is sex, not emotional stimulation. Women want men to be emotional, and that is incorrect. Men are not emotional, we don't really process intimacy outside of physical connection. Remember, the Feminine represents substance. The Masculine wants to experience the substance. Just as the Masculine is the Sword, and is action. The Feminine desires the protection and providing from her Masculine. She also wants Her Masculine to take action and initiative. But by restricting sex from your Twin and asking to be friends, you have indirectly told him that you don't want to be intimate with him, and that he is not worth being intimate with. This is why he runs.

You feel like it is only about sex because you are treating him as if he is a woman, which he is not. You are only taking yourself and your own needs into consideration while abandoning his. If you want to be together, then BE together. Stop restricting sex and telling him 'no'. Men don't process love through the heart primarily, but through the sacral. Women process it primarily through the heart RACO™ first and then through the sacral.

***"I caught my Supposed 'Twin' watching porn when I went to visit him. Is he a creep?"*** Men are frowned upon with the same sexual behaviors women also engage in. If a woman watches pornography, she will not be looked at the same way by society verses if a man watches pornography. Porn became part of the early 21st century culture. Although most people (both men and women) who watch porn do not let it be known, it is part of the modern world in a way.

The porn industry is full of women, and not enough men.. It is not only men who watch porn, and sadly the porn industry is overwhelmed by too many women and not enough men. But still, men are frowned upon by most of society if it is known they are watching porn. Do men not have a Nature-given right to express and engage in their sexuality? Remember, a man and a woman is the same Entity, just expressed in two different ways. If you have a poor perception of men's sexuality, that is only a poor perception of your own sexuality.

No I am not talking about men having sex with minors, or engaging in illegal or immoral (ex. incest) sexual behaviors. Whether he is a creep or not can only be determined if he engage in illegal sexual behaviors such as sex with a minor, intentionally chases women for sex, or has a sex addiction, which would mean he needs help. If you caught your Twin watching porn, did you ask him WHY he watches it? Did you ask him if he is struggling with depression or with being able to have a healthy sex life with REAL women? Or is this all about labeling your Twin as a creep over something you may not understand?

This sounds harsh, but if he is your Twin, you both are single, of legal age, and not biological family, it would be more beneficial if the porn he has is thrown in the trash, and the both of you go out on a couple dates and then have sex with each other. Men and women were designed and made to mate and have sex with each other, real, physical sex. Not watching a digital representation of two other people having sex. Men and women have to make their way back to the natural, Nature-created ways of engaging with each other.

*"Whenever I have sex with my Supposed 'Twin' it trigger all of my insecurities. The sex is so good, but I feel so unworthy after. Why do I feel like this?"* Insecurities and feeling unworthy can stem from a variety of mental and emotional health issues from trauma, abuse, heartbreak, trust issues, and improper upbringing. Although it is easy to assume we want a good mate, and an even better sex life, this can be different in real life. Having amazing sex and a good mate can and does trigger people. This is especially true in a society where some people are born in dysfunctional families. They grow up in a society where dysfunctional relationships and marriages are common. When someone meet another person who is not dysfunctional, and have amazing sexual experiences with them, this is foreign to the person. They are unable to process what is going on. It is so different than what they have experienced all of their life, how they were raised, and what they have accepted as social norms.

Our Twin will trigger any and all insecurities that are within us. This is for the purpose of what is called purging. Purging is what bring the insecurities to the surface so that we can identify them. From there, we can choose to release the insecurities, to change how we think and feel about things. You have to develop a new way of thinking and feeling about love, relationships, and sex. It is not that your Twin is doing anything wrong or attempting to make you feel insecure. It is great that the sex is so good, but if it trigger you, you have some healing to do. Visit the chapter in this guidebook named 'Soul Ascension' for information about various healing practices.

*"I love my Supposed 'Twin' and want to be with her, but she keeps withholding sex and says that I only care about sex. What should I do?"* I am

not surprised. Over the course of my life with personal experiences with woman, observing others, and helping others, I have noticed that some women do not understand men very well. We are treated as if we are woman, as if we are emotional and don't have testosterone. Women interpret our biological drive for sex as: *"He doesn't care about my feelings."* A woman's need for emotional stimulation is in direct relation to a man's need for physical stimulation. Physical intimacy is not only sex, but involves other things such as shoulder rubbing, hugs, kisses, cuddling, ext. Both sexes need verbal and mental (seduction) stimulation.

If your Twin tell you that all you care about is sex, then she withhold sex, this can come from a few different things. She is either manipulating you, has some kind of sexual or emotional trauma/insecurity, or she simply does not understand that intimacy and sex is a requirement for a healthy relationship. Since she is the one who has put you and the relationship in this position, you will have to be the one to make a change. You will have to tell her that her restricting sex from the relationship is HER not caring about you and that you want to leave. Never stay with someone who withholds intimacy like this. Physical intimacy and sex is a requirement for a healthy relationship. This is what bonds two people together, and unfortunately many women do not realize the emotional stimulation they seek actually come from this bonding (from physical intimacy).

It doesn't matter if she is your Twin or not. You know what your needs are. She know what her needs are. She is expecting you to give to her needs while restricting yours. This is her attempting to control the relationship and manipulate you into getting what she wants without giving what you want. Now if you are the kind of guy that does not want a relationship or commitment, but just want sex, then it is important to state that with her. If you have done so already and she restricts sex, she likely wants a relationship or commitment first without giving you your needs. You will have to let her go.

***"I'm so mad and hurt. I found out my Supposed 'Twin' had sex with another woman, he even lied to me about it. Why is he having sex with another woman if he says he loves me and has the best sex with me than anyone he has ever had?"*** *"Your Twin will never cheat on you."* This is one of the most common statements I hear from Twins and others. This is next to *"Your Twin will never abuse you. Twins can't abuse each other."* That is until they actually get cheated on or abused by their Twin. The reality is that Soul Twins are still human and people at the end of the day. They are still subjected to improper upbringing, societal influences, trauma, and all the other things that cause normal people to cheat or be abusive with their mates. I will never say that a Twin can't be a cheater or abusive, because then I would be leaving out the Twins who DO experience them.

The thing about love and sex, you can love someone but still have sex with someone else. You can also have sex with someone and not even love them. It is important to distinguish the two. They are separate. Love is an emotion which come from hormonal changes in the body. Sex is an energetic stimulation through nervous system and sensorial engagement (Mutual Energetic Resonance).

It isn't pleasant to be cheated on, even more so by someone we are all told could never cheat on us. This make the situation worse. You went into it with expectations that this person is your Soul Twin, and they will never cheat on you. But here, you are slapped with the reality of cheating, lies, and abuse from them.

Just as with normal people, it is easy to assume that if we are having sex with someone and they mention that they love us, that they'll never cheat. It is wrong to cheat. You have a right to be angry and hurt. But it is not good to hold onto the anger and hurt. Your Twin may or may not change their behavior. What would you do if your Twin continue to cheat and lie to you? Do you want to live the rest of your life in anger, hurt, and grief? You can change your own behavior. You can put your foot down and not tolerate the cheating and lying. You can leave. Just because they are your Twin does not mean you have to tolerate their bad behavior.

People who cheat and/or lie have their own reasons for doing so. There isn't one reason why people cheat. But some common reasons include, carelessness, they love you but don't respect you, manipulation, not getting their sexual or emotional needs met, societal programming which make cheating and lying seem like normal behavior, an impulsive response to issues in the relationship, vindication, ext.

## FOR MARRIED TWINS

*"Why do I want to have sex with them when I'm married? I want to so bad, but I don't want to destroy my marriage and break up my family."* These are common thoughts and feelings with married Soul Twins. If you met your Twin while one or both of you were married to other people, this likely caused some issues. The Twin Soul connection is a highly sexually charged one. The energy between Twins is intense, especially sexually. BUT, you are married. How can you be married to one person but have such a strong sexual attraction to someone else (your Soul Twin)? This is a huge problem.

Most people will want to stay in their marriage and not cheat. But when the sexual intensity and emotions for your Twin is so high and you find yourself slip, what do you do? Many married Twins have ran into this problem. They are married to one person, but are pulled to and drawn to another person (their Twin). Just because someone is married, does not mean the ability to be sexually attracted to someone else will magically disappear. Now, I am not a marriage counselor, and once two people get married, I believe that they are the choosers of what to do. But here, I will say that cheating is still wrong if you are married. Just because the other person is your Twin, does not justify cheating on your wife or husband. It is still wrong and considered cheating.

If you have not had sex with your Twin while married, it should remain that way. DON'T CHEAT. You are married, you made a commitment and a vow. But if you are having marital issues and wish to divorce, then that should have nothing to do with wanting to be with your Twin. If you divorce, it should only be for other reasons, and not because you want to divorce to go be with your Twin.

But if you have had sex with your Twin while married, you are not the only one who has done so. Many married Twins I have met and talked to seemed to be in a dead-end marriage and want out. They met their Twin while already in process of divorce, or wanting one. Some of them had a good marriage, but after meeting their Twin, things changed. They found themselves questioning where their heart is. They could love their wife or husband to the ends of the Earth, but after meeting their Twin, everything changes. They no longer wanted to be with their husband and found that the Twin Soul connection would always override the marriage. They just couldn't keep and maintain attraction and sexual intensity with their married mate. But they surely could with their Twin.

How you approach sex with your Soul Twin while you are married with someone else should never cross boundaries, create unnecessary conflict, and should never be made out of impulse. I understand some marriages (yes even with some Soul Twins) are open marriages, or one of the people agree to still be with other people. But this is different if the marriage was built on monogamy and remaining loyal to the married mate.

## FOR TWINS WITH CHILDREN

If you or your Twin has children, you or they may have told themselves that they don't want any more children. And because with sex, pregnancy is always a possibility, some people refrain from having sex altogether. That is, until you meet your Twin. Meeting your Twin can rekindle desires for sex, and even to have children. Some people don't want to be with someone if they already have children with someone else. If you or your Twin had children from other people when you met, this could pose an issue.

In another way, if you and your Twin have children together, this can be different than children with others. Because a Twin Soul is such a high energy soul, the children they have together will also be of high energy. The telepathy, knowing where they are, and knowing what they are doing can be felt by the Twins and their offspring. In another way, the children from other people usually are able to feel the high energy between Twins. The children have a draw to both Twins, and may even attempt to bring or keep the Twins together if they are not together. The children will feel like both Twins are their parents. But there are some situations where the children could be repulsed by the other Twin, especially if the Twin is engaged in illegal or bad behavior.

# FOR TWINS WITH A LARGE AGE GAP

Although most people only have sex with others within a small age range (and close to their age), some people will have a wider acceptable age range. They may also accept a much younger or older person. When I was 27 years of age, *PhatPhat* was 25 years old. This would be considered reasonable. But when I was 23 years of age, *Ms. Wonka* was 41. There was a large age gap, I was much younger than her. I was fooled for a few months after meeting her, as she looked more like she was 27 or 28. With my Supposed 'Twin', I am younger than *her*, but not by much. I know in some circles, and with most women, there is a preference that the man is older than the woman, but usually not much older.

As long as neither you nor your Twin are minors, I don't see an issue with it. DO NOT have sex with a minor, even if you think or feel like they are your Twin.

Because at different times of our lives, most people want to have children, get married, or settle down, this will be important to consider if your Twin is much older or younger than you. This is also true for women, as women have a narrow window when they can legally have sex and birth healthy children. Discuss these things with your Twin. Never assume that because you love your Twin and want to be with them that they want to be with you. If one of you are wanting to have children or get married, but one of you is too young or old, this could be a place of conflict.

There are some Twins who separate for this reason. One Twin might want to have children or get married. But if their Twin was too young, or too old, they could have ran and pushed their Twin away, then went to look for someone of suitable age (according to them). The inverse is true, and one Twin might not want to have any children or get married, but the other does not, or they may already be married with children. Take all of this into consideration when thinking about your Twin Soul connection.

Even if you and your Twin have a large age gap, or one of you is a minor, this will not prevent either of you from feeling the intense sexual and emotional energy. You both will still have telepathy and feel each other's emotions and physical sensations. But whatever you do, DO NOT have sex with a minor! Do not let emotions, desires, thoughts, drive, or lust cause you to commit a crime or engage in immoral behavior.

# FOR TWINS WHO ARE A CELEBRITY OR PUBLIC FIGURE

Most people who idolize a celebrity could only imagine being able to meet them, let alone have sex with them. But if your Twin is a celebrity, this add a different spin to the situation.

If your Twin is a celebrity or public figure, you will surely crave for them sexually. You will experience all the telepathy and shared physical sensations.

This could be frustrating if you are not with your Twin, as celebrities usually are rarely single and without constant access to sex. You may find yourself overwhelmed by their energy, as when people are in relationships or have had recent sexual activity, they will also have a higher average energy. This will be unless there is an energetic block put in place, so that you are not always feeling your celebrity Twin's energy when they are having sex. This could also be a dream come true, and beyond if you and your celebrity Twin are together, or are able to be sexual with each other.

If you are a celebrity or public figure, and your Twin is not, you may have found it strange how you could have such an intense sexual attraction to them. This is normal. We don't always have a sexual attraction to the kind of people we think we should. If you and your Twin are not together, you both will still feel the magnetic sexual and emotional attraction. You will feel each other's sensations. If you both are together, your Twin may be overwhelmed by you, due to you being a celebrity on top of being Soul Twins. But you don't have to assume that you are pushing them away or causing them to run. But if they are running, you likely know why.

If you and your Twin are both celebrities and/or public figures, keeping your sexual activities secret could be a challenge. Twins have a lot of energy between each other, especially sexual energy. This can be picked up and seen by other people. This can cause jealousy, stalking, gossip, and other things from other people. Being a celebrity compound these issues as there are already so many people wanting to know your business behind doors. But thankfully as a celebrity, you already know how to navigate being in the spotlight so that not all of your business is out in the open. Feeling your Twin's energy and being sexually drawn to them shouldn't get in the way of your work. It is important to be able to remain level headed, especially if you work with your Twin.

# SECTION EIGHT
# 'RUNNING' OR SOMETHING ELSE?

Before we learn what running is and why it happen in the Twin Soul connection, lets gain a basic understanding of four important things. They are: personality types, love languages, attachment styles, and intelligent quotients. Keep these four things in mind while studying the rest of this guidebook.

## PERSONALITY TYPES

**THE BASICS:** Personality types describe what someone does to 'recharge' their social batteries. It also describe the direction of energy flow. It is important to know that even if someone is an extravert or introvert, during different times of the day, month, year, period cycles, hormonal levels, and their life, everyone can oscillate between different personality types. Also, understand that none of these are engraved in stone. An extravert can have some degree of introvert capabilities and vice versa.

**INTROVERT** – Highly controversial and misunderstood, introverts recharge their social batteries through isolation. The direction of their energy flow is non-inverted, or turned inward. Usually, introverts tend to be more quiet and 'to themselves'. It is important to understand that how much or little someone talks does not determine their personality type.

**EXTRAVERT** – Most of my friends have been extraverts over my life. I love extraverts. They are talkative, are deep wells of information, always are looking to have fun, and enjoy trying new things. Extraverts recharge their social batteries by engaging in social events, activities, and people. They tend to be more talkative and 'open'. Extravert's energy is directed outward (inverted).

**AMBIVERT** – I didn't know until I got into my mid 20s that I was an ambivert. Ambiverts can recharge their social batteries regardless if they are by themselves or by engaging in social events and talking with others. They can bridge the gap between introvert and extravert. Their energy can be directed inward or outward. It is difficult to identify an ambivert, as they are able to recharge in both ways.

**UNIVERT™** – A term I created, a univert™ is a conscious ambivert. Univerts™ are able to consciously and intentionally choose to engage life as an introvert or extravert, at any moment, for any reason. They can recharge in any way. The energy flow in both directions.

## LOVE LANGUAGES

**THE BASICS:** Love languages describe avenues which we give and receive care, intimacy, stimulation, and excitement between ourselves and other people. Everyone has all of these avenues, but not everyone has knowledge, awareness, or proper usage of these avenues. Note that at any given time you might be engaged in one, all, or some of these love languages with your Twin. This may give insight on why your Twin behave the way they do, why you behave the way you do, and how the usage, misusage, or lack of love languages influence your connection.

**DIVINE** – The Divine language is based in your connection with The Most High. It is the avenue which we have life. This avenue cannot be manipulated and functions purely off The Most High and life. Without this in life, one feels lost, without purpose, or always in some kind of conflict with themselves or others. With the Divine Love language, one is always One with The Most High, and they know they are. Life is smooth, easy, and things seem to fall into place without a lot of work, energy, and time.

**ENERGETIC** – This is based in pure, non-physical energy. This is beyond physical and emotional. Those who are soulfully mature and conscious are able to utilize this avenue. A relationship with the energetic intimacy will be highly pleasurable by nature. You both will be able to engage and influence each other and each other's lives through non-physical means. A relationship with high mental intimacy will be easier, with less conflict, and with less time-delay. Things just happen faster with less work. A relationship without this will seem to require a lot of physical work, time, and energy.

**MENTAL** – Those who are more mature and aware will want mental stimulation, and not only physical or emotional. This is based in intelligence. This can translate into verbal stimulation, conversation, and comprehension. A relationship without mental stimulation feel like there is a disconnect, or a mismatch. A relationship with mental stimulation is like: *"I feel so connected to this person"*, and *"Me and this person understand each other and life so well."*

**PHYSICAL/SEX** – Touching, kissing, rubbing, presence, and even sexual activity (with those who are not family and minors) make up physical intimacy. Physical intimacy is not limited to sex. Since we have a physical body, and we are mainly mammals, we are sexual creatures. We all, to some degree, have sexual and physical desires and cravings. The physical love language is basic and considered the foundation for the other languages. A relationship without physical intimacy will feel more like a friendship or family and not sexual or romantic. A relationship with physical intimacy will have the feelings of being bonded and 'pleased'.

**EMOTIONAL** – Because we are heavily influenced by hormones, and hormones cause emotions, this becomes a love language. Feeling pleased, secure, and stimulated emotionally is part of all of our lives, particularly for women and those who are very emotional. A relationship without the emotional stimulation will feel 'boring' and dull. A relationship with the emotional stimulation will feel exciting and hold our attention.

# ATTACHMENT STYLES

**THE BASICS:** All energy has to flow, and it has to flow in a direction. Attachment is our own energy, emotion, and thought going toward someone or something. They have to go somewhere, toward something or someone. Here, we will look at attachment in the sense of our energy, thought, and emotions going toward another person. Note that attachment can change in intensity and toward different people throughout the day, month, year, and our lives. Note that it is possible to oscillate between different attachment styles.

**CONFIDENT (AKA SECURE)** – In your most healthy state of being, you will be confident-attached. This is the result of having your energy, emotion, and thought engaged with things and with people who are healthy and beneficial for you. Your attachment to those things or people create harmony, abundance, and excitement.

**FEARFUL** – Oh snap! The beginning of trouble, fearful-attachment is when someone is attached to things and people out of fear and not out of confidence. This fear based attachment can also be inverted to create avoidant and dismissive attachment styles which are explained below. Fearful-attachment does not necessarily cause someone to want to run from love, but it can cause someone to put up walls or push away the people they love and who love them. Unfortunately, many people with fearful-attachment actually cause people to chase after them, the very thing they might not want. It can also cause people to abandon them and not want to be around them because they might seem to always be 'running', 'playing hard to get', 'closed off', or 'not interested.'

**ANXIOUS** – Different than fearful-attachment, anxious-attachment cause one to overthink or overemphasize the people they are attached to. This can be seen as chasing behavior, stalking, controlling, or someone who has to constantly be close to who they are attached to. This can smother and push away other people.

**SCATTERED** – This attachment style come about when someone is sexually, emotionally, or romantically involved with multiple people at one time. The attachment is constantly changing people. The person will seem hot and cold, or one day so interested, and the next day not caring. Scattered-attachment can create unnecessary confusion and drama. Someone with scattered-attachment will seem impossible to get a commitment from or get into a monogamous relationship. They are too scattered to keep their energy and attachment on one person.

**AVOIDANT/DISMISSIVE** – These are inverted attachment styles. They are the opposite of confident (secure)-attachment. It is an attempt to avoid becoming attached, or to dismiss the purpose and usage of attachment. This is usually done out of fear or manipulation. But this is not to be confused with someone who avoid becoming attached to things and people who are toxic and not beneficial for them.

# TYPES OF INTELLIGENCE

**THE BASICS:** Intelligence is complex. Intelligence can manifest in a variety of different ways. Source is pure intelligence in its most raw form. It is also how a life form utilize its innate abilities to survive and thrive in an environment which has lots of obstacles and challenges.

**XQ (SOUL QUOTIENT)** – Also the source of morality, those with high XQ are conscious and aware. They have experienced enough of life to know that life is not physical. Even what looks physical is actually energy vibrating on a very low frequency, so low that it appear solid. They understand that there are things in life which are not seen by the human eyes or heard by the ears, yet have profound influences on the physical aspects of life. They are aware the Ahmen Most High's existence, and that The Most High is the one who favors, protects, and give abundance. They utilize XQ to experience abundance and soul power in life.

**IQ (INTELLIGENT QUOTIENT)** – This form of intelligence is based in one's mentality. It is their ability to rationalize and process their experience of life. Someone who utilize this understand that just because there are other people on this planet, does not entitle those people to do things for you, or to learn for you. Those with this form of intelligence tend to become leaders, philosophers, authors, scientists, and other similar things. They THINK their way through life. They take matters into their own hands rather than wait for or expect someone else to do things. They are aware that their life and reality is based on their mentality and content of their minds.

**SQ (SOCIAL QUOTIENT)** – Since humans are mainly mammals (actually a variety of different animals), we are also social creatures. There is a sense of interdependency and networking with other people. Those who are aware of this, take advantage of this natural human resource. They invest time, energy, and other things in people. They understand that it is necessary to engage other people in a way that is beneficial for themselves and others.

**EQ (EMOTIONAL QUOTIENT)** – The foundation for human intelligence begin with emotion. Since humans are influenced by hormones, and hormones cause emotion, this is the foundational intelligence. If one cannot live wisely due to being overpowered by their emotion, this can put a damper on their success in life.

**AQ (ADVERSITY QUOTIENT)** – Life is in such a way that there are challenges and obstacles for all of us when we are younger. Only the strong, wise, conscious, and active will overcome those challenges and surmount the obstacles. Through AQ they were able to continue on with their lives, still reaching for success.

## WHAT IS RUNNING?

Anyone who has spoken with Soul Twins or been involved in the Twin Soul community have likely heard of 'the runners' and the 'runner Twin'. It is highly problematic and controversial. Let's take a look at what running is in the Twin Soul connection, why it happen, and why the runners run.

Running can take different forms. We know physically what running look like. We can keep it simple and say that running can be seen as something good, or it can be the cause of such things like fear. Running looks like a car on fire, and the driver getting out the car and bolt away quickly from the burning vehicle. Running can also look like the mail man pulling up in the drive way when you are waiting for a present to come in the mail. You move quickly towards the mail man to see if they have your package.

In the Twin Soul Collective, running hasn't been anything wonderful. Many DFs (and some DMs) have experienced their Twin 'running' from them. This come in the form of physically running, running in the sense of not sharing feelings, not wanting to reciprocate intimacy, no contact, lack of communication, closed hearted, or attempting to avoid feeling the connection.

# THE 'RUNNER' TWIN

Soul Twin Runners, also known as the Matrix Twins or Divine Masculines, are members of the Twin Soul collective often derogatorily referred to as narcissists and toxic. Do not be fooled, however, as the DMs/Runners are a mirror image of the Divine Feminine. Soul Twins are one soul. The DM reflects the DF's nature, and the DF reflects the DM's nature. They are actually ONE entity.

But the more I learned about Soul Twins, the more Twins I met and helped, the more I realized that the DM/Runners are actually not as bad as the DFs claim. But the DFs are not so innocent either. Just as with all things I have learned in life, people cannot admit their own wrong doing and bad behavior, but are quick to point at other's. I didn't realize until it was too late, but I walked into a room full of DFs who were talking bad about their DMs, and treated me the same. This changed everything I thought I initially knew about Soul Twins. Things were very different in real life than they were portrayed on the internet.

But not all Twin's situation is the same, and there were also a lot of DFs that did not complain but simply wanted to share their story. There were also DFs that knew why their Twin was behaving the way there were, and it was not always because the DM was toxic.

It was wide spread over the internet. *"Why doesn't my Supposed 'Twin' want me?" "Why has my Supposed 'Twin' blocked me and won't respond?"* They (the DM/Runners) were called runners. They were said to be afraid of love. They were called toxic and NARCS who couldn't identify or love a good woman if she was standing in front of them. But are these folk really running? There is a reason for everything, and everything for a reason.

Where should a man go where he can be a man and not be shamed? I also had to stop engaging with some female writers on Quora.com because unfortunately they had the mindset that a man isn't allowed to comment on any of their posts. They will flag you under harassment if you see any situation different than they feel it **NEEDS** to be. The feminist, gynocentric society made me sick to the stomach. And the Soul Twin community wasn't any better. The internet in the Twin Soul corner was filled with hatred, anger, and disgust toward the DMs/male Twins because unfortunately people don't seek to understand. People are quick to label someone as toxic or narcissistic when their behavior doesn't match what we feel or think it should be.

But this means there need to be leadership and truth in the Twin Soul collective. The DFs need to be lead into a better way of looking at their Twin and themselves. There needs to be truth in the Twin Soul collective. The 'runner' and the 'chaser' are nothing but our own soul breaking free from attachments to things, beliefs, behavior, places, and people that are not healthy for us or for our greater benefit. The soul is simply becoming aware of itself. The soul is waking up from Separation Illusion™.

# SOMEONE LIKE YOU

In human psychology, the perception of one's self being *"good"* and *"deserving"* is so great, that when an individual set out to find a mate (for whatever reason), the tendency to look for someone who is just like them is an unconscious standard. You would love to have someone just like you. If they are just like you, they would understand you and know you inside and out. It would make an easy relationship and there would be instant and lasting attraction. If they are just like you, they would be a perfect fit just for you and you both would have lots of fun. Or so you think...

The reality is that no one is like you. There really is only ONE you. Someone else can share that same surface level qualities, behaviors, or activities; but at the core, we are all unique in our own way. Many relationship issues arise from an inability to accept the other person's differences. It is also the fact that people aren't always up front and honest about what they really want and who they are.

The Twin Soul connection is no different. Even with mirroring and shared emotion, synchronicities, matching birth marks in the same area, whatever,...our Twins are still unique in their own way and fashion. I saw that the Masculine energy wasn't well understood and was usually pushed to match the Feminine energy in ways that it's not designed to.

I have always seen and observed what we call Masculine and Feminine, as actually One energy that is behaving in two different ways. It is like one day you have a really good day, and you are happy and want to throw a party or do something fun. On a different day you feel weighed down by your external environment and have a lot of things to do. So, you put your hair in a ponytail and get to work. You are the same person, but behaving in two different ways. Likewise, the Masculine and Feminine is One energy behaving two different ways, and the man and the woman is a physical representation of this.

Feminine energies post Feminism of the late 1900s became overpowering. This was due to the nature of the world where the Feminine was accepted as something that everyone must strive to accept and the Masculine as an example of what to avoid. The Feminine energy is lovely in Her own right, with wonderful attributes like gentleness, nurturing, emotion, forgiving and youthfulness. But without the Masculine being the Masculine and exercising His powerful and necessary attributes, the Feminine is left in a place where She feels unhappy, tense, unprotected, aggressive, and fatigued by carrying the weight of life. We have to leave behind the beliefs and teachings of the matrix system which say the men and Masculine energies are toxic and troublesome. We have to change how we think and feel about men and the Masculine energy.

# MASCULINE ENERGY COMPREHENSION

I define masculine energy as 'action'. I use the Divine Sword to represent the Masculine. Most if not all of you reading this have already met and engaged with your Soul Twin. You have likely met soulmates and karmics. You have tried the best you could to find love, in the worst of people and in the best of people. But still things may not have turned out the way you desired, even with your Soul Twin. Some of you are either fed up with the Twin Soul journey, can't even find or connect with your Twin at all, or you don't want to even be bothered with them. But think about this for a moment.

It is mentioned a lot that the Divine Feminines are the Spiritual Twin and the Divine Masculines are the Matrix Twin. I know there are some that are mixed matched. Now, there are two levels to the 'matrix', the man-made matrix which is responsible for a lot of the false programing and trauma we suffered growing up. And there is the natural matrix: the elements, the solar system, the plants and animals, the physicality of existence.

Everything has physical and non-physical aspects, and the physical and non-physical can only co-exist with each other. All of us have physical and non-physical aspects as well. We could switch out the two words and say Masculine or matrix part and Feminine or soul part

It can be so easy (maybe it never crossed your mind) to get frustrated when your DM isn't behaving and living the way you feel they should. But remember, they are unique in their own way. They also don't share all the same attributes you do. The Masculine energy behaves differently than the Feminine energy. While you might want to pray, share emotions, have fun, attend lots of get-togethers, and live a more care-free life, the Masculine energy is more simple and less complex. The Masculine will want to focus on gaining and maintaining a physical/material life that will allow them to survive, self-sustain, and 'relax'.

Imagine a life where you have no place to stay, it is difficult to find food, you just can't seem to get a job that keep up with the bills, your health has deteriorated, and it seem like everything you touch either break or stop working. That would be a very stressful life to live. The Masculine energy is concerned and focused primarily on these things, so that life is smooth, simple, and of some comfort and productivity. Some of the DMs have been so traumatized and brainwashed by the matrix programming, they might not even attempt to have their lives together. They might even use people for those things.

The Masculine energy is more about foundation, risk, action, and living a simple, predictable life, whereas the Feminine energy is more about having the least responsibilities, feeling happy, exploring new things and people, and sharing those experiences with others. They both complement each other. Imagine, though how it would be if your DM tried to make you more like themselves. You would probably get frustrated and feel like they are trying to control you or make you into someone you aren't. I think seeing people for who they are and allowing them to be their natural selves take the pressure away. It also allow the other person to not feel like someone is attempting to change them or disregard the things about them that actually might not be so bad.

If we can allow the DMs to be the DMs and truly give them the space to heal, then we might see more of them reconnecting with their DFs. We have to change our perspective of the DMs away from *"They are toxic and narcissistic"* to something else. We have to trying something different! Imagine if all your DM wanted from you was someone who doesn't go around calling them toxic and narcissistic. Imagine if all they wanted was someone to listen and understand WHY they live and behave the way they do. They are The Masculine, not someone who want to ruin your life.

In what ways has your DM behaved that is different than the way you do that you initially thought was toxic or 'bad behavior' and later realized it wasn't what you thought? Was there ever a time you tried to bring your DM to be more concerned about metaphysical and emotional matters and yet it seemed they were only focused on money, material things and/or physical intimacy?

## WHY THE 'RUNNERS' RUN

Why do the DMs run? Only they truly know. They run for their own reasons. Based off what I have seen and heard, they run because they have too many fears, insecurities, and trauma that surface when they meet their DF. They run as a way to avoid dealing with those things. It is also common for them to run because they are overwhelmed by the Twin Soul connection, and this signify they have not learned how to manage energy and emotion. The energy and emotion swell up and cause pain, confusion, and chaos within themselves. They avoid or suppress the energy and emotion rather than let them flow.

I think the males/runners with Soul Twins have painted a clear picture. This is the fact that when they are emasculated, put down, and forced to be 'soft', it actually turn them toxic, selfish, and incompatible with a woman's natural feminine energy. It doesn't make them behave better, it doesn't make them treat others better, and it clearly doesn't make women feel safe and led up a good path. Men are not women. Men need to be allowed to be men as they are, and not forced to 'behave', conform, or be soft.

So, you are able to see how emasculated men negatively impact any relationship dynamic, and even our society as a whole. This is also true for Soul Twin men. But this is how some men fail themselves and society, because some men allow themselves to have their balls removed and authority taken from them. Men are supposed to stand their ground and be firm, not be 'soft' and compliant as to not offend someone else or come off as controlling.

**POSSIBLE REASONS WHY YOUR TWIN RAN**
- Ran from being loved
- Insecurities
- Fear
- They never ran, the DF wanted them to chase, and they didn't
- Trauma/baggage
- Their DF was toxic or in an unhealthy state of mind

- Being responsible
- Having to put in the work of maintaining a healthy relationship
- Gameplay/manipulation
- Thinking or feeling they can find love somewhere else, although it is never a 'better' love, but rather a love and connection that is less intense and triggering than with their DF
- Energetic blockages that causes them to run
- A need to self-protect their heart from possible pain
- Fear of rejection
- Not wanting to be vulnerable
- Their DFs running from them
- Unwilling to communicate their feelings/thoughts
- Not wanting to let go of their old life and karmic situations

## DON'T OVERWHELM YOURSELF

Both the DM and DF can get overwhelmed by the Twin Soul connection. The runner is usually heavily triggered. Their trauma, fears, and insecurities surface when they meet their DF. The DF is overwhelmed because they feel the immense love for and pull toward their Twin, yet there is no reciprocation of love and communication. This increase anxiety and 'chasing' behavior in the DF.

DMs can be overwhelmed by the intense love from the DF, a love they have never experienced and feel unworthy of. The energy they feel from the connection that never go away. The energy and connection seem to always override every other connection they attempt to become involved.

They might fear getting hurt because of things that has happened when they were a child or earlier in their life before meeting them. The fear can come from a parent that left them or abused them. It can come from someone they were in love with who hurt them. We all have our own reasons. After someone experience something painful, they usually will not want to experience that again. So, if they meet someone or end up in a situation that remind them of the pain they felt before, they might run from the fear of it happening again.

## AVOID RELATIONSHIP JUMPING

It is reasonable if a relationship simply did not work for reasons beyond the two people's control. Sometimes relationships run their course. But then, there are situations where getting into a relationship with someone may not be done for reasonable purposes, and in a way that is healthy. I have heard from many DFs, that their DM (and even some of the DFs) jumped into other relationships after meeting their Twin. Common reasons I have heard are due to attempting to get over the intense emotion they have for their Twin, manipulation, attempting to 'move on', vindication, or not being aware that the person was their Twin.

I don't think these are reasonable purposes for entering a relationship. It also put the other person in a situation where they are entering a relationship with someone who likely does not love them, a relationship that is not built on a healthy purpose, and one which cause more conflict between the Twins. Rather than jumping into a relationship for the above mentioned reasons, I think it would be more wise to either work things out maturely with your Twin, or remain single and do some healing and contemplation.

Within the Twin Soul community, I also see where Soul Twin separation is confused with typical problems and mistakes commonly made in love, dating, and relationships with normal people. It seem like it is common belief that Twins are SUPPOSED to separate, and that this separation is only Divinely orchestrated. But after digging deeper, I have come to see and learn that Soul Twins usually have separated due to issues in love, dating, and relationships common amongst normal people. Soul Twins are not excused from those mistakes and problems. They still suffer the consequences of poor decision making and bad behavior.

## THE STRONG AND LOVING DIVINE MASCULINE

Contrary to popular belief amongst DFs in the Twin Soul community, not all DMs are toxic or abusive. You may actually be surprised to find that many DMs are actually not the kind of people many DFs describe them to be. Since the online Twin Soul community has been heavily occupied by female Twins, and most Twin Soul content online is created by the same, there is naturally a huge bias in favor of the female Twins. *And then there are 3rd party influences which intentionally create fake accounts and post fake content which makes Soul Twins appear to be toxic.* What could actually be a smaller percentage of Twin Soul men who actually are toxic or abusive, has been inflated to seem like they all are.

But some DFs do experience a truly toxic, abusive, or troubled DM.

In reality, you may find that the male Twins are not as they are projected to be. Relationships and people are complex. Add in being Soul Twins, and now you have added layers of complexity. What I have seen, is that most of the 'They are toxic and abusive' is either non-existent, exaggerated, mutual, or in fewer cases one-sided. Remember, Soul Twins are One soul. The energy is shared. It is not realistic for one Twin to call their Twin toxic, and project themselves to be innocent and free from any bad behavior themselves.

Our Twins are a living, breathing mirror of our own being. If they are toxic, then you have that in YOU as well, in some way, and to some degree. If you cannot admit and identify that, then this will be part of your ascension. You will have to come to awareness that you are only pointing the finger at yourself and calling yourself toxic and abusive. It could even be that you found yourself attracted to or getting involved with them. You have had to learn to put your foot down and not tolerate bad, selfish, or lazy behavior.

**NON-EXISTENT** – Just because someone say or claim that their Twin or their mate is toxic, abusive, or on bad behavior does not always mean they are telling you the truth. Sometimes people, relationships, and situations do not happen the way we want. Some people may have a hidden agenda or seek to be controlling or manipulate the social dynamics. Sometime the issues and problems claimed against the male Twin are non-existent.

**EXHAGGERATED** – This is similar to the non-existent claims mentioned above. Except with exaggerated claims, it is made to seem like things are worse than they actually are. Or, that their Twin's non-harmful actions were harmful.

**MUTUAL/ONE-SIDED** – This is probably the most common of the four I have seen. Because a Twin Soul is a split or spread soul incarnated in two bodies, there really is only one person. Many of the problems and issues between Soul Twins are mutual, in some way, and to some degree. Even if our Twin is truly toxic and abusive, and we are not, we have to ask ourselves how we can have a deep love and chase after such a person. This is how the DF or chaser can express toxic behavior in their own way. It come from enabling and feeding into the DM/Runner's toxic behavior. This is probably the most difficult part of the Twin Soul journey: recognizing, admitting, and changing our own bad behavior and toxic ways.

## A WORD TO THE DMs

Who is that mysterious person? Why did they chase you and love you so much? You likely enjoyed them and their presence. That person is someone who you share the same soul with. Even if you never felt any intense emotions, energy, or a magnetic pull toward them, they still stuck out and caught your attention. For some reason, you were unable to remove this person out of your life. Even if you tried ignoring them, dating other people, or moving to another country, you still somehow came across them, dreamt of them, and were contacted by them.

They chased you because they realized sooner than you that you both shared a unique connection. Your DF/Chaser had an intense attraction toward you. You stood out to them, just like how they stood out to you. They loved you because the connection you have with them cause intense feelings of love. They couldn't help themselves. Even if you did not feel good enough for them or capable of being happy with them, they still loved you.

Your DF/Chaser's behavior was probably strange to you in the beginning. I assure you, they were not copy catting you. What you experienced is what is commonly known as *mirroring*. This is not the same as having a lot of similarities with someone else. This is not the same as someone mimicking you. Your DF/Chaser is a living, breathing reflection of yourself. Because you are one soul with them, you both seemingly are just like each other, as if you are male and female versions of the same person.

You likely know how much confusion and conflict you have caused your DF/Chaser by running from them and ignoring them. This is also true if you entered relationships and sexual connections with others but not with your

Twin. If you have struggled to stop running, it is important to know that your Twin chasing you is also the same as you running from them. it is just mirrored inverted. Your running behavior is reflected in them as them chasing you and vice versa. To ease the running, you need to identify the reasons why you ran. Was it a fear of rejection? Have you been hurt by someone you loved and gave everything to?

After identifying why you ran, you want to make some changes to how you think, feel, and behave. If you have a fear of being abandoned, you have to release the fear. Replace the fear with harmony and confidence. If someone hurt you in the past, your Twin is not that person that hurt you. You have to separate that experience and pain from your connection with your DF.

You are experiencing a soul awakening and ascension. This is why you and your life changed so much after meeting your DF. It may not feel or look like a spiritual awakening. To you, it may seem like your life fell apart and everything changed. This is the external changes due to the soul awakening and ascension. Many DFs also wonder if their DM will ever forgive themselves for running and causing their DF the pain and suffering. They wonder if their DM will ever rekindle the love and relationship and stay with their DF permanently, rather than running again and again.

If you and your Twin have conflict with each other, it helps to reach out and make things better. Communication is the foundation. Don't assume that your DF doesn't care about you or that they see you as below them. If you don't talk to your DF and come to a place of understanding, you both will continue with the running and chasing cycles. Do something different this time.

## 'MATRIX' TWIN + SOUL TWIN

There is the soul Twin, which represent one expression of the soul. And there is the Matrix (Earth) Twin, which represent a different expression of the same soul. The soul Twin is not necessarily the DF or Chaser.

While both Twins usually have traumas throughout lifetimes, the Matrix Twin is often particularly plagued with trauma and fear which result in becoming disconnected from the Most High and their own soul. Runner Twins are here to bring a message to the world that no matter how traumatized, no matter how broken, no matter how much they have tried to keep away from the Most High, that can be still change their life around and reconnect with The Most High and their soul. The Soul Twin is the Earth Twin's guide, protector, and lover. The Soul Twin find them in their darkest moments, when they need the Light.

The Soul Twin represents the Higher Self, and the Matrix Twin represents the Shadow Self.

The Soul Twin brings the Matrix Twin Home, back to Ahmen The Most High, and to Source Frequency. This is actually the soul awakening and taking the ascension path. The soul is making its own way back Home. The Matrix (Earth) Twin brings the world Home. Be not fooled by comments from non-Runner Twins longing for their runner to awaken. Believe me when I tell you that once the Matrix Twin finally take the ascension path, you will realize that they are truly special and are a product of all of the hell they have been through, but above all else...still worthy of it is All. The DM is only a reflection of yourself. YOU have to awaken, and take the ascension path.

Your job as the Soul Twin be a Light in the Dark. It is to light the path for them to awaken. If you're calling them a narcissist or the spawn of Satan, you are only sending that energy back to yourself. The purpose of the Twin Soul journey is to bring your Twin Home so you can bring the world Home together. As you awaken and ascend, so does your Twin, and so does the world. It is about worldwide awakening and ascension of everyone on Earth. But if your Twin choose not to at all, your Twin, just as you, have to make the choice themselves. You can't force them.

## END THE RUNNER'S TRAUMA AND NEGATIVITY

Even though many of the DMs and Runners have traumas and fears, they unfortunately live in a way which create more trauma and fear. This create a cycle. They feel stuck, like they want to heal and better themselves, but just can't. When they enter a relationship or connection with someone else, this can create a toxic connection. This can push other people away, cause people to attack them, and even position others to enable their bad behavior. Sometimes the DM/Runners really don't mean to push their DF away, hurt them, or create unnecessary conflict. They have a lot of fear and trauma they never released and healed.

Fortunately, this is where the soul journey come into the picture. After meeting their DF, the DMs are also thrusted into a soul journey. Their lives will change. They are forced to face their fears and trauma. Many of them attempt to run from this, and their DF. They might ignore the DF, jump into another relationship, or try to sever the connection so that they don't have to face their trauma and fears.

DMs/Runners will still have to anyways. Many of the ones who continue to avoid ascension and the connection with their DF, their lives usually turn upside down. They might lose everything, people leave them, and they may find themselves being alone. Some of them might get into a relationship, marriage, or sexual thing with someone else. In the new connection, they end up feeling out of place, with the wrong person, and miserable. They don't feel fulfilled, happy, secure, and with a sense of purpose.

For DM/Runners in these situations, the soul journey will continue knocking at their door. They could run for 30 years, get married to someone else, even have a baby, and yet, the connection with their DF will still remain. Life will still seemingly pull them into ascension. They have no choice. Once the DM/Runner stops running and surrender, their life will change for the better. The ascension will accelerate, and they will no longer hold onto fear and trauma.

## HOW RUNNING AFFECT THE RACO™ SYSTEM

Usually running, abandonment, and ghosting are the result of RACO™ blockages and misalignments. Here the RACO™ system has blockages which prevent constant, smooth energy flow. The misalignments cause internal friction and conflict. This internal friction and conflict is all the result of the person themselves and nothing external. It is important for the ascension, purging, and healing to take place so that the blockages can be opened and realigned so that the RACO™ system function in a way that is harmonious.

## THE 'RUNNER'S' PURPOSE

Quality communication is an important and necessary part of any successful and fulfilling relationship. But why is the Twin Soul connection plagued with no contact, ghosting, messages left on read, blocking, and closed off feelings? You've given your Twin nothing but love and wanted the best for them. Why would they break off communication like that and leave you out in the cold? *"Why can't I know how he's feeling?" "I wonder what's going on in his life, hopefully he isn't with another woman." "I wasn't trying to stalk her, she's just so guarded with everything, I just want to make sure I'm not being lied to or if she's hiding something."* These are some things you may have thought or felt about your Twin.

But really, what have they been up to? No contact, ghosting, messages left on read, not answering your calls or emails,...how COULD you know? You've been left to assumptions, fear, anxiety, stress, and even worry. But really, what has he been up to? Most of the time we assume the worst. Most of the time it never was as bad as we thought it was, and even after knowing what our Twin was up to all along, we wished we wouldn't have assumed the worst at the end of the day.

Meeting our Twin is never just a coincidence or just another man or woman. We met ourselves, everything about ourselves, good, bad, fugly, inside and out, and even our deepest wounds, traumas, passions, and desires. How have you handled seeing all these things in yourself after meeting your Twin? Everyone will respond differently. Some may blow up in anger, some may become controlling and try to force their Twin to change their behavior, some may do what they can on their end to make things better. How do you think your Twin experienced all his good, bad and ugly, and wounds and trauma being reflected back to him?

**NOTE TO DFs:** I know a lot of men, me being one myself, take to isolation and self- reflection when things become too chaotic and overbearing. You've felt all along that your Twin was running. But what if he's been working on healing his own wounds and trauma? What if he is getting himself out of that dark place and walking the path of ascension? From what you've seen on the outside you might feel otherwise. But the Twin Soul connection forces us to self-reflect and handle our own problems being reflected back to us.

If your Twin engaged in substance abuse, gambling, giving himself to no-good women, lying, ext., these are behaviors and things that were most likely there before you met him. You may or may not have made them worse depending on how you responded to him triggering you. Many Twins already had trauma, fears, and other things before meeting each other. It is not that Twins cause each other to behave bad. But thankfully, the Twin Soul connection is on an automatic ascension path. Soul Twins have the opportunity to change their lives around.

But since the both of you have met, you pushed your Twin to go inside and do what he has had trouble doing all along. You flashed the light on everything that he has been holding onto and things that need to change. You exposed everything that isn't good for them and everything that IS good for them so they could begin working on themselves. You may have felt like your Twin hated you, didn't like you, or didn't want to be with you. But you did the one thing that no other woman can do for him, you showed every part of his being to himself. You are his road map to a better him. You are the flashlight that allow him to see his dark place so he know what he can do to free himself. Only he can free himself.

If the DM/Runner is truly toxic or completely closed off, when the DF/Chaser stops chasing them, the DM/Runner will be thrown into DNOS (Dark Night Of The Soul). They will be purged and freed of all of their traumas, fears, and blockages. In this situation, it is important to know that if the toxic DM/Runner attempt to come back, the DF should not feed or enable bad behavior.

## QUICK QUESTIONS

***"How do I get my Supposed 'Twin' to stop chasing me?"***
You can't make someone stop chasing you. Chasing is the result of being attached to someone, mixed with some level of fear or anxiety of loss, conflict, or third party situations. Your Twin likely feels intense feelings for you and a magnetic pull toward you. If someone feels or think the person they love is out of reach, distant, may abandon them, or is involved with someone else, this can cause them to chase. It can also be the result of manipulation.

If you don't want you Twin to chase you, then you need to set boundaries. You need to verbally tell them that you don't enjoy them chasing after you and why. It does not have to be stated in a way that sound hurtful or mean. You are doing this for the purpose of allowing your Twin to know they do not have to chase after you to keep you interested in them, or to keep you in their life.

***"My Supposed 'Twin' is toxic and treats me poorly but doesn't want to acknowledge it, what should I do?"*** That is a stressful situation. It is frustrating when someone is on bad behavior but does not want to admit or acknowledge that. Stand up for yourself. It does not matter if they are your

Twin or not. It does not give them a free pass to mistreat you. Don't accept their poor treatment anymore. Even if they all of a sudden try to come back, stand your ground. Just because someone return, or say they have changed, does not mean they have actually changed.

### *"How do I get over my Soul Twin?"*
I think all Soul Twins have tried to get over their Twin at some point in their journey. With other connections, it is possible after some time and effort to get over someone. But the Twin Soul connection does not allow this. Years, decades, and even lifetimes can pass, and still you will have a connection with your Soul Twin. You could jump into another relationship, get married to someone else, or have other sexual partners and still feel the connection with them.

Don't try to get over your Twin. Many have tried, and all have failed. Those who have attempted to get over their Twin didn't do anything but fight and wrestle with something they can't get rid of. Instead, learn to live with the connection. Not matter what energy you feel from them, the dreams, energy, or magnetic pull, you have to become stable and secure within yourself. Attempting to wrestle with or get over your Twin can actually cause you to feel them more. It can make the connection more intense. You cannot run from yourself.

Trying to get over your Twin is like trying to break yourself. Your Soul Twin is YOU in another body. Let the connection take its course. If your Twin is toxic or on bad behavior, still, attempting to run from the connection and 'get over them' won't do much but create confusion and frustration.

### *"Does the Runner feel the same way for the chaser as the chaser does for them?"* Since Soul Twins are one soul, the Twins feel the same way about each other. There is only one soul, one emotion, one mind. But I understand how DF/Chasers don't always see it that way. If their Twin is not displaying love for them, the DF assume that their DM does not feel the same way. This is even more true if the DM/ engage others romantically and sexually, but not their DF.

It is not uncommon for Twins to hide their feelings or keep their heart from their Twin. This can confuse the other and make it difficult for them to know how you feel. If you love your Twin, they love you as well. If you want your Twin to be in your life and open up, they feel the same way. But it cannot seem like that if their behavior is contradictory to yours.

### *"Does the runner feel when the chaser stops chasing?"*
Just as when the Chaser feel when the Runner stop running, the Runner does feel when the Chaser stop chasing. Twins are ONE soul, not two, a dozen, or five. There is only one soul. So as the soul awakens, it realize that it has attempted to run from or chase after its Self. There is no need to run from or chase after your Self. Only realization is needed. So at this point, both the

Twins become secure and stable enough to eliminate the running and chasing behavior.

When the Runner stops running, the DF will feel like she has lost desire and need to chase the DM/Runner. She may also start running at some point, and then settle into being self-secure and stable. The Twins commonly swap between running and chasing, at least once during their journey. When the Chaser stops chasing, the Runner gain a sense of relief, as if a huge weight has been lifted off their shoulders. But this is not always pleasant. Many, DM/Runners feel hurt, lost, and abandoned after their Chaser stops chasing. Some attempt to go back to their chaser because those feelings become so intense, they have to make sure their DF is still around. This can cause cycles of running and chasing, and the Twins swapping roles (the original chaser runs, the original runner chases, and they swap back and forth).

***"Does the runner also experience repeat numbers, synchronicities, intense dreams, and telepathy as the chaser does?"*** All Soul Twins will see synchronicities, repeat numbers, have dreams of their Twin, and experience telepathy. It is all part of the soul journey and ascension. But just because they see them, does not mean they recognize what and why they are seeing them. The Runner experience all of these things, but they may not know why.

# SECTION NINE
## 'CHASING' OR SOMETHING ELSE?

### FEMININE ENERGY COMPREHENSION

I describe feminine energy as 'substance'. I use the Divine Gate to represent the Feminine. I describe masculine energy as ' action' or 'motion'. Put the two together and what do you get? Energy in motion. Substance in motion. The feminine energy is also foundation. The masculine energy build on top of this foundation. As anyone who has built a house or designed an automobile, they know that there has to be a foundation, some sort of structure. Masculine energy is structure. The feminine energy by itself is raw, uncontrolled energy. Like electricity, there has to be a circuit board which electricity can flow through for that electricity to be useful and not destructive.

The Masculine and Feminine is ONE energy. It is just that the ONE energy is expressing its Self in two ways. You cannot separate masculine and feminine energies. They are ONE, and function as One. Attempting to separate them cause destruction, imbalance, disharmony, and stagnancy. In the same way, men and women are created to function as ONE. The man represent the Masculine, and the woman represent Feminine. Children are a mix of their father and mother. They are the Masculine and Feminine mixed genetically. Therefore, we all have a mixture of masculine and feminine energy to some degree. This is true, even though women tend to have more feminine energy, and men more masculine energy in their natural state. A healthy man will have mostly masculine energy, with a small amount of feminine energy, and a healthy woman will have mostly feminine energy, with a small amount of masculine energy.

Although men are masculine and women are feminine in their natural and healthy states, it is possible for the energies to become reversed. When this happen, men have too much feminine energy. They begin to behave more like women and lack a sense of strength, logic, self-guidance, and productivity. They can also appear to lack ambition, don't stand up for themselves, are easily annoyed, and emotionally reactive. Likewise, when women have too much masculine energy, the begin to behave more like men. Women with too much masculine energy can become very destructive, self-centered, manipulative, workaholics, and sexually reckless. Overworking themselves can cause their physical health to deteriorate. They can suffer from depression, unreasonable anger, abnormal menstrual issues, and victim-mentality.

Now just because someone dress, walk, talk, eat, or sit a certain way does not mean they are not in the correct energy. It is difficult to judge one's character, morality, energy, and other things only off how they look. That is not a wise thing to do. Life is complex, people are even more complex. Sometime a man who has too much feminine energy can appear externally to be masculine.

That is until you have been around them long enough. Sometimes a woman who has too much masculine energy can appear very feminine on the outside. That is until you see her behind closed doors, get too close to her (emotionally, sexually, ext.), and or attempt to take the lead on anything.

But when men are in the masculine energy and they are healthy, we see the strong, confident, leading, logical, and productive beings they were designed to be. When women are in the feminine energy and are healthy, we see gentle, submissive, confident, passionate, and productive they were created to be. When society has a lot of masculine men and feminine women, society is well structured with lots of love, fun, and production. When society has a lot of feminine men and masculine women, society lack appropriate structure and there can be a lot of hatred, drama, destruction, and lack of production.

## THE 'CHASER' TWIN

Many of the female Twins call themselves and each other the Soul Twins. They are also commonly called the Chaser Twin, due to many of the male Twins running from them and the Twin Soul connection. Many DFs have taken the masculine seat, while the DMs the feminine seat.

But in the Twin Soul collective, the energy can be reversed. This mean that the Twins are not in their correct energy, masculine and feminine. Part of their journey is to take the correct seat and energy: the man in the masculine/soul energy, and the woman in the feminine/Earth energy. This is more balanced. This does not mean that women are not soulful and men lacking grounding. We all have both aspects. Anyone who has been involved in any spiritual group, religious practice, ext. know very well that women can be very soulful.

Men need to sit in the soul seat so that they can be led by The Most High, and so they are balanced with their innate masculine energy. Women need to sit in the Earth seat closer to the Earth, so that they are balanced with their innate feminine and emotional energy. Too much masculine mixed with Earth is no good, just as too much feminine mixed with soul is also no good. There need to be balance within and balance between men and women for love, truth, harmony, fun, and productivity to reign in society.

## WHAT IS CHASING

No, chasing someone as usually mentioned in the Twin Soul community and other circles is not necessarily chasing someone physically. Unless someone took your purse, they are running from the police, or they dropped something of theirs, there is no need to chase after someone. People don't physically chase other people just because. There has to be a reason and a cause. Someone can chase after another person for a relationship, validation, or because they feel entitled to that person.

In the Twin Soul collective, it is commonly seen as the female DF Twins who chase their DM. this can be for a variety of reasons. Every Twin's journey and experience is different. Chasing usually happen because we have needs or wants for certain things. But if there is a degree of difficulty, challenge, or distance from being able to obtain those things, chasing can happen. This cause someone to direct their energy, time, and attention toward the object or person of their desire. They can become attached.

When women chase, usually it is because they have found a man they are naturally attracted to. Or, he behave in a way that is masculine. The man catch her attention. But if he is unavailable, not wanting a relationship, or he seem to not be interested, some women find themselves chasing after him. But the inverse can be true. The man could also simply be toxic, abusive, and careless, and some women might still find themselves chasing after him. When women (men included) chase, it can be for a variety of reasons.

Chasing should not be confused with calling, texting, asking someone out, investing time (or energy) in a relationship or someone. This is not chasing, but considered investing (aka pursuing). It is good to invest in your relationship or person of desire. Pursuing carry a different kind of energy. It is not done in fear, from codependency, or being manipulated. Pursuing is healthy, but chasing isn't, depending on the situation and people involved. Remember, people and relationships are complex.

**DF/SOUL TWINS MIGHT CHASE DUE TO:**
- Wanting to feel Loved
- Wanting to give love
- Insecurities
- Fear
- Attachment (not necessarily bad)
- Trauma/baggage
- Codependency/neediness

# FEMALE TWINS ENDING STALKING BEHAVIOR

I didn't realize the commonality of stalking between Twins until being involved in the Twin Soul community for the first few months. It seemed like most of the stalking was done by the DMs. Again, this is strange, as how can someone ignore you but stalk you? After some more time, I also learned that some DFs stalk as well. If Twins are not together (aka separation), this can certainly happen a lot. Because one or both Twins run from the connection (but they still love each other and feel the connection), they wonder what their Twin is doing.

They wonder if their Twin is involved with someone else or if they have moved far away. Stalking through social media, in the metaverse, and in person have been the three most common ways I have heard of Twins stalking. But when the Runner Twins abandon their DFs and jump into other connections, this can trigger anxiety and fear in the DF. The DF may stalking their Twin to know their whereabouts and what they are doing. Has your Twin stalked you? Have you stalked them?

The thing with stalking is that it usually does not help the connection with your Twin. This is especially true if your Twin know that you are stalking them. As much as you may want to know what your Twin is doing and where they are, stalking can never replace communication and conflict resolution. If your Twin has blocked you or mentioned they don't want anything to do with you, still, stalking won't help the situation. It would be more beneficial to accept the loss or rejection and move on rather than chasing and stalking.

## CHASERS END OVERWHELM AND PAIN

Many Chasers also experience a lot of overwhelming emotions, energy, and pain during the Twin Soul journey. This is common in the beginning, but with some Twins, can last years or decades. They might even go through cycles of pain and overwhelm. The overwhelm can be from a variety of things. But the connection is very intense. This intensity is not like with karmics and soulmates. The intensity cause triggering, purging, and even kundalini awakening. It can be physically, emotionally, and energetically painful.

In the beginning, after meeting my Supposed 'Twin', I found myself overwhelmed by the intense body sensations, dreams, repeat numbers I seen EVERYWHERE. I wanted to focus on learning how to invest and make money in the stock market and cryptocurrency. I wanted to concentrate my mind on a new business idea I was in the middle of planning. But for some reason, this woman could not get out of my head. Hearing her voice in my head, feeling her body sensations, and not wanting to sleep so I wouldn't dream of her plagued my days. Fortunately I found a way to bring myself above water.

Do you know why you were in so much pain when your Twin blocked you, slept with another person, or abused you? It is because you met yourself. It is because your emotions became so intense toward this person, you lost control. Their behavior did not improve, or got worse. Or they simply seemed inhibited, and did not reciprocate the same level of love, respect, and attention you wanted. This is painful. Then you were not able to move on from them or get them out of your head. Your Twin also triggered you often and you may have went through a kundalini awakening. Your life flipped upside down, or things all of a sudden changed. This all can be overwhelming and painful. If you were married or unable to be with your Twin physically when you met them, this is another complication.

As a DF, part of the journey for you is to get back into the feminine energy. That is your safe, happy, and secure place. You have to get into a place where you do not chase after things and people who do not love you or respect you. You have to get to a place where your emotions don't dictate your actions. You have to BE and not *react*. You have to consciously choose to not allow your trauma, confusion, or insecurities to cause you to be hurt more by someone who is unavailable or toxic.

Fortunately, women are strong creatures, and they eventually mature. They realize that just because they love someone, that person may not necessarily love them back. They learn that they can do a lot good for someone, yet that person may not reciprocate. That good thing about most DFs is that they actively seek to learn what it is they are experiencing. They want to know what it all mean, and why they are going through it. The internet in the Twin Soul corner is filled with endless questions and discussions from female Twins. They want to share their experience and gain more knowledge.

Just as the DMs were initiated on a soul journey, so have the DFs. It may not have happened the way you like or imagine. Most soul journeys and initiations don't. They can be painful, wreck one's life, and last years, or even decades. Especially as a woman, this can seem like death, since women tend to be more emotional than men. The emotions mixed with all the pain, lose, and confusion can create a lot of overwhelm.

**NOTE FOR DMS:** What do chasers experience on the journey? Most of the DFs just want their DM to come back to them. They want to enjoy life with their Twin. They want to see their DM better themselves. The DFs don't mean any harm, even if they have their own problems. Many of the DFs had childhood trauma in the form of abuse, abandonment, loss, controlling/manipulative parents, toxic relationships, or other unpleasant things. No woman wants to live her life in those things. Your DF likely does not hate you. But just as you might not understand the connection, so can they.

Even if you had problems with your DF, running and attempting to make things work with someone else isn't the right way to handle things. If you are able to contact your DF, they likely want to hear from you. If you know you have done or said things to cause them pain, they will likely accept an apology. Your DF is not your enemy. If you blocked them, please unblock them. Blocking your DF does not make things better for you or her.

## WHEN HE RAN

It has happened to me a few times. There be a woman who I meet, and happen to enjoy talking with. In the beginning, everything is wonderful, then she disappear. Now I am 6'3" and dress well. I'm obviously in my masculine energy with a little feminine energy on top as a bonus. I have been told all my life by so many people that I am handsome, easy to get along with, funny, and a hard worker.

To any person, i would sound like a catch for a woman. But truth be told, and I have heard this a few times, that I seemed too good to be true, I overwhelm the woman (she is not used to someone like me), or she liked me TOO much, and felt out of control of her emotions. These things cause them to run. But I don't and never have chased women. I have never had to, and don't ever plan to. But this phenomena is very interesting and deserve a mention, as it might help you in overstanding.

Being too good of a catch can actually cause people to run or pull away. If they have any trauma, been abused, experienced parental abandonment, cheated on, or have other similar issues, this negatively impact their emotional health and mentality. Because of these, they might go through years being involved with romantic and sexual partners which are no good for them. They may have thought or felt it was normal. But these partners and relationships create further trauma, baggage, and emotional instability. Mix that with multiple partners, and now you have someone who cannot be with someone who isn't toxic or abusive. They have lived in toxic and abusive relationships. It is normal to them. The person can become toxic and abusive and may not realize it.

When they meet someone who is not toxic or abusive, but is in their correct energy (masculine or feminine), they can't trust if this person is hiding something, if they are pretending, or they simply don't feel good enough for them. They might not see them as a good person to be with due to their upbringing or traumatic relationships.

Men in our society especially deal with these issues due to the destruction Feminism, Women's Empowerment, and the MeeToo movements have created in men's upbringing as boys, in the work place, and even in the dating market. They lose trust for women and begin to think that women are out to destroy their life and peace. The men begin to engage in toxic and abusive behavior as well. It is likely your Twin is repelled by your feminine energy due to these reasons. He may not feel good enough for you. He might have unresolved trauma and baggage preventing him from being with you. He may not be in his masculine energy and not allowing himself to be with you.

As a female Soul Twin, know that you are different in a way from karmic and soulmate women. There is just a different charm with Soul Twin women. It is beyond how they dress, boob size, or anything like that. As a Twin Soul woman, you are naturally eye-catching, and can hold the attention of a room without trying. Twin Soul women are always attractive and carry a mysterious energy that isn't known in any other kind of woman. DMs can see and sense this, and this can cause them to run. The DMs likely felt like they met a woman they didn't know what to do with. Their DF was too different and unique, unlike other women they have met in their lives. Twin Soul women also tend to be strong-hearted AND strong-minded. They are intense people.

All of the Twin Soul women I have met in person are like this. There is not one who wasn't mysterious, intense, or exciting in some way. The DMs also have these in their own way. The Twin Soul connection is truly unique, intense, and life-changing.

## THE NON-RUNNER DM

It is easy to assume that if a man is not chasing or pursuing you, that he isn't interested. Social norms, entertainment, and even parents could teach relationship and mating dynamics which are not normal. You may have misunderstood something that is natural but not widely taught or known. That is the fact that men are not supposed to chase women, but women are supposed to pursue the Alpha men, the males who follow The Most High. Because men were created to seek The Most High and build a life for himself and future family, his time, energy, and attention MUST be directed toward those things. If a man's time, energy, and attention is directed and focused on chasing women, he will be turned away from The Most High, and not have built or established anything for himself and future family.

Men were created to keep their focus and attention on The Most High, and not on women. The Divine Hierarchy was abandoned in society in the 1900s and early 2000s. Things were set up so that men were made to chase women and women were made to withhold from the men, or turn from them entirely. This is contradictory to the Divine Hierarchy. It doesn't matter if you disagree with the Divine Hierarchy, that is how it is. The Divine Hierarchy is not man-made, but set in place for good purpose.

When society is set up contradictory from the Divine Hierarchy, great stress and conflict arise between men and women. This trickle down to the children, and the children begin engaging in harmful behavior to themselves and others. This is learned behavior they observe between their parents as well as other men and women. Since men are created to keep their focus on The Most High and not on women, it is common for women to assume some men are not interested in them. Or the women constantly attempt to get the attention of certain men. If they are unable to get or keep certain men's attention, they deem him as being uninterested. It is important to not confuse a man who has his energy directed toward The Most High or making the world a better place from a man who is running. Men don't run from woman. If a man is running from a woman, that has more to say about what the woman is doing and not the man.

## DIVINE FEMININES END TOXICITY

It isn't only the DM's responsibility in keeping the connection alive and healthy. Relationships and connections are a two-way street. Both Twins have a part to play, and I have seen and known many DFs to actually be the cause of WHY their Twin is running or unresponsive (but are not aware of this).

It is possible for a DF or female Twin to be 'toxic'. We always say "no one is perfect" but does that only pertain to half the population (men)? I have met a few DFs in person, and even more online. I know from engaging with many DFs that it IS possible for problems and issues to come from the DFs. Some DFs claim their DM 'ran', when he never ran, he simply left due to undesirable circumstances or her bad behavior. These caused me to look at Twin Soul connections and problems with more scrutiny, below surface.

Some DFs DO have an abusive, unavailable, or toxic DM. Their lesson to learn is not to try and make their DM come back and to not put up with their bad behavior. It is to break the attachment to their toxic or abusive DM. This is because if the DM is like that, the DF feed and enable the DM's bad behavior by loving them, desiring them, and wanting to be with them. The DF in this situation has to ask herself, why does she love someone so intensely who is abusive, ego-driven, manipulative, emotionally unavailable, or toxic?

After some time, some DFs get tired of the whole situation with their DM and might attempt to jumping into other relationships. Although leaving a toxic or abusive relationship can be a good thing, it is not healthy to jump into another relationship just to get over someone. Although entering a relationship or connection with a new person can give us a new start, it is not healthy to do this while having baggage, trauma, and influence from another person. It is important to cleanse ourselves emotionally and energetically after leaving every relationship with every person. Not doing so bring residue and baggage from previous relationships and invite them into the new one with the new person, and the cycle of toxicity and abuse is carried over.

It is common to see on the internet that Soul Twins are supposed to separate. But most of the time the separation is from common problems and mistakes made in love, dating, and relationships. It is not because they are supposed to separate. Just because someone is a Soul Twin does not mean they are perfect. It does not mean they are free from making mistakes or mishandling relationships with other people.

Some DFs and Chasers feed the toxicity in relationships by enabling bad behavior. Although they may claim their Twin is toxic, abusive, cheating, or unavailable, many fail to see how attached to and in love they are with the same person. This is not healthy. There is nothing wrong with a woman being attached to and in love with a man. But when that man is engaged in destructive, abusive, and toxic behavior, her enabling also say a lot about her. It is important to not assume your DM is toxic or treating you bad because a previous lover hurt you. It is important to not assume your DM is ignoring you just because you hear from so many other DFs about their Twin ghosting or blocking them.

Treat your Twin Soul journey as yours. It is unique. If you are attached to your Twin and they are obviously not healthy, you need to redirect your emotions, time, and energy away from them. But if your DM is doing good for himself and others, there is nothing wrong with being in love with him. Your heart is safe there.

## WHEN THE DF IS INNOCENT

The reality is that not all men can be trusted with your heart or body. Unlike when you were a little girl and the world looked colorful and fun, the real world has men who wish to take advantage of women. Many DFs have experienced some degree of emotional or physical abuse, molestation, rape, or manipulation when they were younger. This commonly was from a family member or one of their first romantic/sexual partners. Fewer may have experienced one or more of these devastating things from a complete stranger.

I don't care what anyone say, it is NEVER moral, appropriate, or justified to physically or emotionally abuse, rape, molest a girl or woman. But unfortunately in the real world, there are men who think otherwise. This has been a cause of mistrust, anger, and heartbreak for many DF Twins. By the time they meet their DM, they have baggage, trauma, trust issues, or fragmentation from other men. This can cause issues between Soul Twins regardless how good or bad of a man their DM is. Although specifically unknown, my Supposed 'Twin' suffered some kind of trauma from earlier in *her* life which caused *her* to have huge anger and distrust toward men. This severely impacted our connection. I saw the situation as something I could not do anything about when I met *her*. I figured the best thing for me to do was leave and not bother *her*. Although trauma and baggage should never be wished upon someone, some people don't want to change or be helped. If *she* didn't want to be helped, I wasn't going to attempt to. I left it up to *her* to do something about her own issues, while I put time and attention on changing my own problems.

## RELATIONSHIP AND ONENESS

*"They are going to meet each other this weekend. He randomly called her and asked her out. They are going to be in Union!"* First, there is no such thing as separation. What you really mean is a relationship, or romantic situation. Since Soul Twins are one soul, there cannot be a marriage. People confuse what they see happening physically with Soul Twins and use that to determine if they are in Union or not. Union is not a relationship. Union is not about getting married. Union is Oneness Consciousness™. If Soul Twins are only in Union if they are in a relationship, married, or having sex, then that would mean whenever they divorce, separate, or are not sexually active with each other, they get taken out of Union. That is crazy!

No! Union is a state of consciousness where you experience and know that everything is One. You and your Soul Twin are One. You no longer see your Twin as 'someone else', 'another person', or 'someone I need to marry'. You come to the realization that nothing you do will separate you from this person. You no longer attempt to run from them or chase after them. You no longer attempt to jump into other relationships, marriages, or sexual endeavors to try and get over them or get them to chase you. Everything changes. Just because Twins are in a relationship or married does not mean they are in Union. Most Twins meet their Twin and enter a relationship, have sex with them, or get married several times before breaking up or getting a divorce.

But Twins can be in Union while not being a relationship, not having sex, or not being married. That is because Union is a state of consciousness, not a relationship, sexual, or marriage status. It is important to not get caught up in the internet hype or what is socially popular. It Twins want to be in a relationship or get married, they have to choose that, just like anyone else.

**GUEST** – *"You met some Twins in person? How was that like?"*

**MR.J** – "Meeting Twins in person has been an eye-opening, mysterious, but very informative experience. It has changed everything I thought I initially knew about Soul Twins. I have only met one DM in person, but a few DFs in person. As with normal people, things are good in the beginning, then problems arise...Unfortunately I can't share what I experienced with them for legal reasons. Sometimes people think you are talking about them and get offended or triggered and before you know it, you are standing in front of a judge."

## 'CHASERS' CAN EASE THE LONGING

What is the longing for your Twin you feel? This is a combination of attachment, the magnetic pull of the connection, and lack of Oneness Consciousness™ mixed together. Attachment is normal, and can happen to anyone. It is not necessarily a bad thing, depending on the people and situation. We all can experience a magnetic pull to some people, especially those we are close to. Although the magnetic pull with Soul Twins is different. Because Soul Twins are one Soul, there will always be some degree of magnetic pull toward each other. Magnetic pull does not mean chasing, it is just a sensation of energy. But the lack of Oneness Consciousness™ is the major player in the longing you feeling. Separation Illusion™ in Soul Twins can run strong.

The Soul wants to find its way to Oneness Consciousness™. This is the main source of longing. It is not that you long to be in a relationship with your Twin. That is more rooted in hormones and attachment. But deeper down, at the core, you actually long for Oneness Consciousness™. Once Twins reach the surrender stage, the Soul has realized Oneness Consciousness™. The Soul no longer chase or run from its Self. The Twins realize that running from or chasing after their Twin is useless. They ease the running and chasing and allow life to happen on its own. They find peace, stability, and security within themselves. The Soul is back home, in Union Consciousness™, and with Source frequency.

You can ease the longing by not resisting or fighting the energy and emotions you feel. Later in this guidebook, you will learn how certain healing and meditation practices can further ease longing, chasing, and running energy.

## QUICK QUESTIONS

*"Does communication, sending texts, and calling my Supposed 'Twin' make me needy or a chaser?"* Communication doesn't make anyone needy. Communication is NECESSARY for healthy friendships, family connections, romantic/sexual relationships, and marriage. We have been lied to about the whole 'no text back' thing. It has nothing to do with not looking needy or easy.

As far as messaging him, as I always say, always express how you feel. Not communicating is always worse than communicating something, whether you feel it comes off as needy or being easy. When you text or contact him, it's important to look at it from the perspective of simply communication and conversation, and nothing more.

*"I'm the chaser, but I blocked him and decided to go on a date with someone else. But why is my Supposed 'Twin' running? I can't trust to open myself up to them I don't want to get hurt. I would rather not focus on him or the connection."* It is very clear here that you do need to focus on yourself, but it is not because of your Twin but because you are exhibiting selfish behavior. It's reasonable to block people who are attacking you or causing you, but to block someone just because you want to focus on yourself? Do that, and save him the stress of engaging with someone who is selfish. You did the right thing. Go and focus on yourself, and learn to not be selfish.

The spiritual community has preached this too much, that we have to leave people and not focus on people in order to reach enlightenment. This is far from the truth. In fact, doing these things will hinder your ascension progress and only cause more abandonment trauma. Have you even considered how he will feel or think of you when he finds out you blocked him? Blocking people is rarely a reasonable way to dealing with issues with other people. Now, if he did or said something that caused you harm, he wouldn't be able to come back and apologize and make amends because you have him blocked!

It is likely he is 'running' because you blocked him then went on a date with someone else. This behavior is not attractive to a man in any way. This is what push men away. But if this is your Twin, they are only reflecting you back to yourself. The fact that you blocked him, went to be with someone else, and don't want to open your heart in fear of getting hurt is reflected in him as running behavior.

*"Is it possible the runner wasn't running but the chaser wanted their Twin to chase after them? Their Twin didn't chase after them, so they called them a runner."* This is more common than you think, especially if the female Twin has kept her heart closed, or held back because she wanted her Twin to chase after her or initiate things. This surely isn't the way to go about any kind of connection or relationship. The whole time they think their Twin is running and doesn't love them, they actually have not invested much into the connection, and their DM thinks they simply aren't interested in them, later to find out the DM had great love for her and wanted to be with her. But whatever she was doing (keeping her heart closed off, little to no contact unless the DM initiated, clinging to a different man to see if her DM would get jealous and chase her, ext.) caused him to think she didn't want him, she was uninterested, or she simply wanted to be with someone else.

I see this happen a lot with DFs, and sadly the same dynamic has caused years and decades of unnecessary running/chasing, confusion, and miscommunication with some Soul Twins. We have got to start being open, honest, and direct. Running, pulling energy away, and closing off the heart doesn't work very well does it?

### "How do I get my Supposed 'Twin' to stop running?"

For one thing, you can't change someone else's behavior. You can influence their behavior, but ultimately they choose. Second thing, if your Twin is running, that could be for a variety of reasons. But understand that one or both Twins running from the connection happens at some point, and for a certain time with all Soul Twins. But I suggest not to find a way to get them to stop running. Instead put your attention and focus on your ascension.

### "How do I attract my Supposed 'Twin'?"

Your Soul Twin is the polarized opposite of your Self. You attract them by being in the correct energy (feminine for women, masculine for men), and by your ascension. Your ascension and the raising of your energy is a conscious choice and effort. You have to put in the work. As you raise your energy, you will meet your Twin at some point during your ascension path. It is going to happen, don't force it or look for it. Just focus on your ascension and it will happen as a result.

### "How do I move on from my runner DM?"

If your Twin is toxic or unavailable, definitely don't chase after them. It is reasonable to not chase after your Twin, but put your time and energy into bettering yourself and your life. If you want to move on from them, understand that you will still think about them and feel their energy regardless. You want to get to a place where you are not actively attempting to think of them. You are not affected by their energy, thoughts, or choices. This is how you move on. It is a process. It is not about getting into a relationship with someone else or attempting to keep them at arm's length.

### "If unknowingly you have caused your twin a lot of hurt, which made them run, and there is no communication at all, how can you apologize and amend things?" If there is no communication then you can't apologize or amend anything. But if you can leave a message of some sort, then you can leave an apology message. If they have blocked you or you don't have a way of contacting them, then you will have to release the situation. You can say their name and speak out loud that you apologize. Then simply remove your mind and emotions from the situation. Forgive yourself. Also, whatever you did or said to cause them a lot of hurt, change your behavior. Look at it as a learning lesson.

### "I feel pulled in by my Supposed 'Twin'. I have tried to get rid of the feeling, but nothing works. Why does it hurt to miss your Soul Twin?" The pain you feel is most likely because you are trying to get rid of the feeling, mixed with feeling the pull. You are trying to avoid and run from the connection, so that is where the pain comes from. If you relax and let the connection be and do as it pleases, you won't be burdened by it.

*"Is it only the Runners who go through an awakening? Or do the Chasers go through an awakening too?"* If the chaser no longer thinks of the runner, this is a good sign the chaser has surrendered. But the DM and DF go through the awakening together. It is a joint happening. The Chaser come to ask themselves why they are chasing after someone who is emotionally unavailable, no contact, always going after someone else, or is toxic. They will realize that Chasing the runner is a waste of time and energy. The Chaser may very well get tired of chasing! The person might not even be their Twin. They could be chasing anyone! Maybe that is why the person doesn't want anything to do with the Chaser.

In other situations, the Chaser is the one who was actually the Runner or toxic one in their relationship. They realize that they have done or said things to cause their Twin harm. They will them attempt to find their Twin. The Chaser is going through an awakening.

*"How can I tell if the person I love that's of high status is my Supposed 'Twin', and what are some signs you get when you're not in Union or have made contact with?"* I'd recommend not mentioning to them, or anyone else that they are your Soul Twin. It won't make a difference or bear any weight at the end of the day. It could actually cause more harm than good. It would be wise to allow them to discover the Twin Soul reality themselves and come to meeting you when the time and place is appropriate. There are things in life we shouldn't force, we are already on track going in the direction we need to go. Just let the ship sail and you will reach the necessary destination. Rather than worry about your Twin and their status, put that energy and time into bettering yourself and your life.

Union is not a relationship. It is Oneness Consciousness™. This is your ascension, making your way back to Oneness Consciousness™ and knowledge of reality. Through Oneness Consciousness™, you realize that your Twin is YOU. There will no longer be a need, urge, or compulsion to chase or run from your Twin, because it will be clear as day that they are you. There is no need to run from or chase your Self.

## NARC BEHAVIOR EXPOSED

It is unwise to assume that mental illnesses are NARC behaviors are gender based. Mental illnesses and NARC behaviors can happen in either gender. As much as many female Twins claim that their Twin is toxic and a NARC, it is possible for some female Twins to have NARC behaviors and mental illnesses. This put a different spin on the Twin Soul connection because in society, it is usually seen as men having mental illnesses, while females are excused for their NARC behaviors. Just because someone is a Soul Twin, Twin Flame, or soulmate does not make them free from mental illness.

Many Twins who have a mental illness or NARC behaviors find that the connection with their Twin is difficult, stressful, or impossible for them to be together and stay together. Mental illnesses and NARC behavior in some female Twins is a cause of DMs running and not wanting to be with their Twin. Some mental illnesses cause erratic and or 'backwards' behavior which make being with them and around them problematic. This is beyond something like ADHD. The DMs simply don't want to deal with their Twin's bad behavior.

On the other hand, if a DF has a mental illness or NARC behaviors, this could be a cause for her to run or feel insecure about the connection. It is strange to her that she is so in love with and attracted to someone in a way she has never with anyone else. But because of her conditions, she doesn't feel good enough for the connection. Or she might do or say things which she know hurt her Twin or cause issues, but her Twin may not know of (or the full extent) of her conditions.

If you are a DF with any mental health issues, it is important to relay that to your Twin so that they are aware. It is also important to be careful doing this, depending on your Twin. Some people take other people's conditions as a means to control, manipulate, or bully them. If you possess NARC behaviors, you likely won't identify as having them, as generally those whose have NARC behaviors deny that anything is wrong with their behavior.

It is better to seek help for your mental health issues than to chase after someone for love or a relationship. Get your mind and soul right, THEN seek a relationship or mate.

# 'SEPARATION' OR SOMETHING ELSE

What is separation? You may be thinking about seeing two people break up and leave each other. Or you may think about dividing up your laundry and separating them based on fabric or color. But with Soul Twins, separation take on a different meaning. This section will explore some important things to know about what many call 'separation'. You will learn shortly why I put 'separation' in apostrophes.

Usually, in the Twin Soul collective, the term 'separation' is used in a way to describe seeing what look like two different people not physically together. This is incorrect. Because a Twin Soul is one Soul in two bodies, the Soul still being one even after splitting or spreading; there is no separation. Even physically, all of our bodies all come from the same Earth and cosmos. Even physically we are all One entity.

In the Twin Soul community and in some spiritual circles, you will commonly hear 'separation consciousness.' Separation is not consciousness, but an illusion. It is what I call Separation Illusion™. 'Unity Consciousness' is another one. The term *unity* suggest there are two or more which need to be united. So, there cannot be any such thing as unity consciousness if all is one and one is all. There is only Oneness Consciousness™. Oneness Consciousness suggests that all is already one, there is no need to marry or bring things together. What most actually mean when using 'separation consciousness' and 'unity consciousness' is Oneness Consciousness™.

## 'SEPARATION' ILLUSION™

Separation IS an illusion, a false 'reality' you've been programmed to function under. *"How do I know if I'm in separation illusion?"*

- You see everyone as individual and separate
- There is the behavior of treating certain people with more respect than others, as if some are more worthy than others
- If things go bad, you always blame someone else even if you have done or said something to take part in it
- You commit crimes thinking or feeling like you can get away and it won't have any impact on your life or the lives of others
- It is easy for you to always make yourself the most important person in the room and make others less than in your mind
- Every failed relationship is the other person's fault and there is a failure to recognize that you keep giving yourself to the same person (a reflection of yourself) who only looks different on the outside

**GUEST** – *"What about running and chasing? Can that be separation?"*

**MR. J** – "What we perceive as running, chasing, separation, ReUnion, and role reversals are actually the mind processing this reality as separate. It is just our mind. The mind function for survival and attempt to separate and categorize everything. This is the opposite of Oneness Consciousness™. When you are in Oneness Consciousness™, you clearly see that everything and everyone is One. There is no running, chasing, separation, or division. Union, (aka Oneness Consciousness™) happen when we live consciously, so that no matter what happen in the 'external', we remain secure, at peace, and self-sufficient."

## TWIN SOUL 'SEPARATION'

Some say that all Twins are meant to go through a separation phase, especially one in which the Runner Twin jump into a relationship/marriage, or flings with those other than their Twin. From engaging with other Twins, I have seen this is not always the case. But the majority of DF/Chaser Twins do experience their Twin going to be with someone else at some point in the journey.

**I HAVE FOUND 3 DISTINCT REASONS:**
- Lack of sharing feelings and communication from one of both Twins
- High degree of baggage, trauma, and fear which cause one or both to be afraid of love and being close to someone in fear of being hurt or hurting the other
- One or both Twins have engaged in harmful behavior toward their Twin which caused the other to lash out in return or run

So here, Twins not being together is not because they are *supposed to* separate. One or both Twins decide to abandon or leave their Twin. This behavior is one or both polarities of the Soul attempting to avoid the awakening and ascension process. You cannot avoid the process. All that will happen is that you or your Twin will experience hardship, run into those who cause the same issues, or be pulled back to you and the connection. There is no running, there is no hiding. If Twins want to be together, it shouldn't take excessively long periods of time. A few years is reasonable, but 30 or 40 plus years is just one or both Twins dragging the connection along and resisting coming together for their Divine Purpose. If one or both Twins are married and/or have children with someone other than their Twin, more time is reasonable.

## SOUL TWINS KARMIC DEBT PAID

You have probably heard from some spiritual folk about people having karma. What is karma? Karma is simply consequences (which can be favorable or unfavorable) from our thoughts, choices, and behavior. For every thought, choice, and action, there are consequences. The same is for every relationship in our life. The karma here is shared and mutual between those in the relationship. Relational karma is never one-sided, it doesn't matter who did or did not cheat, or lie, or caused problems. Soul Twins can have karma between other people, as well as with each other. Some believe that Soul Twins are only good people who never do anything wrong and are nothing but love and light.

But that is far from the truth. Again, that is fairytale fantasy thinking and not reality.

All Soul Twins have some degree of karma between each other. It is not uncommon to find Twins who are in conflict with each other, or have done or said harm to the other Twin. This create karma. Since all Twins are on an ascension path, their unfavorable karma need to be ridden. But when Twins meet each other, if they create unfavorable karma between each other, this can put a damper on their ascension. It is important to not create unnecessary conflict with your Twin. The same things which hurt normal people (like cheating, lying, abuse, ext.) will also hurt your Twin and yourself. Do not create unfavorable karma. Treat your Twin with respect and love. If they are toxic or on bad behavior, you can remove yourself from their presence. Never enable bad behavior from anyone, Soul Twin or not.

## ENDING NO CONTACT

Ghosting, blocking, moving away, no reply, denial of feelings, running from intimacy, and other similar actions are common with Soul Twins who do not understand what they are experiencing. This is especially true in the beginning of their journey. Usually it is the Runner who engage these behaviors, but DFs can as well. If their Runner Twin is toxic or on bad behavior, eventually the DF will come to realize their Twin is not changing. At this point, the DF might block their Twin or not reply. They have simply gotten fed up with their DM or Runner's behavior.

It all make sense. The endless life problems, health issues, financial struggles, failed relationships/marriages, traumatic experiences,...we experienced the pain of abandonment, of Separation Illusion™. But Union would be the opposite. It's the most blessed life we can live. You experienced Separation Illusion™ with your Twin, and experienced how horrible it was. You will experience Union and eventually come together with your Soul Twin. You will experience that life can be amazing and wonderful on all levels.

I have seen so many Twins extend their time apart from each other physically beyond what is reasonable. So many Twins get caught up in ego wars, playing the blame game, going no contact, blocking, leaving to be with others, negativity on the internet, hating or being afraid of their Twin. Before they know it, years and even decades have passed, yet they STILL think about their Twin and feel the magnetic pull toward them.

After running from my Supposed 'Twin' just one time (August of 2020) and putting a block on my phone, I can't imagine why and how anyone would want to live through that year after year. I know how painful and difficult the Twin Soul journey can be. But as other Twins have a choice, so do I. I experienced it, and know that it is not worth blocking your Twin. For some reason, when you block them you get this overwhelming energy and feeling that you have done one of the most wrong things in your life. Especially if your Twin find out that you blocked them, knowing the hurt and pain you cause them is unbearable.

Don't make this mistake. NEVER block your Soul Twin. It will just make matters worse and keep the two of you apart from each other.

After removing the block, I did try to reach out to my Supposed 'Twin' but *she* had taken down *her* social media, would not contact through phone, and I couldn't find a way to contact *her*. So I just accepted it for what it was and started to really get myself and life together. I knew there would come a time, sooner or later, we would regain contact with each other, and I wanted to have matured and ascended since the last time we interacted. If *she* ever did want to reach out to me, *she* would *see* I took the block off and it's safe for *her* to contact me. I decided to keep my phone unblocked permanently no matter how bad things might get. I'm not blocking *her* out any more.

## THE PAIN OF 'SEPARATION'

The physical and emotional pain of missing your Soul Twin is overwhelming. This is especially true in the beginning when you meet them and first separate. It is a horrible feeling. But eventually, all Twins come to learn that they were never separated, and not meant to be separated. They will understand that whenever they attempt to harm or separate from their Twin, they cause themselves and their Twin harm. It is not worth it. During the 'separation' phase, most Twins get lonely. Even though many DF Twins complain about their Twin being with someone else, there is a difference between moving on, and being alone. Most Twins still feel and deep emptiness and loneliness while being separated from their Twin, even while involved with others.

### LONELINESS IN 'SEPARATION':
- Little to no attention
- No sex, or unfulfilling sex
- Others are partnered up and look happier than you do
- Insecurities surface
- Addictions increase
- Dating isn't the same
- Increased stress, depression, and illness

## TWIN SOUL RESEARCH FINDINGS

So what are common things Soul Twins find on the internet when researching what they are experiencing during separation? Let's have a quick look below:

**'SEPARATION'** – This is probably the most searched thing next to "Why is my DM running?" There is just something about being so drawn to someone who you seem have trouble pinning down that makes you wonder why you are separated from them.

**ASCENSION** – Because the Twin Soul journey is a soul journey, eventually you will come across the term 'ascension'. Ascension is simply how souls mature and ascend back to Source frequency, and Oneness Consciousness™. The same way a child mature and grow physically, souls can mature energetically by raising their frequency, harmonizing, and purifying their vibration. This simply mean you will become more conscious and aware of things which less mature souls are not.

**CORD CUTTING** – There is at least one time when all Twins wanted to get rid of the connection they experience with their Twin. There are those who do what is call a Cord Cutting. This simply sever any attachment and energetic cords between two people. This work well with normal people. But with Soul Twins, it does not work at all. In fact, may Twins who have attempted to cut cords with their Twin report that they only felt the connection stronger than before. NEVER cut cords with your Soul Twin. It can also prove deadly, as you'll learn later in this section.

**CARD/PSYCHIC READINGS** – If someone's Twin is unresponsive, they might attempt to get the help of a tarot card reader. It is a form of energetic reading. The reader use energy channeling and cards to gain information about a particular person. It is like being able to look at what is going on with someone, but it is all energetically. It is being able to get information about what is going on in a certain person's life, how they feel about someone, or why they chose to make a certain decision.

**TWIN FLAME COACHES** – Oh God! Anyone who knows me is aware of a great disdain I have for some Twin Soul 'coaches'. I am not normally like that. But I have met so many fake Twin Soul 'coaches' that I cringe hearing anything to do with a Twin Soul coach. Between admitting of not being a real Twin, to lying about being 'in Union', and charging unrealistic money for books and courses have all been common issues with fake Twin Soul coaches. It is nothing more than a money scheme, a way to profit off Soul Twins who don't understand the journey and don't have an appropriate leader. But there are some good Twin Soul coaches who are not about making money. They want to help Twins and share truth about the connection.

Sadly, many Twins become misled and waste large amounts of money (literally) thinking they are finally going to get their Twin to come back. The issue is that the whole Twin Soul journey has nothing to do with being in a relationship with someone. It is not about trying to get someone to come back. It is only about soul ascension and awakening. If it was about a relationship, it could be done with the various people Twins be with sexually and romantically before they met their Twin.

**ENERGETIC CHANNELING** – Not far from tarot card reading, channeling can get the same results, just not using cards. Channelers might use other items, or none at all.

**REINCARNATION AND MEETING THROUGH LIFETIMES** – Commonly mentioned in some spiritual circles, it is about a soul returning to Earth to continue Earth school. But Twins can and do meet each other while in Earth schools. But also understand that there is not multiple life times. There is only One life. It is just that whenever a soul returns to Earth, the memory is whipped or hidden. When the person is born, they are either unconscious of their previous experiences on Earth, or they don't have the memory.

**AKASHIC RECORDS** – Imagine if you kept getting speeding tickets and citations for running red lights. They would go on your record. Or if you commit a crime, it will go on your record. Well, there is an energetic form of this phenomenon. It is called the Akashic Records. It is a record of actions and events from your previous, current, and future life experiences.

**PAST LIFE REGRESSION** – Those who can gain access to the Akashic Records are called Past Life Regressionists. While wanting to understand who your Twin is and why you met them, a Past Life Regressionist could help you gain knowledge of some actions and events which happened with you and your Twin in previous life experiences.

**PERSONAL PAST LIFE REGRESSION EXAMPLE** – I have full access to the Akashic Records. In a previous life experience, my Supposed 'Twin' and I were 'forbidden' lovers. There were people attempting to keep us apart. It mostly had to do with a mob which had overran the country. If my Supposed 'Twin' and I got together, we would have exposed the mob, and their operations.

**THE RISE OF THE DIVINE FEMININE** – I assume this to have been coined by a Feminist. But there isn't only the rise of the feminine. There is a collective awakening. It is not gender based. If the Masculines make progress in their ascension, it is simultaneously reflected with the Feminines, and vice-versa. The ascension is not separate, but on a collective level. It is important to not get caught up in what people do physically or their exterior behavior to attempt to determine if they are ascending or not.

**REIKI** – If there was a hospital for Soul Twins, it would be a place where reiki is performed. Reiki is a form of energetic healing. It does work and has obvious and lasting effects.

**THE RACO™ SYSTEM** – This is another one commonly found online while researching Soul Twins. There can be some confusion though. Some circles may say there are seven RACOs™, some dozens, and others only two or three RACOs™. During a kundalini awakening I had one time, I saw my own RACO™ system and of two other people. It appears that the RACO™ system only has three centers. It is like there are two openings and between the openings is an energetic center which is the balancing point of the two openings. The middle one is the heart, the upper is the crown RACO™, and the lower is the root RACO™. It also appears that the crown and 3rd eye RACOs™ are part of the same energy center. It is similar to a battery. Charge go in through one part, and out another part, and charge is stored somewhere between the two. There are other, smaller energy centers, but they don't bear the same weight as the three. It might be that some spiritual circles identify the smaller energy locations as major centers. But there certainly is a root, heart, and crown/3rd eye RACO™.

## TRUTH ABOUT 'SEPARATION'

We have to stop preaching separation and complaining about Soul Twins being in separation. Duality and separation DO NOT exist. They are illusions. There is polarity, but that should not be confused with duality. Dual suggests that there are TWO. There is only Oneness, and not two. The ascension is to bring you back to that. Believing in duality and separation, and living by them has caused so much chaos and destruction in the world. Whoever is teaching you to be separate from your Soul Twin and believing in duality is selling you a meal that will make you sick. Eat from truth and you will feel well and alive.

It is just that too many Soul Twins do not have the knowledge and guidance they need to come and stay together. Usually do to similar issues that normal people experience, many Twins find themselves apart from their Twin and struggle to come and stay together.

Most people experience separating from the other person, although it usually happen toward the end and not the beginning of the relationship. Soul Twins experience separating from each other, although it happen in the beginning. Normal people come together to separate, while Twins appear to initially 'separate' but later come together. I know it sound weird, but reality is different than it appear on the outside.

Separation doesn't exist. We only THINK it does because of how the mind works. The mind sees things as separated from the other. But when someone become conscious, they will realize and see that all things really are One. Everything is just One energy. In reality, Soul Twins are never separated. It is one Soul. Not two souls in two bodies. Because it is one Soul, even though there be what look like two bodies, still there is no separation. Even with the bodies, they both come from the same Earth, the same soil, so even physically there is no separation.

What happens after separation will be up to you and your Twin. You both have the power to create the life you want with each other, or to remain separate. Pour your time and energy into being a healthier you and declutter your life of people and things that don't aid in your ascension, happiness, productivity, or peace.

## 'ROLE REVERSAL'

Each Twin has a different experience as far as who is the chaser, and who is the runner. But the role reversal is nothing more than Twins not being in the correct energy when they meet. Sometime after they meet, they eventually get into the correct energy. Men are designed to be masculine, and women feminine. But when society has changed in a way which push women to be masculine, and men feminine, this create a huge issues when the sexes attempt to engage each other. When the sexes are not in their correct energy, the only good thing which can come out of it is nothing.

But if Twins are not in their correct energy when they meet, this will surely cause them to separate. Men generally clash with masculine women, and women generally are not attracted to men who are feminine. This out of place dynamic simply does not work with normal people, and it doesn't work with Soul Twins as well. Are you a woman who is very masculine? It could be the very thing which caused your Twin to run. Are you a man who seemingly struggle to attract your Twin (or any other woman)? You are likely not in your masculine energy.

Women are attracted to masculine men like flies to a lightbulb, but part of being masculine is being assertive and taking the initiative. If you are going to be involved with women sexually or romantically, you need to exercise your masculine energy. Approach women, talk to them, ask them out, check them when they cross your boundaries and when they are on bad behavior, be driven to do great things, and various other things go along with being masculine.

The same is true for women who are feminine. Do you follow your Twin's lead or are you defiant? Are you openly sexual with your Twin or do you withhold and talk about being friends? There need to be a critical examination here with regard to which energy you are in. Feminine women always win, and masculine men make things happen.

We all do have both energies, but yet, men are designed to be in the masculine energy, and women in the feminine energy. Why the Chaser becomes the Runner, and the Runner the Chaser will be different for each set of Twins. But usually, which ever Twin chased first, realizes that chasing someone who is closed off, unresponsive, emotionally unavailable, or toxic is useless and a waste of time and energy. They will just cause themselves more pain and suffering. At this point they give up the chase and 'move on'...not to another relationship or person, but they move on in the sense that they see they have some things to work on. When this happen, the Chaser's life will improve in a lot of ways.

Whichever Twin was the Runner first, they also have their own reasons why they ran. It could be a fear of love, insecurities, overwhelmed by the Chaser's energy (from chasing), issues from the Chaser, ext. But when the Chaser stops chasing the Runner, the Runner will feel the energy of the Chaser leave. Now the Runner is free and does not have the weight of the connection overpowering them. At this point the Runner will miss the Chaser a great deal. The Runner may not necessarily begin chasing their Twin. They will also have things they need to do, trauma to heal, old beliefs that need to be changed or let go, ext. Once the Runner stops running they will eventually go back to their Twin. But the Runner's life usually falls apart while they are running. So they will have things that they will want to do and take care of before they go back to the other Twin for good.

# CORD CUTTING

What is this and why does it even exist? I thought part of the agenda of choosing to become a Twin Soul was to become aware that separation is an illusion? Why do some Twins try to separate from their Twin by attempting to cut the connection?

Cord cutting is very dangerous, and I don't advise anyone to do it under any circumstance. You are not only harming your own life but also the life of your Twin! Cord cutting is painful. I do not want to wake up in the morning or be in the middle of doing something and then feel like I can't breathe or someone is stabbing me in the heart! Let's look at this from a legal perspective. What if you try to cut the cord between you and your Twin and you end up hospitalized and your Twin dies? And what are you going to do when the local authorities engage an investigation and find out from your post online, someone you have messaged, or the psychic you visited to do the cutting with, that you were 'cutting the cord' with the person who suddenly and unexplainably died?

We are supposed to become aware that separation is an illusion. It's the attempting to separate that is painful, not the connection or the fact that you are tied to your Twin. Your Twin is YOU, and you are your Twin, so why attempt to 'separate' yourself from yourself? I don't think it is wise or beneficial to cord cut. You are engaging in a behavior that is harming your Twin and they can be hospitalized or even die from it!

Can we be adults here and approach the Twin Soul journey with a sense of maturity? I know we are healing and learning, but I think trying to cord cut your Twin show a lack of respect for life. Can we be more considerate of our Twin and their life? How do you think your Twin would feel if you cord cut and they suddenly felt horrible? Even worse, they found out it was you; they would trust you even less and see you as a threat and that would cause even more problems. Would you want them to do that to you and you feel sick and like you are about to die?

DO NOT CORD CUT.

Cord cutting...a seemingly great idea, can be deadly.

## CORD CUTTING VS CORD DETACH™ RECIPE

But one thing that does work is what I call the Cord Detach™ recipe. Unlike cord cutting, the Cord Detach™ recipe only remove artificial cords that are attached to someone for the purpose of syphoning energy, or to connect two people energetically for the purpose of manipulation or to destroy their lives. The Cord Detach™ recipe is unable to break the connection with your Twin, but it can detach artificial cords that were hooked to your energetic system. These cords usually come from family, long-term colleagues, particularly romantic/sexual relations, and of course, dark entities. They also come from trauma (opens a wound where a cord can be attached), unhealthy addictions, and misuse of certain practices which involved opening portals for non-physical entities to enter. Cord attachments aren't necessarily bad, they happen naturally in certain situations, but cord attachments can also weigh you down, bring emotional and psychological instability, and drain your energy.

NEVER perform cord cutting or cord cutting rituals. Organic cords behave like biological tissue, and cutting an organic cord (such as with your Soul Twin) will be unsuccessful, or the cord will immediately repair itself and remain connected. Only artificial cords can be permanently removed.

Running and chasing might be simple relationship issues that the Runner doesn't want to deal with, and the Chaser pushes onto the Runner. I think it is normal behavior that we all get fed up with someone after a while when the connection isn't smooth and just don't want to be bothered. We have the habit of pushing all the issues and problems onto the other person whenever trouble arise. No one likes to admit when they haven't been on their own best behavior. And I don't think we behave truly as adults by running from the problems rather than dealing with them in a way that isn't centered around finger pointing or playing the blame game.

## QUICK QUESTIONS

**"Does separation mean the Soul Twin journey is over?"**
Separation is an illusion. You are never separated from your Twin. Even if you are not with them physically, you are still on the awakening and ascension path.

**"If my Supposed 'Twin' doesn't come back, will I get a new Twin?"**
No, you won't get another Soul Twin. You only have one Soul Twin. Your Twin is YOU in another body. There is only One You. All Soul Twins will eventually come together. The dynamic is the way it should be, to 'separate' in the beginning and then come together, rather than to meet and be together only to leave each other. But you and your Twin are always the same Soul. Don't worry about the physical person you see. If the physical person is not in your life, then enjoy your life. If they are with you, then enjoy their presence. Seek to always be at peace and secure within yourself regardless if they are physically there or not.

**"Does God choose when, where, and how Twins experience a ReUnion?"**
Where did you get the idea of ReUnion from? If everything is already One, there can't be a ReUnion. To reunite suggest that things or people where once together and then separated, and then brought back together. Everything and everyone is already One. This is the foundation of the soul journey, to bring us back to Oneness Consciousness™ so that we are aware everything and everyone is already One. There is no separation. All that happens is we lose consciousness of everything and everyone being on, and regain that awareness. But that doesn't mean that things magically separated. They were still One all along.

**"Why are the majority of Twins not physically together?"**
It is important to not get too caught up in the physical person. There is a purpose for the physical as far as incarnation to directly engage this physical reality and procreation. But many Twins are not physically together simply because one or both chose to not be together. Just like with normal people, it has to be a choice to be together physically. God does not have any hand in it. The choice is left to us. But due to common issues and mistakes made by normal people which cause them to not be together, so do many Twins also make the same mistakes and have similar issues.

**"What causes Twins to separate?"**
Each Twin who left their Twin will have their own reason why they left their Twin. But common ones are: lack of or poor communication, cheating, abuse, lying, being unavailable (already married or with someone), not being in the correct energy, not finding their Twin physically attractive, and various other things. Specifically with Twins, triggering, mirroring, and the intense energy can also cause them to separate.

**"What causes Twins to reunite?"**
After Twins have spent some time apart, they both realize that life just isn't any good without their Twin. After attempting to make things work with others, they eventually both realize they are meant to be with their Twin. But some Twins experience a different dynamic, where their Twin was on bad behavior or did not want to be with them. Their life improved when they left the situation and put their focus on bettering themselves.

**"Do runner's always return?"**
Runners always return, eventually. But the important thing to remember is that the journey is not about waiting for the Runner to return. It is a soul journey. You shouldn't try to worry about or force your Twin to come back. Instead, invest the time and energy into your ascension and making your own life better than it was.

**"Terrence, if your Twin is avoiding the connection and running, are you going to date or be with someone else?"** I have been asked this question by a lot of people. After meeting my Supposed 'Twin', I decided I needed to take a few years to focus on the new path The Ahmen Most High laid before me. Everything began changing in my life, in a good way, and I wanted to take full advantage of this. Unfortunately, as my experience has been in life with women, if they don't support the man in his endeavors, they become HUGE distractions, and even liabilities. I mean, the time, energy, and money that a woman who is not supportive would take, all could be directed to transforming my life. Fortunately, I have never been the kind of person to chase after women, or make a woman first priority. So it was easy for me to break the attachment to my Supposed 'Twin' and pull myself out of the mud so that I could focus on things that were actually important.

During the time of meeting my Supposed 'Twin', I was single and not dating anyone. I was in the middle of educating myself on learning how to make money in the stock market and cryptocurrency and coming up with a new business idea. So I decided to take a break from dating or getting involved with women to focus on my ascension and transforming my life. I didn't start getting involved with women again until after I moved to Alabama.

Fortunately, my Supposed 'Twin' isn't the only woman on this planet, and I know that I will always have plenty of options when I choose to be with someone. I know I can date and have fun, but if a woman is going to be with me on a serious level, she is required to support me in my ascension, personal, and business endeavors. I don't want baggage, I don't want a liability, and I definitely don't want a headache. I chose to keep my options open for other women to come into my life. No Shame In The Game™.

**The ending of this section will be combined between the DMs and DFs. It will highlight some issues caused with Soul Twins due to the cycles of running, chasing, and 'separation'.**

## FOR MARRIED/DIVORCED TWINS

Soul Twins meeting each other while one or both are married to someone else is a common issue in the Twin Soul community. Most people won't want to step out of their marriage, especially if the marriage is stable and children are involved. Those who meet someone who is married might not want to get involved since they are off the market. But being a Soul Twin put a different spin on these things.

When a Twin meet their Twin and they are married, walking away from their Twin can pose problems for both. The married Twin wonders why they are so attracted to this person, but they feel like they can't pursue them because they are married. But the other Twin might feel like it would be wrong to pursue a married person, even if they are their Soul Twins. While separated from their married Twin, they feel their Twin all the time and just can't seem to get them out of their head. That magnetic pull is ever strong.

If you are separated from your Twin and they are married, you probably feel like you don't know what to do. You don't want to pursue them and break up their marriage. But then you love them so much and can't get them out of your head. If you are the married Twin, you likely don't want to break up your marriage either to pursue this mysterious person. A common phenomenon I have noticed with married Twins is the dissolution of their marriage with others. It seem like after meeting their Twin, the marriage become stale, unstable, or the marriage was already in trouble. Time after time, divorce eventually was filed by the married Twin to leave their married partner.

You might be thinking that this is good, and now the Twins can be together. But it does not always result in Twins coming together. Some Twins divorce but then their Twin gets married to someone else, enter a new relationship, or no longer want to be with their Twin. Others come together but don't always stay together or get married. DO NOT divorce your partner just to chase after someone you feel like is your Twin, whether they are your Twin or not. But divorces are so common and Twins always end up together. If you choose to divorce, do so at your own risk, I am not a legal professional, lawyer, or marriage counselor.

Some Twins marry each other. But this does not mean they are in Union or Oneness Consciousness™. I have seen some Twins marry each other only to later divorce and separate. It is a reality that is difficult for some to accept. Sometimes they separate while still being married. It is like Twins are supposed to be together regardless of who they are with when they meet, even if one or both is married to someone else. The Twin Soul connection always override all other connections.

## FOR TWINS WITH CHILDREN

It's painful when you have children with someone, and you become separated from them. But when that person is your Twin, you have now been struck in the heart and soul. Your Twin is YOU, and your children are a reflection of you and your Twin. Losing them is seemingly more painful than children with a normal person. Twins can certainly end up in family court. Just as an absent or abusive parent can be traumatizing for children, it is also for the children of Soul Twins. It is important to know that having children on the Twin Soul journey can also create extra problems for your ascension. If you have children under unfavorable circumstances with someone else or your Twin, this can be problematic. But children under favorable circumstances with the right person at a reasonable time can do good for your ascension.

If you have children with your Twin and you both are separated, you will have to resolve the issues so that you can all come back together. If your Twin won't have you around the children for whatever reason, you might have to let the situation go. If you have done or said things to your Twin or children, this may be the cause of the separation from your Twin and children. This is the time to accept that you have done or said things which were harmful in some way. You have to change your behavior, and if possible apologize to your Twin and children for whatever was done or said.

## FOR TWINS WHOSE TWIN IS DECEASED

Probably the ultimate form of separation for some, death for most people is heartbreaking. Living without your Twin can be unbearable for some Twins. Because their Twin is no longer on Earth, there won't be any relationship, sex, children, or marriage to look forward to. But one thing, because the Twin Soul journey is a soul one, and Twins are One Soul, there is still a non-physical connection. You will dream about your Twin a lot, feel their presence, hear them talking to you through telepathy, and even feel them touching your body. But most Twins who I have met whose Twin is deceased somehow are actually more peaceful and secure after their Twin is gone.

# FOR TWINS WHO ARE FAMILY MEMBERS

Family are the first people we meet and engage with. They set the stage for our life experiences. But family isn't always a good experience for some people. Generational curses, conflict between members, and grudges. But what if your Soul Twin is a family member? What if the both of you are not talking and avoid each other? Usually we never have to chase or run after a family member for any reason. But separation does happen between Soul Twin family members. During the separation, the Twins will still think about each other. The high energy, mirroring, and triggering could make it difficult to live in the same household.

You might have to have your own room on the opposite side of the house, or live somewhere else entirely. But as family members and Soul Twins, you will need to resolve whatever issues are there. It is too much to live life with grudges, conflict, and trauma from issues with family members, even more if they are your Soul Twin. Living with your Twin in the same place can be difficult. This is because the energy between Twins can amplify and become very intense when they are near each other. The telepathy is stronger as well as being able to tell where they are at and what they are doing.

# FOR TWINS WITH A LARGE AGE GAP

*"My Supposed 'Twin' is much older than me. She doesn't want anything to do with me." "Why is my Supposed 'Twin' so young and I am much older?"* These are not uncommon questions with Twins who have a large age gap. It is difficult for Twins with large age gaps to come and stay together, even impossible and illegal if one or both are minors. Usually this is because of social conditioning which make it abnormal for a large age gap between two people who are romantic or sexual. Even friends who have a large age gap between each other is unacceptable with some folk. Worse is when others shame those who are much older or younger, or attempt to keep them apart.

This in itself can be a cause for separation with some Twins. One of the Twins don't want to be caught with someone who is much older or younger than them. They abandon the connection. But because they are Twins, they still feel a magnetic pull and intense love for them. In some situations, a third party influence has wedged the Twins apart. The third party does not approve of them being together. In other situations, one of the Twins is a minor, and the other Twin (not wanting any legal issues) run from their Twin.

What to do when you want to be with your Twin, but you are much older or younger than them? What to do if you are much older or younger than them and just can't find yourself being with them? These are important questions to ask.

Whatever you do, NEVER have sex with a minor. If your Twin is a minor, hands off! But if the both of you are of legal age or older then a sit down discussion or phone call might be necessary. A lack of or poor communication is a very common problem which destroy relationships and keep people apart. You and your Twin need to have a talk, make sure both sides are comfortable being with the other, and set some boundaries. *"I understand that but what if their friend or a family member keep them away from me?"* Third party influences can keep people separated or in conflict with each other. This issue will have to be discussed between you and your Twin. It is likely they will have to dissociate from the person who is wedging the two of you apart.

## FOR TWINS WHO ARE A CELEBRITY OR PUBLIC FIGURE

If your Twin is a celebrity or public figure and not with you, you might think you'll never be with them. If they are married or in a relationship with someone, this can prolong separation. What can you do if you are unable to communicate with them? What to do if they do not want anything to do with you? If your Twin is a celebrity, you are looking at a reflection of yourself. They are you in another body. Your Twin has set the bar and standard. One thing you can do is bring yourself up to and even beyond that standard. Put the time and energy into your ascension and bettering your life.

If you are a celebrity or public figure but your Twin is not, there could be an issue here. Even though most people dream of meeting a celebrity, the reality is that many people might become very insecure and not feel good enough if the person they have feelings for is a celebrity. If your Twin is running from you, this is likely the cause. If you are able to communicate or send a message to them, let them know that you do love them and that they don't have to feel like they aren't good enough. But if you are a celebrity and they are not, you both might live in entirely different worlds. Your celebrity status might make it difficult to bring them into your world.

It is also a possibility that you don't want to speak with them or be around them because they are not a celebrity. But then, you can't get them off your mind, and the magnetic pull is ever so strong. You have kept yourself from them and that's why the two of you are not together. Your Twin may very well want to talk to you and be in your life. Just because they are not a celebrity does not make them less than a person. New celebrities are created every day, and they could be the next one.

If you and your Twin are both celebrities and/or public figures, being separated might seem like a good way to keep the paparazzi away. One or both of you might even have a secret affair out of the camera's view. But why keep it a secret? Is it a fear of losing gigs or your career if your Twin is deemed someone you are not supposed to be with? Is there a lawsuit or legal issues which keep the two of you separated? Or do the both of you work in entirely different industries which make it difficult to stay together? Celebrity status can make it difficult for Twins to come and stay together. But this may be a challenge for you or your Twin to overcome so that the both of you can come together. Don't let the paparazzi or third party influences run your life, especially your love life. Your Twin isn't someone to abandon or someone who has come into your life to bring your name down. They are a reflection of yourself.

## NARCISSIST TWIN IN SEPARATION

NARC tendencies can cause Twins to not want to be around each other. If one or both have NARC tendencies, it can make it difficult for them to stay together. The Twin who display NARC behaviors can make the other Twin want to run and not want anything to do with them. This is even worse if both Twins display NARC behaviors. If this is the case with you, being separated from them might actually be beneficial for you. Usually those who have NARC tendencies destroy the lives of those around them, and even more the self-esteem and mental health of the same people. Never put up with other people's bad behavior, Soul Twin or not.

On the flipside, you might be the one who has displayed some NARC behaviors toward your Twin and is the reason why they ran. Sometimes people can't look at themselves in the mirror and admit that they have some tendencies which make it difficult or impossible for others to be around them or open their heart to them. Sometimes people come right out and tell you that you are not treating them fairly, but do you listen to that? Do you make changes to your behavior and treatment of them? Or do you continue to behave the same way, then wonder why people leave, or even attack you? No NARC behaviors, get rid of them.

# THROW AWAY ABUSE, HEARTBREAK, TRAUMA, ADDICTIONS, & BAGGAGE

**GUEST** – *"Terrence, why would you write a whole section about abuse? Twins would never abuse each other!"*

**MR. J** – "I used to think the same thing when I first joined Quora.com. But after years of research and meeting other Twins, I came to realize Soul Twin abuse is a reality and more common than otherwise believed. Also, for Twins who have been abused by others or their Twin, I don't want to leave them out in the cold. So this section is specifically dedicated for Twins who have experienced trauma, addictions, or abuse in their life. Let's get started!"

## END OF ABUSE

Most Twins have experienced abuse of some kind, at some point in their lives, usually when they were younger. They could have been abused by a family member, a lover, colleague or even a stranger. Just as with normal people, abuse can be traumatic. It can cause someone to become toxic, bitter, or jaded. Before they know it, they might find themselves abusing others, knowingly or unknowingly. But what is the foundation of abuse?

Our family are the first people we meet. They set the stage for our initial impressions about human behavior and society. But what if those who are your family are not of a loving, respectful, and responsible nature? What if they take advantage of the small size, strength, and innocence of a child? As parents, there is a duty to protect, provide for, and nurture each child they have. But not all parents or care takers do these things in the way children need. There can be physical, emotional, sexual, divination, and even financial abuse. Divination abuse can come in the form or performing witchcraft on children. Financial abuse can come in the form of taking money which is designated for child care or making the children work jobs and taking the money from them.

A lack of intimacy and nurturing is also traumatic. Going unheard, absent parents, verbal abuse or withdrawal, and other things can traumatize children.

There are two things to look at: words and touch. These two things are foundational with a pleasing, stable, and lasting relationship, yet they are the two most problematic things in our society. These issues begin in the household, usually as children. A mother might be physically abusive, or the father might say a lot of harmful words to the child. Every situation is different.

**WORDS:** Who don't like being told *"I love you"* by their lover or person of desire? Words are important. What we say, how we say them, when we say them, and their alignment to our actions are all important. When we are children, it is important for parents to speak favorable words over us and about us. This is what build a healthy self-esteem and emotional security. But there are situations where children might get verbally, physically, sexually, or emotionally abused by their caretakers or family. This negligence and abuse can traumatize the child. Then when the child gets older and engage in romantic and sexual relations with others, the trauma and abuse suffered negatively impact their relationships. This is also true with Soul Twins who have been traumatized or abused.

**TOUCH:** One of the only 3 things (marriage/romantic commitment and children are the other 2) that identify romantic, sex-based connections is that of sexual intimacy. Children are an outcome of sexual intimacy. Touch is necessary, just as words, in the stability, pleasure, and longevity of any romantic relationship or connection. Words feel good, and so does touch (or physical intimacy). Physical intimacy doesn't only include sex, but does include the physical actions to back up the words. Other physical intimacy include hugging, cuddling, and kissing. Now obviously parents and family are not supposed to have sex with the children. But there can be non-sexual hugging and cuddling, and kissing on the forehead. When the child gets older, they will have had healthy, non-sexual physical intimacy. When they engage in romantic/sexual relationships with others, they are able to have a healthy sex life.

But the reality of human life is that some children might get abused. In their youth, one or both parents might hit them (not the same as Purposeful Discipline™), engage in sexually inappropriate behavior, or not physically nurture the child altogether. This can negatively impact the child's self-esteem, mental, and emotional health with regard to physical intimacy. When they get older, they might find themselves pursuing or letting in other people who abuse them physically, emotionally, or sexually. The same is truth for some Soul Twins. Soul Twins do not get a pass on abuse. Many Twins report sexual, emotional, verbal, or physical abuse of some kind from when they were younger. Usually it was from a family member.

## WORDS AND TOUCH

Not everyone is good at expressing both (words and touch). Some cast off one and hold firm to the other, and some utilize and express both. But they certainly are important for a secure, pleasing, productive, and exciting connection with anyone. This is also true of Soul Twins. In some situations one or both Twins might withhold or restrict verbal/emotional or physical intimacy. There might also be the misusing words or physical/sexual abuse in some situations.

Due to trauma, unhealthy parental teaching, previous abusive relationships, and other things, it can be normal for someone to utilize more words or more touch than the other. Some people grew up in a home or environment where one was favored over the other. Some people go through their years and never learn or understand that the one they don't utilize is a reason for their failed relationships.

Those who physical intimacy, but don't always show it (through actions, or physical intimacy) do so for their own reasons. Those who show affection but don't speak it do so for other reasons. Abuse is a reality in some Soul Twin's lives. Unfortunately, it does not always come from their family or a previous lover, but could come from their own Twin. Fortunately, all Twins are on the ascension path. Eventually all Twins heal from their abuse, or let go of their own abusive behavior (if they were so themselves).

## END OF HEARTBREAK

Heartbreak come from being emotionally and energetically attached to someone, and then being abandoned, cheated on, abused, or the attachment forcefully or undesirable severed. We've all had our heart broken, even Soul Twins. Heartbreak is also traumatic. It can lead to harmful behaviors toward other people. Many Twins report having had their heart broken by a previous lover or their Twin. Many DFs and Chaser Twins have been hurt by their Twin's running, lack of reciprocating intimacy, and being sexually/romantically involved with other. But DM Twins also have their hearts broken when they experience abuse (verbal, emotional, sexual, or physical) from their DF. The DMs feel hurt too, when they see their DF with other people. Because many Runner Twins were not widely on the internet or open with their Twin, many in the Twin Soul community did not know. But fortunately, more and more DMs are appearing online and sharing their experiences.

## END OF TRAUMA

Trauma and baggage come from abuse, heartbreak, having sex with those who possess fragmented sexual energy, loss (family, wealth, health, ex.), breakups, and excessive romantic/sexual partners. As these negatively affect normal people, they also affect Soul Twins. Most Twins have some degree of trauma when they meet each other. Part of the meeting and journey is to heal the trauma and release the baggage. It is part of the ascension path. Fortunately, trauma can be healed.

## END OF ADDICTIONS

Are you a Soul Twin suffering from addictions? People might call you delusional for identifying as a Soul Twin, and crazy for acknowledging that you have been abused or have an addiction. Sadly, popular media does not want to admit that even Soul Twins suffer from abuse and addictions. But addictions can be different for Soul Twins than with normal people. Soul journeys and the ascension path is not what people think it is. It can be overwhelmingly difficult, painful, traumatic, and at time unbearable. Many Soul Twins find themselves developing some kind of addiction to cope with the dark side of the soul journey/ascension.

**ALCOHOL** – Because of alcohol's affects, it can be a way of escape for those who have trauma or a lot of problems in their life. It take their mind off what has happened, or what is going on. It eases their emotion and mind. Or at least temporarily. What happens, as with all addictions, the person has to continue with it over and over. For the person to remain at ease, they need continual usage or access to their chosen avenue of escaping their trauma or troubled reality.

**SEX** – Sex addiction is probably one of the most dangerous, yet under the radar addictions out there. What might seem like 'just dating', 'sex work', or 'casual fun' can actually be a sex addiction. It is a way to feel loved, boost self-esteem, and confidence. Whenever the person begin feeling bad about themselves, their life, or something that has happened to them, they must have sex to feel at ease. Sex addiction is a mighty animal all by itself. It is one of the most difficult for someone to free themselves from.

**SMOKING (MARIJUANA AND TOBACCO)** – If someone is not into drinking, smoking certain substances might be the ticket out for them. Cigarettes, marijuana, and other substances provide the ease and escape. But unfortunately, just like with all addictions, the person has to continue using it to keep up with the relaxed and detached feelings. This can result in developing cancer for some. For those who smoke marijuana, it can result in a change in brain chemistry which alters the person's psychology and therefore behavior.

**HARD DRUGS** – Cocaine, meth, heroin, and other hard drugs destroy a person's physical, emotional, mental, and energetic health. Although they provide a deeper escape, they can also cause more damage. I have not heard of any Twins being on hard drugs.

**OTC DRUGS** – Painkillers, anti-depressants, and stimulants make up other addictions. The Soul Twin journey is very overwhelming and painful for some. A Twin might find themselves resorting to anti-depressants to help them to cope with life difficulties and the chaotic Twin Soul journey. But these OTC drug addictions are not good for their health.

**SUGAR/FOOD** –
**GUEST** – *"How did food make it to this list of addictions?"*

**MR.J** – "Believe it or not, food can be a coping mechanism. But in some, it can turn into habitual use, leading to addiction. Sugar is a big culprit. Others such as meat, oily, and fatty foods can be a way to 'feel better'. Weight gain or health issues can come from over eating and eating the wrong foods attempting to escape from life and personal problems. Fortunately, I have never heard of or encountered a Twin who was overweight due to overeating or poor eating habits."

**LEGAL DISCLAIMER:** "I am not a medical professional or doctor. If you are having health issues, seek the help of a trained and licensed medical professional."

**ATTENTION/DRAMA** – For some Twins, low self-esteem and high insecurity can cause them to engage in attention seeking and drama causing behavior. They feel better about themselves if others give them attention. Or they might create conflict and chaos with others because, well, if their life is a mess, they feel other's lives should be as well.

All of these addictions negatively impact one's health, life, and relationships with others. If a Twin has any addictions, they can cause separation and other issues with their Twin and ascension path. Unfortunately, some Twins destroy their health and/or life through addictions. Fortunately, due to the Twin Soul journey being a soul one, they have the power to bring themselves out of these addictions and then help others to do the same. Most Twins leave their addictions and recover from them. After, they help others to leave their addictions and begin a new and healthy life.

## THROWING AWAY BAGGAGE

Baggage come from your energy being fragmented, or possessing fragmented energy from others through romantic/sexual partners. They also come from trauma from insecure and fragmented romantic/sexual partners. Their trauma gets transferred to your energetic field. This can have a negative impact on your emotional, psychological, physical and energetic health. All of a sudden, bad things start happening to you after having sex with someone or getting emotionally attached to someone. This is because their trauma, baggage, baggage from those they were sexual with, and demonic influences affect your life since you are now connected to them. To get your life back, you have to leave such individuals, break the attachment, and do an energetic cleanse.

When people hold on to baggage (usually unknowingly) and become sexual or romantic with someone else, the baggage negatively impact the relationship. It becomes a matter of time before the relationship ends. Bringing baggage into a new relationship is not wise (and energetically sanitary). The same way you do not take the trash from your house and take it to your friend's house and leave it on the floor, why do people bring baggage from previous relationships? There is emotional baggage, energetic, and mental. This baggage need to be released and ridden before getting into a new relationship.

You might be surprised how many people are walking around who are traumatized and have baggage. Most people don't know. You can't just look at someone and see it, at least those who are not aware. To the aware, it is easy to notice when someone has trauma or baggage. Just like physically someone can have wounds on their skin or carry bags in their hands or back, the energetically aware notice non-physical baggage and trauma. Most people are not taught that baggage and trauma is created after being abused, abandoned, or toxic relationships. They are not taught how to energetically clean themselves and take the trash out.

They end up going into new relationship after new relationship and usually experience the same problems over and over. It is because the trauma and baggage is influencing and controlling the relationship. Soul Twins also have trauma and baggage when they meet each other. Part of their journey and ascension is to become aware of this so they can cleanse themselves and release the baggage. For me I had trauma and baggage from familial abuse and abandonment.

## LETTING GO OF ABUSE

Have you noticed that many people who report abuse live with or lived with their abuser? Many of them don't leave, and some never make it out alive. The first step to healing from abuse is to get away from those who are abusing you. It might be difficult if you are younger. No family should abuse each other. You might have to get some money and income before leaving. If you don't have another place to go, then you might have to get your own place or roommate with a friend or colleague. The next step is to break all contact with the abuser. After leaving them and breaking contact, you are free to start your new life. But before you do, you will need to go to therapy or get some help. Abuse can wreck your emotional and psychological health. If you can't get a soul guide or help, you might have to get a hobby or begin a career doing something you enjoy doing.

## LETTING GO OF HEARTBREAK

Heartbreak happens. It is just temporary hormonal overload and temporary trauma. Heartbreak heals with time. You might need to do some meditation and spend some time alone. It is not wise to jump into another relationship if you are experiencing heartbreak. All that will happen is once the heartbreak is gone, you find yourself in a relationship or with someone you don't actually love or want to be with. You would have built the entire foundation of the relationship on something that is not rightful and honest.

## LETTING GO OF TRAUMA

Trauma take a longer time to heal from. It also require some degree of work, depending on the severity and type of trauma. Just as with abuse, whoever is causing you to become traumatized need to not be part of your life. You need to move away from them and ensure they cannot follow you or engage your new life after healing. Healing trauma is more complex. Usually it is not enough to let time go by because trauma is more severe than heartbreak. You need real emotional, mental, physical, and energetic help. You can learn some healing practices in the section of this guidebook named: Soul Ascension.

## LETTING GO OF ADDICTIONS

Depending on the severity of the addiction, you may or may not need help. Some addictions require help such as those of hard drugs and sex. The foundation for breaking addictions is to remove yourself from the people and environment which cause you to engage in the addictive behavior. You will also need a withdrawal period. This is the time your body and mind need to go without the addictions. This can be difficult for some people, as time without engaging in their addictions can cause them to become extremely anxious, violent, depressed, angry, and even suicidal. You also need a new life plan created. You need new people, places, and influences to replace the older addictive ones. You need people who are doing favorable things who encourage you to better yourself and life. You need to get into a new environment with newer, healthier activities to engage.

## LETTING GO OF BAGGAGE

Releasing baggage is easy, yet it is the least thing people do between relationships. Just as trash and clutter is created in our home which need to be disposed, baggage is created during relationships. That baggage need to be ridden before moving onto the next relationship. *Releasing baggage is possible with different practices, and for different purposes:*

**ENERGETICALLY** – Probably least known and acknowledged, your energetic health can take a heavy blow during and after a relationship or marriage has ended. There might also be some witchcraft and certain practices intentionally performed on you to cause harm to you by the other person. You will have to engage in healing and cleansing practices to free your energetic field of any impurities and demonic influences. Reading books, reiki energy healing, following the guidance of a healer, certain types of music, gemstones, and certain social gatherings can all cleanse and amplify your energy to its full vibrance.

**PSYCHOLOGICALLY (MENTALLY)** – This form of baggage can cause you to choose partners who exhibit toxic or abusive behavior similar to your previous mates. You are not thinking logically, and so you pick poor partners. Another aspect of this is not going about the relationships THINKING, but only by emotion. It is important to utilize both emotional and mental energy. They both go hand in hand. Another part of psychological baggage is thinking that all men or all women are the same. It can also result in thinking that there are no good lovers out there or that no one is worth your time. It is important to have a healthy mentality when entering new relationships.

**FINANCIALLY** – Some people mix consumer debt or financial responsibilities with their mate. But when the relationship or marriage is broken and people separate, these mixed financial responsibilities can negatively impact your financial health after leaving. It is important to eliminate any consumer debt and financial burdens before entering new connections with others. You must ensure that your financial life is stable and abundant. Never bring consumer debt and financial burdens into a new relationship and place them on your new mate. All this will do is put strain and stress on the new connection.

**EMOTIONALLY** – Emotional baggage is caused from attachment mixed with certain things such as cheating, lying, or emotional abuse. This baggage is more difficult to identify than physical baggage. Someone with emotional baggage might attempt to avoid catching feelings for someone out of fear of getting hurt. They might also treat the new person as if it is one of their previous partners. For example, if they were lied to and cheated on, they might accuse the new person of cheating, or treat them as if they are. Emotional baggage is also the result of being involved with someone for a prolonged period of time, and then breaking up. Maybe their lover died, broke up with them, or moved on to a different mate.

**PHYSICALLY/SEXUALLY** – Physical baggage can come in the form of material things. If you have items from the person, you might have to dispose of them. You will also have to move away from the person and not contact them. Sexually, attachments and energetic connections are created. You will have to redirect this attachment. You will also have to detach the energetic cords using the Cord Detach™ recipe described later in this guidebook. If you do not do these things, your energy will become fragmented. This means that part of your energy is left with the people you have had sex with. Even if you no longer have feelings for the person or think about them, these cords will still affect your emotional, mental, and energetic health. The more sexual partners you have, the more fragmentation. Too much fragmentation can lead to depression, anxiety, confusion, fear, sexual prohibition, or hypersexual behavior. The last part is to disassociate that person from any new person you meet. You cannot meet someone new and treat the new person as if they are a previous experience you have had with someone else. You have to look at the new person as a new and fresh opportunity.

## SEXUAL AND ENERGETIC SHOWERS

Although sexual activity is commonly referred to as 'dirty', it is actually very healing and cleansing when engaged in its natural, Nature-created way. When sexual activities are not, they can create baggage, trauma, fragmentation, and impurities within your system. Just as we take showers with water, soap, and put on clean clothes to clean our physical bodies, we also need to take energetic showers to clean away sexual impurities and fragmentation. This can be done in a variety of ways.

**SEXUAL CLEANSING:** Washing your private areas every day, disassociating from sexual partners which have cause you harm, reading books and ingesting positive content on sexuality, spending more time in nature and around animals, detaching cords from previous sexual partners using the Cord Detach™ recipe, getting your aura and energetic field cleared, using gemstones, and other more complex energetic practices. These all cleanse your energetic field, sexuality, and aura.

After doing a full energetic and sexual cleanse, you can further cleanse your system by finding an STD-free, and energetically clean person to engage in sexual activity with. Sex in its natural, Nature-created way is actually very healing and cleansing. Just because someone is physically good looking, is popular, has money/resources, or make you aroused does not mean they are energetically or sexually clean.

# FRAGMENT RETRIEVAL

Retrieving fragments is more complex. There are people who specialize in fragment retrieval. You are essentially detaching the cords and attachments to all the people you have had sex with. You are taking your energy back from those people and connections so that they no longer influence you or your life. You are free of their energy and influences. This can also help the other person to some degree, depending on how much fragmentation they have from other people. Be careful when searching for someone to perform fragment retrieval for you. There are people who won't do anything but take your money and make you think or feel like they have done something or there has been some change.

# CONCLUSION

Soul Twins go through a lot. But fortunately, Soul Twins don't have to remain victims to abuse or continue using addictions. Part of your ascension will be identifying some or all of these things in your own life, and with your Soul Twin. Once you are aware, you and they can begin healing and making some changes. You will need the help of others: guides, healers, teachers, doctors, soul guides, and those who listen but don't judge. It is a group and collective effort. If you find yourself attempting to avoid people, or if you lock yourself in your house, you are keeping people from helping you. If you seek healing, you will find a healer. If you are willing to learn, you will find your guides and teachers. If you want to be heard and understood, you must become open and friendly with others.

# QUICK QUESTIONS

**"Could Twins be toxic or abuse their Twin?"**
Many Twins have experienced hardships and loss in life which can cause them to become toxic or abusive toward others. Soul Twins are still subjected to common human issues. But fortunately, because they are on the ascension path, they will find their way out of treating themselves and others bad. Soul Twins are also here to experience life and learn lessons. We are not perfect.

**"Why do so many Twin Souls have trauma or addictions?"**
You might be surprised that most people have (to some degree) some form of trauma or addiction in their life. Many Soul Twins are born in abusive homes, or toxic environments where the people were harming each other. These negatively impact and influence Soul Twins, just as they can anyone else. But since Soul Twins are on a soul journey, they usually experience more severe or prolonged hardships or abuse. This is actually part of ascension. It is to challenge the individual to find the Source and Light within. It's an inside job. It is to turn inward. It is part of how souls ascend and mature. An easy life make a weak man (or woman). But a difficult life make a man (or woman) of strength, humility, knowledge, experience, and wisdom. It is about acknowledging that the Light and Dark, the ups and downs of life are All working together for our benefit long term.

*"My Supposed 'Twin' tells me he loves me but is distant, won't touch me, and doesn't do anything special for me. Why is that?"* It sound like it is easier for your Twin to love from a distance, or not be fully involved with someone. It's easy to slide in an *"I love you"* text to someone, but takes a lot more time, effort, and confidence to show them through action.

Ask your Twin directly why he only expresses his feelings through words and not through actions. Also, look at yourself. Do you only give out words with no or little action to back them up? Sometimes we complain about the things people do (or don't do) when we do the same.

*"My Supposed 'Twin' is the Runner, but she's the woman and I'm the DM. But she is abusive and toxic. Why has she called me abusive and toxic when I loved her?"* So I am aware that when many Soul Twin women have mentioned that their Twin was/is abusive or toxic, sometimes this is not true. **FOUR SITUATIONS APPLY:**

1. She is actually abusing him, and this is just a cover up to keep herself out of trouble and gain social leverage over the situation. (she isn't necessarily abusing him in response to him doing it to her, if he is abusive).

2. She has confused normal male behavior as 'toxic' or 'abusive' due to mis-parenting or false teachings from movies, social circles, TV, social media, or dating coaches.

3. She also may simply be unable to be with a man in his natural masculine state due to her own personal insecurities, lack of soft-skills, too lazy to put in the work to make a good relationship, or too much baggage and trauma from previous relationships. She might also be too masculine, and that is not going to mix well with a man.

4. And of course the fourth situation, is when a DF actually is not the abusive or toxic one, but her DM is. But of course this is not always the case.

## FOR MARRIED TWINS

When Soul Twins marry each other, then later divorce, heartbreak, trauma, and baggage can be created. Just because they are Soul Twins does not mean they will part ways peacefully. It is important to heal and release baggage and not hold onto grudges or look at your Twin as the reason for the failed marriage.

## FOR TWINS WITH CHILDREN

Some say that bringing children from a different person into a new relationship is baggage. This hold some truth. Children are naturally a liability, and not an asset. Children can be very expensive to take care of. They cost a lot of time, energy, resources, and attention. Children only become an asset once they are of age and they can be productive and provide beneficial things to their parents and society.

But what about when Soul Twins have children with each other? What if they separate, or there is abusive behavior from one or both Twins? What if one or both Twins have an addiction? These things are a reality in the lives of some Soul Twins. They could traumatize the children. It is important to see that having children with someone is a big responsibility. It is wise to heal and cleanse before having children with anyone, whether they are your Soul Twin or not. If you have already had children with someone or with your Twin, you can still utilize some cleansing and healing practices to heal trauma and release baggage.

## FOR TWINS WITH A LARGE AGE GAP

Although I have never heard of a Twin who was being abused by their Twin who is much older or younger, there have been some accounts of addictions, trauma, and baggage. Through life most people accumulate baggage and trauma. Smoking cigarettes or drinking alcohol can easily turn into an addiction. Soul Twins who have a large age gap might experience their Twin with an addiction. Many times, the addictions come about from early life hardships or trauma. They might also come from carrying too much baggage and trauma into the later years of life. It is never too late to go through a thorough cleansing and healing.

## FOR TWINS WHO ARE A CELEBRITY OR PUBLIC FIGURE

Celebrities also can have hardships and trauma in life. They are not free from developing addictions or even becoming abusive when the cameras are turned off. People forget that celebrities are still human. They still have emotions and are not perfect. This is also true for celebrity Soul Twins.

If your Twin is a celebrity or public figure you probably don't know the full extent of their life. On the outside, they might appear to be happy and successful. But there could be more going on beneath the surface. It is important that you see them as still human. If you are a celebrity or public figure you likely know that other celebrities go through hardships, addictions, and even abuse. You might have even been subjected to abuse from another celebrity. Your Soul Twin might not know of or even believe it.

If you and your Twin are both celebrities and/or public figures, keeping abuse or addictions out of the spotlight can be difficult. Jealousy and others peeking in your business can create further challenges.

How can celebrities deal with baggage, trauma, abuse, or addictions? It is the same as mentioned throughout this section as it is with everyone else. You might have to remove yourself from certain people, change environments, and utilize certain energetic practices or objects to free yourself from the bindings of addiction, or abuse. It might not be as easy since you are in the spotlight. But as a celebrity, you can use that same spotlight to help others heal. This can be a great opportunity for you.

## DESTROYING THE FOUNDATION OF NARC TENDENCIES

Hurt people hurt people. But some people enjoy being hurt. Some enjoy hurting other people. Some people take pleasure in harming others, some don't even comprehend harm against others or themselves. Calling people NARCS and attacking or abusing them is toxic is no better. If someone is a NARC, leave them alone, literally. Let them be, rather than calling them names and attacking them just because you might feel or think they are a NARC. Many people who are claimed to be NARCs are normal people who just have some degree of trauma, baggage, or addiction. Just because someone is called a NARC, does not mean they are one. Just because someone behave or does things that isn't agreeable does not make them a NARC.

Claiming someone as a NARC and then attacking them or doing harmful things toward them is wrong. Just because you FEEL or THINK someone is a NARC does not make them one. You could be attacking someone who is not a NARC, and it isn't justified. All you would be doing is attacking someone who has been abused or traumatized who actually needs some therapy or help. If they are treating you bad or doing things you don't agree with, leave them alone. If they are engaging in illegal behavior, contact the local authorities.

# ASCENDED SOUL

You have likely heard the term 'ascension' somewhere. No, it is not about climbing the corporate latter, or making your way to the top of a social group. It is about soul ascension though becoming more conscious and is about making your way back to Source frequency, and to Oneness Consciousness™. After realizing Union and vibrating on Source frequency, you can create your reality as you like. But for many on the ascension path, it can seem like life is too difficult, too many bad things happen, confusion and loneliness is the norm, and they have no control over anything in their life.

## WAKING FROM A DEEP SLEEP

100% of suffering is Self-created. As someone ascend, they come to the awareness of how they create their own suffering. Through this awareness, they can consciously make different choices. But there is also a such thing as being asleep (being in Separation Illusion™) in a way which is not physical. Someone's physical eyes can be wide open, yet they are unaware of what is in plain sight around them.

## THE TWIN SOUL AWAKENING

On the surface, it can look like one person is running while the other person is chasing. But the Twin Soul is actually in process of awakening, and what we see externally with the Twins is real time action. The soul simply becomes aware of its Self upon the meeting of the Twins. Soul Twins are soul counterparts, so it really is one Soul in what we see as two physical bodies. But the body isn't the person. The body is only a vessel to engage this holographic experience commonly called '3rd Dimension' or 'physical'.

When we see the action of one Twin 'running' and the other Twin 'chasing' this is the Soul having some level of resistance and compulsion to become aware of its Self. When Twins meet, the Soul simply sees a mirror of its Self as what looks like a second person. The 'Runner' Twin is the polarity of the Soul which is resistant to 'looking at its Self in the mirror' and so they do all they can to look the other way. The 'Chaser' Twin is usually the compulsive or anxious polarity of the Soul, so they do all they can to CONTINUE looking at its Self, and to remain attached to this 'other person' they are so drawn too.

As the Soul become aware what is going on, it will see that it is only causing its own pain, confusion, and conflict. So the Soul will begin to make some adjustments so that it can be secure, in truth, at peace, and vibrating on a high frequency. Eventually, the 'Runner' will release their resistance (and fear) as the 'Chaser' release compulsion (and anxiety). The Soul will heal and realign the non-soul parts of the Twins (mind and body), become harmonically vibrant (ascension), and will live consciously and not in resistance, compulsion, or fear. The Twins will permanently draw closer together as the Soul becomes aware of itself and makes the necessary adjustments. This is why it is called the Twin Soul JOURNEY. It is a process and a journey.

## ASCENSION COMPREHENSION

Ascension is when a soul take the journey of ascending into higher consciousness and intelligence. Everyone is on a soul ascension path to some degree. But most people get caught up in the ways of the world and entangle in things and people which distract them from the ascension path. But fortunately Earth is a soul school, and people eventually mature enough that they are no longer distracted.

Soul maturity is not based in time, but in Conscious Choice Experience™. Souls mature by experiencing different aspects and events of life and of the Higher Self and the Shadow Self. They make choices, analyze the results of those choices, and make new choices. This is all done through either the conscious, subconscious, or a combination. Souls do digress on their ascension from time to time, but this is part of their ascension. Soul ascension also require a foundation, which digressions provide. It is necessary to experience what most people think of as 'dark', 'bad', or unfavorable experiences. These provide a backdrop for positive experiences. Earth is a place where 'duality' is experienced. This help souls to learn and ascend.

What is an Automatic Default Ascension™? This means that a soul chose to take the ascension path all the way. They are upper graduates in a way. They have a huge appetite for learning, as well as teaching and guiding others. They are brave by taking the risk of taking the ascension all the way. They chose to not take the same pace, or stray as other souls. Soul Twins are souls which decided to take the ascension path all the way by splitting or spreading, then incarnating into more than one body. When the Soul meets its Self in the other body, it is a way for the Soul to look at its Self. This is the Divine Mirror. It is like a non-physical mirror, a mirror for the Soul to look into to see what lessons it can learn to advance in the ascension path.

Fellow Soul Twins can help each other with ascension (especially if their Twin is not physically present).

## KARMA

Karma isn't a bad thing. Karma means 'wheel' or 'cycle'. All relationships are a cycle, and have cycles within them. People also behave in cycles. We sleep and are awake during a certain time of the day. We also seek mates in cycles, depending on hormones, our age, and other variables. I think the word karma has become to mean something bad because American society has fallen apart on a social level, and with relationships and marriages. Because of that, there is too much negative karma in relationships and marriages. But karma is simply the consequences of our choices and behavior. Karmic consequences are the 'effects' and 'outcomes' of our behavior and choices.

Karma can be good, if the right two people are together. Rather than abuse, lies, cheating, usury, and other similar things, the relationship will be of love, honesty, commitment, productivity, and mutual pleasure, as it should be, at least in theory. Karmic debt can be considered to be the accumulation of unfavorable consequences from our decisions and behavior. Karmic debts came come in different forms, from attachments to abusive family members, having killed someone, unhealthy addictions, using people at their expense, and various others.

If you have karmic debt, you will have 'weight' to different aspects to your life. This weight can make certain areas of your life appear to be lacking in abundance, full of conflict, or simply undesirable. People can carry emotional 'weight', mental weight, relationship weight, sexual weight and others. Weight is obviously heavy and taxing on your system, especially the more you have. Karmic debt can create stress, confusion, and conflict. Letting go of the weight makes you free. Part of ascension is to let go of this karmic weight.

Soul Twins can carry karmic debt, just like anyone else. When they meet their Soul Twin, they will have the opportunity to become aware of their karma. This is beneficial because Soul Twins are one Soul. When you meet your Twin, they are a living, breathing mirror of your Self. This mirror of your Self will aid in identifying areas in your behavior, your actions, mentality, and lifestyle that create unfavorable karmic debt.

## REMOVING EMOTIONAL BLOCKAGES

In the context of the ascension process, what does working through emotional blocks mean?

Ever seen the plumbing of a newly built house or apartment? Clean water come in one way, pass through the showers, sinks, and toilets. The water then exit a different way. If there were trash or build up in the plumbing somewhere, there would either be a loss of water pressure, or the sinks or bathroom will clog, and the water won't drain efficiently.

The same is with our ascension. Any blockages in our system, whether they be emotional, psychological, physical, or purely energetic, will cause disruptions or stagnancy. This can lead to sickness, emotional health issues, poor decision making (psychological blockage), or inability to manifest the life you want (energetic blockages).

Clearing emotional blockages will allow emotion to flow freely, and in a more harmonized manner. This allows the individual to FEEL peaceful, happy, and 'light', rather than anger, sadness, impulsiveness, drained, or depression.

# PUTTING FEAR IN A COFFIN

There is something about this one emotion. Animals certainly become fearful. Every second of their life, they have to be alert. At any moment, they could be attacked or chased after as food by a predator. But people also have fear. Sure we don't have claws, long sharp teeth, or a poisonous tail. Fear in humans can be related to wanting to protect their own life from harm or death. But there is another reason. This is more of a social and sexual fear. Humans are sexual creatures, and social as well. There is a need for social acceptance. There is also a drive for mating, just like with animals.

There are plenty of food, water, single people, and social gatherings. Why would someone fear not being accepted, rejected, or not having the things they need in life? Due to social programming, poor upbringing from abusive, toxic, or absent parents, someone can develop fears. They can have fear of loss, rejection, or not being good enough. While being involved in the Twin Soul community, I have noticed many Twins report having fears. Some of those fears caused them to run from their Twin, others cause them to chase after their Twin. Those fears also influenced their behavior toward their Twin.

Do you have any fears? Can you identify where they came from?

Part of the ascension path is to let go of our fears. Holding on to and acting out your fears can create unfavorable karma and negatively impact your life. Write down a list of your fears. Then write where each of the fears came from. Next, write what you can do to eliminate those fears. For example, if you have a fear of being lied to, become someone who always speak truth and honestly. Another example, if you have a fear of abandonment, understand that no one is in our life permanently. People come and go. You have to learn to enjoy them when they are in your life, and let them be free when it is time for them to go.

# INFORMED AND WELL-GUIDED

Along the ascension path, you might find yourself feeling stuck, not knowing what to do, or where to go. You likely seek the help, truth, and guidance of other people. This is good. But know that not everyone may have your best interest in mind. There are those who might take advantage of you, whether it is financially, energetically (psychic vampires or witches), sexually, or socially. You might have to do some research on anyone you plan on following as your human guide. Fortunately, there are plenty of gurus, old souls, teachers, soul guides, coaches, and experienced scholars who DO mean good. I see regularly some Twins have been misinformed and misguided about the truth and reality of the Twin Soul journey. Be mindful who you follow, and why you follow them.

# SOUL GUIDES

Imagine having to take a long, treacherous journey and not have a map or guide. You have no protection, or supplies for the journey. You know along the way, you'll experience difficulties, set-backs, danger, and loss. For the life journey here on Earth, we are all given guides. They are non-physical and sometimes physical (other people). They are called Soul Guides. There are Soul Guides which stay with you all your life. Others come and go, depending on the situation at hand, and if you know how to welcome them. For the physical guides (other people), they usually come and stay for a time, then go. You might have one or a small group which you stay with long term.

Be mindful that your human soul guides might not come in the form you want them to. They will not necessarily be of an economic class, gender, skin color, social status, or dress that you agree with. Part of the ascension path is moving into higher levels of consciousness and intelligence utilization. At first, you might unknowingly reject some of your human soul guides. Once you mature to a certain place in your ascension, you will understand have to discern everyone you meet. You will understand that not everyone you meet is an average person. Some people come into your life during appointed times, for specific reasons.

Once you get to a certain place in your ascension, you might find yourself being a teacher, guide, or leader of other people. We are all a student and a teacher. We are here to learn, and teach what we learn.

**DURING YOUR ASCENSION, YOU MIGHT ENCOUNTER OTHER ENTITIES:**
**ASCENDED MASTER** – These are those who have advanced far up the ascension path. They have done so well with their ascension, they can guide, protect, and teach others. Ascended Masters usually keep their non-physical form to retain the highest energy. Some ascended masters may choose to incarnate in a physical body here on Earth so that they can have a certain kind of impact on other's lives in a more direct and physical way.

**GURU** – In reality, we are all gurus. We all learn from each other just as we teach each other. But some are identified specifically as gurus. These are those who invest much of their time and energy guiding and teaching others along the life and ascension journey. They have profound and lasting favorable effects on people and on the world.

**ANGELS AND ARCHANGELS** – Even though many people do not believe angels exist, for those who have experienced a real angel or Archangel cannot deny their existence. Their presence is so obvious and breath taking that just experiencing their presence alone can profoundly change the mentality, consciousness, and life path of anyone who has caught glimpse of one. Angels have such a presence that even if your third eye is not open to see one, FEELING their presence alone alert you that something very divine and powerful is near. You won't see an angel with your physical eyes. You can only sense them through extrasensory avenues.

Angels are beings which are closest to The Most High and Source frequency. They carry out the plans and orders for The Most High. They aid in the protection and guidance of human life and other responsibilities. Once you find yourself in a certain place in the ascension path, seeing angels with your 3rd

Eye is possible. It is also likely that seeing an angel might spark ones awakening. Whatever it takes for a soul to ascend right?

# KUNDALINI AWAKENING

Common descriptions of Kundalini awakening mention energy moving up the spine, or up through the RACOs™. The energy move up into the head, or crown RACO™. Heightened consciousness and mystical experiences are mentioned to be the result of Kundalini awakening. But there is more to it.

What is Kundalini, and how does it cause an awakening of consciousness? We all possess Kundalini energy. It is said that the energy is dormant at the base of the spine, and rise during an awakening. But I want to suggest something different. Kundalini energy is present in the whole body and energetic system. But this energy has weight depending on its vibratory frequency, and tend to pool near the feet or root RACO™ when it is of a low frequency. That doesn't mean that the Kundalini isn't everywhere else. Kundalini is essentially the 'God Within Us'. Source and The Most High is within us. They have hid themselves there so that the only way back Home is to turn inward.

When the Kundalini gets excited, its vibration is stimulated. This stimulation give the Kundalini a lighter weight, because it is vibrating at a higher frequency. This is experienced as various sensations throughout the body, but particularly the spin, back, and head. The energy then rise to the head, or crown. Since the pineal gland and pituitary gland is in the head, they are stimulated by sunlight and Kundalini. This stimulation excrete substances which open a non-physical portal or gateway which allow experiencing of the non-physical aspects of what we see as the physical world. Research the pituitary and pineal glands to see their effects.

It is reported by many who have Kundalini awakenings to receive knowledge, understanding, and wisdom about things they did not know before, or were not taught. It is also commonly mentioned seeing non-physical entities such as Archangels, Thrones, Soul Guides, demons, and demonic entities. Interesting patterns, structures, and activity are also mentioned. There are also reports of people becoming mentally or emotionally ill after having a Kundalini awakening. Kundalini awakenings can be dangerous if the person's body cannot handle the energy or their emotional/psychological state is not ready.

I don't recommend anyone pay someone or have someone activate their Kundalini. It is really dangerous. Reiki for healing purposes is okay. But your Kundalini is not an energy you want to try and control. LET IT DO ITS OWN THING. Kundalini awakenings can be painful and even kill you if you aren't physically, emotionally, and psychologically prepared. Fortunately, many on the soul journey or going through ascension experience Kundalini awakening. There are also trustworthy gurus and energy specialists who can safely help your Kundalini to excite without risk of death.

Personally, I have had many Kundalini awakenings since the age of 3 years. They have become a normal part of my life. During the ones I have experienced, my feet and legs tingle, and a powerful but gentle energy move up my spine and back, and into my head. Once in my head and crown area, there are usually cold sensations and a great high pressure feeling inside my head. Sometimes the pressure is so intense, it literally feel like someone is standing on my head, yet my head does not get heavy. Some Kundalini awakenings happen while I'm asleep, and these tend to be more intense, as there is more detach from the physical body while sleeping. These sleeping Kundalini awakenings happen with loud sounds which are similar to wind blowing, electricity, popping, and flowing water.

The results of these Kundalini awakenings leave me in a state of pure bliss, inner peace, calm, and many times very horny and orgasmic. They also are followed by a pouring of knowledge, understanding, and wisdom which I did not have before, and was not taught. These Kundalini awakenings also commonly cause my cell phone and laptop to malfunction. If I go to a store after experiencing a Kundalini awakening, usually the cash register will stop working. One time I went to 4 different stores just to buy some snacks because each of the cash registers all of a sudden stopped working!

Kundalini Awakenings can result from certain practices such as meditation, yoga, near death experience, and pranayama.

If you speak with someone who know about Kundalini awakening or research it, you will also hear about the Kundalini referenced to a snake or serpent. Just as a snake coil, so does the Kundalini up the spin. But I want to bring you to awareness of three other representations of Kundalini I have observed. Not everyone's Kundalini function the same. They are the Lizard Kundalini™, Dragon Kundalini, and the Phoenix Kundalini™. In reality, there is only One Kundalini, but it can take on different expressions. Just like snakes, even though dragons and phoenixes are considered mythological, they are also reptiles.

Most lizards, although they have limbs, cannot stand up or fly. They can climb and leap. There are few kinds which can stand, run, and even catch flight.

A dragon is like an oversized lizard with wings and slightly different body proportions and joint angles. It is said that snakes once had the ability to stand up, much more than a king cobra, but not with feet. The snake lost is privilege to rise up. This is to symbolize people losing consciousness (the fall) and entering Separation Illusion. Their schooling, challenge, and game is to regain consciousness through ascension. It is their awakening.

A dragon can not only stand up, it can fly.

The mythological phoenix can also stand up and fly. The fire represent pure Source frequency. The fire also represent alchemy, transformation, as well as pure, raw energy. It is symbolic for pure, raw consciousness and intelligence. The Phoenix Kundalini™ represent the highest form of awakening and ascension. It represent the highest form of consciousness and intelligence.

*"Do all people have dragon or Phoenix Kundalini™?"* It's not that there are different types of Kundalini. The energy is the same. It is all One energy. But the Kundalini can take on different expressions. The Kundalini behave in cycles, from ash, through the reptile representations, finishing at the phoenix, and going back to ash. It's a cycle of transforming and increasing consciousness and intelligence.

It might seem like this would be boring. But each time around, the challenges, game, and experience is different. It is like playing a video game or in an AI simulation. You start off with a character with certain attributes and abilities. You play through the AI sim or video game. After beating the game, you get to start fresh, with a different character. Each time the difficulty, challenges, and processes change. It is never ending excitement really! No one life is the same.

From phoenix, to ash, to lizard, to snake, to dragon, to phoenix, and back to ash. They are cycles of someone's soul growth. Most people spend a lot of time in the lizard and serpent Kundalini. Few seem to make it to the Dragon Kundalini and Phoenix Kundalini™. Those of the later recycle back to ash and then work their way up in a new world, Universe, or dimension. They are ascended masters. Many gurus have the Dragon Kundalini and some the Phoenix Kundalini™. Some souls (such as Archangels, split/spread souls, angels, ext.) have Dragon Kundalini or Phoenix Kundalini™ by default.

*"How do I know which Kundalini I have?"* Remember, there is only One Kundalini. But let's look at it for the sake of answering the question in a way that is understandable. Since each one represent Kundalini functioning to a certain level (as far as consciousness and intelligence), we have to look at each person's level of conscious choice and intelligence utilization. Now we can't just look at someone and tell. It is not based on physical or worldly things such as social status, skin color, gender, education level, income, or personality type. It is purely based on intelligence utilization and conscious choice.

Someone who has a high level of conscious choice do not look back at their previous choices and think *"Wow, did I really do that?"* or *"Well, that wasn't such a great idea."* Now granted, we all have mis-takes, none of us are perfect in human form. But those who have a high level of conscious choice make choices and decisions purely by consciousness. Less and less do they make choices out of impulse, compulsion, or just because everyone else is doing something. Someone who has a high level of intelligence utilization do not need to read lengthy books, spend top dollar for education or courses to learn things. They seem to learn quickly and easily, even to such a great degree to challenge those who are educated and taught by someone else. They seem to have a direct connection to knowledge, understanding, and wisdom itself. They process information easily and quickly.

Those of the Dragon Kundalini and Phoenix Kundalini™ tend to be gurus, and very wise and powerful teachers and guides. They invest much energy, time, and resources for the benefit of others. They display an inability to be purely selfish or only live for personal gain. They are on a frequency of awareness where it is obvious to them that everyone around them is actually themselves in another body. So, outwardly, they seem to have a great appetite for helping other people in whatever way they see favorable.

## SEXUAL ENERGY

It is also said that sexual energy and Kundalini are one and the same. I see it as truth. But this does not necessarily mean just because you have sex your Kundalini will awaken, or that you will somehow become super conscious or intelligent. Sex is primarily designed for the purpose of producing offspring. Most people who have sex attempting to satiate hormonal cravings, financial gain, manipulation, or to 'feel good' generally do not tap into the deeper and more profound sexual experiences. This is because sex is not a physical activity, but an energetic excitement. It is not enough to rub bodies together. The physical body is only a projection from our mind, it is a very thin barrier of energetic entrapment.

The kind of sex most people desire to experience can only happen through higher forms of consciousness and intelligence. They have to be of higher frequency and power. Sex is an energetic activity!

One Soul Twin woman who contacted me for help constantly complained about not feeling anything when having sex with men. She mentioned that it is because *"sex is just masturbation with two people."* Or at least that is what *she* FELT. This person did not have a healthy mentality or perception about sex. She also had sexual trauma from when she was younger which caused her to feel that someone else has to make her sexually pleased.

I asked her if she wanted to see why she felt about sex the way she did. After consent, I performed reiki energy healing on her. I basically excited her own Kundalini and energy body to a safe level. I also opened her crown RACO™ (which was blocked) and grounded her root RACO™ (which was disconnected from the Earth grid). Not much time after she mentioned that she was so horny and aroused (wet) and didn't know why. I told her it was the same energy I mentioned that is the Source of pleasure she has desired to experience, that energy being of her own.

But it was too much for her. Days of being wet and horny without any physical touch or stimulation was something she wasn't expecting. She claimed that she felt amazing those days, but having to change her underwear so often was annoying. After bringing her energy back down, she had a completely different outlook on sex. I decided to reset her energy and

Kundalini a little above where it was before, and left her RACOs™ how I set them so that she could have better sexual experiences.

This was also a learning lesson for me. I didn't know those kind of results would come about! But it show that sex is primarily not a physical activity, but an energetic one. This also mean that emotions and a person's mentality is tied to sexuality. How do you FEEL about sex? What do you THINK about sex?

Kundalini Awakening: If it doesn't happen to you, it doesn't make you any less aware. They can feel good or painful, it depends. It will happen when your Soul and your Self is ready.

## DNA STRANDS INTO SINGLE BEAM OF LIGHT

DNA is not just a physical thing. It is also consciousness and intelligence in a code format. It is also energy and memory. Notice that DNA has what look like two strands, which have connections in between. There is actually one strand. You can look at one side representing masculine energy and the other feminine energy. Really there is only One Energy, just functioning in two different ways. They function in polarity, in mirrored opposites. So there is actually one strand of code made up of polarized opposites of the same energy. This single strand is of Light and Power. It is pure energetic code. As someone progress in their ascension path, this code will be recoded and upgraded. Then it will be recoded and upgraded some more. The DNA has to continually be upgraded so that it can cause the body to change in a way to support higher frequencies and power of energy.

## TRIGGERING WONT LAST FOREVER

Triggering is not Twin Soul specific. Everyone gets triggered in some way, to some degree, and it can be from anything or anyone. The triggering is when you are responding to external (projected) stimuli, their words or actions based off of too much emotion. It is when you are not in Oneness Consciousness™, but too focused on the physical. If you utilize more logic and consciousness, the triggering will lessen.

This triggering is for the long term benefit of you and your Soul Twin. This triggering will lead to all the healing you and your Twin need in order to be around each other without feeling the urge to run or chase. It is perfectly normal and part of the journey. Even normal people trigger each other, although not as severely as Soul Twins.

## END OF DNOTS (DARK NIGHT OF THE SOUL)

No, this is not the name of a super-villain movie. I describe Dark Night Of The Soul as experiencing the deep 'dark' side of your soul. Your Shadow Self. This is not to be confused with society's or media's representations of 'dark'. It has nothing to do with anything that is evil or negative. Even negative isn't a bad thing. A battery has a positive and negative part which work together to accept, store, and release energy in the form of voltage and current. Dark Night

Of The Soul is experienced by everyone on the soul journey or ascension path, at some point, and to some degree.

It is possible to have a DNOTS at any time, even before meeting your Soul Twin, and after meeting them. If you are having a DNOTS, you are being purged of the trauma and dense energies in your system. But you have to go 'down there' to do this. The soul journey and ascension path is not all light and love. It has its dark and painful moments. If your Twin is triggering you, then this is a good thing. Eventually there will be little to no triggering and no DNOTS after the trauma and dense energies are no longer in your system.

All Soul Twins experience DNOTS. Even your DM or DF. Even if it does not look like they are 'awakening' or going through it, they surely will if they haven't. Also understand that an 'awakened' DM does not chase after women. This is not how men behave who are in their natural state. Men were created to put their attention and focus on The Most High and Divine Purpose, and not chase after women. Women were not created to chase men, but to PURSUE men who have a connection with The Most High, and is about his Divine Purpose. This does not mean an awakened DM or man will ignore you, ghost, or treat you as if you don't exist. This also does not mean if a man reads scriptures, claims to be of a god, or is a religious leader that he is connected to The Most High and about his Divine Purpose.

Women were created to Divine Gate keepers, and to also look after offspring. Many males complain about difficulty getting women to be with them or difficulty getting sex with women. That is because women were designed to not open the Divine Gate to men who are asleep and not about their Divine Purpose.

Men can take part in taking care of offspring, but it cannot pull them away from their attention and time toward The Most High and their Divine Purpose. Many female Soul Twins sit back and wait for their Twin to make a move on them, and usually this result in her feeling like he is running from her. All that has happened is that she has met someone she feel something with and want to be with him, but she has let the opportunity pass. Men pursue The Most High and Divine Purpose, women pursue men who are pursuing The Most High and Divine Purpose. The woman was created to pursue The Most High and Divine Purpose THROUGH a man who himself is pursuing The Most High and Divine Purpose. Pursuing is relational investing. You are investing your time, energy, and attention into someone and something that is of great benefit to yourself, them, and other people.

The children see their father and mother both pursuing The Most High and Divine Purpose and this is favorable. The children will then be able to naturally pursue The Most High and Divine Purpose as they age and mature. This is the Divine Circle. I realized it is not a hierarchy because no one is at the bottom or top. We are all One! So, rather than saying 'Divine Hierarchy', it is the Divine

Circle. See, we are learning together! Even teachers and guides are still students!

## PURGING

Kundalini awakening and DNOTS cause purging. Purging is not killing or murdering people. Purging is the release of trauma, pain, and other people's fragments, demonic influences, and dense energies. Purging can be painful and seem like the person is emotionally bi-polar, impulsive, or out of control. But after the purging is complete, you are left with someone who is free of the above mentioned things. They will seem like they never went through the purging. They might lose weight, have more vibrant skin, smile more, and seem younger and more lively. They'll be more logical, intelligent, aware, and purpose-driven.

## EGO DEATH TO SELF LUMINATION

This subsection include a journey I experienced where my Supposed 'Twin' and I went through the 'ego death'.

To be honest, I don't know what ego is, and I don't include that term in my personal vocabulary. It seem to me that word is used and thrown around without a common, solid definition. Usually, when I see it or hear it somewhere, it sound like the person is saying that the other person is 'full of themselves' or behave in a way as if they are above or better than everyone else. A more common and understood term for this would be 'arrogance' and not 'ego'. The dictionary definition of the word 'ego' means 'self'. Self is definitely not bad, or something that we should throw away. Please do not commit suicide!

We all have a mind, even Soul Twins. The mind is not good or bad. It is just a tool that is used to process information we take in mostly through the body's senses. Soul Twins will have a very deep and sharp mind, as they take in more information, at faster rates, and at higher qualities. This is good and useful for them, because having a deep and sharp mind is necessary for Twins to navigate this chaotic world and social environment. But the mind can get in the way. It is like having to constantly clean and organize a house that keeps getting dirty and messy. This is why some say that the mind need to be quieted or relax. It is that it is easy to be too much in the mind, and not in the soul.

This is what is meant when you hear some speak of 'releasing' or 'dissolving' the ego. What you should do is let the ego be, and transcend into conscious choice and intelligence utilization. This will naturally cause you to not be too much in the mind. Rather than feeling and thinking through everything, SEE and OBSERVE. This is why introverts are so powerful because they SEE and OBSERVE before they make choices. They are not emotionally impulsive or allow the contents of their mind to make the choices. They make choices out of consciousness and observation, they are natural scientists.

The ego doesn't die and can't die. The ego is the Self. The 'ego death' you hear others mention is when someone is not in Oneness Consciousness™. The person see everyone as separate. Because of this, they live, behave, and treat other people in a way as if they are separated from everyone, not realizing everyone is themselves in another body. They are caught in Separation Illusion™.

# A MEDITATION

I saw this while meditating one day. You have to completely let go of your old life and old ways of thinking, choices, and behavior. Soul Twins will be cleansed, purged, decluttered, refreshed, and rebooted. It is painful, exhausting, and chaotic, but stay strong!

As we pass away from our old selves, and on to our glorified selves, we'll feel at times like we are overwhelmed or having our soul beaten to death. We'll continue to lose (and release) things, people, places, beliefs, behaviors, and addictions to make way for the new. Hold on tight the road will be rocky, but you'll eventually come to smooth grounds!

**HERE IS WHAT I SAW IN MY SUPPOSED 'TWIN' AND I'S 'EGO DEATH' EXPERIENCE:**
I heard the sound of church music playing. Then I found myself inside a church building with a lot of other people (other Soul Twins). There were two caskets up front near the altar. I noticed my Supposed 'Twin' was walking ahead of me. The first casket had the body of a man in it, in a tuxedo. The head wasn't there though, but there was a box where the head would have been and it said 'ego' on all sides of the box.

My Supposed 'Twin' looked in the casket and started crying. I looked in, shook my hand (as if I was waving goodbye) and then closed the casket.

Then *she* walked over to the next casket. A *woman's* body was in it, and also had a box where the *head* would have been and it also said 'ego' on it. *She* started wailing, and actually fainted. Some people caught *her* though, before *she* could hit the ground and put *her* in a seat.

I looked in the casket, shook my head, then waved my hand, and closed the casket. Then I walked over, and stopped in front of my Supposed 'Twin' and looked at *her*. *She* looked at me and stopped crying for a moment. Then I walked up toward the top of the altar where pastors preach and *she* started wailing again.

Once I reached the top and turned toward the audience, my whole body lit up and turned into a bright light, and then the whole place was filled with a bright light, then I came to my senses.

**GUEST** – *"Hey what is that ringing in the ear?"*

**MR. J** – "There are three things I know of which cause ringing in the ear. I will mention two here, and the other in a later section. The first is what we all experience. The brain does make noise. It is a powerful computer. But that is one kind of ringing which is mostly constant. Sometimes too, that constant ringing is coming from our ears, from too much loud noises. But you may be experiencing random ringing of the ear that is loud but lasts a short time. This can come from the releasing of memories and information which no longer need to be stored in the brain. It is said that the ear ringing is when the brain receives downloads. That could be true, but the brain is constantly processing information, so that is not the case."

## ROLE REVERSAL ~ CORRECT THRONES

Do roles reverse in the Twin Soul connection? I don't think the roles reverse, but the energy the Twins find themselves in does change. Men were created to be in the masculine energy and the women in the feminine. But due to social conditioning, upbringing, trauma, heartbreak, personal beliefs, and social life, people end up not in their correct energetic positions. Men are commonly pushed into the feminine energy or has his masculine energy suppressed. Women are commonly rewarded and praised for being in the masculine energy.

In essence the roles don't reverse, but Twins commonly end up in the incorrect energy. On the Twin Soul journey, most Twins get the chance to experience both energies and decide for themselves. I know I hated the years when I was younger. Nothing in my life worked the way I know it should. That is until I met my Supposed 'Twin' and saw how much *she* was in the masculine energy. It seemed like *her* being too much in the masculine energy had a negative impact on my life when I was younger, even before we met. After meeting *her*, my whole life changed, and my life started happening the way it naturally should as a man in the masculine energy. I also noticed the changed happened during the switching of the ages, from the Piscean Age to the Aquarian Age.

Unfortunately, my Supposed 'Twin' refused to get back into the feminine energy after we met, and it negatively impacted *her* life. Because I held firm to the masculine energy, my life changed for the better. If my Supposed 'Twin' went into the feminine energy after we met, things would have been much better for *her*.

Which do you choose? How did you feel being in the masculine energy? What about the feminine energy?

## SOUL REBIRTH

The ascension process is just that, a process. Rushing the process might do more harm than good. Ascension is a process and not meant to be rushed but experienced. Allow the process to take you through ascension. After the Kundalini awakening, purging, and 'ego death', there is the 'rebirth'. It is not physically being reborn, although the body will change significantly on a DNA level and with the nervous system. This 'rebirth' is when you are out of Separation Illusion™, and in Oneness Consciousness™. You are in the Soul and not in the mind or stuck on the physical. You are vibrating on Source frequency.

## ASCENSION AND THE RACO™ SYSTEM

The RACO™ system will certainly be cleared and realigned during ascension. Just as it is important to have a healthy body, free mind, and stable emotionally, it is important that the energy system be free of demonic influences and impurities. The RACO™ system can be subjected to impurities, blockages, and misalignment. It is important for the impurities to be removed, blockages opened, and misalignments realigned.

## ASCENSION SYMPTOMS

**GUEST** – *"What are some ascension symptoms?"*
**THERE ARE MANY, HERE ARE SOME BELOW:**
- PHYSICAL DISCOMFORT OR SICKNESS
- UNEXPLAINED PAIN OR SENSATIONS IN CERTAIN PLACES IN THE BODY
- CHANGE IN EATING HABITS
- FEELING UNATTACHED TO YOUR CURRENT LOVER
- MYSTICAL EXPERIENCES
- SUDDEN LIFE CRISIS AND DIFFICULTIES
- PEOPLE LEAVING YOU
- DEMONIC ATTACKS
- EMOTIONAL INSTABILITY FOR NO IDENTIFYABLE REASON

**REPEAT NUMBERS** – 222, 1111, 555, and other repeat numbers are commonly seen by Soul Twins and those on the ascension path.

**DÉJÀ VU** – Just like with 'ego', déjà vu seem to be a term which everyone has a different meaning. From someone who experience déjà vu a lot, I can tell you it isn't anything bad. Those who experience déjà vu experience 'I've been here before' or 'I seen this before' or 'This has happened before'. It is as if, just before something happens, for a split second, it is like you know that you have done it before, or you were there before. Déjà vu is you *remembering*. It is proof that you are awakening and in Oneness Consciousness™.

**RINGING IN EAR** – Doctors will claim ringing in the ears is hearing loss. Even though there is a certain kind of ringing which is the result of hearing loss, what many who are going through awakening are experiencing are of different things. One of those is simply the sound of normal, harmless brain activity. The brain does make noise. The other is the brain having short moments of overload due to high incoming energy. The brain has to quickly make some reconnections and process the energy. This can be heard as a loud ring. On a deeper level, ringing in the ear is also common among those who have a demonic entity on their crown. Someone who is being attacked from psychic vampires or have someone performing witchcraft on them can also experience earring. It can also come from demonic influences.

**SYNCHRONCITIES** – You just pulled into the parking lot at the local grocery store. As soon as you step out and close the door, you noticed that the next 3 vehicles next to you, the drivers got out and closed their doors at the exact same time as you. Or you are driving down the road, and all of a sudden realize every single pickup truck in front of you and behind you are all the same color. There are no other vehicles you can see. Or every time you have to do something or be somewhere, it seem like you arrive right on time. Not late, not early, but right on time. Or you have a sudden restroom emergency, and run to the nearest restroom. As you run, someone just happen to open the door wide just as you would have had to stop to open the door. Then you get to the restroom and the janitor JUST finished cleaning it and left the door open. These are examples of synchronicities. Everything seemingly happen right on time. Not too late, not too early, but at the right time.

**OBE (OUT OF BODY EXPERIENCE)** – If you are incarnated in a physical body, you can DETACH from that body enough to experience deeper and higher dimensions of reality. You don't really leave the body, but detach from it just enough. Leaving the body is death. Ascended masters can leave the body and pick it back up. But they don't engage in such behavior, because at that level of consciousness, every choice is a conscious one. There is no purpose for picking up a body just to leave it.

**BEING DRAWN TO NATURE** – This is a common one. Big cities with few trees, grass, animals, lots of paved ground, lots of machines, bots and computers pull us away from nature. The natural environment is where the body came from. Many realize that living in big cities and following the crowd has pulled them away from Nature, health, and Oneness Consciousness™. So, they spend lots of time in nature.

## WHAT REALLY IS HEALING?

You have probably heard a lot about Soul Twins having to 'heal separation' or heal to bring their Twin back. Why do we have to purge, cleanse, and heal as Soul Twins? Why can't we just go on a date with our Soul Twin and get into a relationship with them and walk into the sunset happily ever after? It could be that easy, like the other connections you've had, but unfortunately it isn't that simple. The rewards are greater, but so is the work necessary to earn those rewards.

When we come to Earth, it doesn't matter how high of a vibration we are or how much soul maturity we have attained. As we live on Earth through the years, we pick up on the energies, influences, and ways of the world. This means that we suffer some things along the way that cause us pain, trauma, fear, and loss of awareness. We end up accumulating these experiences and traumas as we age. This is energetic clutter and trash. If we connect too much to the Matrix, we also end up with belief systems and ways of living that resonate with the world but not that of The Most High or Oneness Consciousness™.

As you age, eventually you realize you are accumulating these things and need to heal and purge to get them out. If you don't, you accumulate all kinds of trauma, worldly experiences, and information that is actually harmful to you and your Twin Soul connection. It is similar to not taking the trash out in your house. If you don't take the trash out, it all accumulates and before you know it the house stinks, has bugs and no one wants to live with you or visit, not even your own Twin!

This serve a good purpose in one way. You and your Twin accumulate worldly experiences and information that cause Separation Illusion™ and low vibration. When you meet your Soul Twin, the process of ridding Separation Illusion™ and releasing low vibration begin. Mirroring and triggering happen, then Kundalini awakenings, purging, cleansing, and healing.

If you are avoiding the process by not healing and allowing the purging to work its magic, you become the thing that blocks the connection between you and your Twin. If you only focus on what your Twin is doing in the 3D-Physical and not healing, you will be like a dog chasing its tail, going in circles and not going anywhere or making progress. Your Twin is your guide. They are YOU. They did not show up in your life to cause you pain and suffering. The pain was already inside of you, and you chose to suffer by not healing and releasing the trauma and low frequency coding.

When your Twin trigger you, it's an opportunity to heal and regain some health in the connection. When you choose to allow yourself to be triggered and heal, you and your Twin will be one step closer to a healthier connection. When your Twin trigger you and you choose not to heal, but play the blame game, fight and argue, go after other people, or avoid them all together, you take a step backward and have to make another trip around the circle again.

So, how do we heal? Everyone can find that answer if they look within. Turn inward. Ascension is an inward journey. As we go in, and make changes within, those changes reflect as changes in our outer projected world. I can't and won't tell you how to heal. Only you know how to do it, and your Twin is your guide. But the basis of healing as a Soul Twin is allowing yourself to be triggered by your Twin and realize the triggering doesn't happen to cause you more pain, but to release the pain and trauma that is already in you. The mirroring is natural and will never go away. Your Twin is YOU, so what we call mirroring is basically seeing and experiencing everything you are in your Twin. If you see something in the mirror you don't like, it is an opportunity to self-reflect and take care of the issue within yourself.

If you want to improve the connection or relationship between you and your Twin, it is necessary to begin your healing. Avoiding the connection, filling up your life with substances to fill the place of your Twin, running after other people, and running from your Twin and the triggering is not healing. I have gained a lot of progress in my Supposed 'Twin' Soul journey by actively healing.

If your Twin isn't texting back, running to other people but not you, abusing substances, or ignoring you, then you can definitely make a difference by beginning your healing work. You will be so happy when you see it reflecting on your Twin's side. A healthier you is a healthier Soul Twin. Get to work!

## HEALING PRACTICES

Many of us suffered abuse, abandonment, toxic families, and undesired situations that created the trauma we lived with. All of that over a long period of time create a lot of wear and tear on one's body, mind, emotions, and energy.

It's important when healing, to match that in reverse. What you feel in your body, hear in your ears, see with your eyes, and feel with your energy and emotions. We have to introduce daily activities that repair and heal our being and system. Healthy music like love songs or worship songs do well, body-specific foods (what YOUR body likes), physical exercise and stretching, reading books, time in nature and natural environments, time isolated from people and noises (meditation), aromatherapy, salt baths, and most importantly to remove ourselves from the people, places and things that are sources of the trauma. **A little a day goes a long way:**

- Healthy food choices
- Meditation
- Journaling
- Energetic showers and salt baths
- Reiki sessions
- Yoga and cardio exercise
- Acupuncture
- Isolation
- Join a community of people who are of higher consciousness and intelligence
- An understanding/listening friend to talk to
- Remove items from your life that remind you of your past traumas
- Love songs and religious music
- Remove certain hormone-disrupting foods (sugary snacks, processed foods, fast food ext.)
- TIME - healing takes time, it's not an overnight thing

I use the OMAD (one meal a day) and intermittent fasting (eat within 4-hour window, fast rest of the day). My body like these two the most. Your body might favor meats with fat. Or it might favor plants only. Or it might favor the omnivore option with only certain meats. Fasting isn't for everyone. You will have to experiment with different eating habits and fasting types to see what your body likes. Food can be just as toxic as excessive alcoholic and other drugs. The body of one who is high frequency does not need a lot of food, and certainly not any kind of food!

Be conscious of what you eat!

# JOURNALING

Journaling is very effective. Write down EVERYTHING, all of your feelings, thoughts, desires, traumas, fears, doubts, ext. I have been journaling since my teenage years. I also learned how to write from journaling for years and years. I recommend my tried and true method of daily journaling mixed with daily meditation. It is important to write your feelings down and review them later, rather than reacting to situations by how you feel in the moment. *You might have to hide the journal in a place so certain eyes won't see what's in it.*

If you don't have a journal, you can purchase some healing specific ones from me. The link to purchase is in the ending section of this book named: Other Books By Author.

# MEDITATION

Meditation is very effective. The most simple but effective form of meditation is to sit in a quiet room or place with no people and no distractions. Close your eyes and just sit. Allow any thoughts, feelings and urges to pass you by. Don't identify with any of them, and don't allow any of them to make you get up to go do something. If you have the urge to eat, or reach for the phone, ignore them. Sit as long as you can. If you get bored, agitated, or anxious, then this kind of meditation will benefit you the most. If you can't sit for at least 30 minutes in a quiet place alone and do absolutely nothing and be perfectly fine, your mind/emotions/desires are overriding your soul. The more often and longer you do this meditation, the more calm and peaceful you will become, and you will slowly detach from the 3D and uncontrollable life situations. Your stress and anxiety levels will drop dramatically.

I call this RESET Meditation – not being affected by or influenced by the 'external' (projections of your own mind). I can't trade mark meditation because it has been around since the beginning of time! Meditation is ancient! The Egyptians knew of and fully utilized the power and purpose of meditation. But daily meditation is so that you can essentially hit the RESET button, emotionally, mentally, and energetically speaking. It also aid in your physical health, because emotional and mental stress is destructive to the body.

# RACO™ CARE

**REMOVING IMPURITIES** – This can be done with salt baths, showers, mist sage, getting out into nature (especially around trees), walking barefoot in the sand or grass, and gemstones.

**OPENING BLOCKAGES** – The root RACO™ is like the negative or ground terminal of a battery. It ground energy and rid the circuit of static, interference, and noise. The crown RACO™ and 3rd eye RACO™ are like the positive terminal. They are the gateway for energy to flow in. The heart RACO™ is the center. It is like a holding place for energy, which is where we also experience breath and emotions. Of course, energy flow in and out in the heart RACO™, in a different manner.

A blocked root can seem like you have a lot of unhealthy emotional and mental things going on. A blocked crown can severely impact your awareness and ascension. A blocked heart can make you not speak and use your voice and words to change your experience of reality. It can also make your relationships very 'dry' and 'cold' with a lack of intimacy, affection, and warmth.

Opening blockages usually is based in action. For root, you need to spend more time in nature. If you are always inside the house or a building, and always around computers and electronics, this can block your root. Too much social media, news, and some forms of entertainment can block your root RACO™.

For crown and 3rd eye RACOs™, it is important to engage in practices which cause you to be more conscious and utilize intelligence and not emotions. It is also important that you have more advanced teachers and guides so that you are not trying to lead yourself. They can help keep you in the right direction and doing things which will aid in keeping you healthy and receptive. Detoxing your body also helps these two RACOs™. It is important to eat what YOUR body needs. There is no universal way of eating. Everyone has different DNA and genetics, and everyone's body is different.

For heart RACO™, you need healthy relationships. You must take care of yourself. Do you shower daily and put on clean clothes daily? Do you keep your living space clean and organized? You must also engage in healthy social activities with those who respect you and have a sense of love for you as well. If you are always getting into relationships and connections with people who abuse, use, or mistreat you, this can create a blocked heart RACO™. Look at all of your current relationships and connections. How are they benefiting you? How are you benefiting them?

For heart RACO™, it is also important that you come from a place of honesty, transparency, warmth, respect, and love. Likewise, you must surround yourself with people of the same. Anything like trauma, sexual abuse, cheating, lying, or abandonment from others can cause your heart RACO™ to have a blockage. Be conscious that you do not become bitter, angry, vindicative, or jaded after experiencing these things.

**REALIGN MISALIGNMENTS** – The RACO™ system is a simple one. But your RACOs™ must all function together, as One. Your root, heart, and crown RACOs™ must all be free of blockages and impurities. You align them by doing all of the above things, and make it part of your life. As you do this, your RACO™ system will remain clear, unblocked, and of high vibrance.

# ENERGETIC PROTECTION

As you progress through life and ascension, you come to want energetic protection. You realize that you don't only need physical protection.

But here, there are some simple things to protect your energy from other people. There is a reason why people say to be careful who you spend time around. Other people can have influence over our behavior, choices, and mentality. Be conscious who you associate with. Some people might pretend to be your friend or kind to you just to get certain information. Just because someone is kind to you does not automatically mean they are trustworthy or have good intentions. This mean that you should not make assumptions about people just because. Be aware and never believe people just because they are saying it.

It is common for the same people who are jealous, envious, or vindicative against someone to be kind and friendly with that same person when they are around them.

Also, be careful who you live with. There is just something about living with people that can change a lot of things in your life. All of a sudden bad things can start happening. Or you might notice you just can't stay in a good financial place while saving money on splitting rent. Or you start having unexplained health issues. It can also manifest in good ways too, depending on the person. You have to really know someone first before you live with them. Never roommate or live with someone you just met or don't know.

It is also important you don't have sex with people you don't know. It is not enough to have sex with someone just because you think they are good looking, you heard something about them, they are popular, or you like how they dress. Many people (women in particular) regret having had sex with someone after the activity has already been done. It is too late by then. Always choose your sexual partners wisely and do not rush. Most people don't understand that having sex with someone cause that person's energy to mix with their own (fragmentation). If that person has had other sexual partners, the person will also be taking their energy. This can cause certain unexplained physical, emotional, and mental issues which a doctor might tell you is just work-related stress.

**GUEST** – *"Whoa! I never thought about all of that sexually! But what about blocking other people's energy?"*
**MR. J** – "Simply do not identify with other people's energy as your own. It's more a mental thing than doing trickery to block other people's energy. Keep from people who you know are not good for you, or who mean you harm."

It might not be a good idea to block other's energy out, because you will block EVERYONE'S energy, and this could have a negative impact on your family, friendships, and relationships. It is a good thing to feel other's energy. It is also possible that trying to block someone's energy could actually cause you to feel them even more because then you are focusing your own energy on them, and this create a positive feedback loop. You will need to not focus on other's energy or identify them as your own.

# QUICK QUESTIONS

**"Why are the DMs sleep but the DFs awakened?"**
I don't see one Twin as being awakened and the other isn't. It's just that too many people don't see what is obvious. Or they don't want to admit to what they see. The DFs are not necessarily more awakened than the DMs. The question I ask is how can someone be so obsessed and love-crazed about another person if they are so toxic, abusive, unavailable, and no good (cheating, lying, ext.)? Some DFs also ignore what is obvious.

Some Twins have had to walk away from their Soul Twin because they were as many have described as 'toxic', 'narcissistic', and 'abusive'. You may not possess the behaviors yourself but chasing after and desiring people who do also isn't very healthy. Our Twins came to show us to ourselves, to show us all the things (good, bad, and fugly) that prevent us from living the truly satisfying and blissful life we all desire. They show us all of our own traumas and inner conflict that cause us to manifest a life and relationships that are not healthy or fulfilling.

The same way you may have seen your Twin resist change and lead a healthier life, you resist as well, just in different ways. Letting go of any and everything that does not bring you security, peace, and clarity is a good way to break the resistance. Accepting things and people who do bring you the above mentioned things is taking the path of lesser resistance, and therefore opening up a smoother and less chaotic life path.

You may have to learn to not accept other's bad behaviors, while your Twin has the lesson of learning to change their own bad behavior. The Soul (You + Your Twin) is learning both lessons. As the Soul leave anything and anyone who cause the above mentioned issues, the Soul also learn to embrace those people and things that bring favorable things.

**"If I am married or divorced does that keep me from ascension?"**
Just because you are divorced or married does not mean you are kept from the ascension path. People become initiated into ascension through marriage in different ways. Sometimes the marriage has issues that are beyond stressful and problematic. At the end of the marriage, it awaken them on a deeper level. They see things and people differently, not in a bad way. They just come to realize somethings regarding relationships, people, and social activity is different than what they were taught or previously believed.

**"Does having children take me off the ascension path?"**
Although children are costly (financially, attention, energy, ext.) they don't necessarily take you off the ascension path. Many who are soulfully mature

have children and families. Some people's soul journey begin when they have children. They look at the person they had children with and then their children, and get to experience an obvious Oneness with their family. Their children looks and/or behaves just like their parents and this experience can change someone on a profound level.

### "If my Supposed 'Twin' died does that mean my Supposed 'Twin' Soul journey is over?"

Your Soul Twin's death does not indicate an end to your journey. Many Twins whose Twin died report actually feeling more peaceful, secure, and happy sometime after the initial pain and grief. Your Soul Twin just doesn't have the physical body. Many Twins who report their Soul Twin dying also mention higher levels of energy. They also commonly say they feel their Twin more.

### "If I'm a celebrity or public figure does that restrict me from being on the ascension path?" Why would social or celebrity status keep one from the ascension path? Just like others, public figures and celebrities can also be initiated onto a soul journey and ascension. Nothing keeps them from doing so except their own choosing.

### "Is ascension only for people of a certain skin color?"

Although some groups and people claim that only people of a certain skin color can be soulfully mature, soul ascension and the ascension path is not about skin color. The ascension path and soul journey does not care about what gender, skin color, or social-economic class you belong to.

### "Can narcissism be healed?"

This is a 'split-between-two' parties kind of question. One side will say that narcissism cannot be healed, and it is a permanently mental or emotional health issue. The other side will say that NARCs can be healed and changed their behavior. But have YOU properly identified a real, clinically diagnosed NARC? I think too many people call others NARCs not knowing what they are talking about. Really, they do this to verbally and emotionally attack someone. Or if that person is not behaving the way they want them to, they call them a NARC.

The only ones who truly know if narcissism can be healed are NARCs themselves. If there be any NARCs who know they were NARCs and were able to permanently heal and change for the better (with evidence to show), then they would give you a more clear answer to this question.

### SILVER NUGGET

Why do we say an elevator is going 'up'? Why do we see a plane, and say that it is going 'up' in the sky? Where and how do we get direction? I know that we use this to describe what we observe in the environment and physical world. But to those who are awakened, they can see things in a different way. They realize that what is called 'physical' is actually a mentally projected phenomenon. If it is projected, where is up?

For the ascension path, you take this path by what is called 'turning inward'. Rather than physically walking a path, the ascension happens by becoming more conscious and aware. To do this, it is required to 'turn inward'. Turning inward is transitioning from Separation Illusion™ to Oneness Consciousness™. INSIDE IS UP. TURNING INWARD IS ASCENSION. Taking an elevator up a building is just a projected, holographic phenomenon. You are not really going up anything. But turning inward is going up.

IT'S UNION SEASON™!

# SECTION FOURTEEN

## SOUL TWINS UNITED AND THE END OF KARMIC WARFARE

**GUEST** – *"What is this about a soulmate lie? What is the lie?"*
**MR.J** – "We will get to that in a moment. But first, let's take a deeper look into what the four soul types are."

**There are four soul types:** Cosmic/ET, StarSeed, monad, singular
**There are three subtypes:** Soul Twin, Twin Flame, karmic

Note that there is only one Soul. The one Soul can function in different ways, and this is where the various souls and subtypes come from. The Soul can take on different behaviors and functions.

## WHAT ARE KARMICS?

Karmics are Earthling and younger souls. They are the most common. Karmics are not necessarily bad people. It is not necessarily that they are less able to have a healthy or stable relationship, they just function differently than Twin Flames, soulmates, and Soul Twins.

Since karmics are Earthling and younger souls, they usually hold a lot of Earth energy, meaning the connections with them are usually more physical (hormonal) and based on social norms. Some Twin Flames and Soul Twins have trouble staying together, because unless they have enough Earth energy (grounding) or enough soul maturity, the energy between them is too intense. Earth ground energy. Part of Twin Flame's and Soul Twin's coming to Earth is to learn how to stabilize this high frequency energy. It is part of their ascension.

Karmic relationships can still be fulfilling. What is meant when people mention karmics, or karmic relationships, are simply those which are not split, spread, or monadic souls. Most people are karmics or Twin Flames. With Twin Flames, this is why you see groups of people who behave, dress, live, and even look similar. They are likely Twin Flames. Remember, Twin Flames are souls which multiply in pairs (male and female being the pairings). The Twin Flame soul can continue to multiply and spread just like fire. This doesn't mean karmics are lesser or less desirable. Karmics can be family members, friends, coworkers, and even romantic partners. Karmic connections, especially if you are a karmic, seem to feel like what is 'right' or common amongst most other people.

Since karmic relationships are more connected to Earth, they seem easier. One might assume that the person they are with is their Soul Twin, because the relationship doesn't have all the intense energies and conflict that Soul Twins have. But they might actually be with a karmic.

Karmic relationships generally all have an expiration date, even if they get married. There is a reason why most people have had multiple relationships (and sometimes multiple marriages). Humans are polygamous. Karmic connections can also have their issues and problems. Because they are less mature souls, they tend to take relationships with others as 'fun' or something they are supposed to do based on social norms, and not out of conscious choice and purpose.

Karmics - temporary, come and go, fun and easy, usually are relationships that are difficult to keep together permanently, serve no purpose except to feed the lower self (food, sex, shelter, attention, social activity).

## SOULMATES COMPREHENSON

Things are going to get confusing and different here. But what most call 'soulmates' are actually called Soul Twins.

Because there is only one Soul, there can't be any mating on a Soul level. The Soul is already One and doesn't need any reproducing or 'bringing together'. Mating is an activity centered around producing physical offspring (babies, cubs, kittens, puppies, chicks, ext.). A physical body is needed to engage the physical world, and mating creates those physical bodies. Soul can't and does not mate. Soul Twins are one Soul in two bodies. The mating is all physical, even though what we experience as orgasms and sensations are purely energetic and not physical.

So, there is no such thing as a soulmate. What people mean when they say 'soulmate', are Soul Twins. All Soul Twins are polarized, one Twin the masculine (the male), and the other the feminine (the female). When the Soul in each body reach a certain frequency, the physical meeting takes place, and people call them soulmates, but they are only together physically, the Soul is still One entity.

## TWIN FLAME COMPREHENSION

It is important to look at names, terms, and definitions carefully. Just because a term is used by people when labeling something, does not mean it is correct.

First things first, ask yourself what the nature of fire is. What does fire do? It spreads and multiply right? You likely know what twins are. So if you put 'twin' and 'flame', together, what do you get? No, not JUST 'twin flame', but something else as well. It is that this spreading and multiplying nature of fire has a 'twin' reflection of its Self. So, this mean that Twin Flames are souls which multiply and spread in pairs. They are polarized. Twin Flames are monadic souls by default. They can be Earthling souls, but also cosmic, ET, or StarSeed souls. It is likely you have been told that you only have one Twin Flame. And that is true, but then in another way, it go deeper than that. See, if you are a Twin Flame soul, you have polarized reflections of yourself. You have multiples.

Remember, the nature of fire is to spread, and multiply. The monad which Twin Flames come from, can also be of various frequencies, just as fire can burn in different intensities and at various temperatures. Because of these things, there are multiple Twin Flames, although there are no false twin flames or catalyst twin flames. Twin Flames are groups of souls which come from the same monad. Twin Flames can take on similar behavioral and even physical characteristics.

Twin Flames are beings born from a single source of energy (a monad). Their souls are born from that single source, almost like a father and mother giving birth to children. They share the same soul blueprint since they function as one unit with other souls from the same monad. This is a Soul Family. They are not necessarily romantic or sexual. Twin Flames experience a soul connection. This soul connection allow them to have a deep sense of knowing upon seeing or meeting each other. They share certain things such as telepathy, dreams, 'knowing' them like they are your best friend though you JUST met them, synchronicities, and other mystical phenomena.

Not everyone has a Twin Flame, or Twin Flames. If your soul is from a soul family or monad, THEN you will have Twin Flames. Twin Flames can incarnate in multiple bodies.

## SOUL TWIN COMPREHENSION

A Soul Twin is a soul which experienced a split, or spread. The split is almost like the soul copying itself and dispersing the attributes on the middle plane (the Divine Mirror), which looks like a mirror is in between. Souls can polarize and incarnate in pair bodies. This is why there are men and women. This is why everyone has a Soul Twin, a mirror of themselves. The men are the masculine polarity incarnate of the Soul, and women are the feminine polarity incarnate of the Soul. Split souls, even though they appear to be physically separated, have telepathic capabilities and behave as if they copy-cat each other, because the soul still function as one even though it is split.

Spread souls are 'spread' into two bodies. Spread souls are just that. The soul is 'spread' into polarizing energies (one masculine, the other feminine) and what looks like an energetic cord is created (the part in the middle which looks like it is stretched). Spread souls take on similar characteristics as split souls. They also are telepathic and behave as if they are copy-catting each other.

Soul Twins are like a romantic couple. They are not Soul Family, but romantic and sexual in nature.

We all have the capability to become a Soul Twin, or the ability to split or spread. But generally, souls do not split or spread until they reach a certain frequency. This is because souls of high frequency cannot incarnate in one body. The frequency and energy of the soul gets too high. Souls can choose to split or spread if they wish to incarnate in the 3$^{rd}$ Dimension.

Soul Twins are not divided in half, but their energy actually increase after splitting or spreading. So you have an increase of frequency after the soul split or spread. This explain why Soul Twins are overwhelmed and even haunted by the energy they feel with their Twin and the connection, because the energy is very high and powerful.

**NOTE:** Just because you share a lot in common with someone, they look very good, or they make you feel a certain way does not necessarily make them your Soul Twin. All bodied souls are influenced by hormones, and sometimes people take hormonal activity as someone being their Twin Flame or Soul Twin. They do not understand that they are only under the influence of hormones which drive them to become emotionally attached to someone.

Soul Twins - (living, breathing mirror your Self), eternal, never ending. Can be full of conflict and drama or Divine bliss and love depending on the Souls frequency – The Twin's ability to work together, serve the Higher Self, heal and let go of matrix programming

## COSMIC AND STARSEED SOUL TWINS
The cosmos is always expanding (and contracting, in cycles). It is always moving energy around. This mean the energy FEELS higher because the energy is constantly moving at higher speeds and changing forms. The energy is higher frequency and more resonant.

Soul Twins can be Earthling, ET, cosmic, or StarSeed souls. The only requirement is that the soul has split or spread.

# THE REPLACEMENT
I have seen this in more than a few places online, and from other Twins. It is said that *"If your Twin doesn't come back, you will be getting a replacement."* Now, this couldn't be further from reality. The thing is, some people who think they are experiencing a Twin Soul connection, ARE experiencing a Twin Soul connection. But someone who has met one of their Twin Flames can surely go to be with others. They may or may not have a Soul Twin, but they will have many karmics they can be with. But if the person has met their Soul Twin, they won't be getting a replacement. You can't replace your Self. If you have met your Soul Twin, they are your Self in another body. There are no replacements for Soul Twins.

I have also noticed that this was predominately female content creators who mentioned things related to someone else coming to replace their Twin or similar things. But let's be real here, if you can't make a relationship work with anyone else, why would you think if ANOTHER person comes in, things will magically work perfectly? The reality is that no one is perfect. No relationship is perfect. Many people are fooled into thinking that there is a perfect lover somewhere out there. The only perfect lover out there is yourself!

You only attract the caliber of mate based on YOU, whether they are Twin Flame, Soul Twin, or something else. It doesn't matter who show up, if you are not on a certain energetic frequency, if your lives are not able to mix and mesh harmonically together, it will be no better than the others you have dated and gotten together with, only to separate. I know it is a common thing amongst women to want to move to the next person if their current relationship is not going the way they feel it should. But with a Soul Twin, there is no moving to the next person.

All that will happen is that you'll be haunted by the energy, telepathy, and sensations of your Soul Twin. Soul Twins who have attempted to sever, run from, or move on from their Soul Twin commonly report that they only feel their Twin more. They end up grieving and regret leaving their Soul Twin, as if they have just done the most wrong thing in their entire lives. Understand that it does not matter what type of soul, connection, or person you are dealing with, if they are toxic, abusive, unavailable, or treat you poorly, those are reasons to not stay with someone.

But on the flip side, just because things are not working out with someone does not mean to just abandon the relationship and then chase after someone else, or sit and wait for a replacement to show up. Many people do not realize they have done and/or said things to cause the same issues in relationships they complain about. Many perfectly healthy and fine relationships get abandoned. And in the other way, some people remain stuck in toxic connections and relationships because they believe they have found their Twin Flame, soulmate, or replacement. They feel like they should throw out all logic and self-respect and allow a potential murderer, rapist, child-molester, or felon to mistreat them, abuse them, and use them. And the sad part, the person likely isn't their Soul Twin at all! They have fallen victim to a master manipulator, or a real NARC.

## ENDING KARMIC WARFARE

It might come as a surprise to those who have not researched Twin Souls, or engage with them in the Twin Soul community, but third party issues also abound. I still shake my head every time someone reaches out to me, or I meet a Twin in person, and they go on and on about how a third party keeps getting in between them and their Twin. It seem like most of these third parties simply just want to stay with their Twin, but in other situations, it is like these third parties WANT to keep the Twins separated. It is as if they know something about Soul Twins that we don't know...

Imagine if meeting your Soul Twin was as simple as a walk in the park and never required a huge life change and inner change. Imagine if we could just meet our Twin and the progress to Union was as simple as exchanging some texts, calls, going on a few dates and within a few weeks be in a committed relationship. Then after a couple months a random proposal happens and before you know it, you are pregnant with your Twin's child, and roses are falling from the sky, and angels appear to play the music of heaven.

But those who are Soul Twins know how far from the truth that is, and it just isn't that simple. Many Soul Twins met their Twin while they were living with or married to karmics. Some met their Twin but during the Running/Chasing and separation, they found themselves with a karmic. Karmics of course aren't your Soul Twin, but they can certainly feed off the energy between you and your Twin and cause destruction to your life.

Too many Soul Twins hold on to these karmics for different reasons. But karmics aren't truly for us and some can derail our ascension. Karmics can reel you in and keep you locked down by being sweet and making you comfortable in a place where it can be difficult to focus on your ascension.

Some karmics aren't very happy with themselves or their own lives, and attempt to sabotage Soul Twin relationships. Other karmics are like puppet shows, only there to keep you distracted and comfortable in a place where your ascension will stagnate. Other karmics are there for a period of time to teach you a lesson or to cause some trouble in your life to get you out of being lazy and complacent. The fire does warm the pot and make the water boil!

Karmics aren't necessarily bad, and all in your life serve some purpose. But holding onto karmics who mistreat you or keep you off the ascension path isn't wise. Karmics won't rescue you from the soul journey or your Soul Twin, so leaving your Twin for a karmic will only cause you further confusion and problems. Choosing a karmic over your Soul Twin is not an act of self-love or love for your Twin, but an act of abandonment and carelessness. If you know in your soul that your Soul Twin is the one to choose, why choose someone else who you know is not soulful to be with?

Now for one thing, I don't like calling people karmics because it can make it seem like there is something wrong with them. Or, like there is something about them that makes a relationship impossible or too difficult and therefore they are meant to be left. Karmics are not all bad people. But you need to evaluate how, and who are aiding you in your ascension.

It is also possible for some karmics to be jealous of what Soul Twins experience. They might attempt to keep Soul Twins apart from each other, downplay what they have, or pedestal their own relationship.

**NOTES:**
- Karmics are abundant, Twin Flames are common, but you only have one Soul Twin (if your soul went through a split or spread).

- A Twin Flame or soulmate does not necessarily make a better partner or relationship, just as a 'karmic' does not necessarily mean the person is bad or not good for lasting, healthy relationships. The 'karmic' souls simply function differently, and are usually Earth-bound souls.

- Everyone has their own reason why they choose to be with a particular person. Connections and relationships are complex, and it isn't always a straightforward answer. It is common though, for one Twin to avoid their Soul Twin and desire to be with others due to being overwhelmed by their Twin, not wanting to face their fears, not wanting to change, or actually because of the other Twin's behavior. Sometimes it is simply just them choosing who they feel is the more favorable partner.

- Karmics and Twin Flames are not primarily romantic or sexual. Soul Twins are sexual and romantic by default, as they are a polarization of the same soul. They experience something beyond hormones, physical attraction, and social norms.

- Never jump into a relationship with someone other than your Soul Twin after you have met your Soul Twin. When Soul Twins meet each other, it is time to graduate from karmics and Twin Flame connections. You'll only prolong separation and cause pain to everyone involved, including yourself. It's sickening to see people who have so much love for each other go in the complete opposite direction and cause so much confusion and pain when it's obvious who they should be with. It's not difficult, we just make poor choices, and everyone suffer for it

## WHEN KARMICS DON'T WORK

You might hear from some that you need to leave your karmic to meet your Twin Flame (or Twin Soul), or you need to leave your Twin to meet your soulmate. I suggest to not abandon people just because you have a dopamine rush to move on to something 'better'. Please understand the ascension is not about chasing after someone or looking for someone to be with. It is said by many mature souls that if someone need to be in your life, or you are supposed to partner up with someone in this lifetime that you WILL be with them. There is no need to stress, worry, or panic. What I recommend to focus on is being the healthiest, most vibrant you. You attract what you ARE. If your state of being, way of living, and way of treating others is poor, how can you expect someone else to want to be with you?

## QUICK QUESTIONS

*"I've met my Soul Twin, but the connection is too overwhelming. He does not want to be with me. Am I supposed to leave this connection for a karmic or soulmate?"* I say this all the time, once a Twin meets their Soul Twin, it is time for them to graduate from Twin Flame and karmic connections, not run to them. You have already been with karmics and other types of connections, why would you want to go BACK to them? Karmics and Twin Flames will still serve their purpose, but your Soul Twin is the one you should be with. No one graduates high school and when they are handed their diploma, turn it down and ask to retake their classes! Take your diploma! In the same respect, accept your Soul Twin!

***"Do Twin Flames meet a karmic before meeting their Soul Twin?"***
Everyone meets karmics, not only Twin Flames and Soul Twins. Karmics are the most common and standard connections. Meeting a karmic before meeting your Soul Twin has no importance or relevance. They simply were the last person you happened to be with when you met your Soul Twin.

***"Are Soul Twins happier with karmics than with each other?"***
It is common and more likely than not, that the Soul Twin who is involved with a karmic is not happy or stable in that relationship. They will be haunted with dreams, intense energy, signs, synchronicities, redirects, and heart pulls (toward their Soul Twin) while with the karmic. The Soul Twin connection will always override all other connections. Because of this, the Twin will eventually leave (or be left, or kicked out by) the karmic.

***"Why do I still have strong feelings for my Supposed 'Twin' Soul even though I go with a soulmate?"*** You can't leave yourself. You can't separate from your own soul. What you are feeling is trying to make things work with someone who isn't your Soul Twin. Your Soul knows this isn't the correct choice which is why your feelings have gotten stronger. It is also likely that you are feeling your Soul Twin's emotions. They might be hurt by you choosing to be with someone else and not them. They also know that you and they are supposed to be together, but because you left them and chose to be with someone else, that has hurt and confuse them. Those strong feelings increasing also are the result of hormones. We tend to miss people when they are not around.

***"Why can't I stop thinking about my Soul Twin even though I am with a soulmate?"*** You can't stop thinking about them because they are YOU in another body. They are your own soul. Just because you go to be with a karmic or someone else does not mean you will forget about or move on from your Soul Twin. You might physically be with someone else, but your mind, emotions, and soul are still with your Soul Twin.

***"Does everyone have a Twin Soul?"***
Everyone has a Soul Twin. But unless your soul has split or spread, you won't meet a specific physical person who is your Twin. You will experience your Soul Twin purely as a energy. It will seem like you always attract people, and it is always based on your own physical, emotional, mental, and energetic health. People are not physical bodies, but frequencies of energy which incarnate in a physical body. Your Soul Twin is a frequency of energy you experience in your romantic and sexual partners. Once your soul split or spread, then your soul will have the ability to incarnate in another body, and that is when you will have an incarnate-Soul Twin. But at the end of the day, we all have a Soul Twin, and they are our own Soul, whether they come to you as a specific person, or as an energetic form in different people (based on your frequency).

***"Are we supposed to leave our Soul Twin for a soulmate or a karmic? Why do I have trouble falling in love with my soulmate or a karmic after I have***

*met my Soul Twin?"* You aren't supposed to fall in love with someone else, not after meeting your Soul Twin. Upon meeting your Twin, it is time to move on and away from being romantic/sexual with others. Your Soul Twin is purposeful in your life, and not a random occurrence, or someone you need to run from to go be with someone else. That defeats the whole purpose of the Twin Soul journey. Soul Twins ARE meant to be together. It is unbreakable and the intense love, heart pull towards them, the sexual cravings for them, thinking about them day in and day out, being madly in love with them,.....none of those signify needing to abandon the connection to be with someone else. Those are all obvious signs of who you need to be with and why.

If one has spent YEARS and DECADES being in romantic and sexual connections with karmics and/or Twin Flames, why do they need to go back and be with more karmics and Twin Flames after meeting their Soul Twin? That would be so unnecessary and backwards; in that situation, it would have been better for them to not have a Soul Twin, and never meet them so that they can remain with their karmics and Twin Flames.

### *"My Supposed 'Twin' and I had issues so we decided to leave each other to be with other people. Are we still going to end up together?"*
After meeting your Soul Twin, it isn't possible to have the same depth and intensity of love and connection with someone else. If you are in relationships with new people, why are you concerned with not being together with your Soul Twin? You both made the CHOICE to be with other people. It is counter-intuitive to do this and then wonder if you two will be together. Why not have stayed single and work out what ever issues you and your Soul Twin had, rather than you both going to be with other people?

### *"Why does my Soul Twin leave me repeatedly for karmics?"*
Everyone has their own reasons why they choose to be with a particular person. The reason why your Soul Twin won't stay with you could be for so many different reasons. Your Soul Twin surely know why. It could range anywhere from them not feeling good enough for you, to you having done or said something to cause them to not want to be with you and all in between. If you know for sure you haven't done or said anything harmful to them, you likely are dealing with someone who simply chooses others over you, whether they have feelings for you or not. In the other situation, if you have done or said harmful things toward them, then these are likely the reasons why they leave you for karmics.

### *"Can Soul Twins dream about each other before meeting physically?"*
Soul Twins can certainly dream about each other while having not met physically yet. Remember, this is a soul journey. And Soul Twins are already One on a non-physical level. The dreams will definitely come about after meeting physically, and can be more intense.

# SECTION FIFTEEN

# SURRENDER, THE GREAT REALIZATION

It has been a long inner battle hasn't it? Lots of running, separation, pain, chasing, and confusion, amongst other things. After doing all of that, you find your Self in a different frequency of energy. You are no longer chasing after your Twin, but you don't run from them either. There is no more pain, confusion, or frustration. At times, you may even feel dull, and very calm. But you are also very conscious. You are thinking about a lot of things, and have even more 'Aha!' moments. You have surrendered!

Surrender is when the soul stop resisting ascension and becoming conscious. When Soul Twins surrender, they stop running from and chasing after their Twin. It is when the Twins become conscious that they cannot run from or chase after the other Twin because their Soul Twin is their Self in another body. The Twins do not always surrender in the same way. Don't go looking for physical or external clues to see if they have surrendered or not.

The surrender stage is when there is a relax and peace with the Soul Twin and ascension.

Unlike relationships with Twin Flames and karmics, with Soul Twins, it is inescapable. You were able to rack up karmic debt with others and assumed escape. But not with your Soul Twin. Your Twin is YOU. You can't run or hide from yourself, and neither the karmic debt you have been stacking up over the years, decades, and lifetimes.

But some Soul Twins continue to try and run from their Soul Twin or 'move on'. Unfortunately, there is no moving on from your Self. Still think you can get away? Absolutely not. There is no running from your Soul Twin (your Self), breaking the connection (with your Self), or moving on from your Twin (your Self).

## THE JOURNEY FORWARD HOME

You've probably gotten so accustomed to your Twin not responding, ghosting you, and not giving love back that you've surrendered and stopped chasing. But why haven't they returned? Doesn't Union come after Surrender?

There is a reason why female Soul Twins commonly experience what they do with their DMs. It is for both Twin's awakening and ascension, not just the DMs. Many DFs were deep asleep when they met their Soul Twins. But it is easy to assume that if the DM is running or doesn't want to communicate that their DM is asleep. There is more going on here than what is seen on the surface.

You see, your Twin is no ordinary person. If your Twin just loved you and communicated, and did all the things you wanted, you would not be able to look yourself in the mirror. You would not have been forced to look deep within yourself and realize that you still have some trauma, fears, and other things to work out of your being. You have been involved with Earthly people in your life. After meeting your Soul Twin, you felt and knew the kind of love they are capable of, but was heartbroken when they did not reciprocate and or was closed off. It was all for a reason and good purpose.

You might not want to admit it, but you haven't always seen your Soul Twin in the best of perception. You may have met them in the worst part of their life. You probably looked at them as just another person with problems, although one you have felt a deep and unbreakable attraction too. You tried to 'get them' to wake up and see the light. You tried to make them aware of all the love you've given them. You even took the time to explain everything and make them see the potential you have together. But why did none of that work? It worked mostly with other people, but why not with them? The more you tried, the more they ran, ignored you, and disappeared.

You might think this sound funny because in some ways that might seem like it's true, but in other ways they might seem worse than any. You see, on Earth, there has been a major spiritual war taking place; two forces fighting for control and ownership of the planet and its inhabitants. As Soul Twins, we are here on purpose, and it is to help raise the vibration of Earth and usher in a new world. *"That's great! So, how come he is still asleep and not responding to my messages and calls?"*

It's normal for us to want to be in control. But wanting to control someone can cause more harm than good. *"I know, but why would my Supposed 'Twin' behave like this? If they woke up earlier or when we met, we would be in Union by now and fulfilling the Divine Mission!"* Oh, it is seemingly that simple, but unfortunately it isn't. Many have had to learn the hard way. Your Twin choosing to keep from you might be necessary for you to see that it isn't only them which need to heal and make some changes to their behavior and lives.

When Soul Twins come together, they have a profound effect on the people and environment around them. If they come together too soon or too fast, the opposite results can happen that the Divine has in mind. It could cause them (and the people around then) more harm than good. Soul Twins have difficult lessons to learn and healing to do, and that takes time. It's a process, one which should not be rushed.

*"But why would they initially not want anything to do with me? Why not have both of us partially awake so at least we can have a good friendship until we get into Union?"* That sounds like a good idea! But remember, it all has to be carefully planned and timed, so that it cause more good than harm.

Your DM is the man. He hold the heaviest of the weight, weight that could crush and kill or weight that could knock out the destructive energies on Earth and lay down a new and stronger foundation.

When the Earth is full of hate, murder, theft, fraud, lies, slavery, conflict, greed, hunger, and other things, Soul Twins come in to shift the energy away from these. These things have to be replaced with new ones, ones that bring love, save lives, protect life, bring harmony, peace, productivity, truth, resolution, and sustenance.

Your Twin being away from you has allowed both of you to gain Earthly experience, knowledge, and understanding. These all come in handy. We know how and why certain forces do what they do, and that's a huge advantage. Your Twin will be with you when the time is right, when The Most High is ready to send you both out after training is finished. Fortunately, that time is soon! It's Union Season™! It's time to take Earth back! You've gotten too used to calling your Soul Twin a liar, cheater, careless, heartless, and other things too uncensored for me to mention. This will only prolong the process. You must refrain from doing these things.

Your Soul Twin is YOU. YOU CANNOT call yourself a princess or queen then turn around and call your Twin a scumbag. That would be you calling yourself a scumbag! You are smarter than that! Try something different this time. If you are willing to call yourself a Princess (whether you are one or not) then you should also be calling your Twin your Prince. How you perceive your Twin is how you perceive yourself.

## THE JOUNREY FORWARD HOME PT. 2

The Soul Twin Collective has been in a major shift. The Runner/Chaser dynamic is over. We have all heard it so much that it has been easy to feel that our Twins will never return to us, or if they do, it will just spark another separation. But just imagine for a moment your Twin returning to you and things being different, much better than ever. You've gotten so used to your Twin ignoring you, going no contact, and running into the arms of others that the feelings of your Twin returning (and staying permanently) leave you in doubt, disbelief and distrust.

Anyone who has ran long enough know that it is exhausting. Only so much energy can be expelled. Your Twin will eventually get tired. I remember a few months after running from my Supposed 'Twin', I got so exhausted, I just gave in. I surrendered to the ascension process and began healing and making changes with myself and life.

Nothing can truly keep the Runners running. Each and every one of them will eventually get so exhausted from running that they'll surrender by default and accept the ascension process (and you!) as it is. Because your Soul Twin mirror everything in your own being, behavior, and life, it is important to not look down on our Twin. Even if they are up to no good, or have mistreated you, remember, life and ascension are not always blue sky, white clouds, and sunshine. Your Twin might be your Shadow Self. Twins who have realized Union, see their Twin for who they truly are, and it's definitely not the negativity and conflict we see on the outside.

Only the strong, wise, conscious, and ones who take proper action will make it through. This journey is not for the weak which is why Soul Twins are so rare. Even in the Soul Twin community, we see Twins who can't handle seeing themselves in the mirror or the intensity they feel with their Twin. But things are different this time, and seasons do change, and the light is meant to shine in the dark.

Your Soul Twin will return when you humble yourself and finally realize your Twin has been showing you to yourself all along. They are the journey and pathway to the Union you seek. You have been running from yourself which is why separation seemingly prevailed. You are the Union you have been seeking. You finally realize you can't change your Twin, you can only change within yourself what they mirror back to you.

Surrender bring a peaceful state of being. You won't feel the urge or compulsion to chase after anything. You no longer stress over people or things not flowing smoothly in your life. Surrender is a wonderful place to be. From here, you won't feel much push or pull from external influences. You'll be able to do activities without anxiety, stress, confusion, anger, or frustration. From surrender, a CONSCIOUS life can be lived through choices without emotion or desire getting in the way.

It is not a bad thing to feel peaceful and like you don't want anything else from life. In time things will change better for you without having to force anything.

## THE FEELINGS OF SURRENDER

*Surrender.* It sound like a blue sky, waves reaching up the seashore, and hands up in the air with soft music playing. *Surrender.* It sound like a big smile on someone's face after letting out a big sigh. *Surrender.* It sound like the light shining in a dark place followed by a light breeze with birds singing.

But Surrender isn't always so wonderful. Entering the Surrender Stage will affect everyone differently and everyone similarly at the same time. The beginning of Surrender can be uncomfortable and so peaceful at different times. But no matter how you feel when you enter the Surrender Stage, it is always an event worth congratulations! You've gotten the hard stuff out the way! Congratulations!

**PEACEFUL** – Entering the Surrender Stage can bring about a deep sense of peacefulness where there is no stress or worry about your Soul Twin. There is no stress about what (or who) they are doing. This deep peace can be a wonderful feeling, or it can be annoying because it can keep you in an actionless state. The sense of peace can make you inactive and not want to get up and do anything. This doesn't last forever. You will eventually readjust to this new-to-you frequency and find yourself not only getting things done, but doing them with a great sense of purpose and enjoyment.

**PANIC** – The beginning of the Surrender Stage isn't always pleasant. When you are so used to 'feeling' your Soul Twin, when you no longer 'feel' them, it can bring a sense of panic. *"How come I don't feel him anymore?" "Is the connection gone?" "Did something happen to him?"* All kinds of questions will surface. But you will realize soon that your Soul Twin is still there, but it doesn't feel like it is because the energies have harmonized well enough. After a while you will start feeling your Twin again, as Soul Twins are always pulled together after they both Surrender.

**HAPPINESS** – This is the one we all want. Who doesn't want to feel happy? After Running/Chasing for so long, entering the Surrender Stage can bring feelings of great happiness, as you are no longer fighting the ascension process, your Self, or your Twin. You are FREE!

**SADNESS** – This is an unexpected one. Why? You would think anyone Surrendering would feel happy and at peace immediately. But sadness is possible. This can happen for a number of reasons. It can happen due to feeling uneasy about hurting your Twin and causing them to run and missing them. It can come from the release of pain that your Soul Twin caused you. You surrendered but you feel sad because you didn't want your Twin to hurt you, and you didn't want to hurt them. You realized that you didn't have to chase after your Twin or try and change their behavior or run from them. The sadness is temporary and will go away, it's a final release, let it leave you.

**EXPECTANCY** – Entering the Surrender Stage can bring the feeling of expecting something to happen. You know things are different. But you know they won't stay the same, and something grand is going to happen soon. This can feel wonderful, or it can feel uneasy, especially if that something grand doesn't happen right after you surrender.

The Surrender Stage is a stage that can take a little getting used to. It can happen suddenly and catch you off guard.

It is perfectly normal to not feel your Twin once you surrender. This is because there is little to no push-pull or energetic friction (resistance) in the connection. It doesn't mean they disappeared or have forgotten about you, it's just the energy is riding smooth and not on rough terrain. There is less energetic resistance. Surrender is wonderful, but once you are in the Union energy, you will permanently be free of the push-pull and energetic friction. Keep on healing and ascending!

## FOR MARRIED/DIVORCED TWINS

If you are married to someone other than your Soul Twin, you might find yourself feeling like you are with the wrong person. Even if your partner is a good person and treat you well, you may still feel like the marriage is over. Once reaching surrender, you might find yourself wanting to leave your marriage. If your Twin is (was) married, you might get sudden news that they are divorcing their partner, or that their partner is divorcing them, and they are perfectly happy with that. The Twins will come to the realization that no one else is for them, except their Soul Twin.

## FOR TWINS WITH CHILDREN

Has your Soul Twin not want to be with you because you have children? Or did you not want to be with them because they did? At this point, the Surrender Stage, both Twins will realize that children from others still doesn't change or break what they have. They will realize that nothing keep them from their Twin, not forever. They realize that just because you have children already does not make you less than their Soul Twin. You both are still one Soul.

## FOR TWINS WITH A LARGE AGE GAP

If your Twin is much older or younger than you, this could be the very cause of the separation. But you and your Twin will both realize that it is perfectly okay for an age gap.

## FOR TWINS WHO ARE A CELEBRITY OR PUBLIC FIGURE

If your Twin is a celebrity or public figure, in the Surrender Stage, you no longer stress about meeting them. You no longer care what they are doing or who they are with. You accept the situation for what it is.

If you are a celebrity or public figure, you take a reconsideration. Your Twin begin to look more appetizing! You want to meet them and get to know them. you realize that it is perfectly okay to be with someone who is not a public figure or celebrity.

If you and your Twin are both celebrities and/or public figures, there will be less care what the paparazzi do or others think. Neither of you will care what the media has to say about anything. You realize that your Soul Twin is YOUR business, and no one else's.

## WHEN NARCISSISTS LET GO

There is a common belief that NARCs never change. But it is possible for NARCs to give up their behavior. Even they become tired and bored, with destroying people's lives and hearts! If your Twin had NARC tendencies or behaviors, you will see them differently in the Surrender Stage. You no longer find yourself calling them toxic or any negative things. You simply just let them be to figure things out on their one. *Life is still working on them.* Likewise, your Twin will become aware of their own toxic ways, and how they destroy their own lives and the lives of others. They will realize that their own suffering is their own cause and no one else's.

# SECTION SIXTEEN

## UNION

**GUESTS** – *"Yay, finally! Union!"*
**MR. J** – "Alright, calm down, I know you all are excited. But CONGRATULATIONS! You made it! This is your Ascension Graduation! But there is more, you've only passed training. Your real work begin from here. The last four sections of this guidebook will reveal some important to know things. They will point you the rest of the way."

But what is Union? Throughout this guidebook, you have seen me mention several times that Union is not a relationship with a person. You have seen me say that Union is actually a state of consciousness, Oneness Consciousness™. I understand, you want to be with your Soul Twin physically. You want to be with them romantically and sexually. But that is all physical. Union and ascension are about non-physical things.

Also know that Union and ascension are not specific to Soul Twins. Even karmics and Twin Flames can be on the ascension path, or experience Oneness Consciousness™. But as Soul Twins, you are on an Automated Default™ ascension, meaning you will go through ascension and realize Union anyways. It is because you chose to do so before incarnating here. Your Soul decided to take soul ascension all the way.

## EQUILIBRIUM BETWEEN SOUL TWINS

No one understand the Soul Twin journey better than Soul Twins themselves. We experience it all, the good, bad, and fugly. We experience the lows, highs, and all in between. The best part is we get to live through it all and come the other end healthier, stronger, wiser, livelier, and of course more conscious than we were before.

Once Soul Twins realize Union, they don't automatically come together physically. Remember, Union is a state of consciousness, not a relationship with another person. If Soul Twins are already One, there is no need for comparison, bringing together, or merging. But for the sake of it, most Soul Twins do come together physically sometime after realizing Union. Some are together, but only as friends, family, or colleagues, while some don't come together in a relationship or marriage, at least not in the current lifetime.

Soul Twins can certainly be together physically before Union, but don't always stay together, and it isn't always harmonic or pleasant. Fortunately, when Twins do realize Union and come together physically, they forgive all their issues between each other. They no longer have anything against the other Twin. The Twins fully overstand and innerstand that their Twin is themselves in another body. They are now able to be together permanently.

## UNION SYPTOMS

- Constant open and aligned RACOs™
- No fear of death or loss
- Being unable to see people as separate
- Random feelings of peace, bliss, and joy
- Always optimistic (but realistic) no matter what is going on
- Seeing your Self in everyone around you and everyone in your Self
- People and animals are completely drawn to you
- Seeing synchronicities regularly
- Never forcing things
- Many mystical experiences, especially while in meditation
- Inability to perceive 'loss' or 'lack'
- No longer fight or resist change
- Not just 'feeling' connected, but KNOWING and EXPERIENCING Oneness with everything and everyone
- Awareness that your 'outside' world is actually a holographic projection of your inner world
- People enjoy and even crave your presence
- Just your presence alone cause favorable and positive changes to the environment and people around you
- Experiencing a flow of life energy going in and out of you
- Operating in conscious choice and intelligence utilization
- Surges of energy and orgasmic sensations in the body

## SOUL TWIN SPECIFIC UNION SYMPTOMS

- Not feeling a push or pull energy from your Twin
- Unable to worry or stress about your Twin
- Inability to see your Twin as separate from you

# UNION FORSIGHTS

It started on September 27, 2022. I went to bed as normal. What happened that night had me rolling with laughter the next morning. I had dreamed of being in a high-rise hotel. The floors were patterned carpet, and the windows were tall. It was very luxurious and expensive looking. Some of the walls looked to be made of a fine stone. There were lots of us in there. Music was played and most everyone danced. There was hot food and cool drinks. Most of everyone were women and there were a few men, although other men slowly entered the hotel to celebrate. I woke up still hearing the music and heard some horns blown. I fell back asleep and was still in the hotel in the dream. Everyone had their own room. This was a celebration in the Soul Twin Collective. We were all behaving like a bunch of kids with no adults around and no responsibilities. Ha!

Each night I dreamed of more partying and celebrating. I thought it would stop after 2 or 3 nights, but no, the celebration dreams kept coming in. One night I appeared to be in a small gymnasium. The bleachers were filled with people. I was out in the court. Everyone was quiet for a moment, until I walked over and joined the crowd. Then everyone cheered, some even holding up alcoholic beverages.

About two after that, I had a very vivid and intense vision. I saw a crowd of mostly women (a few men were in the crowd). They all looked very happy and excited about something. My vision zoomed in on one woman. She had long brass, reddish colored hair and pale skin. She cheered on. I woke up and had a vision of an entity that had pom-poms on each side. It looked like a rounded cube with no feet or legs. The entity was happy and excited and uttered *"You! You!"* While tossing the pom poms around.

In another dream I had it was of being at a beach with a lot of women (and a few men). The women wore bikinis and the men shorts. The water was so clear we could see the sand, fish, and ocean items through the water. Some of the Divine Feminines did not know how to swim so they were being taught by other DFs. At that place there was food and music. Everyone was having fun.

## MERGED: THE THIRD ENERGY

You have likely heard of a soul merge between Soul Twins. Although the Soul is already one, for the sake of it, let's look at what this means. Because Soul Twins are One Soul in two bodies, physically, when they are together, this create a third energy. This third energy is non-physical in nature, but give an open space for children to be birthed. It is the mixing of their frequencies and energies that create the third energy. The third energy has energies from both Twins. It is like when a man and woman has a baby together, the child take on characteristics, energy, and behaviors of their paternal and maternal parents.

## ONENESS CONSCIOUSNESS™

Imagine this. You are a tree, and the tree is you. How so? Look at it this way. The tree take the carbon dioxide you exhale and use that to make oxygen. You breath in the oxygen, and make carbon dioxide. Look, you and the tree have a silent but important Oneness! The same soil the tree grew out of, your body also came from, by the eating of food. Since food is grown from the same soil, and you eat that food, you and the tree come from the same soil. You and the tree exchange the same gases back and forth. You and the tree are One, and because of this, you and the tree give each other life! The tree also take nutrients from the soil to make fruit and nuts that you can eat. When you eat the food, your body will absorb some, and release the rest as waste. The waste goes into the soil, and fertilize the soil. The soil being fertilized give the tree health and allow it to take more nutrients from the soil to make more food. So, you and the tree are like one entity, self-sustaining.

This is the same with the Masculine and Feminine, whether you are a man or a woman. The Masculine and Feminine are One entity. They give life and sustenance to each other.

And, this is the dynamic you have with anyone you mate with. But when it isn't self-sustaining and mutual, it can make you feel unloved, angry, used, annoyed, confused, aggressive, or unhappy. But that isn't an issue with the other person, you must question what is going on within yourself. Two healthy individuals always produce a healthy dynamic. When you are with someone is it sustaining, mutual, and enjoyable by the other person? In a simple way, the Feminine represents substance, and the Masculine action, and the Masculine puts the substance into motion. But the Feminine must be open and trust the substance (Herself) with the Masculine. Is the substance within (and that you give) of love, confidence, honesty, affectionate, and of trust? Or is it of hate, low self-worth, dishonesty, jealousy, and distrust? Is the Masculine within you only giving out to others protection, guidance, and truth, or is it giving out usury and deception?

Men must function under a healthy masculine energy and women a healthy feminine energy. Soul Twins must redirect their attention away from the man-made matrix system, and back to the Most High. They must live their life as a Divine Being and not as a slave to the man-made matrix system. They will lose all fear, doubt, and trauma, and will walk in full confidence, love, and healthy self-esteem.

Male Twins must live for the Most High and Divine Purpose and discard toxic behaviors, addictions, and emasculation. Female Twins will be drawn to their Twin, but not when their Twin is engaged in toxic behaviors, addictions, and emasculated. Female Twins must discard their need for drama, control, and attention. They will crave the nurturing and presence of her now healthy masculine. But Union, is not a relationship, but a Oneness of energy. Relationship suggests that there are two, and the two need to unite. Union suggests that there is already One, and no need for any unification, only realization of Oneness.

The final stage is Union. Most in the community use the term 'Union' to describe a relationship with their Twin. This is incorrect. Union is a Oneness of energy, and not a relationship. Relationship signifies there are 'two'. Union is already One, and so there is an impossibility for relationship. All you have to do is realize that you are already One with your Soul Twin.

Both Twins may or may not *appear* to reach Union at the same time. When they are in Oneness Consciousness™, THEN they are both in the proper energetic state to have a lasting and harmonious relationship on a physical human-to-human level. If one or both attempt to have a physical human-to-human relationship with the other before they both are in Oneness Consciousness™, this will cause the running, chasing, and separation that many Soul Twins suffer from and complain about.

**GUEST** – *"What is ReUnion?"*
**MR. J** – "I know you are probably thinking that ReUnion is when Soul Twins come back together and are now in a relationship or married. But that is not

what ReUnion is. For there to be a ReUnion, there had to previously be a Union. Now, Union is not a relationship or getting married. Union is Oneness Consciousness™. So, when souls become entrapped in Separation Illusion™, they are not in Oneness Consciousness™ (aka Union). But as they progress through life and their awakening, they come back to Union, or Oneness Consciousness™. ReUnion is the coming back to Oneness Consciousness™. It is the cycles of becoming conscious, going into the unconscious, back into the conscious, and the cycles repeat."

## SURRENDER, UNION, AND THE RACO™ SYSTEM

The RACO™ system is now free of blockages, impurities, and demonic influences. The change in energy flow through your system now support a healthier you and therefore more fulfilling life. Your life will seem to be so much better. It is not only important to have a healthy body, but healthy energetic system as well.

## QUICK QUESTIONS

**"Does The Most High choose how and when Soul Twin Union happens?"**
Soul Twins will realize Union if and when they CHOOSE to put in the work. They must accept the ascension path, as well as their Soul Twin as mirror of their Self. It is a matter of choice; it's in our hands, not the Most High's.

**"Do Soul Twins remain in Union once they reach Union?"**
Yes. Remember, Union is a state of consciousness, and not a relationship. Fortunately, once someone realize Union, they don't revert. They wouldn't want to! The grass surely is greener on the other side over here.

**FOR DIVORCED TWINS**
You may have divorced your Soul Twin, but you both are still One. No need for court papers! You both now realize that it is not about marriage, but truly realizing and experiencing Oneness with the other on all levels, physically, emotionally, mentally, and energetically.

**FOR TWINS WHOSE TWIN IS DECEASED**
Your Twin might not have a physical body, but you are still One with them. You don't feel the least bit separated.

**FOR TWINS WITH A LARGE AGE GAP**
Even though they are much younger or older than you, that doesn't mean that you are separated. You are One with them despite the difference in incarnation age.

**FOR TWINS WHO ARE A CELEBRITY OR PUBLIC FIGURE**
If your Twin is a celebrity or public figure, they no longer feel out of reach. They no longer feel out of your league, but you feel One with them. You see life completely different now. You don't put yourself down any more. Your self-esteem is healthier, your confidence is on fire, and you are secure within.

If you are a celebrity or public figure, you realize that people shouldn't be judged by income level, social status, clothing, or other similar things. You realize that it is the person themselves that is important.

## NARCISSIST AWAKENING

Just like with anyone else, NARCs have to choose to change their ways. They have to come to the realization that the life they experience is of their own choosing. They have to come to realize that the harm they inflict on others, is the destruction of their own life experience. Can it happen? That will be up to them to decide to change their ways and treatment of others.

## SILVER NUGGETS

# THE MUSIC OF UNION

Don't we all enjoy music? There is music for our happy days, sad days, when we want to dance and party, music for relaxation, and even music that pump up the adrenaline in our body.

One of the most powerful structures of music is the trio. Just three different instruments playing in harmony with each other provide a good mix of simplicity, complexity, emotion, power, and sense of purpose. A very popular trio in Western music i56ts drums, vocals, and guitar. With these three, the drums provide rhythm and weight, the vocals the melody and emotion, and the guitar the airiness and sense of heaven. When the three instruments are tuned and played in harmony with each other with a sense of purpose, beautiful music is enjoyed by those who hear.

The human trio is a powerful band. Mind, soul, and body make the human trio. The body is the heavy and dense frequency of energy, the soul the colorful and expressive aspect of energy, and consciousness the airiness or ethereal aspect of energy. When each part of the human trio is healthy, balanced, and tuned to work in harmony with each other, the human play beautiful music as it walk the path of life. The music is love, peace, joy, youthfulness, wisdom, empathy, power, resilience, excellent, patient, righteous, intelligent, and conscious.

When was the last time you sat down and evaluated all three of your instruments? We give others plenty of attention and want them to give us attention. But when was the last time you gave your Self (your Trio) attention? How would you know if the guitar is out of tune, the drums sound saggy, or the vocals sound scratchy and unsure? How has your body been functioning? How are your emotion and state of mind? Are your desires healthy or harmful? Do you feel full of life and sensitive to energy around you or do you feel sluggish, insensitive, and unable to connect to the more subtle communications of the world around you? Are you truly aware and conscious, or are you just following whatever the crowd is doing?

When your Trio is healthy, balanced, and playing in harmony with each other, people will enjoy the Music that you are. What we call music, is harmonized vibration. If your Trio is unhealthy, imbalanced, and dissonant, other people won't enjoy the music. When those three parts of our Self are functioning as One in a harmonious way, we are no longer *just* body, soul, and consciousness. But we become the incarnated Oneness and Harmony that All is and is All.

How does your music sound? You might feel like it sound good, until your Twin come around and play the same music back to you! If you don't enjoy the music your Twin play, maybe one or two (hopefully not all three!) of your instruments need some retuning, detoxing, or alignment. We want to create beautiful music that magnetize others and heal them. We want to create music that uplift and empower others to look at their own Trio and see if they need to work on themselves so their Music also sound good!

Now imagine you and your Twin's Trio in perfect health, balanced, and tuned in harmony with each other. When you both play together, now you have a simple chorus! Now you can really create music that is heavenly and ethereal that will show the world where Home is and how to get there! That's the music of Union!

## BUTTERFLY WINGS

This is an urgent message. You have been through this too long, your Twin not texting back, your Twin ignoring and ghosting you, your Twin seemingly refusing to leave their wife/husband or karmic. This has been going on for too long. Maybe you feel stuck like nothing you do allow you to progress and move forward. Maybe you see and want better things for your Self, but you feel tied down to your current life circumstances.

I have heard a lot about female Twins being angry and sad that their Twin is behaving this way; running from her, ignoring her, not leaving his old life behind to be with her in the new life, ext. I have seen some talk about their Twin being 'in his ego' or 'in HIS shell'. But I am aware that there is no shell that even exist, except the illusionary one we create and believe to exist. The ego isn't necessarily a bad thing, and the same ego your Twin has, is a mirror of your own.

YOUR TWIN IS NOT STUCK. YOU ARE NOT STUCK. If you are experiencing your Twin not contacting you, ignoring you or remaining with his karmic, he is in a COCOON. Like butterflies, when they want to ascend and experience life from above, they have to transform into a new entity that can elevate and remain off the ground. But before they can fly, they must transform from a caterpillar. This require them to be in a COCOON.

You might feel like you have your life together and you are just waiting on your Twin to get his life together and leave his karmic. BUT, the only way he can do this, is if you also do your part! I think the mirroring between Twins is either not considered enough or Twins haven't truly grasped the reality of their Twin mirroring their Self.

Your Twin is in the cocoon. The cocoon represent Separation Illusion™. He know how to fly already, and you know this. But he can't because he is still in the cocoon. You are not in a cocoon and therefore free to fly. BUT, you can't fly because your Twin need to work WITH you for you to fly. It's a joint effort. Sitting and waiting for your Twin to change or come back, or you 'moving on' to other people is the very cause of your Twin remaining in the cocoon.

The cocoon is VERY uncomfortable! I know from experience because I was once in my own cocoon! It is HOT, uncomfortable, and outside forces can attack it. Neither you nor your Twin want to be in this cocoon. Both of you want to fly. Your Twin know how to fly, but that darn cocoon! How can he leave the cocoon? How can you FINALLY have your Twin back and in your arms? A joint effort is required. The old way of waiting for the other to initiate or do all the work or take the lead will not work. This is a team effort. Both are required to work together.

If you feel like you have everything together and are waiting for your Twin, how about trying a different method. You have been doing this too long, and it is mirrored in your Twin waiting on you also! The wait is OVER! It's time to break through the cocoon and fly. BUT, the cocoon is intentionally woven so that one person will not be strong enough to break through. It is required that the combined energy and effort of both Twins is needed to break through. If you have been stuck in a situation you don't want to be in but can't get out, if you have been waiting for your Twin to change their behavior and come back to you, you have lowered your frequency to where neither of you can break the cocoon!

**NOTE:** The cocoon is the place of transformation. It is where DNOTS, kundalini awakening, and purging happen. It is an uncomfortable, but necessary place to enter. Once the transformation is complete, the ascension (increasing of consciousness and energy) break the cocoon. At this point, the Twins are no longer bound (or enslaved) by their own ego, insecurity, procrastination, hormonal desires, social norms, self-sabotage, or fear.

You might feel like you have already done all the healing and preparation you can. That's good, but what about your energy? What about your consciousness? See, we have built and wired the circuit and machine, but we haven't turned on the battery so the POWER can flow! Turn on the power! Re-evaluate every area of your life and your Self. Continue to heal and detox. Be the best you, you can be. You made progress but you got too comfortable.

Also, all the energy you give to those other partners, this is a huge energy leak between you and your Twin. I am not talking about lesson learning from karmics and others we have contracts with. I am talking about the people you go to, to fill the perceived void or disturbance within yourself due to your Twin not giving you attention and reciprocity. These individuals are forced and are not soul contracts! Raise your energy and LEAVE these people who you know in your heart are not there to help you and obviously cause you even more harm and emptiness.

As you ascend and raise your energy, so will they. YOU are your Twin, and your Twin is YOU. The jointed raising of energy will BREAK the cocoon (Separation Illusion™)! If you want to fly, you have to fly along with your Twin. You can't do it without them. But you surely can do it with them!

# BUTTERFLY WINGS PT.2

When caterpillars want to transform, they have to undergo a self-destruction process. They enter a cocoon then turn into a gooey mess. Inside the cocoon they self-destruct, then particle by particle, rebuild themselves into a butterfly.

It is the most frustrating and heartbreaking thing to have to live through, your beloved Self not engaging with You. They left you alone, left you on read, they went after other women but not you. They closed themselves from you and ignored you. On the outside it seemed like your Soul Twin (You) didn't want anything to do with you and they were deep into themselves. How can someone who is a mirror of you do this to you? You never meant them any harm, you showed them plenty of love! How could they do this?!

In the first part of BUTTERFLY WINGS, I talked about how you and your Twin are One. You both exist and function as One. But the thing is, there is a cocoon that seemingly separate you and your Twin. The cocoon appear to be around him, but not around you. The cocoon 'separate' you both from each other. You are outside the cocoon, and he is inside the cocoon. You may feel it is as easy as just telling him to break out of the cocoon. He should stop being selfish and care more about you and not just himself! But ahh, the Oneness prevent the situation from being one sided. What happen with one Twin, is mirrored to the other Twin. While it may be as easy as telling your Twin to leave the cocoon or you smashing it with something to get him out of there, this action will only cause both of you harm.

You see, your Twin is in the cocoon for good purpose. And it is a process that isn't good to be rushed. You tried before to get your Twin to wake up and get him to be aware of the Oneness. This only caused more conflict, confusion, Separation Illusion™, and pain. But what does work is when you actively focus on healing, bettering yourself and your life, and engaging your ascension. This will cause both of you to transform into higher frequency beings with a sense of harmony. As you both ascend, you transform, and as you both transform, the gooey mess turn into a butterfly (a high frequency being). You are the Twin that is outside the cocoon and want to fly but can't fly because you have to fly together with your Twin. Your Twin is in the cocoon and can fly but can't while he is in the cocoon. In order to break the cocoon (illusion of separation, identification with ego) you both have to ascend TOGETHER. It's a team effort. The days of having the other person do all the work while you sit back and reap the benefits are long gone.

The transformation process has finished for many Twins and those Twins (who are still in the cocoon) will begin emerging. They and their Twin have healed and ascended enough that the cocoon can no longer hold due to the energy being too high for it to maintain its structure. It has been a long, confusing, frustrating, and painful process for many to go through.

I want to congratulate you for going through the process and even though at times you wanted to give up and attempted to, you always came back and tried again. Seeing your Twin emerge from the cocoon will be an amazing experience. I emerged from my own cocoon, and it is well worth to go through the journey! Your Twin is worth it! Your Twin is you and of course you want your Self! Don't you?

If your Twin is still in the cocoon, rest assured that the cocoon (illusion of separation) is not even real. As you heal, better yourself, allow yourself to be triggered, and live your best life, that energy will reflect in your Twin and their energy will rise while in the cocoon and break the shell. But this won't happen if you are running, chasing, trying to cord cut your Twin, and pointing out your Twin's faults when you get triggered, and refusing to heal. If you want to see a change in your Twin, YOU have to change. When you are triggered it's an opportunity to identify a part of yourself which you can work to improve or change.

Will you be ready to fly when your Twin (YOU) emerge from the cocoon? You've had moments when you gave up and ran, you pushed them away, you blamed everything on them. You did want to love and give them everything while they ran and went to be with someone else. When they return will you feel the same way? Will you still hold them in your heart? You loved them at their worst, surely you can love them at their best! You loved your Self at your worst (Shadow Self), you surely can love your Self at your most luminated and conscious (Higher Self)!

Get ready! The energy is high, and the cocoon can't hold! Your Twin is about to emerge! This is what you have been waiting for so, so long!

## BUTTERFLY WINGS PT.3

They (YOU) are free! The energy has gotten too high and powerful for what that cocoon can hold. They've broken free from the cocoon now, still wiping the crust from their sleepy eyes and looking around to see what's going on. They are no longer held down or closed off, they are free to fly! Your Twin was in a long deep sleep, and it's good that they were. Had they woken too early, neither of you would have experienced life, learned lessons, and matured in the way that you both needed to ascend and experience Oneness Consciousness™.

You've been frustrated for too long, sad, angry, depressed, confused and doubtful. But now it's time to put all of those behind you. You can't fly carrying those heavy emotions. LET THEM GO and fly with your Twin! Fly together! You can fly now that they are free from the cocoon. It's going to take a little time and practice to get those wings dry, stretched, and warmed up!

# GATE & SWORD™

One of the ways I see the feminine energy and masculine energy is the Gate & Sword™. The Feminine is the Gate (or gateway, or portal). The Masculine is the Sword. The Gate is where everything come in and go out. It is the Divine Door, or Divine Gate. She is the Divine Creator. The Sword is the Divine Warrior (the Divine Protector and Divine Builder). The Feminine creates, and the Masculine builds. Think about it. You can use a blade to protect yourself from harm, but you can also use a blade to hunt, take plant foods, and to perform work. The Sword is also the Mind, or Intelligence of The Most High. The Divine Gate is the Heart of The Most High.

**Source frequency** = Divine Gate + Divine Sword
**Source frequency** = Divine Heart + Divine Mind

You have to have a man and a woman. The woman has the womb, and the man is the sword. Together, all needs are met. Together, life is abundant, there is protection, food, shelter, peace, joy, creativity, travel, and productivity. The Divine Gate need the protection of the Divine Sword, but the Divine Sword need the Privilege Of Passage of the Divine Gate. They go hand in hand!

# SWEETHEART (A BEE STORY)™

Once upon a time, there was a sacred place called Middleland. In the center of Middleland was the biggest honey comb on the continent. This honey comb was called SweetHeart. It was green in color on the outside, due to the kind of nectar and pollen from the flowers in Middleland. It also came from a type of grass and fungi which grew around Sweetheart. But It had a problem. The flowers in the land could not produce the kind of honey needed to support such a massive honey comb. The bees could not fly far enough to outside flowers without dying. The mother bee, Setthora, was filled with anger, stress, and insecurity, with the bees. She felt like the bees were lazy and not working hard enough.

There was a bee named Absaar. He was the only blind bee in Heartland. Even though Absaar could not see, he could still feel the differences in the energy of the surrounding air. He could smell both pollen and nectar from flowers, and honey from SweetHeart. He was still able to get nectar and pollen from flowers in Middleland. But the mother bee was most angry and dissatisfied with Absaar, because he was the bee which brought back the least nectar. The mother bee, Setthora, bullied Absaar most of the time. This caused Absaar to wander in the field longer, as he did not want to deal with the mother bee's anger and frustration. It made him sad and feel inadequate. Due to his blindness, he would sometimes bump into other workers, and they would get mad at him. The other bees picked on him and gave him a hard time. The only bee that did not pick on him was Moura.

Moura felt sad to see how Absaar was treated. She did not like the other bees because of how they bullied Absaar. She felt like he tried the best he could. Even though she attempted several times to comfort him, Absaar would fly away or deny that he is of any benefit to the colony. He didn't want Moura to see how insecure and lacking in confidence he was inside. He had a love for her, because she was the only one that did not make his life miserable. But still, he felt uncomfortable around her, like he wasn't good enough. He kept himself closed. Moura could not spend too much time attempting to comfort Absaar, because the mother bee did not like to see her comforting him.

One day, Absaar crashed into something while out in the field. He couldn't tell what it was because he was blind. It felt like a flower, but he could not smell any pollen or nectar from it. On his way back to SweetHeart, he happened to enter the honey comb the same time Moura was leaving. They smacked into each other, kissing each other. Moura was thrown back into the comb. Absaar hit the ground. He felt very disoriented. Moura came and apologized and asked if he was okay. *"I didn't mean to kiss you!"* Absaar yelled. *"It's okay, I know you've been wanting to kiss me for a long time."* Said Moura. *"What are you two doing! Get back to work! I need nectar now!"* yelled the mother bee, Setthora.

*"I'm sorry, I have to go."* Absaar said. Moura watched Absaar fly recklessly into the field. But he noticed something strange. He could no longer smell the honey from SweetHeart, or the nectar from the flowers. Somehow, his senses changed after kissing Moura. Absaar flew through the field smashing into other bees and flowers. The other bees in the field bullied him. Absaar flew away, somewhere below the brush. *He hid himself.*

After some time, Moura wondered where Absaar was. She hadn't seen him for a long time. She went looking for him. After a little searching, she found Absaar sleeping under a flower that was very large and had very colorful leaves of purple, orange, white, and black. She went down to where Absaar slept. He looked tired, stressed, and dried up. Eventually Absaar died right there in front of her. *"Absaar!"* she yelled. She kissed him, then laid next to him, crying.

After some crying, she heard a loud SNAP! She turned quickly and felt a drip of something on one of her wings. She hadn't realized, but Absaar had come back alive after the loud SNAP sound, and he looked at her. She stood between him and the large flower. Moura took the substance that fell onto one of her wings. It was nectar from the large plant which they were under. But it was nectar which none of the bees could get out of the flower. She tasted the nectar and was strung with an intense energy. Then she heard a voice. *"Moura!"* said Absaar. When she turned around to look at him, he was pleased with Moura's beauty. *"Absaar, you are alive! But how is it you can see me? I thought you were blind? I thought you were dead."* Moura asked. *"After you kissed me, my senses changed. Whoa! That is a huge flower! How pretty!"*

yelled Absaar. Moura turned to look up at the flower, but Absaar really wanted to say that Moura was pretty.

Moura looked at Absaar and spoke *"Taste this nectar. It's from this large flower."* Absaar tasted the nectar from the large flower and all of a sudden both Absaar and Moura where overwhelmed with energy. They heard a loud buzzing noise, but couldn't identify where the noise came from. (it came from within themselves). The energy caused them to draw close together and kiss again. Another loud SNAP sound came from the large flower. All of a sudden, the flower, named Amsi, began to ooze with nectar. *"Wow, Absaar. This flower has never produced nectar! This is the same flower you crashed into the other day."* Said Moura. Absaar said *"How do you know?"*, still stimulated from Moura's kiss. *"Well, um, I watch after you. I don't like how the bees and mother bee bully you."* She said. Absaar felt insecure, but then he also noticed how beautiful Moura was. She was the first thing he ever saw when his eyes opened. *"I just want to bring the mother bee nectar without her anger destroying the honey comb. And thank you for watching after me."* He said.

Moura said *"But look! This flower is making nectar now! Somehow we made this flower to start producing nectar. Let's take some back to Setthora and see what happens."*

*"I don't want to."* Said Absaar. *"You have to stop feeling bad about yourself. They pick on you because you don't feel good about yourself."* Moura said. Absaar thought for a moment. He looked at Moura, enjoying her shining beauty and clear confidence. Then he looked at the Amsi flower and noticed the circular purple, orange, white, and black patters on the squarish, lobed leaves. Then he looked at SweetHeart and was dissatisfied at all the anger, stress, and insecurity amongst the bees and mother bee. He also did not realize how big the SweetHeart comb was. It stood high, even above the trees. *"Let's get this nectar and take it to mother bee. We need to get rid of all the anger, stress, and insecurity in there."* Said Absaar. Moura smiled big and was pleased with Absaar's sudden confidence.

The two of them gathered some nectar from the Amsi flower, but struggled to handle the energy from the nectar. This nectar was surely different from any of the other flowers. The only way they could contain the energy was to fly and keep moving. Absaar flew toward SweetHeart, and Moura followed. When they entered SweetHeart, mother bee was angry to see the two of them together. But then she noticed something different about Absaar. He was looking right at her in the eyes, something the mother bee never seen Absaar do. When she looked at Absaar in the eyes, she saw Moura. The mother bee turned and looked at Moura, and saw Absaar in her eyes. The mother bee was now confused, as she could not tell which was Absaar and which was Moura.

*"Mother bee Setthora, take this nectar. I apologize for any anger or stress I have caused in Middleland and in SweetHeart. Forgive me and take this nectar."* Said Absaar. Moura followed *"It's from a different flower that*

*Absaar and I found."* Mother bee took the nectar and ate. She wiggled, bounced, and twisted as the nectar was more pure and potent than she expected. *"The heavens be opened! Purification and power be here!"* yelled the mother bee. The other bees stopped for a moment and looked at SweetHeart, Setthora, Absaar, and Moura. SweetHeart began to shake and buzz, before it started to glow an orange and white light. *"Moura and Absaar, bring me more!"* said mother bee. The other bees followed the two to the Amsi flower. They all took from the flower, but only Absaar and Moura could take nectar from the large flower, as the nectar was too pure and potent for the other bees.

So the other bees took nectar from the other flowers in the field, and Absaar and his beloved Moura, only took from the Amsi flower. The mix and ratio of the two nectars created a new kind of nectar which was different than anywhere on the continent of Middleland and the planet. Eventually, Middleland began to expand and build honey combs in other lands and on other continents.

The honey from these honey combs fed all the homeless and poor. Even the mighty kings and warriors of other lands used the magical honey from SweetHeart to symbolize the powerful bright Source of All life. Those from all over went to SweetHeart, located in Middleland, to visit Moura, Absaar, and the Amsi flower. Eventually, Absaar and Moura birthed little bees which also took nectar from the Amsi flower. Absaar and Moura became well known and even died together in old age. Moura-Absaar were buried in front of the Amsi flower. An image of them kissing was impregnated in a stone slab using various rare gemstones such as green aventurine, carnelian, lapis lazuli, quartz, and obsidian. Those who visited the stone and flower were forever changed, just by the energy alone from the Amsi flower, stone, and Moura-Absaar.

**NAME MEANINGS**
Absaar – sight
Moura – light
Amsi – reproduction, creation
Setthora – thunder

# SUNRISE: THE JOURNEY INWARD

As stated earlier, my awakening began at the age of 3 years, from a series of very vivid and powerful dreams. I didn't know what was happening, or why I was experiencing what was happening to me.

When I was a child and teenager, I found the world, people, and environment to be too harsh and toxic underneath. Although things appeared to be a certain way on the outside, I saw things on a deeper, more subtle level which I found very disturbing. Due to certain things in my life such as family issues, unexplained health issues, identity issues, and various others, I found myself in isolation. When I was not in school, outside riding my bicycle, or with family, I *hid myself* in my room. The door would be locked and the window blinded, so no light came through. I wanted to block myself (really a self-protection mechanism) from the outside world I saw at the time as being unaccepting of me, as well as harsh, toxic, and unstable.

I did not know that I was engaging in a practice called meditation. I thought I was just keeping myself away from the dramatic and chaotic world. This routine meditation mixed with the profound dreams, set the foundation for my ascension in my twenties and thirties.

I also enjoyed getting up early in the day to go outside and watch the sunrise. I did the same later in the day, watching the sunset. I was very much pleased and in awe at the phenomena that most people did not really pay attention to. To me, watching the sunrise and sunset was part of my daily routine. It was common to feel intense energies, buzzing, laughter, prickly skin, and tears while watching the sunrise. The sunset was more calming and relaxing. Little did I know, this practice was something people from ancient civilizations did to feed the non-physical aspects of themselves. The light from the sun entering the eyes, passing through my energetic field, and shining on my forehead caused something in particular to happen. It is called the opening of the third eye. It is also certain substances excreted from glands inside the head, the pineal gland and pituitary gland.

This caused me to become aware of things that other people seemed to be oblivious to. It fueled intense dreams, strange bodily sensations, the gaining of knowledge without having read a book or taken a class, and the awareness of an entire non-physical world underneath what most people call physical. It was like my eye was wide open, able to see the Hidden and Unseen, all from this daily practice of focusing on the sun. This, mixed with meditation, laid the foundation for my ascension and soul journey.

High school was a very exciting but also stressful time for me. In one experience, life treated me well. In another, it seemed like I was the devil or Satan everyone said was no good and needed to be casted into hell. The turning point is when I got news that my Father passed away. It was heartbreaking. It brought me back to the time when he and I were outside playing basketball. Because of his tall height, and me still being a child at that time, I literally had to look up to see his face. On the basketball court, in one quick moment, the ball was in my hands. I looked up and noticed my father standing in front of me, looking back at me. The sun was right behind his head. The sun looked like his head, and his head looked like the sun. It's a sight I still remember this day. This mystical moment happened not long before he passed away.

Ten years later, I got news of my mother passing away. In a similar, yet different situation, I also had a mystical experience before she passed. It was that one day, we were at a Neighborhood Walmart. I parked my car in a parking space to wait for her to come out of the store. She was going to give me some money to borrow, but she needed to go to the ATM first. I opened the door of my car and put one of my feet on the ground and looked at the sun. The sky was full of vibrant colors. A few minutes later, my mother walked in front of the door, while I was looking down. By the time I looked up to look at her, the sun was right behind her head. It was as if her head was the sun, and the sun was her head. Immediately, I was reminded of seeing the sun right behind my father's head. That day, it was difficult to interact with other people or do my daily activities. The only thing I could think about was what had just happened.

Right before both my parents died, I saw the sun directly behind their head. I just couldn't get that out of my head. I knew these things were not coincidence. They all happened for a reason or a purpose. Of course being young, you don't want to die. But if I saw the sun behind both of my parent's head before they died, I figured that I was going to die as well. We are all an intricate and complex mix of our parents. I was going to die. But by this time, I was aware enough to know that this was not going to be a physical death. I still couldn't put my finger on it.

The year after my mother passed, I had a few dreams. I kept dreaming about meeting some famous people, and seeing dragons flying. I had dreams of going in and out of buildings with a group of people, setting free people who were bound. In other dreams, I seemed to be attacked by strange creatures, and even weapons fired at me from people I knew in real life. Something was going on. Obviously, these people in real life were not harming me. They weren't of any concern. Something deeper was going on here. I realized that this death I was to experience was a sort of 'ego' and identity death. I knew at that moment that some bad things were going to happen, that some major changes were about to happen to me and my life that would be very painful and unbearable.

In the latter half of 2020, after the passing of my mother, and meeting the strange *woman*, I knew for sure that I was in the middle of a soul awakening. I was going through the DNOTS, Kundalini awakening, purging, triggering, cleansing, my life completely fell apart, my physical health suffered, and it seemed like no matter what I did, nothing went right. But I kept the trust in myself, in Ahmen The Most High, and whatever process I was going through. I simply had to endure. I already had the knowledge that I was going through an 'ego' and identity death, a great transformation. That sun said it all. This was what the gurus and ancients from Egypt were talking about when they talked about enlightenment and 'Know Thy Self'. I was on the ascension path, the path to Union, or as I say, Oneness Consciousness™. It also symbolized the Energy and Fire within me rising.

I was remembering who and what I really Am. I was coming to the knowledge that most had forgotten or that was hidden from them. The transformation was real, and lasting. It caused me to have a profound effect on the lives of other people, fortunately in a favorable and just way.

# SECTION SEVENTEEN
## THE DIVINE MISSION IN ACTION

You have likely heard of the term 'Divine Mission'. What exactly is the Divine Mission? Are Soul Twins here to fulfill a certain mission? Let's take a look. But for there to be a mission for anything, there has to be some kind of conflict which need resolution.

## THE DIVINE MISSION

Various kind of souls and beings come in and out of Earth to cause different changes to the human species. Soul Twins are powerful beings which come here to bring positive change to the world. For Soul Twins, The Divine Mission is when they live their life for the benefit of everyone and not just themselves.

They are here to help the world heal and change its ways, by raising the energy to break the veil of Separation Illusion™. They help to reveal those things which have been hidden by certain people, entities, and systems. Soul Twins also reveal all of our inner wounds, trauma, fears, and blockages that prevent us from experiencing the pleasant, stable, and truly fun life we all desire to live

The Divine Mission is a responsibility and privilege. The Soul Twin community should help each other with this Mission and should not live solely for themselves. The rest of this guidebook will reveal somethings which may be part of The Divine Mission in some way or form.

## THE FLAMES OF THE TWINS

How do you feel? What do you think about? How do you perceive the people around you? What kind of words do you speak to others and with what intention? How we feel, think, and perceive ourselves and others around us is the very energy we send out into the cosmos. This is then reflected back to us in our own life. Our state of being and awareness is also important. That same energy not only create our reality and experience of life but is also felt by the people around us. Our inner life and mind is projected outward and affect the people around us, whether they are aware or not. It does whether you are aware or not.

Soul Twins are forged in the Fire of the Soul. The energy they radiate outward is like a flame that alchemize everything that is not of Truth, Knowledge, Life, and Abundance. But from birth we do pick up impurities and harmful programming from life experiences in the matrix. These impurities and harmful programming affect our energy. A realized, conscious, and pure individual will burn hot, and that radiance will raise the vibration of the people and even the environment around them. An individual that is unaware, and with impurities will burn at a lower temperature and the radiance will not have a favorable impact.

How does your flame (aura, EMF, and words) affect the environment and people around you? Does it attract people, send them running, make them feel happy and peaceful, or does it cause them to feel uncomfortable and irritated? I'm not talking about attracting people or them feeling good around us because of money, status, or good looks. I'm talking about your energy here.

We can feel the effects of our own flame from our Twin, because our Soul Twin is our Self and their flame burn the same as ours. Your Soul Twin serve as your guide and mirror. If you want your flame to burn brighter and cause healing and ascension of others, it's important to realize that your Twin will always have the same flame as you. This provide the perfect opportunity to self-reflect and make some adjustments or do some healing. Sometimes what we call triggering or our Twin behaving in a way that we don't like, is actually our own flame mirrored in them. It is not always a 'comfortable' experience. Once you are burning pure, you won't feel triggered by your Twin any more.

Your flame also affect you too. It's your energy that radiate out of your being. What you radiate out, come back to you. If you want a happier you and a purpose-filled life in every area, pay attention to the energy you send out. When your flame burn brighter and more pure, so will your Twin's. When you and your Twin realize Union, you both will be able to merge your flames into a larger and more powerful one. This will cause an exponential effect on other people and the environment. Imagine if that flame burn and radiate truth, love, righteous behavior, knowledge, power, and peace!

How is your flame burning? If you want to know, look at your Twin. How do you feel? How do you think? How do you perceive and treat others? What are your intentions and behaviors? How does your Twin feel about you? What do they tell you about you? These are all areas and opportunities to purify our flame and shine bright that break down the illusion of separation and light away the darkness in the world.

## THAT ORANGE ENERGY

In the summer of 2021, a Soul Twin I met off Quora.com led a journey session for me. A journey is kind of like meditation and energetic channeling. It also work with past life regression.

In this journey, I was a 4-year old boy in Egypt. In the journey, I walked down into a pyramid. As I went through the pyramid, I noticed a mysterious orange energy. I got brighter as I went through. The closer I got to the orange energy, the more energy I felt in my body. Along the way, I saw a wizard and an animal which looked like a mix of a dog and a wolf, but it had no eyes. The animal was a pet I had in Egypt. The wizard was dressed in a purple and gold rob. The wizard had skin that was so dark it had a purple tone to it. It was pure melanin. The wizard held an orb in one of its hands. It appeared as if the orb was the Earth.

Then, I was no longer inside the pyramid. I found myself out in the cosmos, amongst the stars and suns. Then I saw my Supposed 'Twin'. She had on gold plated armor and had a sword. She smiled back at me. I also saw a planet which looked like it was vacant. Usually planets have a glow to them, but this planet did not. It was Earth after it was first created. It had rocks and meteors going around it in a ring.

At one point, I had to stop the journey because the energy got too intense. The orange energy was so intense, my body was vibrating intensely, my skin was prickly.

The woman who led the journey for me sent me an audio message about her thoughts on the journey. It is interesting that she mentioned 'He's in on the secret'.

This orange energy is Source energy. It is pure consciousness and intelligence. We are not taught in schools about the Energy that reside within us. But the Egyptians knew of this Source energy.

# SECTION EIGHTEEN

## 'RESTRICTED AREA. TOP SECRET. NO TRESPASSING.'

**THE EAGLE GUARDS** – *"You can't come in here, restricted area. You need to leave."*

**MR. J** – "No, it's all good. Let them in. They made it this far, it wouldn't make sense to not let them go all the way."

**GUESTS** – *"Yea, we want to learn more! Please let us see more!"*

**THE EAGLE GUARDS** – *"You all are safe to pass."*

**MR.J** – "Alright, before any of you come in here, know this. Those of you who have made it this far have shown a willingness to learn the basics. But if you all are hungry for more, for something deeper, then this is for you. But proceed at your own risk. Let's go!"

**GUESTS** – *"I have a feeling this is going to be life changing!" "Yea, this will be interesting!"*

**DISCLAIMER:** "I am not a government entity. I am not affiliated with or work for any government entities or organizations. I do not represent any government entities or organizations." – Terrence Johnson

Let's start out simple, then get into the deeper stuff. But first, I want to mention something for you to keep in mind while studying this section. I want to introduce what I call the 1% Rule. It is only a very small percentage of people in any group of people who actually facilitate and act out the majority of the crime and unrighteous behavior. This one percent has a small effect on the 98%. On the other far end, there is a different kind of 1%. This small percentage of people in any group facilitate and act out righteousness and favorable behavior in any group. They have a profound effect on the 98% of the other people. So the 98% are influenced by two different energies, so they must all make a decision on what to trust and how to behave. Of course, the 1% is not a fixed number, or exactly 1% of the population. It simply point to a very small number of people who have small or great influence on the rest of the population.

You have two different types of 1% leaders, or those who influence the masses. Everyone has a choice who they want to follow. That 1% can have an unfavorable (and greater) influence on the masses of people. The other 1% can have a favorable influence on the masses of people. It is rarely that large percentages of people or group of people facilitate unrighteous behavior. It is really a very small percentage which influence and push the masses to engage in unfavorable behavior. The saying *"One bad apple spoils the bunch"* still ring true. We all have a choice, choose wisely and consciously.

Let's get started!

# AVOID FAKE TWIN FLAME ACCOUNTS

Imagine messaging someone on the internet or metaverse. After a short time, they seemingly disappear, and you never hear from them again. Then you meet and begin messaging another. Rinse and repeat. Then you notice certain accounts post AI-generated pictures, and writings that seem to not be original. The wording does not flow and connect like a stream of linked thoughts. Then you come across other accounts where they all always follow the exact same people, and upvote all of the same posts. When you reach out to these accounts, you never hear from the person, or if you do, they immediately attempt to get you to purchase their services and want you to follow them and upvote their content.

Welcome to fake twin flame accounts. *"Why would anyone want to create a bunch of fake accounts?"* Well, remember, humans do enjoy drama. Although humans are intelligent, that doesn't mean they don't engage in sub-telligent behavior. People have their own reasons and motives why they do what they do and behave the way they behave. But know that not all twin flame accounts are backed by a real person. It is one person, or a small group of people who create dozens, hundreds, and even thousands of fake accounts. It is all to boost their own content upvote and follows. This is to appear to have a large audience and large amount of upvotes. This attract real people, because people tend to go after and trust whatever is popular or trending. *"Are you saying this is content popularity manipulation?"* Yes. Now don't assume just because someone has a lot of followers or upvotes that it is a fake account. There are still some who are real people and create original content.

# LEAVING DECEPTIVE TWIN FLAME COACHES

I understand this journey is not about a relationship with your Twin, but about your ascension back Home, to Union (aka Oneness Consciousness™). Through Oneness Consciousness™ and being luminated, you know who you really are, and what you are capable of. You are able to create the life and experience you want. No one, and nothing is in the way anymore, because the Conscious

One is aware that only they can get in their own way.

The authentic Twin Soul coaches are not there to profit off Twins at their expense. They only want to share their experience, knowledge, and truth for the benefit of other Twins. They know they can make money elsewhere, and they do not have to take advantage of Soul Twins.

You can identify authentic Twin Soul coaches because their primary drive is not about money. Their primary drive is to aid Twin Flames and Soul Twins in their soul journey. The know what Union and ascension really is, and they are aware that everyone is given the opportunity for ascension. They never pedestal themselves, and they behave like they have normal lives just like everyone else. They are aware that the Twin Flame/Soul Twin experience is not all pretty and glittery. They don't flash their money and expensive material possessions. They are logical and also don't force expensive courses and books on people. The biggest one, they create favorable and reasonable outcomes and results in the lives of those they help. They are aware that not everyone wants a relationship, marriage, or children. They also tend to sway and reel large masses of people. Remember, never follow the herd. This is a game we are all in, and the only ones who pass are always a few out of the many.

They also overstand that they have to protect their Twin's identity, especially if their Twin is a female. Unfortunately, there are people out there who target and attack Twins. It is important to never share your Twin online or out in the open for everyone to see unless you have your Twin's consent and they don't have a problem with it.

But there are Twin Soul coaches and guides who are real Twins. They create content, books, and courses which are priced reasonably, they make themselves available to help Twins directly, and their teaching is based on real, ancient knowledge and practices. We all need help at times in our lives, even Soul Twins. Having a guide or coach can be of great benefit to your Soul Twin journey. Just be conscious of who you are being led by.

## SPELLS EXPOSED: AVOID THE TWIN FLAME TRAP

**GUEST** – *"Terrence, why is this man still chasing after his Twin? He keeps saying how toxic she is and that she took his children from her. And here, there is this woman who says her Twin is physically and emotionally abusive, but she doesn't want to leave."*

**MR. J** – "It sound like they have an attachment to someone who isn't very healthy for them. It doesn't matter if the person is a Twin Flame, karmic, or soulmate, or Soul Twin, why put your time and energy into someone who is treating you like you are less than? How can someone be so in love with someone who is so toxic? There are some who believe that even if your Soul Twin is abusive and treats you nasty, they you still need to be with them and love them. Reasonably, I see it wise to give them their space and focus on bettering yourself and life, rather than feeding time and energy to someone who is like that, Twin Flame or not."

Never allow yourself to become attached to and entrapped to someone who is not for your ascension and greater good.

## DEATH TO ENERGY VAMPIRES

No, this is not what you think it is. This is not a man or woman in a cape with sharp teeth who feed off the blood of others. This is about a different type of feeding. You likely overstand the concept or idea of a vampire and what they do. But here, this type of vampire is of a different nature. Energy vampires don't go around looking to feed off the blood of others, although there are rare accounts of those who do. They crave the feeding of other people's time, energy, and attention.

Energy vampires are not specific to any gender, race, ethnic background, social status, personality type, or dress code. Since those in the conscious and spiritual community (including Soul Twins) are engaged in gatherings, practices, and discussions of things which pertain energy and consciousness, they become the most desired feed for energy vampires. If they are of very high energy and vibrance, energy vampires seek them out. This is why you hear about some Soul Twins, Indigo Children, StarSeeds, and others complain about attracting NARCs or vampires at some point in their ascension. The energy vampires attempt to feed off their high energy. In a way, it is also a challenge to become aware of, and overcome for the growth and maturity of the soul. Your time, energy, and attention are all invaluable.

Energy vampires are not easy to identify, except for those who are conscious enough, and have experience with them. It should not be assumed that an energy vampire can't be that handsome, popular man you saw at the party last night. It shouldn't be assumed that they can't be the person who does a lot of things for you that you feel like you haven't done anything to receive such treatment. They could even be that woman that you are very physically attracted to, or seem very feminine. These vampires can be anywhere; in the store you shop, in the metaverse, on social media, on dating apps, and even in the same neighborhood you live.

When it come to these vampires and their engagement with Soul Twins, it is important to identify them quickly. Do not give them your time, attention, or energy. They are only around to feed off those three invaluables. You will know when you are around one, because that is what they will only be about: taking away your energy, attention, and time. Once they are feeding off you, they either demand more, suddenly disappear, or make you feel like you are hurting them by not giving them those three things.

*"How do I protect myself from them?"* It begin with the knowledge and information about who they are, why they feed, and how they go about feeding. You also protect yourself by identifying them and removing your time, attention, and energy from them. It may even require moving to a different location, or legal action if they stalk you and don't accept your desire to be left alone. Never send pics of yourself, your Soul Twin, or loved ones to an energy vampire. They use them to latch onto your (and your Twin's) energy to feed. Do not continue conversing with them either. If you have to delete their phone number, remove them from your social media, do so. Do not meet up with them in person for anything.

## ILLINTENT WITCHCRAFT & HOODOO DISMANTALED

Most people's understanding of these are based on movies, video games, virtual reality, social programming, and augmented reality. Society at large frown upon those who claim to be real witches and those who perform hoodoo/voodoo. It is looked at as just child's play and only for fun. But again, most people do not go further than what they see everyone else doing. They don't research, investigate human history, or even attempt to meet the people in person and experience it in person. So, they walk around feeling like these things are for entertainment and 'pretending'.

But in reality, witches and those who perform hoodoo/voodoo are real. But don't expect to find them wearing robes with hoods, and waving their hands in weird ways. When you study human history, you find evidence that ancient civilizations performed rituals, did magic, and alchemy as part of their daily lives. In fact, some of them created their entire reality and lives solely off these! It was never 'evil' or 'satanic'. Many of these people actually lived in societies where crime, murder, rape, incest, burglary, fraud, and other similar things were virtually non-existent.

When people say that something is 'satanic', 'evil', or 'demonic', they are usually framing this from religious teachings and scripture of the 21st century and earlier centuries. They have been taught by people, media, entertainment, and others that these things are satanic or demonic. They have no knowledge, overstanding, experience, or truth about what people call witchcraft, alchemy, hoodoo, or magic. So they blindly believe what they are taught. They may even verbally, physically, or energetically attack people who they do not know (who practice these things).

*"Have you met any witches or had people do witchcraft on you?"* More than enough that I know the truth! Most who perform these things are normal people. They have families, colleagues, have jobs or businesses, and seek a fun and comfortable life. But the exception is that they have found and utilize ancient practices which they may or may not use for good purposes. *"But how does it feel like to have witchcraft done on you?"* There can be various side effects. Many report loss in their life (a job, object, person, ext.), or bad things all of a sudden begin happening. They may even behave differently than they always have. Personally, those who performed witchcraft on me usually did it to 'scare' me.

But fortunately, I have been on the soul journey for a long time and am well aware of what goes on. Some of the witches are so advanced in their craft, they know how to disguise their identity. Even if you see something or someone while you are asleep dreaming or meditating, you won't know who it is. But again, being aware, I can know who is behind the witchcraft, and sadly I've had to remove people from my life.

But it is not all bad. Most witches and those who perform hoodoo/voodoo are not bad people. There have been plenty of witches who have helped me in life, usually involuntarily. Not all witches are bad, remember the 1% Rule. It's always that very small percentage of any group which destroys the reputation of the whole.

It is important to also know that most people perform rituals and don't even realize it. Even cooking a meal is a ritual. You set in your mind to create a mix of ingredients which will have a certain effect on your health, or the health of who you are cooking for. You gather objects, ingredients, and then mix them in a certain way, at certain times, and under heat. You might even play some music and dance or sing during the process. You may even speak to the ingredients or objects: *"I'm going to make it spicy!"* *"This will make the flavor pop!"* *"I'm going to burn it just a little so it is crispy!"* *"They are going to enjoy this!"*

You have affected the food in a certain way by doing all of these things. Once you consume the food, now your body will ingest not only the food, but the energy you mixed into the food with your own thoughts, intentions, and words. This is why you may find that certain people who are very aware do not eat just anything, or food that is prepared in any manner. They overstand that the process of creating a meal is a powerful and usually underestimated ritual that shouldn't be taken lightly.

Magic is about changing your reality (experience of life) through visualization, chanting, thoughts, certain actions, and affirmations. It is not necessarily by saying cool sounding phrases and waving a wand. But it is by consciously creating an intention, visualizing the outcome of the intention, choosing the words you speak, acting them out, then speaking affirmations as if it is in your physical reality.

Alchemy is performed by everyone, to some degree, usually subconsciously. Alchemists overstand that if they apply conscious choice and action with certain things, they can improve their personal health on all levels, physically, mentally, emotionally, sexually, and energetically. They overstand that alchemy is a useful tool to transform and elevate their health and well-being, and that of others. It is not about mixing potions in an underground laboratory, although many alchemist do overstand and use the power of herbs and certain substances.

**NOTE:** Never send pictures of yourself or your Soul Twin to people who you do not know online or through communications. They could use them to keep Twins separated, power their spells, and rituals, and to also cause conflict and violence amongst others behind the scenes. They might even behave like puppet masters behind the scenes and use demonic entities and devices to perform their work. Do your research before seeking the help of people you don't know and have never met.

## END OF RELIGION AND ENSLAVEMENT

**GUEST (3)** – *"Well this better not be anything against God! I thought you were a man of God, Terrence! I will not sway from believing in the Lord Jesus Christ, my Savior!"*
**MR. J** – "I knew this would trigger someone."
**GUEST (3)** – *"My father was a Baptist and a preacher, and I stand firm on the Word of God, the Holy Bible! You need to be baptized and stop backsliding! Religion doesn't enslave anyone, Jesus came to set everyone free!"*

**GUEST** – *"Hey, I went to school to study the history of the Bible and all the other Bibles that it came from, and that book has been copied and rewritten so many times I don't see how anyone could believe anything it says! Then one of my colleagues took me on a trip to Egypt and I didn't realize all of those Bible stories were copied from the Egyptians!"*

**GUEST (3)** – *"Jesus is not a copy! I smell foul here with all of you!"*

**MR. J** – "Alright now, you aren't going to call me or anyone else here foul and think that is okay. If yall want to argue about the Bible and where it came from yall can find a time and place after leaving here. If you want to leave, you can turn around and go. No one here said anything against the Bible or Jesus. Most of us grew up in Christian families, went to church, and read the Bible."

**GUEST (2)** – *"Yea, don't call us foul, that's rude! Most of us grew up in religion and still have beliefs today that shape and made our world. Mr. J, what is the enslavement thing about?"*

**GUEST (3)** – *(crosses arms, rolls eyes)*

**MR. J** – "Well, GUEST know more about this since she went to school and to Egypt to studying the history of religion and the Bible. But there are some things you may not have been taught in Bible study or heard your pastor mention. That is all this is about."

As I have said before, most people don't do any research, investigate, or seek to gain further knowledge than what is common. They will believe and conform to what everyone else say and believe. They won't back-trace to find out where something originated from and who it originated from, and why it came to be. It is true. When you study the history of the Bible, you find that it has been copied and rewritten, books removed and added over and over again. This is the same with other religions and religious scriptures. Many of the stories in the current Bible do originate from the Egyptians, although in the Bible many of the words and meanings have been changed. This is why most people struggle to understand the Bible or what the stories mean.

The Bible went through different changes because various civilizations and empires did not want the people to have access to the knowledge of the Egyptians. They wanted to alter the original stories in a way which they could create false truths and gods for the people to follow. If people can follow a god or belief that is not real, they are easily controlled. People who are easily controlled can be taught and told anything, and they will go right along with it. Certain people (usually small groups of men and women) wanted complete dominance and control over the human race for their own benefit. That is human nature in a way. *If someone could, they likely will.* That is why the fall of powerful people and civilizations always happen after their rise. Somewhere down the line, they made the mistake of wanting too much control over the people, or they allowed complete control over themselves.

There are two sides here. You will see people who are so tied to a religion and think it is the way to live, or the way to heaven. But how do they know? Someone told them, or they blindly believe something in a book that has no real life evidence for backing. Their lives usually are not the way they want it to be and they call or pray to god for a better life. But little to nothing change. On the other side, you have those who seemingly have EVERYTHING they could want and ask for, and they claim it is all because of a god they have never met, or from a book that has no real world backing.

What is the one and only thing you know? That one and only thing is that you are conscious and have an experience which you don't know the why, how, and what for. You know that YOU are real, that YOU exist. There is obvious and immediate evidence of YOU! This is why the ancient Egyptians said, 'Know Thy Self'. YOU are the living, breathing, walking evidence. But how come people are led to follow and believe in a god they can't see, have never met, and have no evidence for? Remember the original gods of God? Go to Egypt, there is plenty of evidence for them, and even now, much of the evidence is being destroyed, hidden, or remade to look like other people.

So, many people do not realize they are enslaved to a religion which is based on belief and not of evidence, facts, or reality (meaning it is obvious and immediate in your current experience of life).

If you want a better life, only you can create that for your Self. There is no need to wait for someone to come back to save you from the life you created yourself. If you are conscious, and experience your creation as your reality, why not create a better life experience for your Self? Now, if you want to go along with the Bible or any other scripture, why not decode what is there so you have a complete and deeper understanding of what is there, why it is there, and how to utilize it all to your advantage?

**GUEST** – *"So you realized the Bible has hidden meanings and isn't a collection of events that actually happened?"*
**MR. J** – "Absolutely! I had the same issues when I first began reading the Bible. None of it made sense, and much of it sounded crazy. That was until I did a little research and realized that the Bible had been copied over and changed so many times, it lost its original meanings as they were in Egypt. Over the years I met more and more people who either were getting tired of religious beliefs, or they had been involved in cults which they were led to through the church or certain religious organizations! It seemed like I was shifting from a world where believing a religion was the thing to do, to a world where people were waking up and realized they had been misled and lied to. More and more people who studied human history, the origins of the Bible, and religion began releasing the information and knowledge of what was really going on and it made even more sense."

I'm not saying religion is evil or shouldn't be followed, everyone has to take steps from drinking milk to eating meat and vegetables. I am not a scholar at this, so everyone is up to do their own research. You also have to overstand, that just like many other people, I too grew up in a religious family and environment. I was little. I went to church, read the Bible, got baptized, and all the other things that come along with standing firm with the belief.

But I realized there was so much more going on and what I was doing was part of something that was designed to keep people away from the true knowledge of life. Remember, my awakening started at the age of 3 years old. It really did feel like "Why am I doing this?" "What is this for, really?" "How come this is something I HAVE to do to go to heaven or be labeled a good person?" It really did feel like I woke up and looked around, and others were deep asleep.

## TRUTH UNCAGED

This is a dream I had in late 2022. It reminded me of some things I saw in society at the time. Everything in this dream is symbolic and some things were actual.

In the beginning of this dream, I appeared to be inside of a large building. I stood on the far end of the room. I noticed more than a few things immediately. To my right, a large metal cage housed hundreds of men. Most of the men yelled and screamed. They were drawn to a crowd of women, who were on the left side of the building. There were a few men who were not inside the cage. Some of them stood against the wall, others sat at tables. The cage was locked in several places, so that the men could not escape.

The women were in lingerie, bikinis, or short dresses. Most of them wore heels. The women in the crowd danced, teased, and flaunted sexual energy toward the men, who were locked inside the cage. But even though the women were not in a cage or trapped, they did not try to flee the scene. I noticed more than a few of the women had necklaces around their necks, which had keys on them. I assume those keys worked with the locks on the cage, to lock and unlock the cage.

There were some women who were not in the crowd. These women were not in bikinis, lingerie, heels, or short dresses. They wore casual apparel. These women did not have necklaces or keys with them. They looked at what was going on and did nothing. The men in the cage seemed to either want the women, or they more so wanted the keys so that they could open the cage and set themselves free.

Then I noticed a tall structure at the other far end of the building. At the bottom of this structure where guards with rifles and bulletproof gear. They guarded two elevators, which the entrance to were at the bottom of the structure. At the top of the structure, were a few windows. I squinted my eyes to glance into the windows, to see if I could see what was inside the structure. I then noticed a very small group of people inside. There were all white people, and dressed in white, expensive looking clothing. Some of them stood at the window to look out at the men and women. The others appeared to sit at a table with papers and pens. There were two guards at the top of the structure, guarding the entrance to the elevator.

Above the tall structure, I noticed a dark cloud. The cloud appeared to be a demonic entity. The people at the top of the structure communicated with the entity at times. Then, I was immediately pulled out of the scene. As I was pulled away, I noticed that the outside of the building was a small box floating in the sky. As I was pulled away from the building, it got smaller and smaller. Eventually I was in space, before waking up.

In my notes I took from the dream, it was as if the dark entity had control over the masses of people through those at the top of the structure. The guards protected the people at the top of the structure, and kept the masses of people from entering the structure. They kept them under control.

## HUMAN HISTORY, NOT AS IT'S TAUGHT

*"Humans are the most intelligent species on Earth",* one of my school teachers said, when I was young. "Where did humans come from?" I asked. The teacher looked at me, *"Um, well humans evolved over millions of years into what we are today."*

A monkey or sasquatch looking creature probably come to mind when you think about the first humans on Earth. While many people still have no clue of the origins of humans and men and women, some know the truth. It is quite obvious, just like with many things in life. The truth is commonly hidden in plain sight, but only those who have the knowledge and perception can see the truth.

I grew up in a time where people were told that humans came from monkeys and cave men. But later in my life, genetic evidence revealed that humans are actually comprised of the DNA of a VARIETY of animals. Physically, the human, and men and women, are animals. But men and women have a part of themselves which are not animals.

Humans were genetically created from a variety of animals, but the non-physical part of themselves already existed. That non-physical part of themselves filled the body with Life, Soul, and Spirit. The first people were the Soular People. They were the first on Earth. They are called the Soular People, because they came to Earth from the heavens, or from other planets in our solar system (actually Soular System). These Soular People are still alive and walking the Earth today. The sun give them energy, and feed their higher forms of consciousness, knowledge, and soul power.

But genetic manipulation of the human race is a real and obvious thing. You might think that the Soular People always ruled the Earth, but occasionally, they are overthroned by other people who do not like the power Soular People have. It is widely known in human psychology that people are susceptible to jealousy, envy, greed, and can become excessively hungry for power, control, and authority.

Humans and men and women do ascend, but it is not through millions of years of happenstance. The ascension take place every few thousand, and tens of thousands of years. The changes take place more so because Earth is a living entity, and She mature Herself. The cosmic bodies and systems also influence human ascension. Earth is also a Soul School, or a place for souls to learn and ascend.

# THE GREAT WEALTH TRANSFER: WEALTHY STARBEINGS

There was a time where every person was 'rich', for the most part. Wealth was a matter of directly managing raw materials: food from the ground, natural water sources (creeks, rivers, ext.), metals, land, wood, tools and weapons, cattle, ext. If you needed something, you either went out to get it yourself, or you found someone who had what you needed, and traded them for it.

But over time, humans created fiat money systems. Some of them were backed by real materials and assets. But some of those fiat money systems were backed by nothing. These fiat money systems led to the '*work for money to buy what you need*' societies. If you needed something, you went to work for someone, or got a job, and after performing the work, you received the fiat money. Once you had enough fiat money, you could then go and buy what you needed.

Human history has shown that when fiat money systems which are backed by nothing emerge, the economy experience huge growth, followed by a decline, and then a major crash. The crashes are so bad, that the entire money system and economy experience an overhaul.

I grew up in the early 21st century. There was a common saying of 'the rich get richer, and the poor get poorer'. It was during a time where the fiat money in place, was not backed by any real assets. The fiat money also had inflation, taxes, and high interest rates tied to it, and this caused a lot of dis-ease in the economy. There was a large wealth gap between two groups of people. Eventually, it became three groups of people, the poor, the middle class, and the rich. The poor had little to nothing. The rich seemed to have it all and then some. But the middle class looked like they had a lot, yet because of inflation, high interest rates, taxes, too many (or too high) expenses, and runaway consumer debt, they actually owned nothing. The purchasing power of the money they had was negative!

As I came to learn, there were wealth redistribution systems put in place, so that certain people who had wealth, could accumulate more wealth. This eventually led to a large wealth gap, and large wage gap. Those who had less and less complained that the rich needed to be taxed more, and some hated the rich. The rich wondered why the poor did not take responsibility for their spending habits, seek financial education, and learn to invest their money into business and things which could make them more money.

Whether you are a Soul Twin, karmic, Twin Flame, soulmate, or something else, your financial well-being is your responsibility. It is not the government's, the rich, or your Twin's. If you are not where you want to be at financially, it is important to identify your own habits, seek financial education, and learn to invest the money you get into things that gain you more wealth.

## END OF EXPLOITATION

I grew up in a time where it was common for women to complain about the exploitation of women and children through human sex trafficking, pornography, prostitution, and other similar things. They mentioned that men were the reason why women and children were exploited. But they did not know how much some women are also willing (and paid) participants in these vary things, along WITH men. But, I also saw that they were largely oblivious or didn't care about the exploitation of men. You couldn't even talk about it or mention it. You'd be labeled a woman hater, a misogynist, or rapist!

Boys and men were also subjected those things. But there was another kind of exploitation, and that was using a man's desire for physical/sexual intimacy to get money out of them. This was common in advertisements, dating apps, and even the dating market. It wasn't uncommon to hear horror stories from men who worked hard to take care of their family, or men who had lots of money, to wake up one morning, and everything was gone. The woman they thought loved them, cleaned house, or more so, cleaned out his wallet and bank account.

Advertisements and scams galore depicting beautiful women, sexually dressed women, or phrases which indicate a feminine, sexually innocent female led naïve men and boys to spend money on services and products which did not deliver what was portrayed. I remember hearing about something called MGTOW (Men Going Their Own Way), and it was obvious that these men were the subjects and victims of being exploited.

I don't think it is okay for anyone to be exploited for any reason, regardless of gender. There can't only be 'save women and children from human trafficking', what about men who are also exploited? Why is it not 'Save *people* from human trafficking'? Sadly, much of the exploitation men experience and complain about come from women, and certain businesses using men's sexuality against them, so it is an endless cycle of complaining, finger pointing, and of course, exploitation.

## TRUE ASCENSION IS INTERNAL AND EXTERNAL

Being popular, having a lot of money or resources does not equate to a soul journey or ascension. Ascension is an inside job. Not all who go up the soul path desire or care about gaining resources or money. In fact, some on the soul path find themselves losing attraction to the idea of gaining money or resources. When a person become conscious or realized, they find the shortcut. That shortcut has nothing to do with money or material things, but everything to do with being fully aware and conscious of the things other people don't see. When you are conscious and aware, you see opportunities that others do not. You find ways of achieving your goals and desires without as much effort or resources needed. You may even find that having less is more.

But some people feel like just because someone has a lot of money or resources, they automatically must be mature. Although some who become conscious also attain great wealth and much resources, this is largely not the case for those on the ascension path. Ascension is not about acquiring resources, but about soul ascension, about becoming conscious of reality, and that your experience of reality is a reflection of your Self.

# END OF EMASCULATION: THE RISE OF STRONG MEN

In these next two subsections, we will take a look at the rise and fall of men and women through the reversal or suppression of the masculine and feminine energies. Due to certain conflicts and issues in the late 20th century, especially in America from Feminism and emasculation of men, more and more men have been pushed into the feminine energy, and women the masculine energy. Twins are brought here to take part in reversing this, so that men and women can be put back into their correct, natural energies.

I remember growing up and seeing all the toxic energy between men and women of society. Some women felt like men were the single cause of all the problems in the world, especially the problems faced specifically by women. It was common for man-hate campaigns and man-shaming on social media and in the entertainment industry. The men seemed to mostly not stand up for themselves, as most did not know what was going on, or why the women were behaving like this. Until a big shift happened, the veil was lifted. It was the shift from the Age of Pisces, to the Age of Aquarius. The Age of Aquarius is the age of information. When the shift happened, the veil was lifted. It was as if everything that was kept Hidden, came to Light, and as if those who could not see what was really going on, all of a sudden became aware.

I noticed that more and more men began to see and realize that society was set up in such a way to look down on men, and on the masculine energy. The world and society heavily favored the feminine energy. Suddenly, more and more men realized that the people they thought loved them, or things they thought were normal, surely was not. The men realized they, and their masculine energy had been demonized, exploited, and suppressed. Fortunately, some of these men realized that the masculine energy is not toxic at all, and actually is necessary for a healthy society and world. So, they refused to be emasculated and changed their lives, who they interacted with, and how they went about doing things.

What we are told about the male sex isn't all true. I remember growing up and commonly heard some women speaking things like *"I don't need a man." "I'm the mother and father." "I can raise better kids than any man."* But as with all things in life, if you pay attention to people's actions and the actual outcomes, and not their words, you see the truth. The truth of the matter, is that as more and more women became single mothers, and more and more women pushed their children's father away, the worse some children became. Many of the children became worse as far as their behavior, their ability to learn, and their ability to be successful and handle social interactions with other people in the real world. There was a child-crisis. There was also a man crisis, and underneath all the layers, there was also a woman-crisis.

I learned early in my life that the most important thing in the human race is not money, fame, or material possessions. It is actually a healthy and stable family unit. Fame is attainable, and physical resources will always be here for the taking and usage.

A strong, healthy, complete, stable, and productive family unit is essential. The family unit is not *women and children*. It is a complete family: **MOTHER, FATHER, and Children.**

All around me I observed families that were being destroyed, not because the men did not want families, or because the men destroyed those families, or because the man wasn't being a man. It was because of huge societal changes through certain social movements such as Feminism of the 1900s, the MeeToo movement of the early 2000s, Women's sexual freedom, and Women's Empowerment. A certain group of individuals initiated these movements for the purpose of using and exploiting women to destroy their own households, so that certain entities and corporations could profit (and gain increased control over) the separation and conflict between men and women.

Through these social movements, society PUSHED men out of their households, ALLOWED women to destroy the family unit, and made the same women *feel* like it was normal to do so. These women were completely unaware that they were being used and exploited to destroy their own marriages and families, and it had nothing to do with men being toxic, liars, or the cause of all of life's problems.

**GUEST** – *"Yea but Terrence, you don't know how dating men these days is like. All they want is sex. It's hard to find a man that doesn't want that."*
**MR. J** – "That is what women were told, and they believed it. Remember, what you think, feel, and believe become your reality, and experience of life. If you feel like all men want is sex, all you will attract is men who only want sex. But as said earlier in this guidebook, men and women do not process emotions and desires the same. Women process intimacy, desire, and love through emotions (verbal) and feelings, but men do through physical intimacy. Physical intimacy INCLUDE sex, but is not only sex. It is also hugs, kissing, rubbing, and other forms of physical touch. It is also visually and through the senses, like smell. A woman who dress feminine, smell like flowers, and touch her man is always HIGHLY attractive and appealing to him."

This is simply a misunderstanding women have of how men work. They look at men and treat men as if they are women and wonder why they struggle to find a good man or keep one. They do not understand that the man is a mirror of themselves. If you love yourself but hate men, you are in conflict with yourself. You have inner conflict which influence how you perceive and treat men, and then that is why you experience what you do.

Men want what men want, not what government-entities, large corporations, and society say they want, and definitely not what a woman feel men want. Nature created men to be as they are. Men did not create themselves. Feminism told society that men just want sex, and they are stupid, and women make better leaders and parents. Overstand that we are all sexual creatures, so of course men want sex. Women do as well, maybe not for the same reasons. The majority of men in their natural state (meaning not emasculated) desire that one special woman they can have offspring with. At the end of the day, no amount of sex top having a woman who is devoted to us and the children we have with them.

# END OF FEMINISM: THE RISE OF PURE WOMEN OF BEAUTY

**GUEST** – *"Why are DMs so toxic?"*
**GUEST (2)** – *"I have noticed a lot of toxic DF Twins too. How come they are not talked about a lot on the internet?"*

It is likely, and more common than you think, for many of the male Soul Twins to actually not be the toxic, abusive, fearful people many DFs claim. We have to overstand that societal changes in the mid-1900s to the early 2000s caused a reversal of the energy between men and women. Society became very gynocentric and toxic toward men, and toward women in other ways. Society also pushed women out of their feminine energy. Even though many people made claims of men suppressing women, there was no evidence or proof. This shift in society caused the destruction of the family and man-woman dynamic. Society took and held firm to the notion that men are toxic and abusive by nature, and that woman are innocent, and are always right.

But in reality, none of this is true. And in the decades proceeding this changes, society realized that all of it was a hoax created by the matrix to destroy the family unit, to separate and create conflict between men and women. By this time, it was too late. The damage was already done. Men took it as women became too toxic and unbearable, and that relationships/marriage with women did nothing but caused them to unlawfully lose everything. The women held firm that men are toxic and abusive, and women are innocent, and continued to push their beliefs on men and society. Men turned their backs on the women, and women suffered in the long run due to increased depression rates, suicide, homelessness, physical health issues and diseases, childlessness, and being unmarried in their later years.

All along, the men did not change much, except their perception of women. They used to think women, WERE innocent. Until things changed. Then more and more men chose to not get married, have children, date, or even have sex with women. This paint a completely different picture than what we have been taught.

Although we all do have both energies, still Nature designed men to hold the masculine energy and women the feminine energy. Men and women are pushed to behave and live in the incorrect energy. Many Soul Twins, upon first meeting, feel like they are in the wrong energy, as if the man is feminine and the woman is masculine. Some realize this before meeting their Twin, but it become ever more apparent upon first meeting.

But at the foundation, women not only change society (for worse or better) by giving birth to children, but also by how (or if) they are able to maintain a healthy and productive relationship with the children's Father. Children learn relationships and social activity from the Father-Mother dynamic. If it is toxic, full of abuse, in the wrong energy, one parent not present, ext., the children can take on those relationship dynamics as well, and that become a generational cycle.

The first call-to-action I give you, is to research the origins and purpose of Feminism and Women's Empowerment. It had nothing to do with setting women free from a patriarchal society or enslavement of marriage. It was created specifically to weaponize women against men, and everything that men were created to be and do for the benefit of society.

## AVOID THE 'DIFFERENT MEN, SAME PROBLEM' TRAP

Even in the Soul Twin Community, the men have walked away. Oh, you haven't heard about the women in society complaining about men not wanting to get married any more, or not wanting to ask them out on dates anymore? Oh yes, the same women who complain that all men want is just sex. What is going on with the men? Why are the men behaving this way? For a long time, we were told that men are no good and that they are cheaters and liars, and this, and that, and the other. What kind of effect do you think that has on men (boys as well) after having that message force fed to them and the women around them for so long?

*"They are men, men are supposed to be strong!"* *"It's all just joking, why do men take everything so serious?"* When 'being strong' and 'just joking' turn into men actually being treated the way they have be described for so long, that has a huge effect on the Man-Woman relationship dynamic. It is so serious in fact, that women also have believed it, so much so that they aren't even aware that they are part of the problem. A man running from a woman? Come on, that is an easy one! How can men be so dangerous, and yet they are the ones walking away from women?

They are the ones turning their heads and pulling away from women. A man running from a woman? We were told it is because they are just insecure, scared, can't handle a real woman, or that they are toxic and narcissistic. I'm going to paint a different picture here and suggest that the men are walking away because they have experienced women as the source of the problem (as initiated during the 1900s during the Feminism movements) and not the men. Men don't run from women, it's not in our nature. A man running from a woman send an alarming message. Something just isn't right with this picture.

*"But Terrence, he is so toxic and abusive, and he behaves like he is narcissistic. I know I'm not the crazy!"* But that is the thing. That is the result of what Feminism and society have created those men to be. And people never realized it, until it was too late. It all start when they are boys. And from there the ball just grow bigger as it roll down Snow Mountain. At what point do you think is the point of no return?

That is what the Soul Twin Community has dealt with. The men haven't just walked away because they have problems, it's also because they have to see their Soul Twin with problems as well, which doesn't help the situation. And unfortunately, unlike most women, men walk away at the point of no return. We don't fight battles that are never ending. We eventually get hungry, tired, or horny. What ever happened to '*MAKE LOVE NOT WAR*'?

If you have had problems with your Soul Twin and you just can't figure out why they ran or don't want to talk, you have to try something different this time. And I suggest turning that finger pointer back at your Self. Look at everything you did, did not do, said and did not say (without making excuses or bailing yourself out) that you know in your heart was part of why they ran or closed communication.

The hardest thing for anyone to ever do is to admit when they are wrong and the cause of a problem. And there are some people who truly haven't really done or said anything to them, but what happen is we chose to give our time, energy, sexuality, money, and attention to someone who is not good for us. But because we felt a powerful connection and have a deep need for intimacy and companionship, we tried to turn poison into a healing elixir.

Let's reconsider this. Let's stop running from our own problems. We have to change. We have to do better and be better. Let's stop throwing the blame on everyone but ourselves, because relationships and connections are always at least two way streets, and traffic does flow in both and all directions.

## VACCINES COULDN'T STOP THE RISE OF CONSCIOUSNESS

DNA is the foundation for our health, life-span, and capability. If DNA is changed, it can have beneficial, or deadly effects. The Covid19 vaccine and its contents are highly controversial. Some believe that it is harmless and was created to save lives. Others know that it is harmful, even deadly. But its effects on the health and lives of many who did take it, showed the truth. The human immune system is designed to fight viruses and germs. It actually get stronger from doing so. How did humans get to where they are now, when ancient civilizations did not have vaccines? At best, we find that they used natural herbs, honey, and energetic healing practices to fight against any viral infections, if there were any viruses to be infected by.

Videos of a strange behavior called 'The Spin' surfaced the internet. The Spin is a seizure caused by the Covid19 vaccine. The person would appear to see something, or someone over their shoulder, then begin to spin, before falling to the ground, and eventually dying. In other cases, those who took the vaccine suddenly passed out and died after a certain time after getting the shot. Others suddenly got very sick, and died later.

Evidence was revealed in other countries that the vaccines can cause DNA restructuring, or reprogramming. Other sources said that the other vaccines contained the actual virus, which lead to the deaths of tens of millions of people. *"Are you saying if I got the vaccine I'm going to die?"* Absolutely not. Not everyone who took the vaccine died. And if some of the vaccines don't contain the virus, but contained DNA programs, or DNA restructuring agents, then that would mean that you won't die just because you got a vaccine.

## END OF THE MAN-MADE MATRIX

**GUESTS** – *"We know about the man-made matrix. People were kept under an illusion. They were told how to live and what life was about. But many of them woke up and realized they were living a lie."*
**MR. J** – "That's right. But the man-made matrix failed and has been dismantled. It is because so many people have awakened."
**GUARDS** – *"In the forces, we were told not to tell the public or regular people about the control mechanisms and lies. We had to keep our mouths shut. Good thing we got out of there once we realized what was really going on. We are proud to serve a better purpose for humankind here at EonF!"*
**MR.J** – "Your service is well appreciated, SGs!"
**GUESTS** – *"Yes! We thank you as well!"*

## UFOs, ETs, AND THE SOULAR SYSTEM

There was a time when UFOs and ETs were only something to talk about for fun, or see in a movie. If you mentioned that you saw an alien, UFO, or believed they existed, you may have been called weird or laughed at. But recently, more and more people are seeing UFOs, and encountering ETs. It has gotten to the point to where the government can no longer cover up what they know, and what they have been hiding.

I remember in school reading about the Soular System. In the books the teachers gave us to look at while they taught, I noticed Soular System was spelled: solar system. But I knew that our home sun is not just a big light in the sky, or gases colliding to create explosions and light. The sun is a living entity. It is Soul. And those who come from our Soular System, are the Soular People. They were the first genetically created people on Earth, and they are still here today, and will always be here. Some of the ETs are Soular People, and their spaceships are basically vehicles they use to travel through outer space. Just like we have EVs and other vehicles to travel across Earth, they have vehicles to travel across space, the galaxy, Universe, and even through time.

Many Soul Twins are actually Soular People. They are Soul Twins. It will be interesting in the coming years and decades to see more evidence, and even experience ETs and UFOs become part of our own lives. They will not only be seen in movies, the metaverse, or online. They will also be seen amongst us, in our backyards, when we travel, and in the atmosphere as if they are sky art.

# THE 144,000

It is said that these people are of 'light' and of the sun, and of the Stars. They are people who come from the Sun. They are Soular People. The Sun and the Stars, and the cosmos raise their energy, and this raising of the energy symbolize becoming enlightened, and conscious, and of the light, just like the Sun. It symbolize they are 'raised from the dead' (from darkness, from illusion), and taken up into the sky (from being energized by the Sun). The sky representing higher consciousness, energetic vibration, and mentality. This is ascension and becoming One with THE MOST HIGH, THE LORD OF ALL.

For a long time, I ignored the whole idea of the 144,000. But it was something that kept coming up along my ascension path. One day I decided to meditate on it and see for myself. During the meditation, I saw a group of brown-skinned people, the 144,000. The total number of people in the group was not specifically 144,000. But what I noticed is that all the people in the group had a Bright glow to them.

They identified themselves with their Oneness with the Sun, and the Stars, and the cosmos, and THE MOST HIGH, and with each other. They were people of the Light. They were a small percentage of the masses. They ascended beyond what common men and women were willing, so they became the Chosen Ones (meaning *they* CHOSE to go up the ascension path and became One with the Sun, and with each other, and with the MOST HIGH). The opportunity was given to many, yet only few chose, therefore only few were chosen. THE MOST HIGH being related to Polaris, whose name is MORAEL, because she is the center Star of our reality.

But rest assured, if you think the 144,000 will be all caucasian people, you have been lied to and mistaken.

# WHO AND WHAT TO TRUST (YOU, turn inward)

The best person to trust is always your Higher Self and THE MOST HIGH. But you have to turn inward to gain access to your Higher Self and THE MOST HIGH. That can only come through meditation, self-reflection, and being 100% honest with your Self. Don't lie to your Self. Hold your Self accountable. You have to find that quiet place away from all the noise (people, movies, a job, friends, the media, ext.) so that you can awaken to the truth that is in plain sight. That is the place where you find Your Higher Self and THE MOST HIGH, within. TURN INWARD! In an upcoming book I will publish, I will talk about turning outward, and how to use this energy to create a better external world for yourself and others. Stay tuned!

# SECTION NINETEEN

## END OF THE MAN-MADE MATRIX & PULL-DOWN PROGRAM

### FREEING THE DIVINE FEMININE AND MASCULINE

When I first became engaged with the Soul Twin community, I started having regular dreams of a certain nature. In these dreams, I commonly was with a small group of other people. We had weapons and some gear. We went to, and through, strange buildings. In these buildings we found people who were trapped and locked in rooms and cages. Some of these buildings were protected by vicious animals and armed bandits. I didn't know why I began having these dreams all of a sudden. Then I realize it pointed to the freeing of people from the matrix, including Soul Twins. I was so shocked to see this whole layer of reality in plain view that was filled with so much conflict and warfare on a spiritual level!

I realize a common problem in the Soul Twin Collective had to do with the DMs/Runners being LOCKED and EMPRISONED. It was initially believed that they were just toxic and NARCs just to be that way. But in the spiritual realm there was HEAVY conflict and warfare Soul Twins and lightworkers were involved in. The DMs/Runner's souls were bound and held hostage. The DFs/Chasers were as well, in their own ways. Fortunately, the evil forces failed and were either destroyed or ceased their attacks against Soul Twins and Twin Flames.

This was an energetic war that had to be fought in the higher realms. The rising and ascension of Twin Flames, Soul Twins, StarSeeds, Lightworkers, and Ascended Masters added to the Army Of Light that was needed to set the DMs and DFs FREE. There were also HUMAN souls participating in this.

*The real fight for Union and enlightenment had to be fought within your Self. Your Self need to be set free.*

### TWIN FLAMES AND SOUL TWINS ARE SUPPOSED TO BE TOGETHER!

Twins are not supposed to be separated from each other. Separation between Soul Twins is NOT the work of THE MOST HIGH. The Divine Masculine and Divine Feminine exist and function as One and are not separate from each other. We are supposed to graduate from being in the matrix, from being influenced and blinded by illusion. That's why Masculines have yearnings for the Feminine and the Feminines have yearnings for the Masculine. The Masculine and Feminine are One Energy.

BE WITH YOUR SOUL TWIN, YOUR DIVINE COUNTERPART. WE ARE HERE TO LOVE EACH OTHER, NOT RUN FROM, CHASE AFTER, ABUSE, OR LIE TO EACH

OTHER! WE ARE HERE TO DO THE WORK OF THE MOST HIGH BY MAKING THE WORLD A BETTER PLACE BY SHOWING THE WORLD BY THE LOVE WE HAVE FOR EACH OTHER.

## HOW TO FREE YOUR SELF AND OTHERS FROM THE MATRIX AND PDP

- Meditation and regular time alone
- Change in eating habits (eat what give you good health)
- Exercise
- Time in nature, around bodies of water and non-domesticated animals
- A social circle of people who do things to better themselves and their lives, who don't follow the crowd or try to fit in with everyone
- Detach emotionally from the external, don't react to what people say or do. Your experience of life (the physical world) is only a projection of your mind and emotion
- Find and engage with mature and aware mentors and coaches. Remember, always research who you follow. Never blindly follow and assume someone mean good or is speaking truth just because it sound good or they are popular
- Read books about human history and ancient civilizations
- Grow and eat your own food
- Ensure your sexual and romantic connections are based on purpose, longevity, mutuality, and generosity and not based on money, material things, or social status
- Take the leap and learn business, how to write a book about your life or something you know about, and open a business that help people with something they need. Be part of making the world and people's lives better

# SECTION TWENTY

# THE SOUL TWIN COLLABORATION NETWORK™

**GUEST** – *"I have a feeling this is going to be interesting!"*
**GUEST (2)** – *"Yea!"*
**MR. J** – "This is exciting news for Twin Flames and Soul Twins! FINALLY we have come together, in person, so we can all work together as a team."

What is the Soul Twin Collaboration Network™? Finally, Soul Twins have come together with the Twin! Not only that, but Twins are now collaborating together with other Soul Twins. Twins have come together here in the United States. This is important as government 'leaders' and celebrities have fallen from stardom, given up their career, or gone back to their country. Twins now are the World Celebrities and Leaders, stationed here in America.

**GUESTS** – "Oh yes! The meeting we all had the other day was so fun, informative, and life changing!"
**MR. J** – "I am happy you all enjoyed the meetings! Many more to come!"
**GUESTS** – "Oh man, so many powerful and beautiful people filled the building! So much energy! I couldn't help but smile and laugh. And the food was SOOO good! Oh and it was so awesome to hear from other Twins their amazing business ideas and plans for a better society and world. I am so inspired and confident now in my self and this collaborations between Twins."
**GUESTS** – "It's a big relief and dream come true for us to be with our Twin physically, even married and with children! Did you see how many pregnant female Twins were at the meetings? It is real! Star babies are being born! Yay!"
**GUESTS** – "No more working jobs for us! With talking with other Twins, it seemed like all of a sudden their businesses began making BIG money soon as they came into physical union with their Twin. Since we've been having these meetings all of our businesses have been expanding and making so much money it's taking a mental adjustment. It feels good to always have more than enough, and being able to get what we actually want without looking at the price tag. Appreciation, dividends, and interest from investments are also looking real good!"

Looks like I'll have to add more to this section later as the Soul Twin Collaboration Network™ continue to grow and rise here in America! So many great, abundant, and beautiful things are ahead!

# CONCLUSION

First I want to change something in society. I want people to stop calling other people NARCS. It does not make a person look mature by doing that. Whether or not the person is a NARC or have NARC tendencies, calling them a NARC can be increasingly harmful to them. STOP CALLING PEOPLE NARCISSITIC. We can do better than that, and speak better things over people. Rather than calling someone a NARC, lets change that to *"Life is still working on them."* We are all a work in progress. No amount of money, beauty, fame, resources, or age mean that we are finished learning and growing. Learning and growing are eternal professions!

But I hope this guidebook helped you in some way. And allow your Twin to go through their ascension as well. Remember, they are YOU. Keep this guidebook with you, it'll come in handy when you need it! It's a great tool.

## WHAT I ULTIMATELY WISH FOR MY SOUL TWIN

We have to be honest with ourselves. If we are not meant to be with someone they will always be repelled from us. It just doesn't make sense to chase people who don't want us or value our time, energy, and love. As stated at the beginning of this guidebook, I realized soon after that my supposed 'Twin' was not someone I was supposed to be with. Even though yes, there was mirroring and dreams, those two things alone does not meant we are supposed to be with someone. She was simply a past life connection from a previous lifetime and previous timeline, meaning we ARE not soulmates or Twin Flames.

If you are meant to be with someone in your current life, your two will surely meet each other and it will be MUTUAL. There wont be running and chasing, and confusion. All you have to do is disconnect and move on from karmic relationships, clean up yourself, clean up your environment, and raise your frequency. You'll naturally attract someone who best fits your energy and life purpose. This is what I have been focusing on and am open to meet and receive a true soulmate or Soul Twin when it is the right time.

I have lifetimes of getting married, having families, and 'looking for the *one*'. After doing it so many times, this lifetime I knew would be different. I get asked a lot why I don't feel the urge or need to chase after supposed 'Twin'. That is because I am aware there is no one to chase. There is only to become more conscious and to grow through experiencing life and learning. What look like a person I need to chase or be with, is actually ME. I am *her*. So, all that I see left, is to be a better version of me. To continue ascending through learning and growing. Through that, I can also turn to others and help them by becoming a teacher and a guide.

## WHAT I WISH FOR MY SELF

Those who make it to a certain point will understand this. You have to learn to be patient with others who are earlier in their ascension, and also remain humble. Those two things are what keep you from falling back down the ladder. Oh yea, that happened to me in one lifetime! That was a lesson learned. "Be humble. Be humble." "Stay patient, they don't understand yet. They are learning." I have repeated in my head this and previous lifetimes. To be patient with younger souls, and remain humble are what I wish for myself, and to be a leader and guide.

## WHAT I WISH FOR YOU AND OTHER SOUL TWINS

The most important thing to remember is that life is not about achieving something or attaining something. It is simply about experiencing life. That is how exciting and sustainable life is. Even into all eternity, there will always be new things to learn and experience. So, go out and experience life! Take action! Get up and do it! Your Twin may join you when the time is favorable!

Thank you for studying. Go out and do it! Keep on climbing! And remember, it's Union Season™!

~ Mr. J

**GUESTS** – *"Wow, this was so fun! We learned so much!"*

# SOUL TWINS ON WORLD STAGE

There are more than enough wonderful things about this journey that has the entire world in awe. Soul Twins are now in the spotlight! On stage with mic in hand! **Here are my findings:**

- Soul Twins share a bond that most don't
- Sex between Soul Twins is of the highest experience, intensity, and pleasure
- The Soul Twin journey is an accelerated Automatic Default Ascension™ journey, meaning they are on an accelerated soul ascension which doesn't require being initiated by a guru or cult practices.
- The meeting and engagement of the Soul Twin provide a guru-less (or Self-guru, however you see it) soul ascension. The Soul Twin is a living, breathing mirror of your Self. You get to look at your entire being mirrored back to you as a real person
- The journey awakens Twin to a very high and bright level of consciousness and clear truths
- No one innerstand you better than your Soul Twin
- You learn things about your Self, others, and life, that is not taught in school, by parents, college, social activity, or social media
- Soul Twins find themselves living the life others can only dream of having
- Soul Twins are always very good looking and stand out amongst others
- Meeting the Soul Twin prove that love and stable relationships are not rooted in money, material possessions, or looks, but in healthy attachments, natural attraction, and connection with THE MOST HIGH. Money, material possessions, and looks only add to those, but are not the foundation
- Those in the Soul Twin community help each other, we are a community, so we have to help each other and work together
- We share an energetic and romantic bond with our Twin that inspires others to find and experience something close to that with another person
- A RACO™ system with higher levels of energy holding capacity
- The Twin Flame journey is a huge responsibility and privilege and we don't take it lightly, but respect and honor it for ever

# REVIEW THIS BOOK

Thank you for purchasing this guidebook! Please review and rate this book wherever you purchased it. If the library, website, or eBook provider does not have a rating or review system, use the online Amazon bookstore, Apple Books, or Google Play Books.

Reviews and ratings help drive consumer feedback, book sales, and support for future book ideas.

A three-sentence or single paragraph review along with a 5-STAR ★ ★ ★ ★ ★ rating is highly recommended and preferred! Thank you for the support and feedback!

# AMAZON WISH LIST:

*By sending BTC Bitcoin to the above address, you agree to the disclaimer written below.

**LEGAL DISCLAIMER:** "The author and Johnson Craftworks LLC are not liable for BTC Bitcoin sent to the wrong address or person. Sending BTC Bitcoin to the above address may incur a fee (transfer, processing, international, transaction, or conversion). Cash, debit/credit card, check, wire transfer, ACH/checking, money, fiat currencies, and NFTs are not accepted. BTC Bitcoin sent ARE NON-REFUNDABLE. Johnson Craftworks LLC and the author do not send any communications (or requests) asking for cryptocurrency, NFTs, payment, debt collection, or repayment.

Terrence Johnson accepts BTC Bitcoin and items purchased from the above wish list as gifts. Goods, products, and services are not provided for the receiving of BTC Bitcoin and items from the above wish list. Company ownership, shares, and equity are not provided for the receiving of BTC Bitcoin and items from the above wish list.

# SOCIAL MEDIA & CONTACT INFO

## YOUTUBE: @loveenroe

## EMAIL: contact@johnsoncraftworks.com

# BUY GEMSTONE NECKLACES

Scan this QR code to visit our shop and purchase 100% natural gemstone amulets, pearl necklaces, and solitaire quartz pendant chains with silver hardware!

www.ingramcontent.com/pod-product-compliance
Lightning Source LLC
Chambersburg PA
CBHW051144030726
47504CB00004B/1024